A GARRISON CHASE THRILLER

THE GREATEST GOOD

CRAIG N. HOOPER

www.craignhooper.com

Note: This is a work of fiction. Names, characters, places, and incidents are a product of the author's imagination. Locales and public names are sometimes used for atmospheric purposes. Any resemblance to actual people, living or dead, or to businesses, companies, events, institutions, or locales is completely coincidental.

The Greatest Good/ Craig N. Hooper. – 2nd ed.

ISBN: **978-1-7333755-5-9**

For Janine

To seek the highest good is to live well.

—St. Augustine

CHAPTER ONE

I LIED TO the police and was arrested at ten minutes to eight on an otherwise fine and sunny Southern California morning.

I was sitting on a cold metal chair in a holding room at the Long Beach Police Department. Of course, I wasn't arrested for lying, but the lie did lead to my current predicament. In my defense, I had two decent reasons to lie: one personal and the other professional. Right now the cops were hopefully speaking with my boss to verify my professional reason for lying. My personal reason was too painful to think about.

My left foot tapped the concrete floor. Aside from the humming of the air conditioner, it was the only sound in the room. I glanced at my watch and sighed.

Just as I spun the watch face around so I couldn't see it, the holding room door screeched open and a plain clothes cop stepped in. He looked like a sergeant, maybe a detective. I wasn't sure. He glared at me, then back kicked the door shut. The sound bounced off the cinder block walls and reverberated through the room. The cop took three long strides and stopped in front of the table, but he didn't sit down. Instead, he plopped a manila file folder onto the table and placed a cellphone on top of it. He crossed his arms.

I looked at the phone, then back to the cop. "Did my boss call and vouch for me? He at least confirmed my identity and credentials, right?"

"Your boss didn't call," the cop said.

"Do you want me to call him?" I motioned to the cellphone. "Is that what this is about?"

I reached for the phone, but the cop trapped my hand against the table. He leaned forward and put his weight onto my hand.

"We know exactly who you are," the cop said. "In fact, Agent Chase, a number of cops are hunched over a laptop in the break room watching the infamous video that got you suspended. I guess I should call you 'former' Agent Chase. Isn't that right?"

I yanked my hand out and glared at the cop. A year ago I'd lost my cool with a creepy sexual predator on a popular TV show. The video footage went viral, which led to my suspension. Sure, I was pissed about the suspension, but what hurt the most was losing custody of my three-year-old son, Simon, over the whole thing.

I kept the stare going, debating my next move. Time was ticking, and I was already late for an important job. I stood and spun my watch around. "You've confirmed my identity and occupation then, so the weapons the cops found shouldn't be a problem. And unless you're going to charge me with obstructing justice, which I believe is a stretch, I guess I'm free to go."

"Sit down."

I didn't.

The cop jabbed at my chair. "Sit down now."

I didn't sit. "Are you bent out of shape because of the video?"

"No, I don't give a rip about the video. What bothers me is this..." He slid the phone off the folder and pulled out the paper I'd written my statement on. He waved the paper in the air. "This is garbage, a complete lie, and you know it. Don't you, Gary?"

My given name was Garrison Chase. Gary was not the short form of Garrison. When people called me Gary, I tried not to jump down their throats and correct them. Only Mom could call me Gary and get away with it.

I took a deep breath. "I go by Chase actually. And I'm not a liar. I made a mistake this morning."

He scoffed. "You *are* a liar, Gary."

I balled my fists up and released them, then stepped toward the cop until our faces were eighteen inches apart. The man had even-toned, mocha-colored skin, but it was all pockmarked, like he'd been pelted in the face with a BB gun at a young age. His nationality was beyond me. I watched his Adam's apple bob slightly.

After a moment, he backed off and took a seat in a chair across the table from mine. "So, you work in Cyber Crimes for the feds, but you're currently on suspension and don't have a badge or any sort of law enforcement credentials?"

"Correct," I said, taking a seat. "I trust my boss will vouch for me on the weapons. My suspension's nearly over, by the way."

At least, that was the hope I clung to.

The cop looked at the statement I'd written. "Let me get this morning's story straight. A neighbor calls the cops because he witnesses one person chasing another person. It's just before dawn so it's fairly dark and the neighbor can't make out many details, but he does notice that the chaser is wearing a dark bathrobe and holding a gun, and the chasee is unarmed. So the cops canvass the neighborhood to see if anyone else witnessed the chase. When they come to your door and ask if you know anything about the incident, you tell them you don't know a thing."

"Sounds about right," I said.

He held out his hands. "But you were the chaser. Right?"

"I was."

"And you were chasing an intruder who broke into your house? That's your story?"

"Correct."

He squinted at me. "So you lied to Officer Palmer and Officer Kowalski about the incident?"

"I did, but I had two good reasons to do so. I'm not saying that makes it right; I shouldn't have lied. It was a stupid mistake. I'd do anything to take it back, but that was what happened at the time."

3

"And you didn't tell the officers right away that you were a fed, or former fed, or whatever the hell your official status is?"

"I didn't."

He started scribbling notes on a piece of paper in the manila folder.

I looked at my watch, then wished I hadn't. My right foot started tapping the floor. A few days ago, my boss, Frank Lemming, offered me a job; my first since the suspension. Frank said if the test job went well, he'd lobby his superiors and try to get me reinstated. Frank was going to freak out when he spoke with the cops. Tardiness on my first day of the new job could cost me my career. My lie and subsequent arrest could even cost me more than that, but I refused to entertain that thought.

I wiped my palms on my pants. The cop kept writing. What could he possibly still be writing? Leaning forward, I said, "Can I explain things, give you the quick story and cut right to the chase?"

The cop stopped writing, patted down his out-of-control brown hair, and leaned forward. His hair puffed out five or six inches from his head in every direction. It looked like brown cotton candy, if there was such a thing. I tended to fixate on people's hair when I first met them, probably because I was bald. As soon as my hairline had started receding at age thirty, I'd shaved my head and kept it that way; my way of giving the balding gene the middle finger.

"Fine," the cop said. "Go ahead. Tell me what happened; start at the beginning. And try not to lie."

I ignored the comment and cleared my throat. "So I was in the bathroom when I heard the intruder break in—"

"What were you doing in the bathroom?"

"Really?"

The cop didn't respond.

"Fine. I was on the toilet and heard the intruder fumbling with the doorknob."

"And the door was locked?"

"It was."

He jotted a note. "What'd you do next?"

"Listened. When I heard the latch click into place, I knew the intruder had picked the lock and was inside. The whole break-in was a rookie production, by the way."

"What do you mean?"

"You keep the knob turned when you're closing a door, so the latch doesn't click. Even teenagers sneaking in late at night know that. And about three feet from my front door is a squeaky board. The intruder stepped on it twice. Once, I understand, but not twice. So I knew I was dealing with an amateur burglar, maybe a local teenager with a troubled past, somebody like that."

"What did you do?"

"I bailed. Punched out the bathroom screen window, stepped on the toilet seat, and launched through the window."

"What are you, like six foot two?"

"Six four. What does that have to do with anything?"

"You're a big guy. Why didn't you confront the intruder?"

"I couldn't see if the intruder was armed or not."

"But you said the intruder was an amateur, maybe even a teenager. A person like that wouldn't have a gun."

I shrugged. "Probably not, you're right. But if the intruder did have a weapon and I came charging out of the bathroom, who knows what would've happened? An amateur with a gun is totally unpredictable. I didn't want to take that chance. And besides, I wasn't letting the intruder off. I planned to go after the person."

He nodded and took a note. Then he used his pointer finger to loosen the collar of his dress shirt, which was buttoned to the top even though he wasn't wearing a tie. The white shirt was flawless, not a wrinkle in sight. Either the guy was a wizard with an iron or he paid for his shirts to be cleaned and pressed. Whatever the case, he was obviously meticulous about details. I made a mental note not to leave out a single thing.

"Okay," he said. "After you went out the window what happened?"

"I ran down the alley. When I hit the beach boardwalk at the end of the alley, I doubled back toward my house and stopped at my car to pick up a revolver I keep under the passenger seat. By that point, the intruder was running down the street toward a car."

"What kind of car?"

"A black Monte Carlo."

"Any details about the intruder?"

"A male, for sure. I could tell by the body shape. He wore a black hoodie. It was fairly dark still, so I couldn't see his face."

"License plate?"

"He was in the car and gone before I was close enough to read the plate."

The cop leaned back and patted his hair. "So you didn't call the police to report the break in? And when the cops arrived and asked if you knew anything, you blatantly lied to their faces. Why would you do that?"

"I'm on thin ice with the Bureau," I said. "Been on paid suspension for too long. I finally got a chance to redeem myself when I was offered a job to protect the governor's son, Stanley Tuchek. Maybe you've heard about him and the death threats he received on his Facebook page?"

The cop leaned forward. "You were chosen for that job?"

"Thanks for the confidence boost."

He didn't respond.

I shook it off. "I have no idea why I was chosen, but I was happy to take the assignment since I haven't worked in close to a year. Today is the first day of protection." I looked at my watch and cursed in my head. "I'm already a half hour late for picking up Stanley. My boss will already be pissed, I know him. Beyond pissed, actually. And the governor's probably going to have my head."

"So you didn't want to be late for the assignment? That's why you lied?"

"Yes, like I tried to tell the beat cops earlier, a police report would entail a bunch of questions and a formal statement. All of that takes time; time I didn't have this morning. So I made the stupid decision not to call in about the intruder, and then to lie to the officers when they showed up. The intruder didn't take anything anyway, so I didn't think it was a big deal."

The cop eyed me.

If he knew my personal reason for lying, he wouldn't have been so skeptical, but I was hoping to get away with my explanation without getting personal.

THE GREATEST GOOD

While the cop rifled through the manila file, I sat and stewed over my dumb decisions. I had just finishing brewing a cup of coffee when the cops knocked on my door. After inviting the cops in and lying to them, I offered them some coffee on their way out, probably to assuage my guilt. To my surprise one of the cops actually took me up on the offer. While I went to the kitchen at the back of my house to prepare a cup, the cops got nosy and started poking around my place, which wasn't hard to do since I lived in a 740 square foot two-bedroom bungalow by the beach.

Anyway, I'd left my navy-blue robe in the middle of the bathroom floor. I had no idea the cops would be presumptuous enough to open the bathroom door. When the cops spotted the robe, they figured my story was a total lie, so they poked around some more and found twenty-seven guns in my hall closet. They freaked when they found the arsenal. I tried to reason with them, telling them I was a federal agent, but I'd blown my credibility by lying about the intruder. Plus, because of the suspension I didn't have a badge or credentials to back up who I was, and I didn't have permits for every gun. Most of the guns were my father's. He willed them to me after his death; the only thing he willed me, by the way. Two of the guns were banned assault weapons, and I was pretty sure my father had obtained them illegally.

Dad had been in the ground eighteen months, but he was still wreaking havoc in my life, one way or the other. Of course, the lie was on me, and that was where this all started.

At any rate, the beat cops wanted nothing to do with me or my story, so they cuffed me and hauled me in for more questioning.

The cop cleared his throat. "Now it's my turn to cut right to the chase. The forensics team found something else at your place, which makes me question everything you've told me so far."

"Found what?"

The cop turned and paced toward the window. He stopped a foot from the window and kept his back toward me. "I'm trying to get my mind around this lie of yours."

"What did they find at my house? You need to tell me what's going on."

The cop spun and pointed at me. "You don't dictate the terms. Understand, Gary?"

I put my hands behind my back and balled my fists, then released them and took a slow breath through my nose.

"Earlier you said you had two reasons to lie." The cop stopped pointing. He adjusted his tight grey slacks, then put his hands on his hips. "What was the other reason?"

I opened my mouth, but no words came out.

"You need to come clean," the cop said.

"Fine," I said. "I have a custody hearing in three days that I'm worried about. My ex-wife Gina is some sort of human bloodhound. She has an uncanny ability for sniffing out any story that portrays me in a bad light. She also has a number of friends in my neighborhood that keep an eye on me. I didn't call the cops or tell them anything about the intruder because I didn't want a formal report filed. If a formal report was filed, Gina would find out through the local paper or maybe a friend. She'd use the break-in against me at the custody hearing. She'd convince the judge I lived in an unfit neighborhood with inadequate home security, something like that. She's ruthless. I want to be with my son again; that's all I care about. I lied to the police so I wouldn't jeopardize my future with my son, as well as because I didn't want to be late for picking up the governor's son."

The cop widened his stance, but didn't say anything.

"Obviously the lie backfired," I continued. "Now I'm sure Gina will find out about the intruder, plus she'll find out I've been arrested. I can only hope she doesn't hear about anything until after the custody hearing. I made a stupid mistake that could cost me custody of my son, and my job. I wish I could take it all back. Believe me."

The cop stepped toward me. "I think you're still lying. I think your whole story is fabricated."

"What are you talking about?" I stepped toward him. We were a foot apart. I towered over him by about eight inches. I felt my chest rising and falling too rapidly. "I'm not still lying. I did lie to the cops, but I'm not lying to you. I wouldn't keep lying with everything I have at stake. Didn't you hear everything I just said?"

"So you're sticking with the theory that the intruder was an amateur?"

"Of course."

He brushed by me and grabbed the phone from the table. After fiddling with the screen for a moment, he handed me the cell. "Do you recognize anything?"

I looked at the photo on the screen. "Sure. That's the inside of my house."

"When the police were confiscating your guns, they took that picture."

"So what? It's a picture of my hallway. The door at the end leads to my bedroom. Am I missing something?"

"Look closer, Gary."

I stepped back out of arm's length since my hands wanted to find themselves around his neck. I looked closer. "What am I supposed to be seeing?"

The cop snatched the phone away. He used his fingers to zoom in on the picture, then handed the cell back. "You know what that is?"

I did, but I blinked and looked again just to be sure. What was that doing there?

"I asked if you know what that is."

I was afraid my hands might start shaking, so I sat in the chair and put the phone on the table. I looked at the zoomed-in shot. "You sure that's my house?"

He sighed. "You think I switched pictures or something? Zoom out."

My palms were sweaty, so I wiped my left hand on my pants, then fiddled with the screen until I learned how to zoom out. It was the same photo of my hallway and bedroom door.

"I asked if you—"

I cut him off. "I know what it is, Officer." I sat back and smoothed my hands over my head.

What the hell was going on? I closed my eyes. My heart started pounding. I tried to think about the intruder and what I'd missed this morning, but my son filled my thoughts. I pictured Simon's face. I hadn't seen him in a year, and I wondered how much he'd have changed. Then I had a horrid thought: that if things went wrong now, I may never know how much my son had changed. My heart paused for a moment.

"Gary," the cop said, snapping his fingers. "Now you understand why I think you're lying?"

I opened my eyes and looked at the cop.

I certainly did.

CHAPTER TWO

SOMEBODY WANTED ME dead.

Considering my past, that wasn't too surprising. I had a decent-sized list of people who wanted me dead. Deep down I knew that, someday, I'd have to atone for my past. I just didn't think that would be today; the worst possible day it could happen.

I took a deep breath and looked at the photo for the third time. There was a quarter-sized piece of grey plastic explosive smeared over my bedroom door jamb. A tiny red detonating wire was looped into the middle of the explosive.

The cop took a seat. "Do you know what type of plastic explosive that is?"

"Looks like Semtex. And for the record, I didn't know it was there. I haven't been lying about that. I honestly thought it was an amateur who broke in this morning."

"It is Semtex. Clearly your intruder put that there. Unless, of course, you did. Perhaps you planned on burning down your house for the insurance money?"

I shot him a look.

"Fine. I had to ask. Anyway, Semtex isn't something an average burglar or arsonist would have access to, certainly not a teenager. I'm sure you know that. Right?"

I nodded. Semtex was expensive and hard to find. Only a professional would use Semtex. The intruder wasn't a pro, however. He'd made all kinds of rookie mistakes. Plus, the explosive didn't even detonate. Things weren't adding up.

The cop cleared his throat. "I think there's more to this than you're telling me."

"Give me a second to think." I rubbed my temples.

"You know what I think?" the cop asked, not giving me a second to think. "I think it was a professional who broke into your house this morning, and he had a remote detonator that malfunctioned. I think we weren't supposed to be having this conversation right now. I think you were supposed to be a dead man with a burned-down house."

He paused, probably for dramatic effect. The cop was likely right about the malfunctioning detonator, and probably correct about it being a professional.

"I think this all has to do with your past," he continued, "and I'm not talking about your unflattering video from a year ago. I'm talking about your past past. And this is about payback."

I stopped rubbing my temples and looked at him. "And what do you know about my past, Officer?"

"Enough."

"How would you know about my past anyway?"

A sudden thought came to me. I had it all wrong. Totally backwards. The intruder was a pro, after all, but he didn't want me dead. He wanted me alive.

I rapped my knuckles on the table. "I was wrong about the intruder. Completely wrong. I get that now."

"How so?"

"I think the intruder meant for me to hear him. Letting the latch click and stepping twice on the same squeaky board were deliberate. The mistakes were too obvious. I think the intruder wanted me to know he was there. He wanted me alive and out of the house before he razed it to the ground. So I agree with you, Officer. The intruder probably was a professional."

"Good, now—"

"Now answer my questions," I interrupted.

"What questions?"

"What you know about my past, and how you know it."

"Let's talk about why a professional tried to blow up your house this morning." He eyed me. "How about that?"

"Probably because of my past, which is something you apparently know all about." I paused and tried to read his eyes. The lighting was bad in the holding room and the cop's eyes were set an inch deeper than the average person's. I couldn't even tell his eye color from this distance.

"I do know some things," he said.

"What do you know?"

He leaned forward. "You trained at Pendleton, California in the Marine sniper program and topped out as a gunnery sergeant. After that, you spent nearly two decades doing classified missions without your unit, which tells me you were recruited out of the Marines to be a government operative. But you were still registered with the Marines for those twenty years, which means your operative work was clearly black ops. And—"

"Wait." I held out my hand. "How do you know all this? My past is classified."

He ignored me. "And three years ago you walked away from it all and entered the FBI academy. Left all those years and training behind to take a desk job, not to mention entry-level pay. You work, or I should say used to work, in Cyber Crimes. Cyber Crimes? Come on, nobody with your experience does that."

Being a father gave me a new appreciation of life, which was at odds with my chosen profession. I walked away from my government operative gig two days after holding Simon for the first time. Never looked back, never regretted it once. I wanted to be home to raise my son. I wanted to do everything differently from my father.

I forced Simon from my mind and leaned forward until I could see the cop's face clearly. His eyes had a thin, rust-colored band encircling his black pupils. "Seriously, how do you possibly know these things about me? Who are you?"

"Actually, that's all I know about you, and I want to know more." He grabbed the file on the table, opened it, and pulled out a single piece of paper.

"That file's my jacket?" I held out my hands. "Are you kidding me? How do you have a file on me?"

"I would hardly call this your jacket. It's only one piece of paper."

"It doesn't matter. We're in a city-run police station. It's not like they would have a classified file on me here. Where did you get that?"

He put the file down and crossed his arms.

My nostrils flared. "Are you IA? Is that what this is about?"

"IA? Do I look IA?"

"You do actually."

He laughed. "And you'd know Internal Affairs, wouldn't you? You probably know some IA agents by their first names. Am I right? For the record, Gary, no, I'm not IA."

"Then who are you and what are you doing here?"

He kept his arms crossed and stayed tight-lipped.

"Fine then." I looked at my watch and stood. I walked toward the one-way window. As I walked, my flip-flops snapped against the concrete floor. I suddenly became conscious of my outfit. The cops had cuffed me and hauled me into the cruiser before I could change. I was wearing a faded blue hooded sweatshirt, grey shorts, and black flip-flops. My lack of professional attire, however, was the least of my problems.

"Frank's called by now," I said. "I'm sure of it." I rapped on the window. "Let me out. The governor and his son are expecting me."

"Sit back down," the cop said. "And give me some answers. I need answers."

I spun and walked back to the table. "Not a chance. Not until you tell me who you are and how you got that file."

"We're not in a quid pro quo situation here, Gary."

I didn't know which irritated me more: him avoiding my questions, or him calling me Gary. I wanted to add a few more marks to his face, but I held back. I walked to the door and pounded on it.

"You realize how serious the situation is, right?" the cop said. "You're the governor's chosen protector for his son."

"So that's it," I said, turning. "That's why you're here. The governor sent you. You're working for him."

"The governor didn't send me. I don't work for him."

"So now *you're* lying."

He stood and stabbed his finger at me. "Don't turn this around on me."

We glared at each other.

About ten long seconds later the steel door opened, putting an end to our stalemate. Officer Kowalski, one of my arresting officers, stepped into the room.

"Special Agent Frank Lemming called," Kowalski announced. "He confirmed the identity of Agent Chase. Apparently Agent Lemming also knew about the guns at Chase's house."

In anticipation of Simon moving back in, I had planned on disposing of all twenty-seven weapons. A month ago I let Frank know I was bringing in my father's guns. I didn't want him to go ballistic when I brought in the arsenal. Of course, I was an idiot for not bringing them in sooner.

"I have a few more questions to ask," the cop said to Kowalski. "I hope that's alright."

"Suit yourself," Kowalski said. "But Agent Chase is free to go. If he wants to stay, it's up to him."

I followed Kowalski toward the door.

"Just two more questions, Agent Chase," the cop said.

I stopped. "So now it's Agent Chase and not Gary? Forget it. It's too late for professional courtesy."

"Please."

I looked at my watch. "I have somewhere to be."

I followed Kowalski out the door.

Once the door was closed, Kowalski turned and faced me. "Your boss sure was pissed. Man, does he have a temper. He wants you at work right away. If I were you, I'd avoid him today."

"Work? Why?"

"All I know is the governor's kid is waiting in your office."

"My office? How? Why?"

"Like I said, that's all I know, Agent Chase."

I looked Kowalski in the eye. The young officer was tender-faced, with cherry red cheeks. The rest of his face was bright pink. Everything about the man was puffy. It looked like he'd been hooked up too long on an IV of red food coloring.

"Sorry, Officer Kowalski," I said, patting him on his shoulder. "I understand. They were more rhetorical questions anyway."

He shrugged. "No biggie. Palmer and I will give you a ride. Your boss wants you at the agency like yesterday."

He led me to a side door and opened it. "We'll meet you out front in a few minutes."

Before he shut the door, I said, "One question, Kowalski: who was that officer in the holding room? Is he your boss?"

"He's not. And he's not an officer."

"What do you mean?"

"He's an agent."

I scratched my head. "An agent? An agent with whom?"

Kowalski shrugged. "Don't know. All I know is that about ten minutes after you arrived here my commanding officer got a call from somebody telling him a fed was coming to question you. Then we turned over the questioning to the fed when he arrived. They don't tell me much, Chase. I'm just a beat cop."

I nodded. After the door closed behind me, I leaned against the side of the brick building. An agent? Who sent an agent and why? And what agency? Was another agency involved because I was protecting Stanley? Had the governor recruited some other federal agent to check up on me? Deep in thought, I ambled toward the front of the building and shook my head. That didn't make sense, not at all.

By the time I reached the front of police headquarters, I realized I had more questions than answers. I also realized I had to figure out those answers, and fast. First, though, I needed to smooth things over with Stanley.

I turned left toward the front of the building, then stopped dead in my tracks on my third step. Shocked at the sight of her, I put my left hand against the building and braced myself so I wouldn't fall over.

What was my ex-wife doing here?

Gina had parked in front of police headquarters and was feeding a parking meter next to a car I didn't recognize. I quickly looked around, hoping to see a grocery store or a women's store nearby, some place Gina would be headed; but I didn't see anything like that.

A sickening feeling came over me. I breathed a deep breath of ocean air and watched her. It had been almost a year since I'd last seen her. She'd chopped off her long auburn hair and was now sporting a short, stylish haircut. It was intentionally messy, especially the back of her hair. I hardly recognized her.

Once she finished feeding the meter, she turned in my direction, but she didn't spot me. I hoped she'd cross the street and get far away from the police station. Maybe she had a hair appointment somewhere down the street. However, she looked up at the front of police headquarters. It was clear she was headed there.

Damn. I rushed toward my ex-wife.

"What are you doing here, Gina?" I asked as I approached her.

She looked up, not surprised to see me at all. Shoot. This was bad. I swallowed.

"You're not going to ask about my car?" she said. "It's nice. Isn't it?"

Gina stood beside a brand-new black Infiniti Q45. "I can see it's nice. A five-hundred-dollar car payment isn't part of our alimony agreement."

"My new boyfriend bought me this. You know him, by the way."

I didn't bite. "I asked what you're doing here?"

"You're out already I see."

"Seriously, Gina, what are you doing here?"

She sighed, then resumed chewing on her gum. For as long as I'd known Gina, she always had a stick of gum in her mouth. Whenever I smelled spearmint, I instantly thought of her.

"You're not going to like this, Garrison."

"Just tell me what you're doing here, please."

"Stuart Feldman was the person who saw you chasing after the intruder. He called the police."

I looked away. This was beyond bad. Gina was pals with Stuart. I grabbed at my stomach, as if that would lessen the sick feeling.

"He didn't know it was you," Gina continued, "not at first. But when he saw you being put into the back of the cruiser, he figured you were involved somehow. Remember Stuart and I are buds? He called me right away."

I looked at Gina and tried to remain composed. "What are you doing here at the station exactly?"

"I talked to my lawyer a half hour ago. He told me to come to the station and confirm you were arrested. And..."

"And what Gina?"

She cleared her throat. "And then he said we should file a restraining order if you were arrested."

"A what?"

"A restraining order."

"I heard you. Why on earth?"

She put her hands on her hips. "Do I really have to explain why?"

I stepped back and turned around. My face went hot and my head felt like it was about to explode.

"I can't have my son staying at a place where intruders break in," Gina said. "Where you have guns in your house and you chase after bad people. No way."

"But seriously, Gina," I said, turning around. "A restraining order? You can't."

"I can. And I feel I have to. I didn't want you to have Simon back even before this morning's incident. Not a chance. But my lawyer said you had a right to see him, especially since you've been out of trouble for the past year. So I gave up on trying to fight against weekend custody. I was preparing for the judge to rule that way. Not after this morning, however. I'm sorry, Garrison."

"You have no idea what went down this morning. I don't even know what it was all about quite yet. You can't do this to me."

She shrugged. "You were running after an intruder in your bathrobe holding a gun. Are you kidding me?"

"Please, Gina."

"I know you love Simon, but you can't be with him. I can't let you. I'm not sure if I ever can. What if he had been in your house this morning? You think about that, Garrison? I'm sorry, but you're not getting our boy back. You're a risk and a danger. Clearly you still have issues and a past to deal with. The restraining order may be harsh, but it's what's needed to protect Simon."

I turned away so I didn't say or do something stupid.

A moment later, Gina placed her hand on my shoulder.

"Don't," I said. "Don't do that."

"I'll let you say 'hi' and 'bye' to him."

I turned around. "What? What do you mean?"

"Simon's in the back seat. I was just about to get him out before you arrived."

"What? He's in the back seat?"

"He is. Do you want to see him or not?"

"Of course I do."

Gina pushed a button on her key fob and the back passenger tinted window rolled down. She stepped back a few steps.

I hurried over. As soon as I saw Simon, I beamed. "How are you, pal?"

My son didn't respond. Not a trace of recognition on his face. Simon sat in his car seat and stared at me like I was a stranger.

My heart sank, but I kept beaming anyway. "Pal, it's me, Dad."

Nothing, no response at all.

I ignored the hurt and stared at Simon. The last time I saw him was just after his second birthday. His hair had really filled in over the past year. It was brown, tightly-curled, messy, and just plain cool looking. His eyes were steel blue. He looked like I did when I was three.

"Simon, it's Dad."

Still no response.

"Remember this, pal?" I pulled out my ears and inflated my upper lip, imitating a monkey. Simon used to love the monkey face.

He blinked at me. His upper lip started to quiver.

Gina rushed over. "I'm sorry, Garrison, but he's about to cry." The window started rolling up.

"Wait, stop, please."

The window kept going, so I grabbed the glass with my fingers and held it back. The motor whirred and screeched, then made a clicking sound.

"Stop," Gina snapped.

I leaned in. "I miss you, pal."

"You're breaking the window," Gina said. "And you're scaring him half to death."

I was. Simon's eyes were bugged out. I let go and watched the window continue its ascent, but a second later found myself latched onto it again.

"You do remember me, right? I'm your dad, Simon."

He backed away as far as he could in the car seat. The window's motor made a crunching sound. The smell of burning rubber filled the car.

"You're breaking the damn window, Gary. STOP. NOW."

I stopped. As the window closed, I looked at my son and said, "I love you, buddy, and I miss you, more than you could ever know."

Gina ran around the hood. Before she climbed into the driver's seat, she glared at me. "I have to get away from you, but I'll be back to file that restraining order. If that window's broken, you're going to pay for it. You're going to pay for all this. I should've never let you see him."

She got into the driver's seat, dropped the gear shift into drive, and squealed off.

I stood on the sidewalk and stared at the Infiniti as it roared down the street, but I couldn't really see the car. All I could see was the vision of my son cowering in his car seat, afraid of his own father. A tear welled in my right eye, then burned a track down my cheek.

I quickly wiped it away and looked around to see if anybody was looking my direction.

To my recollection, I've cried three times in my life. Once when I was six I slid down the tallest slide in our local park on my stomach. I face planted in gravel and still have the scars on my face to prove it. The second time was three years ago, while holding Simon in the delivery room. The third was this moment outside the police station.

Another tear bubbled in the same eye and rolled down my cheek.

This time I didn't bother wiping it away.

I lost track of time after that.

CHAPTER THREE

I WASN'T SURE how long I stood in the middle of the sidewalk. Long enough for a tear to dry up, that was all I could say for sure.

As I stood there, I wanted to hate on Gina more than anything. I wanted to think about how awful and unfair she was being, but my mind didn't go there. Instead, I thought about how right she was. How could Simon move back in with me if a professional was trying to burn down my house, and also possibly trying to kill me? A good father wouldn't put his son in a dangerous position like that. Right?

I took another deep breath of ocean air. I had to figure out what was going on before the custody hearing in three days. I absolutely had to.

"You're taking up most of the sidewalk," a voice said.

I snapped out of my daze and looked up. A homeless lady was bearing down on me with her overloaded bicycle. I stepped out of her way just in time.

Leaning against the parking meter, I replayed the encounter with Gina in my mind. What was I thinking? I couldn't believe I may have broken her car window. I envisioned her marching to the judge's bench in a few days. No doubt she'd enter the damages to her car window as Exhibit A in the case against Garrison Chase, worst father in Southern

California. Then she'd tell the judge all about my arrest. Then she'd pull out the restraining order.

I turned and kicked the parking meter.

"You'd better hope it doesn't press charges."

It was Kowalski's voice. I looked over at the cruiser idling in the street. Kowalski sat in the passenger seat. The window was down.

"Get in the back," he said.

I put my head down and climbed into the cruiser; the second time I'd been back there in two hours. The smell of fresh coffee permeated the vehicle. I had a caffeine headache starting, so I tried to focus my mind on that, and not on how screwed I was at the custody hearing. Unfortunately, the pounding in my head reminded me of a judge's gavel banging. I envisioned the judge thumping it down and announcing his decision to deny me visitation, stating that I couldn't provide a safe environment for Simon. Good thing the back doors couldn't be opened from the inside. I wanted to roll out and meet the pavement.

"Your resident agency is at One World Trade Center, right?" Officer Palmer adjusted the rearview mirror so he could see me.

I nodded. To refocus my mind, I stared at Palmer. He was twice Kowalski's age and the complete opposite body shape. Palmer was lean and rigid with square shoulders. No doubt he swam in college. In fact, he looked like an older version of Michael Phelps, but not totally like Phelps since Palmer had normal sized ears tucked in close to his head.

Palmer broke eye contact. I closed my eyes and rested my head on the back of the seat. My mood quickly turned as dark as my vision, so I opened my eyes and looked out the window.

As I watched the ugliness of Long Beach, California roll by, I thought about the federal agent. Why was he sent to question me, and by whom? How did he get there so fast? And why did he have a classified file on me? Unfortunately, I couldn't think because Kowalski kept glancing back at me.

On his third time turning back, I addressed him. "What is it, Officer Kowalski?"

He smiled. His big, red cheeks puffed out even more. "That video. It's outstanding. I just watched it on YouTube with a few other cops at the station. I thought I recognized you when you opened your front door this morning, but I couldn't place where from. I can't believe that was you." He held his hand over the seat for a high five.

I don't high five. It's a rule I follow. Besides, I had absolutely nothing to celebrate.

"Come on. Don't leave me hanging." He pressed his hand closer.

"How old are you, Kowalski?" I asked.

"Thirty-one. What does that matter?"

"Guys over thirty don't high five."

Kowalski quickly removed his hand, then he turned and nudged Palmer. "You saw the TV show or the video, didn't you?"

"Nope, haven't seen it."

"Oh, it's great," Kowalski said, smiling. "Such an awesome story."

"Let me hear it," Palmer said.

Kowalski swiveled around. "You mind?"

I shrugged. I didn't care at this point.

He turned back to Palmer. "Did you ever watch that TV show, *To Catch a Pervert*?"

"I think once," Palmer said. "My wife watched the show, I know that. It was basically a sting operation, right?"

"It was definitely a sting operation," Kowalski said. "The producers enticed these creepy internet perverts by pretending to be a young girl and inviting the pervs over for a good time. Sometimes the men traveled across state lines to visit these young girls, which triggered the feds' involvement. As soon as the men would allude to sex with these minors, the cops would storm in and arrest them. Most suspects would break down and beg for mercy, but not this one eighteen-year-old Marine on a show from about a year ago now. He stonewalled the host, wouldn't say a word, the kid was a real entitled prick, so they turned the interview over to the feds."

Kowalski had a solid recollection of the events.

"The feds sent in Chase," Kowalski thumbed over his shoulder, "to get some answers, but Chase wasn't getting any answers, which really ticked him off." Kowalski looked over his shoulder. "That fair to say?"

"What do you think?"

"Right. So Chase grabbed the kid by the throat—"

"And this was on live TV?" Palmer interrupted.

"Totally, it's awesome. And the video of it went viral on You Tube. Anyway, Chase held his right hand up, palm open, about a foot to the left of the kid's face. He yelled, 'BEATING, soldier'. Then he swung his hand, so the back of it faced the kid. 'OR DISCIPLINE? Your choice, soldier'."

Kowalski mimicked my infamous movements for Palmer's amusement. The beating/discipline thing was courtesy of my father. He rarely talked to me growing up. Most of our conversations ended with his gracious offer of a beating or discipline. He was a tough man, to say the least. After being honorably discharged from the Marines, my father became a survivalist. He led groups of people into the wilderness and taught them survival skills. He loved his job; in fact, he loved being outdoors with strangers more than being with his family.

"So what happened?" Palmer said.

"This Marine perv still didn't talk. I'm not sure if he was too terrified to talk or if he was just being stubborn." Kowalski looked at me. "What do you think?"

I sighed.

"Right," Kowalski said. "I'm not sure either. Anyway, Chase asked one more time, but this time he said it calmly: 'Beating or discipline?' The kid stammered, but didn't actually answer the question. So Chase unloaded. 'DISCIPLINE IT IS'. Then he backhanded the kid a bunch of times."

"Really?" Palmer said. "How many?"

"Six, I think."

"Five," I corrected.

"I can still hear the backhands on the Marine's face." Kowalski laughed. "Sounded like a paddle smacking the water. It was awesome."

Most men who met me had the same reaction as Kowalski. Most women kept their distance. Naturally there was a select group of people who wanted me arrested and fired over the incident, but the FBI didn't want to admit they'd hired an out-of-control agent. Their main PR argument was that I never made a fist. I was suspended and given a year of court-ordered therapy. As I said before, what hurt the most was losing visitation rights for Simon.

"So how did it end?" Palmer asked.

"Three other agents rushed in," Kowalski said. "Tackled Chase and dragged him to another room."

Palmer looked at me through the rearview mirror. "So what's your exact status now?"

"Paid leave, basically suspended."

"But that was like a year ago," Kowalski said.

"It's complicated, gentlemen," I said.

After the video of me 'disciplining' the Marine went viral, Frank took my badge and service piece and told me an investigation was imminent. A year later I was still awaiting the outcome of that investigation. Since I'd been receiving a paycheck for the past year, I hadn't pushed the issue. I figured if I pushed, things may go the wrong direction for me.

"Here we are," Palmer said. The cruiser slowed to a stop in front of my work.

Before I got out, I asked Kowalski, "What's the name of the agent who questioned me? Do you know that much?"

Kowalski shrugged.

Palmer said, "Agent Gates. His first name is Anfernee, something odd like that."

I addressed Palmer. "Do you know what agency he works for?"

Palmer shook his head.

After thanking the officers, I got out and thought about Agent Gates. I was currently dating a woman, Eva O'Connor, who worked for another law enforcement agency. I wondered if she knew who Gates was.

Unfortunately, I didn't have the time to call her. Instead, I hurried into the building. The Long Beach Resident Agency was one of ten field offices in Southern California. Our offices occupied the fourteenth floor of One World Trade Center. Before my television appearance and subsequent fallout, I had an outside office with windows and a view of the Pacific Ocean. Now I was stuck in a former janitorial closet deep in the basement. When Frank called a few days ago to offer me the protection detail, he told me I could use the basement office. He didn't want me hanging around the fourteenth floor, since I wasn't officially off suspension. Yesterday I came in and set up the office. It took less than ten minutes.

As I approached my makeshift office, I thought about Stanley. He was my lifeline to everything that happened this morning. If I smoothed things over with him, and did a good job protecting him, perhaps I could lobby the governor to help with my custody hearing. And I needed all the help I could get. It was a long shot, I knew, but I didn't have any other options. It was worth a go.

I gave a quick knock and entered my office. Nobody was there. I saw a yellow sticky note on the desk and quickly rushed over to it. Stanley, I assumed, had scribbled: 'Went to Long Beach State coffee shop'.

I crumpled the note and pounded on the desk. After a deep breath, I grabbed my backup service piece, a Sig Sauer P226, from the bottom drawer of my desk and tucked it into the back of my shorts. I also grabbed my beeper. I hated cellphones. Didn't like being reached at the push of a button. The only communication equipment I embraced was my office phone. Frank made me carry a beeper, however, in case he needed to get in touch. Only a few people had my actual beeper number.

I looked at my office phone and wondered if I should call Frank to update him. After a moment, I decided against it. He'd lay into me, and I had had a rough enough morning. Next time I communicated with Frank it'd be best to be in the presence of a safe and sound Stanley Tuchek.

I rushed outside and hailed a cab. It took a little over five minutes to reach the campus coffee shop. The place was bustling with over-caffeinated college kids. On a positive note, the place smelled fantastic, like freshly-roasted coffee beans and steamed milk. I could see Stanley sitting by himself at a table on the patio.

The death threats on Stanley's life had turned into a pretty big news story in California, which made sense since his father was the governor. The governor was well liked and respected because of how quickly he turned the state around since the recession. It was important to ensure his only son, Stanley, was well protected.

I ordered a coffee called *Full Throttle*. It had twice the caffeine, which I needed. Since Kowalski took the coffee I brewed for myself this morning, it was now three hours past my usual first cup. My head felt like someone was inside it, trying to pound out the curves with a jackhammer.

I took my coffee and weaved through a maze of small tables and comfy chairs, toward a door that led to an outdoor patio. When I reached Stanley, I held out my hand.

"Stanley, I'm Garrison Chase. I'm so sorry about missing pick up this morning."

Stanley sprang to his feet and pumped my hand. "No problem, Agent Chase."

"You can call me Chase, by the way."

"That may be hard for me, Agent Chase," he said, nodding quickly. Stanley's short, spiky dark hair didn't move at all. The kid had bulging, round eyes. His eye sockets protruded from his head like a cartoon character, seriously.

"I can see that," I said, smiling.

He blinked fast. So far every movement he made was quick, which made him look slightly nervous, and also thirsty.

"You need some water, Stanley? I can get you some."

He plopped into his seat and turned his attention to his laptop. "I'm fine, Agent Chase. Just give me a minute to finish this spreadsheet. I'm right in the middle of something."

While Stanley typed away, I took a seat across from him. Now that I was looking at the kid straight on, I couldn't help but notice how narrow his face was. It looked like his head had been squeezed in a vice at a young age. In fact, his whole upper body was narrow and small, everything but his eyes. I glanced at his feet underneath the table. They were unusually large for his petite frame. The kid would've been a shoe-in for a hobbit part in *The Lord of the Rings*.

"Sorry again about this morning," I said after a minute. "I won't bore you with the details about what happened. Rest assured it won't happen again. I promise you that."

"Not to worry, Agent Chase. When you didn't show up this morning, I figured there was a problem. So I drove my vehicle to your work and went to see Agent Lemming. He set me up in your office and told me it wouldn't be long. After a productive hour there, I relocated to this shop. I come here almost every morning."

"Did you go to college here? Finish when you were sixteen or something crazy like that? Rumor has it you're super smart."

"Actually, I haven't attended college." He pushed up his glasses.

I leaned forward and put my forearms on the tiny round table. "Really?"

"Really," he said, nodding fast. "I've deferred acceptance to MIT."

"Didn't you finish high school a while ago?"

"When I was fifteen."

"So what have you been doing since?"

He sniffed, looked around, then smiled. "It's classified, Agent Chase."

"Good one, kid." I leaned back. "I won't press. No big deal. You almost done here?"

"A little bit longer." He whipped out his phone and started texting.

"Who are you texting?"

He ignored my question, so I went to top up my bad coffee. My headache wasn't completely gone and I had time to kill. When I returned, I sat at the table next to Stanley. "Just in case one of these pretty college girls wants to chat with you." I motioned to the empty chair at his table.

"Funny, Agent Chase."

I worked on my cup of coffee and thought about the federal agent Anfernee Gates. The man must've been lying. He must've been working for the governor. That had to be it. The governor likely had connections in other agencies, so maybe the governor reached out to them for help as well. Maybe he took the death threats to Stanley seriously, unlike the rest of us. Perhaps the governor was concerned about my questionable vigilante acts and wanted another agent to keep tabs on me because I was protecting his son. That was plausible. I mean, I would do anything to protect Simon, so it made some sense. The problem with that theory is, if the governor was concerned about me and my past, why have me on protection in the first place? Why would he let that happen? It didn't add up, not at all.

While I wondered how I actually got the protection gig, I gave my eyes a good rub.

"You okay, Agent Chase?"

I looked over at Stanley. "I'm fine."

"Maybe you should take the day off."

"Day off? I just started. Are you trying to get rid of me already?"

Stanley smiled. "Just testing you."

"Good one."

He turned his attention back to his phone. I leaned back and closed my eyes. It was about mid-seventy today and sunny. While I let the warm Southern California sun bathe my face, I wondered about my morning intruder. What I needed to do was prove to the custody judge that the intruder wasn't a threat. Could the intruder have been an actual burglar and not a professional looking for payback? Maybe the burglar had stepped up his game and intended to start burning down homes instead of stealing stuff. Maybe the burglar had gotten bored with stealing and wanted a bigger thrill. The more I thought about that, though, the more doubts I had. If that were the case, the burglar wouldn't use Semtex. Semtex was too hard to find and way too expensive. The burglar could find far cheaper and more accessible explosives.

I turned my mind off, frustrated that I seemed to be getting more questions than answers. When I opened my eyes, I was blinded by a split-second flash of light. Within milliseconds the light disappeared, but my eyes scanned the surroundings anyway, searching for the source of the flash.

A waist-high wall sectioned off the coffee shop patio. Beyond the wall was a huge stretch of grass that covered about two acres of land. Various concrete paths sliced through the greenness. The paths led to a number of tall buildings that skirted the edge of the grass. Hundreds of students walked in and out of the academic buildings. My eyes swept the area, but I didn't see anything that would explain the flash, though I kept scanning back and forth for another minute. Before long, everything blurred into one. Once again, I gave my sockets a good rub. Maybe I had imagined the flash.

"That coffee doesn't seem to be working, Agent Chase."

I looked at Stanley. "It takes some time. I—"

The flash happened again. I saw it through the reflection in Stanley's glasses. I glanced at the buildings.

"I what, Agent Chase? You're acting strange. You can't even finish a sentence."

I scanned the top of the buildings. A third flash happened. It came from the tallest building to my right. I squinted and saw a rifle barrel peeking over the ledge, pointed right at Stanley and me.

The flash was the reflection from a sniper's scope.

I suddenly hopped to my feet, only to plop straight back down again, then I scraped my chair to the left. Quick movements caused snipers to realign, which bought their targets a few seconds.

"Agent Chase, what on earth?"

The barrel tracked my movements. I saw it. I was sure of it. The shot was aimed at me. I needed to get away from Stanley. I had to protect the kid.

Suddenly my body reacted. I dove left, as far away from Stanley as I could, and collapsed into a ball, crashing to the ground in a heap.

The rifle crack came a second after I hit the ground. The sound seemed to echo longer than it should. Every muscle in my body clenched as I remained in a tight ball. Nothing tore through me, though. I felt no searing pain; and my head was still intact. Plus, there were no gaping holes in my body. I looked up and gasped; saw the worst possible thing I could imagine.

I blinked, but the image didn't change. My mind told me I needed to move, but the gravity of the situation seemed to be pressing me to the ground, rendering me immobile. Everything in me wanted to stay curled up in a tight ball. But I needed to do something. I needed to act. I knew that.

So I scrambled to my knees and headed toward Stanley Tuchek, who lay flat on his back in a pool of growing blood.

CHAPTER FOUR

THE PATIO WAS deathly silent for a couple of seconds, then two girls saw Stanley lying in a pool of blood and screamed. Chaos ensued. Some students dove for cover while others ran around the patio, unsure of what to do or where to go.

I leopard crawled, elbows advancing in unison with the opposite knee, across the concrete toward Stanley. When I reached his table, I yanked it over. The kid's laptop crashed to the ground. I peeked over the table and looked toward the building. The rifle was gone, so I turned my attention to Stanley. He was flat on his back, completely still. His crisp white t-shirt had a growing crimson stain over the right shoulder area. His glasses had fallen off.

"Stanley," I said, patting his neck, searching for a pulse.

I tried both sides of the neck, but couldn't feel anything. I ripped open his t-shirt. Stanley's sternum had a huge softball like divot in the middle and blood was pooled in the center of it. The divot concerned me for a second until I realized it probably always looked that way. My eyes followed the trail of blood up to his shoulder. I wiped away the blood with my sleeve and saw the bullet's entry point just above his clavicle. The wound spurted blood. The kid was still alive.

I jammed my palm against the wound, peeked over the clavicle, and saw a clean exit wound. Using my palm and fingers, I applied pressure to both sides of the wound, then placed my cheek to Stanley's mouth and felt a faint breath.

"C'mon, Stanley, stay with me."

I glanced up at the chaos. The couple sitting closest to Stanley had followed my lead and tipped over their table. Both were staring at me. I motioned to them.

The guy shook his head. The girl looked cooperative.

"Stay low," I shouted. "I need your help." The girl started crawling.

"Stanley." I lightly slapped his face.

No response, so I tried a few more times. On the fourth slap, his eyes fluttered open. Stanley tapped the ground with his right hand, searching for something. I realized he couldn't see, so I grabbed his glasses and put them on.

"Agent Chase?" He blinked, for a bit too long, though.

"Stay conscious, pal."

"What happened?"

"You've been shot."

"For real? Am I alive?"

"You're gonna make it, Stanley. She's going to look after you." I turned to the girl crouched next to me. "Put your hand right where mine is, exactly. Apply steady pressure on the wound."

"I'm a nursing student," she said. "Don't worry."

I turned back to Stanley. "I have to go after the shooter, Stanley. You'll be fine."

"Get him," he said faintly.

I looked toward the building. The shooter was still gone, so I ran to the guy at the neighboring table. "You have a cell?"

His eyes were wide and pupils full. He didn't respond to my question, so I smacked him. Not hard, but not soft either. Finally, he nodded.

"Call 911, now. Get an ambulance here."

I waited until he pulled out his cell and dialed, then I hopped the waist-high patio wall and took off my flip-flops. I sprinted across the grass. At 150 yards away the side of the building came into view, and so did the shooter. It was a man; I could tell by the broad shoulders and choice of clothing. He raced down the side of the building on a fire ladder, which ran down the building's side. The ladder had metal rungs embedded into the brick and a cylindrical cage wrapped around the rungs to protect from a fall. The shooter's hands moved fast down the rungs. His feet weren't moving in unison, though. They slipped over the rungs, barely touching each one in a controlled free fall. It was good technique.

When I was a hundred yards away, the shooter made me. He kicked his feet toward the wall and jerked to a stop, then pulled out a handgun and pointed it at me through the rungs. I zagged to the right, then zigged back left. The shooter knew it would be a tough shot with a handgun, so he stuffed the gun back and continued his free fall. When he reached the bottom of the ladder, he hang-dropped to the ground and sprinted into an alley between the buildings.

I maintained my charge, but was losing ground, so I slowed and pulled out the Sig. When I reached the alley, I stopped running and quickly surveyed the area. The alley was filled with huge industrial-size garbage bins, giant boilers, pumps, and other large mechanical structures. No students wandered the area. Not a soul around. I took a few breaths to steady my arm. The shooter was about seventy-five yards away, a mile for a handgun. He was angling toward a thicket of bushes at the end of the alley. I took up the trigger slack and steadied my arm as best I could with a heaving chest; then I dropped the hammer.

At the last second the shooter angled behind a boiler. My round hissed into the metal cylinder. Water jetted out and steam squealed through the hole. I sprinted after the shooter, but soon watched him slip through the dense thicket of bushes.

When I reached the foliage, I brought my forearms up and crashed through the tangle of branches and twigs. By the time I bashed through and burst onto a maintenance road on the other side of the bushes, I was just in time to see a sedan race away.

A black Monte Carlo, identical to the one I chased after this morning.

The intruder's car.

I charged down the road and popped three shots. One sprayed wide. Another smashed out the rear window. The final bullet lodged into the back bumper. Nothing, however, stopped the car's forward momentum. It roared off. I watched the Monte Carlo squeal a hard left and disappear around the corner. It felt like my future was racing away from me, just like the car was.

I bent at the waist and sucked in some air, for close to a minute. It was all I could do at that moment. After that, I put my hands on my knees and squeezed my kneecaps. I couldn't believe Stanley was shot right in front of me, and that I dove away from him. This couldn't get worse. I lay down with my back against the pavement, not caring if anyone was around and watching me.

As I lay there and caught my breath, I thought about the kid. He'd survive the gunshot, which was the only silver lining. Life with my son was over, however, and my career wouldn't survive. I'd lose my job and my paycheck. And a judge wouldn't give weekend visits back to a deadbeat dad with no source of income. A man who harbors weapons, lies to the police, and can't protect someone else's kid. Not just someone else's kid, mind you, the governor's son, for crying out loud.

I bashed the pavement with my fists, then put my hands over my face and stayed like that for about three minutes. After some wallowing, I resolved to figure out the mess. If I was going to have no family and no job, I wanted to at least know why.

Suddenly I pictured Stanley alive, but unable to use his arm ever again, and the fallout that would occur because of that. I had to get back to him and make sure the kid was okay.

I fought my way through the bushes and back into the alley. As I walked, my eyes focused on the coffee shop patio. Fortunately, an ambulance had already arrived. In fact, it looked like Stanley was about to be loaded into the ambulance, so I picked up the pace.

As I approached the ladder the shooter used, something dawned on me. The shooter hadn't carried a rifle down. It must be on the roof still. I stopped and thought a moment. I had to check the roof and see. Stanley was about to be carted off anyway. I wouldn't get to him in time.

I grabbed a large garbage bin and wheeled it under the ladder. About thirty seconds later I was on the roof. Aside from small gray stones pebbling the roof, not much else was up there. A couple of monstrous air conditioners hummed away. Around the AC units were four steel air ducts growing from the roof like oversized periscopes. To the right of the ducts was a small building with no windows and one door, clearly a covering for the stairwell landing. Around the perimeter of the roof was a concrete ledge about three feet high by two wide. I followed the ledge to the northeast corner where the shooter had set up. The rifle was braced against the ledge. Unbelievable. I couldn't believe the shooter had left it.

I walked over to it. It was a bolt-action RAI Model 500; a .50 caliber beast of a weapon that weighed over thirty pounds. It was way too big for a job like this. Like the Semtex used this morning, it was total overkill. I inspected the rifle, noting a bipod mounted midway down the barrel. I carefully extended the bipod, placing the two legs on the concrete ledge. I didn't want to mess up any fingerprints, if there were any. After propping the butt of the stock on my shoulder, I looked through the variable 24x power scope and examined the shot. I eyeballed the distance to the coffee shop at about 200 yards. There was a ton of commotion at the shop. A couple of cruisers were there and the ambulance was gone.

I pulled back and noted the rifle's settings. The settings on the turrets were spot on. The proper adjustments were made for elevation change, wind, and bullet drop. The scope was dialed in at 204 yards. I would have set up the shot the same way. The exact same way.

Yet the shooter missed.

I tried to get into the shooter's mind. He obviously knew the kid came to the coffee shop every morning and ate outside. That was clear. He likely knew Stanley moved quickly and had habits that involved touching his head. I noticed that within minutes of being around the kid. The shooter would have decided on a chest shot, not a head shot, because the head moved and wobbled much more than the chest. At this distance, and with this rifle, anyone with some shooting experience would hit Stanley somewhere in the chest. Not above the clavicle. I pulled my eye away from the scope.

He missed on purpose. Because this was all about me. The shooter wanted me to dive away from Stanley, to make me look like a terrible protector, not to mention totally selfish. The shooter obviously wasn't out to kill Stanley. He was out to make me look incompetent. Which meant this was deeply personal. Whoever was behind this wanted me alive, so I could experience pain, humiliation, and basically suffer. That was why the intruder gave himself away this morning, so I would escape the impending explosion and fire. That was it; it had to be. The plan all along was to raze my house, but the detonator malfunctioned.

Obviously somebody, or perhaps some government, had found out about one of my black ops missions and was looking for payback. Which meant I was endangering the governor's son.

After blowing out a deep breath, I put my eye back to the scope to survey the scene. Just as I did, the stairwell door behind me burst open. I tensed and stayed in position. Because I didn't want to spin around and look guilty.

"Hands off, Gary." The voice made my blood pressure spike. I heard a holster unclip and a weapon draw. "Step back from the rifle."

I hesitated.

"I'll fire," the voice said. "I promise you."

I slowly stepped back and turned around, and looked directly at Agent Anfernee Gates.

CHAPTER FIVE

GATES STOOD THIRTY feet away, pointing a small automatic gun at me. I couldn't tell what type of gun it was, but I could tell his hands were wrapped too high around the stock and his feet weren't wide enough apart. It looked like he'd never fired his weapon in the line of duty.

"Drop your other weapon," he said. "I saw the bulge in the back of your shorts. And why are you barefoot? Where are your sandals?"

"It's my backup service piece, Gates. What do you care about my footwear? What's your problem with me anyway?"

"I don't care if it's a service piece. Drop it slowly, and it's Agent Gates to you."

"It's Agent Chase to you."

"Maybe a year ago it was, not now." He waved the gun at me. "Reach around slowly."

I didn't.

Steps in the stairwell drew my attention. A moment later Palmer came through the door. Following that, Kowalski waddled through, breathing like he just climbed the Empire State Building.

"Officer Palmer, relieve the suspect of his weapon."

Palmer hesitated.

"Suspect?" I said. Was he that pissed that I'd stormed out on him at the station?

"Officer," Gates barked.

Palmer walked over and relieved me of my weapon.

"This is ridiculous" I said. "The shooter got away and I came up here to follow a lead."

"Ridiculous?" Gates said. "Try cautious. You had a sniper rifle on your shoulder pointed at the scene of a crime. Doesn't seem ridiculous at all to me."

"How did you guys know I was even up here?"

"A maintenance worker heard shots and saw you climbing the ladder. He alerted us to a suspect on the roof."

"That's why you came charging up here?" I said. "Did you even ask the worker a timeline for the shots? And stop calling me a suspect."

Gates didn't respond.

"For the record," I said, "that was minutes after Stanley was shot. At least a dozen witnesses could verify this."

"Listen, Gary, I just arrived at the scene with Officer Kowalski and Palmer. We were alerted as soon as we arrived on campus that a man was spotted on the roof of this building. Naturally, we reacted right away."

"So you haven't been at the crime scene yet? Is that what you're saying? You haven't spoken with any witnesses? You're kidding me, right?"

Gates blinked at me, but didn't respond.

I took a second to breathe and compose myself. "Let me give you the short story then. I was sitting beside Stanley when he was shot. Once he was stabilized, I went after the shooter, but didn't catch him. I fired three shots at his getaway vehicle. I noticed the shooter hadn't brought his weapon down the fire escape, so I came up here to investigate." I walked toward Palmer. "Give me my piece back."

Gates stabbed his gun at me. "Stop."

I detoured away from Palmer and marched straight at Gates, stopping about two feet away.

Gates kept the gun level at my chest. The gun was a Kahr PM9, the same gun the Charlie's Angels used. I wanted to snatch it away and shove it down his throat. It was small enough to fit.

"Tell Palmer to hand over my piece," I said, wiggling my fingers.

"Not until I talk with witnesses at the scene and verify your story."

"You're kidding me?" I took another step, now I was a foot away.

Gates raised the gun at my face. "Stop, Gary."

I was close enough to look down the Kahr's barrel and see the grooves. I seethed. "Quit pointing that gun at me, and quit calling me Gary."

"Kowalski," Gates snapped. "Pat the suspect down and cuff him. He's exhibiting hostile behavior."

Kowalski didn't move, which I appreciated.

"Hostile?" I said.

Gates motioned again at Kowalski, and Kowalski still didn't move. I didn't know the chain of command in this situation, whether Palmer and Kowalski had to listen to Gates. I still wasn't sure why Gates was working out of the Long Beach PD. By Kowalski's attitude, I guessed they didn't have to listen to Gates. Maybe the officers were working with Gates and not for him. Or perhaps Kowalski was stepping up and breaking the chain of command.

Gates sighed and motioned at Palmer. "Do this."

Palmer hesitated, but eventually walked over. He patted me down, then cuffed me for the second time that morning.

"Put him in the cruiser," Gates said. "And hold him there until I get back."

Gates marched down the stairwell. The three of us followed suit. At the bottom of the stairs, we turned right and stopped in front of the cruiser. I debated making a stink and walking away, since I didn't want to deal with Gates and whatever issues he had with me.

In the end, however, I swallowed my pride. I figured Gates was working for the governor, so I knew I had to make things better, not worse. Besides, I wanted to see the look on Gates's face when he came back and had to release me.

Palmer didn't hip check me into the back seat. Kowalski didn't push my head down. A professional courtesy, I guessed. I shuffled into the back seat on my own while Gates had a quick word with Kowalski.

When Gates was out of sight, Kowalski came over and undid my cuffs. "Sorry, Chase, I have no idea what his problem is with you."

"Thanks, Kowalski. It probably didn't help that I walked out on him at the station."

"Probably not. The guy has some beef with you, that's for sure. Listen, Palmer and I are going to the shop to check-in, and to see if they're serving coffee amidst this chaos. Want some?"

"No, but thanks for the offer."

After Kowalski closed the door, I rested my head on the back of the seat. I tried not to think of the implications of Stanley being shot, but I couldn't stop the thoughts. Frank was going to have my head. The governor would go postal, which made sense. I'd go mental if something like this happened to Simon. I couldn't lobby the governor to help with my custody battle now. I'd definitely not get weekend visits back with Simon. Soon I'd be on permanent suspension. I bet I couldn't even get a job on this campus as a cop or security guard.

I glanced around the cruiser. I wanted my hands on something. I needed to squeeze something, anything. So I used both hands and gripped the seat and raged for a few moments.

After calming down, I thought about some of the more questionable missions I'd been on with *The Activity*, which was the black ops organization I used to be a member of. I had a sizeable list of people and/or governments that wanted me dead or to suffer. For about ten minutes I tried to narrow down the list. At the end of ten minutes, I came up with eight solid leads. But I didn't delve further into those leads because the driver's door opened and Gates slithered in. He didn't say anything. Neither did I.

The sight of him made my blood boil.

After close to thirty seconds of silence, he patted at his puffy hair and turned to the side. "Are you ready to start cooperating?"

"Haven't I?"

"I need details. Are you ready to give details?"

"Depends," I said.

"On what?"

"On whether you start talking first."

He narrowed his eyes. "About what?"

"About what you're doing here. About what agency you work for, that sort of thing."

"Again, this isn't a quid pro quo situation." Gates pressed his finger against the Plexiglas partition. "You're the one in the back seat in cuffs, not me."

I brought my hands up and locked my fingers behind my head. If Gates was shocked at my cuffs being off, he didn't show it.

He turned forward in the seat and looked at me through the rearview mirror. "Here's what I know so far, the assumptions I'm working from. A federal agent's house is supposed to blow up one morning, and the kid he's supposed to be protecting gets shot a few hours later. Perhaps the person hired to kill the kid tries to get rid of the protector first. A decent theory, but if that's true, why is the agent being hostile and uncooperative and lying to the police? It doesn't add up in my mind. It suggests the agent may be in on something. Maybe the agent knows more than he's letting on." He raised his eyebrows. "How's that for a quick theory, Gary?"

"Let me remind you," I said, "of your entrance to the holding room. Your lack of formal address right from the start. Your lack of professional courtesy when it comes to firearms. And your constant use of a name I told you I don't prefer. I'm not going to give you an inch until you tell me what your real problem is with me. Not to mention how you came into possession of a classified file on me. And how you arrived so quickly at the Long Beach police station."

Gates spun in his seat. "Maybe the theory goes like this. Everything that's happened today is about *you*, not the governor's son. Like I said in the holding room, this all has to do with your past, with your long list of idiotic vigilante outrages. I know about the Motel 7 operation. And, of course, everybody knows about your infamous TV appearance. So someone's out to make you pay, but they screwed up this morning and had to come back to take you out at the coffee shop. They botched that job, too. Maybe they're not that experienced, a bad shot, who knows? The bottom line, you're now endangering the kid you've been assigned to protect. The governor's son, mind you. I'm sure the governor would be pretty upset to hear that theory, wouldn't he?"

"So you do work for the governor, is that it? And you lied to me about it earlier."

He stabbed his finger at me. "I told you I don't work for him."

I leaned forward until my face was a few inches from the Plexiglas barrier. "Well, then, tell me what's going on. You're obviously obsessed with me for some reason. It's clear you were already investigating me before you got to the police station this morning."

"I don't have to tell you a thing," he snapped. "I'm under no obligation." He wiped at his mouth since a little spit had landed on his lip.

I glanced at the sliding window in the partition. I wondered if I could grab Gates's puffy hair and pull his head through the window, but I blinked away the thought and looked out of the car. Kowalski and Palmer stood a few feet from the cruiser enjoying their coffee.

"Fine then," I said, turning back to Gates. "You talked to the officers at the scene I take it."

"What does that have to do with anything?"

"Everything. Now you know I was on the roof after Stanley was shot. My story checks out, doesn't it?" I tapped on the window and got Kowalski's attention, waved him over. He waddled over and opened the door.

Before I got out, Gates said, "Just tell me what's going on. Is this about you or Stanley?"

I didn't trust Gates, so I didn't say another word. I left the cruiser and walked over to Palmer.

"Can I have my piece back?"

Palmer handed me the Sig.

I turned to Kowalski. "Where's Stanley?"

"Long Beach Memorial. He just arrived there. Before he got into the ambulance, he told a young woman who was helping him to give you this." Kowalski handed me some car keys. "Stanley wants you to drive his SUV to the hospital. It's a white Lexus in the coffee shop parking lot. And he also wanted you to bring this, said it was extremely important." Kowalski passed me Stanley's laptop.

"Thanks, Kowalski."

He winked and gave me the finger gun.

I walked a wide perimeter around the coffee shop. The place was a circus. Four news trucks were already parked at the scene. Each had a satellite aerial stretching high in the air, transmitting the breaking news to the Golden State.

Great. I was in for it.

Wanting to stay as far away from the cameras as I could, I walked an even wider berth around the coffee shop parking lot. There was a bigger circus there. As students strolled by, I had a sudden idea, so I sat on a bench and waited until I saw a male student about my size. I flagged him over. I offered him twenty-five bucks for his green flip-flops and black and gold Long Beach State hooded sweatshirt. I didn't want to go back and grab my flip-flops and risk being caught on camera.

The student must've been a business major because he negotiated hard. In the end, we settled on fifty bucks. I told him where he could get a free pair of black flip-flops if he wanted.

To blend in as a student, I took off my blue hoodie, threw it in the garbage since it had blood on it, and put on the Long Beach State sweatshirt. Pulling up the hood, I walked to the parking lot and found the white Lexus. Fortunately, nobody paid attention to me. Unfortunately, because of the traffic, it took me twice as long as it should have to get off campus and onto the 405 freeway.

While driving up the 405 toward the hospital, I realized I was gripping the steering wheel so hard my knuckles had turned white. I balled my fists and released them, trying to get rid of the tension in my body. What helped me calm down, however, was not thinking about Gates. The man infuriated me.

So I thought about Stanley instead. I prayed the kid was okay and didn't have any long-term damage to his arm. I also hoped he was awake so I could explain to him why I dove away from him before the shot. He had to know I thought the shot was aimed at me. He had to relay that information to his father. I couldn't have Stanley or the governor thinking I was trying to protect myself. I was in enough trouble for Stanley being shot on my watch.

The trip up the 405 was short. After parking, I walked into the receiving area of the hospital and checked in with a lady volunteer at the front desk. I needed to find out the location of Stanley's room. The lady volunteer, of course, was forbidden to give me information for a VIP patient like Stanley, and since I didn't have my badge with me, I couldn't flash it and demand to know his whereabouts.

I sat in the waiting area and debated contacting Frank for the information. But I didn't have to call Frank because at that moment George Pepperstein, one of the agents assigned to Stanley's investigation, bellied up to the volunteer desk asking for a free coffee.

Pepper, as I called him, was a piece of work. He was that guy who lifted a ton of weights in high school so he could push people around, but since then he hadn't lifted anything heavier than a Budweiser King can. Now he was round like a wine barrel, undefined and soft, no tone. He reminded me of John Candy, minus the jovial attitude.

After Pepper got his coffee, I followed him from a distance. I wasn't worried about him turning and spotting me. I was worried the flip-flops would give me away. They made a sharp snapping sound against the hard, polished floor.

Pepper shuffled through a maze of hallways, sipping on his coffee, finally making it to a private room about six minutes later. I stayed back thirty feet, watching the door from an intersecting hallway. Johnny Labonte, the other agent assigned to Stanley's case, sat in a blue plastic chair to the left of the private door. Pepper took a seat on the other side of it.

Twenty seconds later, I approached the private room and addressed them. "How's Stanley, gentlemen?"

Labonte sprung up. "Mag? What the hell happened? You were on protection this morning, weren't you?" He pointed at my clothes. "And what's with the outfit? You going back to school?"

Johnny Labonte was skinny and tall, and his facial features were too pronounced for his thin face. He had wavy, blond hair that he constantly ran his fingers through – a clear sign that he was quite proud of it. I didn't particularly like Labonte, but if I was being honest, I was slightly jealous of his hair.

"Seriously, Mag, what happened at the coffee shop?"

A few guys in the office started calling me 'Mag' two years ago, because of a certain incident involving a Maglite flashlight and a Motel 7. The nickname irritated me, but I never reacted to it because I didn't want to give the guys the satisfaction of it bothering me.

"The kid got shot," I said.

"Heard it was a sniper," Labonte said. "And from quite a distance. Crazy."

"I'm going in, fellas."

"Can't let you, Mag." Pepper stood. His knees cracked from the weight.

"Sure you can."

"Nope, Frank's orders. Sorry." Pepper shuffled to the left and blocked the door. Inflated his chest a bit. "He doesn't want anybody in there."

"And where's Frank?" I asked.

Pepper nodded. "In there with the doc." He pushed out a breath and deflated, as if it had been hard work holding his chest out.

"Also heard you went after the shooter," Labonte said. "Did you catch him?"

I shook my head.

"What kind of protection detail are you running?" Pepper said.

"What about your investigation?" I responded. "You think this is just my responsibility? Tell me about your leads, boys. Obviously we all underestimated the threat on Stanley. What have your keen investigative skills uncovered so far about Stanley's death threats? Sure, I'm in for it. But so are you two."

They both blinked. Pepper took a sip of coffee. Since neither was quick on their feet, they just stood and glared. A moment later the door to the private room sucked off its rubber seal and opened. Pepper and I stepped out of the way. A doctor strolled out with a chart in hand. He didn't look up. I slipped through the door just before it closed.

Frank sighed when he saw me. He held up his finger and motioned me away from Stanley's bed. Frank had grey, thinning hair that was matted to his forehead with sweat, so I knew he was beyond stressed.

"Is he okay?" I asked.

A bunch of machines pumped and hissed away. The cloying smell of cleaners, bleach, and antiseptics filled the room. I hated the smell of hospitals, so I breathed through my mouth.

"He's weak right now from the blood loss, but he'll pull through. He was in pain, so the doc gave him some heavy narcotics. He conked out a few minutes ago; he'll be in and out for a bit. What the hell happened, anyway? How did I arrive here before you?"

"I went after the shooter, then I had a little altercation with the police, which was mainly a miscommunication."

Frank rolled his eyes. "Altercation? Miscommunication? I'm not even going to ask. Tell me you got the shooter, please tell me that."

"I wish I could."

Frank pushed up his sleeves and spun around, like he had to or else he'd explode. My boss was average height and weight, but had a thick, goiter-like neck and disproportionally short arms. He had to buy huge dress shirts to fit around his neck, which meant he always had to roll up his sleeves.

He spun back. "Before we talk about Stanley getting shot, what the hell happened this morning at your house and the cop shop?"

I hesitated to answer.

Frank continued. "You're late for this important assignment. You lie to the police. You were supposed to bring in those weapons a month ago. I can't believe I stuck my neck out for you again, especially after your infamous video, and let's not forget the Motel 7 incident before that. What the hell, Chase?"

"So there was this intruder, Frank." I paused.

"I know," he said, sighing. "The cops told me that."

"How much did they tell you?"

Frank cleared his throat. "I know that someone broke into your house and you lied about it. And then the cops found all those weapons at your house. Why lie, Chase? Why would you do that?"

"I didn't want to deal with the police and be late for picking up Stanley. I figured it was just some local kid breaking in. No big deal."

"That worked out, didn't it?" Frank motioned toward Stanley, then continued. "It's not a good enough reason to lie, you know that. You're smarter than that."

I nodded. "You're right. I didn't want Gina to find out, okay? Remember we have that custody hearing in a few days. In fact, I may need your help with that."

"What do you mean?"

"Gina already found out I was arrested."

"And you want me to vouch for you? Right? Just like I did with the police?"

"I'd be grateful, Frank."

He pointed at me. "You're infuriating." He turned away again to calm down.

I used the opportunity to think about my strategy with him. I knew for sure I'd be pulled off protection, but I really needed to work the case and find out what was going on. Since somebody wanted me to suffer for some past deed, I needed to find out who and clear the threat. I needed to provide a safe environment for my son, and prove that to a judge. Somehow I needed to get on the investigation so I could use all the resources the FBI had to offer. It was a long shot—beyond a long shot actually—but I went for it anyway.

"Something really interesting came up, Frank."

"This better be good," he said, turning.

I went straight to the truth. "The intruder at my house this morning and Stanley's shooter are the same person."

Frank squinted. "How do you know?"

"Same getaway car both times. And I think this all may have to do with my past."

"Great. You mean from your black ops days?"

Frank knew I'd worked black ops, but he didn't know any more details than that.

I reluctantly nodded. "Possibly. I'm not sure exactly, but what's important—"

"No, your involvement is important, Chase." He sighed. "It's absolutely the most important part."

"Okay, granted, you're right, but what's also important is that I have a lead with this organization. I can start working some of my army connections to help figure things out."

"You're kidding me, right? You think I'm going to let you work the case? Really?"

"You need me and my connections. Take me off protection."

"Don't worry," he scoffed. "You're off protection, that's for sure."

"I'll work unofficial on this thing. You won't even know I'm on the case."

Frank stepped toward me. "You're already unofficial. And now you're off unofficial protection. You're going to be nowhere near this kid. I don't want you even talking to him. In fact, don't even look at the kid. I mean it."

"C'mon, Frank."

"You don't get it, do you? When the governor gets here, he's gonna go ballistic."

"I do get it, trust me. We're in for it, I know."

"*We're* in for it? No, not you; try me, Chase."

"That's why we have to figure it out fast. These guys," I thumbed at the door, "are useless. They're probably talking about their fantasy football picks right now when they should be talking about the case. Seriously, listen."

There was loud talk near the door. Frank humored me and walked over and listened for a second. "Dammit."

"Football, right? I told you."

"Wrong, Chase. It's—" Frank stopped mid-sentence and stepped back, just as the door heaved open.

And the governor of California stepped in.

CHAPTER SIX

"WHO'S THIS, AGENT Lemming?"

The California Governor and I were three feet apart and eye level. Ernesto Tuchek, however, didn't look at me. He had his head cocked to the right, looking at Frank over my shoulder.

Frank hesitated. "Uh."

"Well?" The governor prodded.

"Special Agent Chase, sir."

The governor locked eyes with me. "Special? That's debatable." He gave me the once over. "What on earth are you wearing? Is that what you wore to protect my son? Flip-flops?"

I tensed and stumbled with my words. "I had a bit of. I mean, I..."

"Never mind. I don't even want to hear it."

The governor turned and motioned at his entourage to stay outside, then closed the door and took three long steps, stopping at the foot of Stanley's bed. He stood there for a few silent moments, assessing Stanley's situation.

I cursed in my head, then gave the governor the once over. I couldn't believe he was Stanley's father. The two couldn't be more different. The governor was a hairy mountain of a man. He looked like a well-groomed gorilla in a black suit. No kidding. The man was tall and thick with a barrel chest and protruding forehead. He had thick hair the color of squid ink. I had a side view of him and could see his chest hair trying to escape from his white shirt. The hairs dangled over the collar like spider legs.

The governor turned and addressed me. "So you're the infamous Agent Chase. I can't believe Stanley requested you for protection."

Requested me? I scratched my head. What?

"It was your shift this morning, wasn't it, Agent Chase?"

I cleared my throat. "Yes, sir, it was."

"But you weren't at the scene when my son was shot, is that correct?"

"No, I was, just not when the police showed up. I stabilized your son, then went after the shooter."

"I take it you didn't catch him."

I shook my head.

"You knew the shooter's position then, correct? Since you went after him."

"Yes, sir. I made out his position right before the shot."

"I got a report from an agent on my way over here. He told me something happened at the scene, something that concerns me, Agent Chase. A lot." He paused and eyeballed me.

I played along. "What's that, sir?"

"Witnesses at the scene said you dove in the opposite direction from Stanley." The governor stepped toward me and entered my personal space. "You dove away from my son. Really? Is that true?"

I paused and cleared my throat again. Why did I keep doing that? My face suddenly felt as hot as the sun's surface. I cleared my throat for the third time. Damn.

"Agent Chase?" the governor said.

"I made a mistake, sir," I said, swallowing. "I thought the shot was aimed at me. At first it was, but the shooter must've shifted at the last second and aimed at your son. I'm sorry."

He shook his head. "Diving away from your responsibility?" He shot a look at Frank. "Aren't your men supposed to take a bullet for whomever they're protecting?"

Frank wiped his forehead with a handkerchief. He was about to respond, but the governor interrupted.

"Why did I go to the FBI for protection?" he said. "I should have requested Secret Service agents for the job. One of their men would've taken the bullet."

"Sir," I said. "If I knew the shooter was going after Stanley, I would have dived on top of and protected your son, no question."

"But you didn't. Explain to me why again?"

"I tried to get as far away from Stanley as I could because I thought the shot was coming for me. My guess is the shooter aimed at me on purpose. He wanted me to dive away so he had a clear shot at Stanley."

"Great," the governor said, blowing out a breath. "So the shooter is smarter than the protector. You're lucky my son's alive, Agent Chase." He turned to Frank. "Be sure he's off protection immediately. I don't want him near my son."

"Of course, Governor."

Tuchek motioned at me. "Open the door."

I opened the door. As I did, I tried to crush the metal doorknob with my right hand. I stood and waited for the 'get the hell out'. I wasn't sure why I didn't run from the room with my tail between my legs; probably out of pride.

The governor didn't tell me to get out, though. Instead, he shouted, "Agent Hornsby."

Phil Hornsby hustled in. Hornsby held the top position in FBI Los Angeles. He also oversaw the resident agency in Long Beach. His official title was Assistant Director in Charge, which was comical. ADIC was an unflattering and ill-planned acronym, but in Phil's case it was on point.

"Yes, Governor?" Hornsby fidgeted with his grey suit jacket. He wore one of those slim-cut suits, the kind of suit that was supposed to hug a person's body, but Hornsby was so wiry he couldn't fill it out, so the suit looked big and uncomfortable on him.

"Agent Chase is off protection," the governor said. "And I want the agents outside off the investigation. You're taking over, Phil. I want LA running the investigation from now on. I don't care how busy you are. Long Beach can still run protection, but not with Agent Chase on board."

"Understood, Governor."

"And I want three agents around the clock with Stanley. Eight hour shifts this time, no more twelve-hour stints. I want them sharp. Got it?"

Hornsby nodded.

The governor turned his attention to Stanley. Frank motioned at me to get out. I smoothed my hands across my stubbly head and stepped from the room. After easing the door shut, I turned and saw Anfernee Gates ten feet away.

Are you kidding me?

"How'd it go in there?" he said. "Bet the governor wasn't too pleased with you diving away from his son, was he?" Gates patted his puffy hair with his left hand and adjusted his tight pants with his right.

Everything inside me wanted to rush Gates and headbutt him, but I kept cool and refrained. Instead, I brushed by and bumped his shoulder.

"Take care, Gary," he said.

I kept walking so I didn't do anything stupid. Pepper struggled out of his plastic chair and waddled after me. I heard his lumbering footsteps behind me.

"What happened, Mag? What's going on?"

I turned, but didn't stop. "Not now, George."

Pepper waddled after me for another twenty yards until he got tired.

My mind spiraled downhill. I walked back to the reception area and plopped into a chair. I took a few deep breaths and tried to think proactively. I thought about the governor's revelation that Stanley had requested me for protection. I knew first-hand that the FBI rarely pulled protection details. The only reason why our office had ended up with the protection detail was that the governor went to college with Hornsby. So the governor had implicit trust in the FBI. He not only wanted the FBI to run the investigation, but also protection. But why was I specifically requested? I thought Frank offered me the assignment as a test. After a minute of thinking, I didn't have an answer or a theory. I had to follow up with Stanley and Frank about the issue.

As I looked around, I noticed a landline phone on the side table beside my chair. I dialed one of my closest friends, Mick Cranston. Mick and I were both recruited out of the Marines to work for *The Activity*.

We'd worked a number of missions together over the years and I wanted his input on this morning's events.

I couldn't reach Mick on his cell, though, and I hesitated to call home in case his wife, Julie, answered. She wasn't impressed with my television appearance a year ago. Mick supported me over the incident, but Julie had reservations about the circumstances, and about me in general. They had twin girls and Julie didn't think I was the best role model for the girls. She may be right.

Knowing I really needed his input, however, I decided to try Mick at home. Just before dialing, I saw the woman I'd been dating, Eva O'Connor, breeze into the hospital. I did a double take just to make sure it was her.

After a quick blink, I confirmed it was indeed Eva.

She wore her typical power suit. The grey, pinstriped jacket was cut short and fit snug to her body. Her skirt hung just above the knee. Short enough to look sexy without being unprofessional.

She walked right up to me, but didn't sit in the open chair to my left. She stood over me. "When you didn't respond to my email this morning, I knew something was up. And then rumors started exploding about Stanley. What happened, Garrison?"

"I had a hell of a morning, that's what happened. It hadn't crossed my mind to check my email."

She loosened her stance. "Tell me what went down. Tell me in detail."

I motioned to the chair. She sat. Surprisingly, Eva whipped out a notebook and took notes as I recounted my entire morning. At first I thought it was odd, but then again Eva was in law enforcement and worked for the feds, so maybe she was going to look into the situation for me. Anyway, it took about ten minutes to tell my story because Eva wanted all the details. It annoyed me that she never asked how I was.

She kept at it. "I guess that explains why you're dressed like that. Anyway, so tell me more about this intruder at your house. You said you were tipped off. How did that happen?"

"No interest in my wellbeing, huh? Or the fact that I may never see my son again."

Eva pulled closer and grabbed my hand. It shocked me how cold her hand was. "I'm sorry, Garrison, I'm obsessing about details. Are you okay?"

She managed to evoke no emotion with her question. She squeezed my hand and gave me a piercing look with her green eyes. Eva had high cheekbones and flawless, olive-colored skin. So flawless, in fact, that I wondered if she ever spent time in the sun. If she did, I imagined she was the type of woman to wear large sunglasses and an oversized hat to protect her delicate skin from its rays. At any rate, the woman was striking, and I suddenly forgot how annoyed I was with her.

"I'm fine," I said. "Just a little down."

"Understandable. Let's talk more about it tonight over dinner." She stood and looked at her watch. "I have to get back to the office."

"Which is where?"

Eva and I met a little over a year ago at a joint law enforcement symposium. Eva was there representing a classified task force from another agency. A few months ago we bumped into each other again, and we've reconnected a few times since. She can't tell me who she works for.

Eva ignored my question. "Eight fifteen tonight, sharp, for dinner."

I looked at her, not sure if she was telling me the time or asking if that time worked for me.

"Good," she said. "I'll see you at Casa D'Amici."

With that, she spun and walked out.

I collapsed into the chair. Before I could get any thinking done, I saw Frank steam into the reception area and head toward the exit. I turned in hopes that he wouldn't spot me.

I wasn't so lucky. He saw me and changed course.

Frank marched up to me and said, "We need to talk."

"About?"

"Not here, somewhere private. Let's go."

He hauled me up with one arm and led me down a short hallway. We ducked into an empty clergy room. There were two chairs in the room. The walls were painted a dark, serene green. The lighting was subdued and calming, which was in stark contrast to Frank's mood.

He told me to sit while he drew the blinds on the door's window.

"Why'd you lie to me?" He turned and walked toward my chair.

"Lied?" I said.

"Withheld the truth is a better way to put it, I guess. You didn't say a word to me about the shot coming at you. And that you dove away from the kid? Obviously you know how that looks. And obviously this doesn't help your career."

"Thanks for reminding me."

"Tell me exactly what happened at the coffee shop." Frank put his hand on my shoulder. "Let's work through this together."

I didn't like Frank standing over me, so I said, "Have a seat."

He wiped the sweat from his forehead and took a seat. "Alright, talk."

"At first I thought the shot was for me. I spotted the shooter on the roof before the trigger was pulled. It looked like he was set up to take me out, but at the last second he must've shifted."

"Maybe the plan was to take both of you out, but the rifle jammed on the second shot, the one meant for you."

"No," I said, shaking my head. "The rifle was bolt action. One shot at a time, one target in mind. Not enough time to re-rack. Not with that gun."

"So, like you said, he lured you into thinking he was going for you, knowing you'd dive away from Stanley to protect him, then he'd have a clean shot at the kid."

"I guess."

"What do you mean, I guess?"

I leaned forward. "He had a clean line at Stanley, so he could've taken out the kid easily. I shouldn't have even spotted him. It was like the shooter wanted me to know he was there."

"How so?"

"By reflection from the scope. He made the worst mistake a sniper can make, a total amateur move, and he did it three times."

"What do you mean?"

"The objective lens of any scope reflects sunlight, just like a mirror does, or the face of a watch does when the sun's rays hit the surface. Every shooter knows this. Snipers have countermeasures to protect against glare, like a hood for the lens, or a KillFlash."

"KillFlash?"

"A honeycomb-looking filter on an end of a scope that reduces reflective glare. You use a KillFlash when shooting in sunny conditions. But this shooter didn't use one. Everything else he did, though, was professional. His location, his extraction point, his dials, and all his settings were spot on. He knew what he was doing. So he must've been sending me a signal."

"Why would he do that?"

"That's why I need to be on the case, Frank, to figure this out. Why am I not dead right now? This guy had two chances to take me out. Right now I should be sunny side up on a stretcher in the county morgue. But I'm not, and I'm the best person to figure out why. You know how tough it is getting any answers about a black ops unit. But I have an in. I can solve this, I'm your best bet. Plus, I need to redeem myself, Frank. And, of course, I need to stop any further threats on my life."

He stuck a finger in my chest. "Not a chance. I'll subpoena evidence about your old unit if I have to. I'm not going to risk my career over this, or yours. If you still have one. Besides, LA's running the show now and they want a detailed account of what happened the past few days. Hornsby gave me these reports to fill out. You have some paperwork to do. Here's your share." He handed me a decent sized stack. "Get to it."

Before Frank left, I said, "One more thing."

He sighed. "What?"

"Speaking of lies, how come you never told me Stanley requested me for protection? Is it true he requested me? What's that about?"

"Not telling you something doesn't equate to lying. There's a big difference. Get that straight."

"Let me rephrase, then," I said, attempting to smile. "How come you withheld the truth?"

"I wasn't told exactly who made the request. And I didn't think it was that big a deal."

"So it's true, Stanley did request me?"

"I guess. Who cares anyway?"

"Maybe it's nothing. I'm just a little curious. If I remember correctly, you offered me the job as a test assignment, right? As if I had a choice in the matter."

"It's my management style, you should know that by now. I didn't think twice about it. I always offer agents assignments, to make it appear as if they have a say. That way if the assignment turns out lame, they don't whine to me."

"And if they refuse?"

He laughed. "I make them do it anyway. I can count the refusals on one hand, by the way. And in your case, I knew you were desperate to be working again. In reality, Chase, it really was a test assignment. I knew if you performed well on this assignment I would have leverage to get you reinstated."

He paused and put his hands out, showing me his palms.

"I know. I screwed up big time."

"I'm sorry, Chase. I really am. But I do need that," he pointed at the paperwork, "completed by the end of the day."

"So for the record, you have no idea why Stanley requested me?"

"Leave it alone. It doesn't matter anymore, you're off the case."

I looked away.

"Don't do anything stupid, Chase, I know you. And I'm warning you. The paperwork, by 5:00 p.m." He backed out of the room, pointing at me.

I leaned back and thought about doing something stupid.

CHAPTER SEVEN

I HAD TO go back and speak with Stanley and smooth things over. A dumb move, I know, but I figured my career was basically over anyway. Besides, I couldn't sit around all afternoon doing paperwork, not after everything that went down today. Unless I figured out what was going on, I'd likely never see my son again. I'd lived a year without Simon and I didn't think I could do it any longer.

I went to the Lexus and grabbed Stanley's laptop since I'd forgotten to leave it with him. After that, I headed back to Stanley's room, stopping just short of his door. I took a quick peek around the corner to make sure the governor or his entourage weren't standing outside. They weren't, so I approached the room. Labonte and Pepper still flanked the door.

"Is the governor inside?" I asked.

"Nope," Labonte said. "He just left."

"Is Stanley awake yet?" I stepped toward the door.

Pepper pried himself out of the plastic chair. "Whoa, Mag, you can't go in there."

"Is he awake?"

Pepper started to inflate himself.

"Give it a rest, George." I held up the paperwork. "Frank's orders. I'm sure you heard, you're off the case and I'm off protection. LA wants detailed accounts of the past few days, in particular what happened this morning. I need a couple of statements from the kid."

"Frank's orders?" Pepper asked.

I nodded. "He just told me on his way out."

Pepper glanced at Labonte. Labonte shrugged.

"He's awake," Pepper said.

I gave a quick knock and walked in. The hospital bed was at a forty-five-degree angle. Stanley was lounging on it. A couple of pillows puffed out from behind his head. The pumping and hissing machines were at a minimum, but the antiseptic smell seemed stronger. Stanley lit up when I walked in.

"Agent Chase, am I glad to see you, and my laptop." He motioned for it.

"Glad you're doing okay, Stanley, but give it a rest, please." I nodded at the computer while handing it over.

He ignored my comment and drew attention to his shoulder, which was wrapped in a huge sandwich of white gauze. "Pretty cool," he said. "How many times have you been shot?"

"This is serious. Six inches to the right and two inches down, you're dead, Stanley."

"I'm fine, Agent Chase. You sound like my dad."

"You know, Stanley, I dove away from you because I thought the shot was aimed at me."

He nodded. "Agent Lemming let me know. So, you didn't catch the shooter, right?"

"I tried."

"He was far away?"

I nodded. "What do you remember about the coffee shop, anyway?"

"Not much before the shot. After the shot, I remember you smacking me, then the ambulance ride."

"Lightly smacking," I corrected.

"I'm upset with my dad, by the way, for pulling you off duty. It wasn't your fault. And now I have these guys protecting me?" He motioned to the door. "They've talked football for twenty minutes straight. I can hear everything from my bed."

"Sorry, kid, I really am."

"I want you back on protection. I'm going to convince my dad."

"Why'd you pick me anyway? Your father said you requested me. Is that true?"

"It is."

"And why was that?"

"I knew your history, Agent Chase."

"And you still requested me?"

He smiled. "I can't tell you how many times I watched that video of you smacking the Marine around. You know, I always wanted a job like yours. Did I tell you that earlier?"

I shook my head.

"Are they letting you help on the investigation at least?"

"I'm doing an unofficial investigation, on my own time. Off the books, understand?"

"I think."

"Just don't tell your dad, okay? He can't know."

"Got it, I promise." He nodded fast. "I like secrets."

"Thanks." I scraped a plastic chair over to Stanley's bedside and took a seat. I needed to smooth things over with Stanley and get on his good side, so I decided to show interest in his situation. "Now tell me about these death threats and what you've been doing online. Tell me everything."

I only knew a little about Stanley's situation. I knew he'd developed some theories about a popular TV mystery show a few months ago, and that he wrote a condensed version of his theories on his Facebook page. Surprisingly, his theories about the show turned out to be correct, which gained him a large following of fans, or friends, or whatever they're called on Facebook. Somehow he'd turned his success with the television show into a lot of money. Anyway, a few weeks ago, one fan started posting death threats on Stanley's wall, telling him to stop with the theories or be stopped, that sort of thing. The fan had a bogus Facebook account and was ultimately untraceable. Most of us in the FBI thought the governor had overreacted by demanding around the clock protection.

"I'd love to tell you everything, Agent Chase." Stanley hit a button on the side of the bed and the bed hummed to a near ninety-degree angle. "Have you been watching *Stranded* on TV? That's where this all started."

I shook my head.

"Everyone's been watching it. You haven't seen it, really?"

"I watch Food Network and TV Land occasionally, that's about it."

"Well, if you watch TV Land, then you know *Gilligan's Island*."

"Sure. How does someone your age know *Gilligan's Island*?"

"Some of us young kids like classic TV, too, Agent Chase. Anyway, *Stranded* is sort of like a modern-day *Gilligan's Island*. In fact, the premise is identical; a yacht encounters a massive tropical storm and is washed ashore on an island in the middle of the South Pacific. Where the shows differ are the passengers. In *Stranded*, there are twenty-five people on the yacht, all part of the wedding party for a famous celebrity couple. They're on the boat to celebrate the rehearsal party. The interesting thing is that the actors are all B and C list celebrities, and they actually play themselves on the TV show, same name and all. The only actors who don't play themselves are the super couple."

"Super couple?"

"Yeah, you know how big-time celebrities hook up and the media conflates their name. A super couple."

I nodded like I understood.

"So these twenty-five celebrities are stranded and trying to get off the island, but every week something goes awry with their plans to leave, always some sabotage. Another nod to *Gilligan's Island*. The following week viewers learn who was involved in the sabotage and why. There is only one master saboteur, and everyone on the island has something from their past which makes them look like the saboteur."

Stanley's eyes lit up while he paused. He was clearly more excited about the show than I was. I think he wanted me to acknowledge the coolness of the show. When I didn't respond or show any emotion, he simply carried on. "The cool twist is this: Because the actors play themselves on the show, a lot of viewers wonder if the characters' back stories are true in the celebrities' real lives. The producers of the show deliberately used some real-life facts in each character's back story to fuel that speculation. It created a huge amount of buzz for the show. The show really took off when the celebrities started being killed off, one each week, always in an apparent accident, ultimately ruling them out as the saboteur."

He paused. "Cool, right?"

"Sure," I said. "Sounds real cool. So how are you profiting from this?"

Stanley pushed up his glasses and smiled. "Since the show drew thirty million viewers a week, other big companies, American Express for instance, wanted in on the action for advertising reasons. American Express and the network teamed up to create this elaborate interactive website about the show. They held weekly contests in which they gave money away to the viewer who predicted the celebrity responsible for the previous week's sabotage. That's where I came in. I entered the contests and started winning."

I scratched my head. "And how'd you do that?"

"From the start I had a pretty good idea what the show was about. I had a theory of what I thought the writers were trying to accomplish. So when the contests started, I entered my theories and won. I also posted elaborate versions of what I thought had happened in the weekly episodes on my Facebook site. In my postings on the network website, I linked people to my Facebook site to read more. After I won a few weeks in a row, I started attracting thousands of friends every day to my Facebook page. Two months later, I was approaching almost a million friends."

I squinted at him. "A million friends? I don't get it."

"I know, they aren't true friends, just people who wanted to read what I thought was happening on this show. But that's what Facebook calls them."

"Tell me about the money, Stanley."

He leaned forward and looked around. I wasn't sure why.

"The place isn't bugged," I said.

"You never know." He smiled. "Anyway, midway through the frenzy my Facebook page started jamming the server, so I was forced to start my own website. Which turned out to be a gold mine. I used my Facebook page to direct my 'friends' to the new website. Within about a week, the site had had around a million hits. Suddenly big companies wanted to advertise on my webpage. I started selling ad space and raking in the money. And you know the rest."

"Someone wanted you to stop, so they sent death threats and posted them on your Facebook page."

"Yeah, which freaked my dad out and he requested an investigation and protection. I stepped in and requested you, my favorite internet sensation, and now here we are."

"*Stranded* is still running, right? And you're still doing the webpage?"

"Yeah, the show is in the final month of production. My theories have turned out to be correct so far and I'm still posting on my webpage. I have obligations to maintain the millions of hits, to keep the advertisers happy."

I sat back and ran my hand over my head. "The network must be pissed at you, since you're predicting what's happening on the show and taking away the mystery for the viewers."

"Actually, the network supports me under the adage of 'any publicity is good publicity'. They deny any sort of wrongdoing. They're thrilled with the added buzz I've generated. Plus, they've already been investigated."

I got up from the chair and paced across the room, thinking about Stanley's death threats.

"You're antsy, Agent Chase."

I walked back and stopped at the side of his bed. "How much money are we talking about, Stanley?"

He pushed up his glasses. "Enough to buy a Lexus and a house outright."

"Enough to warrant death threats?"

"I suppose." He motioned at his wound. "I didn't take the threats seriously until this."

I paced again until a knock on the door stopped me. Pepper swung the door open before we could respond. He stepped in and glared at me.

"You lied, Mag." He held up his cellphone. "Frank called. When I mentioned you were in here talking to Stanley, he lost it. He's beyond pissed."

CHAPTER EIGHT

I SHOULD'VE GONE straight back to the office and smoothed things over with Frank, but I didn't.

I went home instead. Frank needed time to calm down. When I saw him next, it would be best to have the paperwork completed. Unfortunately, I couldn't go inside my house because yellow police tape was stretched across the front porch. Plus, there was a police sticker on my front door I couldn't tamper with. It looked like a major crime scene. I sighed and wondered if Gina had taken a picture of my front door. No doubt she'd log that picture as evidence against me at the custody hearing.

I pushed away the negative thoughts and drove to a motel a few blocks from my place. *The Faded Blue* motel was one of two motels in town. The other motel was a Motel 7 and I refused to stay there. After the Maglite incident, I refused to stay at any Motel 7, ever.

I checked in with the front desk clerk. He gave me a key to room twelve.

When I arrived at room twelve, I opened the door and thought I'd stepped into the seventies. Orange shag carpet greeted my feet and wood paneling filled my vision. A faint smell of mold combined with sea air lingered in the room. The queen bed had a blue comforter with overlapping orange circle shapes on it. The drapes had the same color scheme and pattern. There was a small kitchen with tiny white appliances. The kitchen table was white and had a chrome edge about four inches thick. The chairs matched the table's style. It was definitely retro, but not the cool kind of retro.

I pulled a chair tight to the table and began Frank's paperwork. It took most of the afternoon to fill out the mind-numbing forms. After that, I went to the motel office to use the free internet on their archaic computer.

Tapping on the dirty computer keys, I logged onto email. I wanted to send Mick a message. For all I knew he could be overseas and not using his cell, and I really needed to hear from him. I had to figure out what was going on and Mick was the perfect person to bounce some theories off.

The connection took forever. While the modem beeped and whirred, I sat and stared out the window. As I gazed out the window, I noticed a car parked across the street from the motel. It was idling, and a little suspicious looking. I went to the edge of the window for a closer look. The burgundy car was police issued, for sure. It looked like a Crown Vic. The side windows had heavy tint and the back window had a lighter coat. I could just barely make out the silhouette of a man's upper body above the steering wheel. He was turned to the side, looking directly at the motel office.

Keeping my eye on the car, I went back to the computer and fired off a message to Mick, telling him to contact me ASAP via email. After that, I turned my full attention to the Crown Vic, which still looked odd and out of place.

I got up and left the office, crossed the street, and ambled toward Stanley's Lexus. I made sure not to look at the suspicious vehicle. As soon as I stuck the key in the door, I heard the Vic's gearshift drop into drive. I looked up and watched the Crown Vic zoom away. The sun shone through the passenger side of the car and lit up the driver from the side. The silhouette of the man was unmistakable, especially the messed up, puffy hair.

Gates? Are you kidding me? Was he watching me?

I leaned against the SUV and thought some more. What was his problem? Was he somehow the key to this morning's mystery? I smoothed my hands over my scalp a few times. I didn't know the answer, but I knew I had to find out. Maybe Mick could find out some information. He definitely had abilities and the necessary security clearance to look into it.

After grabbing the paperwork from the motel room, I headed to work. When I arrived at Frank's office, his blinds were open and his back was to me. He was talking on the speakerphone, which meant he was mildly ticked. When Frank was pissed, he bent over the speaker and shouted into it. He only used the receiver when he was calm.

I waited until Frank hung up. He saw me through the blinds and sighed, collapsing into his chair. He didn't motion me in, but I went anyway.

"What if the governor came back when you were in the room with Stanley?" He held out both hands. "What the hell were you thinking?"

"He didn't, Frank."

"What if he finds out you were there anyway?"

"It's taken care of. Stanley will keep it on the down-low. Trust me. And besides, I was just returning the kid's laptop."

Frank pushed back from his desk and stood. "I can't handle you anymore, or trust you for that matter. I told you not to do anything stupid. You're exhausting." He waved his hand at the stack of papers. "That done?"

I nodded.

"Thorough?"

"Every detail." I put the stack on his desk.

"Good." He pushed up his sleeves. "Now you're done."

"What's that supposed to mean?"

"You're officially not unofficially working anymore."

I held up my hands. "I don't even know what that means."

"Honestly, I don't either. The one thing I do know, however, is that you're making this harder on yourself, and for me."

"I just went to give the laptop back."

"Really?"

"Okay, I wanted to find out why he requested me, and see if I could smooth things over a little."

"Exactly." He pointed a stumpy finger at me. "After I clearly told you to drop it. And don't for a second think I believe you were asking the kid questions for the LA report. Please spare me that lie."

I folded my arms and stared at him. He didn't say anything.

After a few awkward moments, I said, "Do you happen to know of another federal agent working Stanley's case?" I really didn't want to mention Gates to Frank, but I needed any information I could get on the man.

"Another agent?" Frank pushed his greasy hair off his forehead. "From where?"

"I'm not sure exactly."

"What the hell's going on, Chase?"

"An agent by the name of Anfernee Gates has some sort of beef with me. He's been tailing me, and it appears he's investigating me for some reason."

Frank threw up his hands. "Just great."

"It wouldn't have to do with my suspension, would it?"

"No way. Not a chance. That's definitely an internal matter." Frank turned and thought for a moment, then turned back. "Why would a federal agent be investigating you? What aren't you telling me? Actually, I don't want to know. Scratch that question."

I didn't let it go. "Maybe the governor hired him to check up on me. That's all I can think."

Frank eyed me. "Maybe, maybe not." He walked to his desk and sat down. "Who knows and who cares anyway?"

I leaned on his desk. "What's that supposed to mean?"

He pointed at me again. "For the last time, you're off protection and not on the case, so drop it. Now let me get back to work."

"One last thing, Frank, I promise that's all."

He sighed. "What?"

"Are you really putting Labonte and Pepper on protection? I don't think Stanley is in any danger, but I want to be extra cautious, and I don't trust those guys."

"I have to. And before you question me on that, I get your concern, believe me, I share it, but Stanley will be contained by tonight. I think they can handle it."

"Contained?"

"The governor is pulling Stanley from the hospital this afternoon. There are too many entrances and exits to worry about, and too many people in and out of the hospital. He's paranoid, you know."

"Where's the kid going?"

"Home, with twenty-four-hour nursing care."

I gave Frank a look.

"They can at least handle a home assignment," he said. "In fact, I'm going to put them both on the evening shift. One inside the house and the other outside."

"So you're going to double down on two incompetent people?"

"Out." He pointed at the door. "It's not your problem to worry about, got it?"

I opened the door.

"One more thing," Frank said. "The governor wants you to drop off the Lexus at Stanley's house as soon as you can. And then you're done with this case for good, got it?"

I nodded and walked out.

There wasn't a chance I was going to drop Stanley's case. After all, the case was about me, likely from a questionable mission I'd had with *The Activity*. I had to figure out what was going on and neutralize the threat. That way I could prove to the judge that I could provide a safe environment for Simon.

So, instead of dropping the case, I went straight into investigative mode. I took the stairs to my office and checked my email, hoping Mick had responded.

He hadn't.

While I drummed my fingers on the desk, I looked at my office phone and wondered if I should use it. I had a number of buddies and associates in the intelligence world I wanted to call. If Mick wasn't available, I had other options. As I looked at the phone, however, I knew it wasn't a good idea to call from my office. Frank could find out.

I grabbed my old-school rolodex from a desk drawer and drove back to the motel. I set the phone on the chrome kitchen table and got to work, reviewing all my various contacts from my operative days. I settled on six people to call; people I knew were still in government intelligence. All six calls went to voicemail, however. I found a seventh person to call, but when that call went straight to voicemail, I slammed the phone down. I wanted answers. I wanted progress. And I wasn't getting either.

To cool off, I took a walk to my local surf shop to get some new clothes. Along the way, I realized what a hypocrite I was being, since I didn't even own a cellphone. People had a hard time getting in touch with me, so who was I to judge a person who didn't answer their phone? Besides, the number I was calling from was foreign to the person on the other end. The person probably thought I was a telemarketer and didn't dare answer.

At the surf shop I purchased a collared shirt, a new pair of dark jeans, and some Vans shoes. When I got back to the motel, I called the seven numbers again. Nobody answered, of course. This time, however, I left a quick voicemail and told the person to call my beeper number. After that, I showered, changed into my new clothes, and headed to *Casa D'Amici* to meet Eva.

I made it to the restaurant a few minutes early. It was a modern Italian place that Eva said had been featured on Food Network. Naturally, it was busy. What surprised me were the number of servers, greeters, and managers on duty, which added to the overall chaos. Everybody was running around attending to people or trying to look busy. It reminded me of the chaos that ensued on the patio after Stanley was shot.

Eva wasn't there yet so I checked in with a greeter. Two people escorted me to our table. I sat and drank water. Though Eva insisted I be there at 8:15 sharp, she didn't roll in until twelve minutes past that time. She weaved through the tables wearing the same power suit as this morning. Her hair was down. It flowed and bounced with each confident stride. She looked striking. I forgot all about punctuality.

I stood, but didn't pull out her chair. I did that on our first date and she almost popped me in the face.

"Garrison," she said, nodding from ten feet away.

"Evangeline."

She stopped in her tracks. I'd forgotten she had the opposite view from mine. She hated her full name. "Sorry, Eva."

She took a seat, no smile.

"I'll start with a drink," she said. "I know you need one."

"How about a bottle?"

She leaned forward, still no smile. "How about two?"

"You had a rough day as well?"

"You could say that, but not nearly as bad as yours. Tell me more. We didn't get to cover too much at the hospital."

I smiled. "Why don't we mix it up a bit? I'd love to hear about your day first."

She sighed.

"Right," I said. "Can't talk about it."

"Naturally."

The sommelier interrupted us. "Something to drink for you two?"

I ordered a Zinfandel from Paso Robles, California. Eva nodded her approval.

"You're on," she said.

"Let's order first."

"Fine." She picked up the menu.

Since I always ordered risotto at Italian restaurants, I didn't need to look at the menu. I spent the time instead watching Eva over the top of it. The woman was definitely sexy. It wasn't a free-flowing, carefree sexiness, though, more of a clinical sexiness, like a hot female doctor or scientist. Her personality was a challenge, which was what intrigued me about her. I wondered if her personality was truly rigid and harsh, or if it was a product of working in a man's profession. Maybe she just wanted some respect in her profession and carried herself accordingly. All I wanted was to crack her shell, make her laugh, and watch her shake her hair. Heck, right now I'd settle for a smile.

She snapped the menu shut. "So, let's hear it."

"No pad and pen?" I smiled.

She didn't.

"Listen," I said.

"Excuse me, sir." The sommelier stood to my right with a bottle splayed over his forearm. I nodded and he uncorked it, then he poured a splash and slid the glass toward me. Eva jumped in and redirected the glass her way, like a true control freak. I watched her take a sip and swallow, then subtly mop the wine from her lips with the tip of her tongue.

Eva nodded to the sommelier, then told him what she wanted for dinner, even though I was positive she knew he didn't take food orders. To his credit, he never said a word, just nodded along and poured two glasses of wine. I followed suit and ordered.

We took sips, then Eva put down her glass and stared at me. She wasn't going to ask again about my day. She was above that.

I told her everything. I relayed more details about Stanley's shooter, and how I didn't catch him. I asked her about Agent Gates, but she'd never heard of the man. I talked about how I bumped into the governor at the hospital and he yanked me off protection. And how Frank officially took me off unofficial work.

"So what are you going to do now?" she asked.

I leaned forward. "Figure this whole situation out. What else would I do?"

"Do you think that's wise?" Eva slid her slender arm across the table and touched my hand. She had long, thin fingers and beautifully manicured nails. In contrast, her touch was slightly clammy. "What about Simon, Garrison? Won't this jeopardize your chances with custody? Aren't you thinking about him?"

I pulled my hand back. "Of course I'm thinking about him. That's all I think about."

The table beside us looked over. I realized my voice had gotten loud, so I took a second to compose myself, then proceeded in a soft tone. "I know I've basically lost the hearing, and that guts me more than you can imagine. But all I can do is pursue this, figure things out, make a safe home for Simon, and restore my reputation. If I don't, I'll have to send my son cards on his birthday, for crying out loud. I'll have to sneak into Little League games to watch him play. And I won't end up that type of father. I won't. I refuse."

"You're being dramatic, Garrison." She stated it plainly, with a half-smile.

I was about to unleash on her, but checked myself. Eva's comment was probably her twisted way of telling me that everything would be okay. She didn't have kids, so she hadn't a clue what it would feel like to be forbidden from seeing them.

"Well, I have to do something," I said. "What would you do in my situation?"

She took a sip of wine, then leaned forward. "I don't have kids, or even want any for that matter, but if I did, I imagine I'd do anything for them. So, yes, I guess you're right, you should pursue this." She finally smiled, something she should do more often. "Pursue this with everything you have, Garrison. I mean it. To the very end."

Since her smile appeared genuine, I wondered if the ice queen was melting. Maybe I had finally cracked her shell.

Our dinner came and the conversation turned to food for a while. Eva talked about how well her dinner complemented the different nuances of the Zinfandel. During dessert, we discussed Special Agent Anfernee Gates. Eva seemed especially interested in Gates, asking me tons of questions about him and strategizing how best to handle the situation.

I was about to suggest an after-dinner drink when two people walked into the restaurant and caught my attention. They were two people I couldn't believe were together. Two people I never in my life thought I'd see together. It didn't make sense, not at all, not in the world I inhabited.

I watched the hostess seat the couple. I guess my mouth was open or my eyes were bugged out because Eva asked, "What's wrong, Garrison? Your dead father walk in or something?"

I didn't respond. I stared at Gina, my ex-wife, then my eyes locked onto her date. My mind replayed what Gina had said about the Infiniti earlier in the day: 'My new boyfriend bought me this. You know him, by the way'.

I sure did. The bastard sitting across from Gina was my court-ordered therapist, Dr. Frances Julian, an effeminate man I nicknamed Doc Jules. He was the man I was forced to spend an hour with once a week for an entire year.

I grabbed my water glass and downed the contents.

"What's going on?" Eva said. "Don't break the glass, Garrison, your knuckles are all white." She turned her head and followed my gaze. "Who are you looking at?"

"Nobody." I relaxed my grip and took a breath. I looked at Eva and felt my face turn red. I saw raging white spots when I blinked. "It's my stomach, something didn't quite agree with me. I'll be right back." I headed to the bathroom.

"Garrison," Eva said after me.

I ignored her and hurried to the men's room. Naturally, I wanted to charge their table and clothesline my therapist, but I held back. I went to the bathroom and splashed water onto my face to cool down. How could this be happening? It had to be a violation of the therapist/client relationship. There had to be some sort of ethical code he was violating. Right?

I looked at myself in the mirror. I realized my face wasn't getting better because I was gripping the edge of the sink with the intention of crushing it; so I let go and splashed more water onto my face. When I finished, another man rolled into the bathroom. I grabbed some paper towels and took a seat in a stall.

I sat there for some time, reviewing in my mind what I'd actually revealed to Jules.

After that, I thought about the doc himself. When I first met the man, I pegged him as smarmy and untrustworthy. Then a few months later I found out he'd been to college with Gina, and I lost it. The doc didn't seem to have a problem with the connection, but I certainly did. So I looked into switching therapists, but when I learned if I switched therapists I couldn't bank the months I'd already put in, I laid that idea to rest.

I dabbed at my forehead with the paper towels. Perhaps I had everything wrong. Maybe Jules and Gina were just two old college friends having dinner together. But then why would they be at a romantic Italian restaurant?

Nope, I was right. Unbelievable. They must be dating. I knew I should've trusted my instincts with that man.

I banged the stall door open and walked back to the table. About halfway there, the sommelier met me. He matched my stride and handed me the bill.

"She just left, sir. She paid for half."

I saw our empty table and looked at my watch. I'd been gone about thirteen minutes. I looked past the table and saw Gina looking at me.

She smiled when our eyes met.

CHAPTER NINE

I WALKED CALMLY out of the restaurant.

As I did, I tried to breathe smoothly in hopes of dissipating the redness of my face. Outside, I noticed Gina's Infiniti just happened to be parked next to the Lexus. It was a good thing I didn't have my car. If I were driving my green '86 Chevy Caprice, I may have backed up and used the trailer hitch to do some damage to the Infiniti.

I hopped into the Lexus and started driving. The vision of Simon and my ex-therapist filled my mind. Had they spent time together? Had they actually interacted? I envisioned Jules pushing my son in a swing at our local park, then I saw them playing together in the sand at the beach. Tempted to swerve into oncoming traffic, I pulled the Lexus over and tried to force Jules and Simon from my mind.

I rolled down the windows and let the sea breeze in. The sounds of Long Beach buzzed in the background. In an effort to clear my thoughts, I focused on the steady noise for maybe five or ten minutes. I wasn't sure how long. When a city bus pulled in behind me and flashed its giant, bright lights, I snapped out of it and pulled away from the bus-loading zone.

Fifteen minutes later I found myself near Stanley's house. I had to drop off the Lexus, but I also wanted to check up on Labonte and Pepper.

I didn't trust them to do a good job. I felt it necessary to back up Stanley's backup. Now that I was off protection, I didn't think Stanley would be in danger, but I wanted to keep an eye on him tonight and make sure of it. Besides, if I went back to the motel, I knew I wouldn't sleep, not with everything that had happened today.

I parked the Lexus by the red-painted part of the curb on the kid's cross street. Stanley's house was three in from the corner. Most of the Lexus was protected from view, covered by a large bush on the corner lot. Only the windshield and hood could be seen from Stanley's yard. If anyone involved in the case spotted me, I'd pull into Stanley's driveway and tell the person I was dropping off the SUV as requested.

Labonte had outside duty. He'd parked across the street from Stanley's. The cruiser was pointed away from me. I could see the back of Labonte's head. Every thirty seconds his head tilted back as he slurped from a large, Styrofoam coffee cup. Pepper was inside the house.

I settled into the driver's seat and rolled down the four windows. That way I could be alerted to any unusual noises in the neighborhood, and I could hear someone sneaking up behind me, which was a force of habit from my operative days.

I sat, stared at Stanley's house, and found myself alone with my thoughts. Which was a good thing. All day I hadn't much opportunity to sit uninterrupted and think about what was going on. I worked through every player and situation that I'd encountered during the day. Tried to think about as many angles and possibilities as I could. It took a few hours.

After that, my thoughts turned to the governor. I figured he put Agent Gates on the job to watch me. The governor wanted to back up Stanley's choice of backup, exactly what I was doing now. Perhaps Stanley lobbied his father on my behalf, stressing how much he wanted me on protection. Maybe the governor couldn't say no to his son, but he hired another agent to watch me. If that was the case, I could understand Gates's beef with me because, admittedly, I wasn't overly talkative or forthcoming with evidence, and I did lie to the police.

That was a decent enough theory.

Cracking my knuckles, I turned off my thoughts and looked over at the cruiser. It was quarter to three in the morning and Labonte's head was nowhere to be seen. He'd likely fallen asleep and slumped over. Earlier I'd noticed a pocket-sized camcorder in the Lexus's console. I picked it up and played with it until I figured out how to use it, then I left the car and crept to the cruiser, staying in the shadows of the trees and bushes that lined the sidewalk. When I reached the passenger door, I shot a thirty-second video of Labonte slumped over the wheel. Then I slipped into the car, and Labonte sprang up.

"Mag," he said, yawning. "You scared the hell outta me. What're you doing here? You can't be here."

"Two things," I said. "Call me 'Mag' again and you'll personally meet my Maglite flashlight, and it's the big one with four 'D' batteries." I paused.

Labonte looked blankly at me.

"Got it?"

He swallowed and nodded.

"Second, if you fall asleep again while on protection, I'll send this video to the governor and Hornsby." I held up the camera. "I'll be sure to highlight the date and time."

He blinked. "So you've been watching me watch Stanley?"

"Good thing I was."

"But you're off protection and not supposed to be anywhere near this case. That's what Frank said."

I jiggled the camera.

Labonte didn't pursue it further.

"Keep it together, Johnny, at least for the next three hours. Stanley's life could still be in danger. You never know."

Since I didn't want Labonte to know where I'd parked, I left the cruiser and headed in the opposite direction from the Lexus, then I doubled back. I eased into the Lexus and tried to get a few minutes of sleep. After my interaction with Labonte, I knew he'd be awake and on watch for at least an hour before maybe dozing off again.

My mind didn't turn off, however, so I couldn't sleep. I knew I had little time to figure out who was after me, so I came up with a game plan. I'd wait for one of my intelligence contacts to come through. My goal was to find out if there was any chatter about some foreign government getting wind of a previous assignment I was on. I also wanted to connect with Mick and see if he had experienced any threats. If he'd been targeted, then most definitely everything that happened today was about one of my past missions.

I pulled the lever on the seat and reclined. In the morning, I'd return the Lexus and see if I could get some face time with Stanley, see if he'd noticed anything at the coffee shop that I'd missed. A face-to-face meeting was unlikely to happen, however.

As I thought about how to get some face time with Stanley, I heard a slight click followed by a louder whirring sound. A sprinkler suddenly popped up by Labonte's cruiser. It started pelting water against the car. Labonte bolted out of the vehicle with his weapon drawn. I watched him run a full circle around the cruiser, scared out of his mind. It was the only entertaining thing that happened all night.

After Labonte settled back into the cruiser, I knew for sure he'd stay awake until morning, so I shut my eyes and rested, but I still couldn't fall asleep.

About two hours later, just before dawn, headlights filled my rearview mirror and caused me to perk up. A moment later a Ford 500 raced past me on the left, then turned right onto Stanley's street. As the car turned, I glimpsed a woman driver. She pulled into Stanley's driveway.

Figuring she was a nurse, I was surprised to see she wasn't wearing scrubs. The woman wore snug blue jeans and a white V-neck t-shirt. Her legs were short but thin, and her upper body was petite and fit. She had the look and build of a cheerleader. She was small and didn't weigh much, so she would've been the cheerleader at the top of the pyramid.

Before heading to the door, she looked over at Labonte and nodded. She must've been one of the agents from the LA field office working the investigation. Labonte crawled out of the cruiser, stretched his legs, and walked over.

It was getting light, so I could make out her face. She had dirty-blonde hair, cut short and stylish and tousled about. Immediately I thought of Anne Heche or a younger Meg Ryan. The woman wasn't sexy, but definitely cute, real cute.

They talked for a few minutes. Labonte smiled too much and used too many hand gestures. The woman was all business, nodding along as Labonte talked. I could tell she only wanted the facts.

Right away I liked her.

When it appeared that Labonte was relaying his sprinkler story, she turned and walked to the front door. She had a spring in her step and walked on the balls of her feet. That told me she was athletic and in good shape. Now she reminded me more of a professional fitness competitor than a cheerleader.

The woman knocked on the door as Labonte carried on talking behind her. A moment later, Pepper swung the door open and greeted the two with a cheery smile. He had a giant coffee mug in his left hand. He held it up, motioning to the lady to see if she wanted a cup. She shook her head.

Stanley popped into the doorway. His shoulder and clavicle were bandaged and his arm rested at a ninety-degree angle in a cream-colored sling. He looked excited to have more visitors. Labonte stepped in front of the door, turned around, and pointed toward the cruiser. Started talking fast and laughing. I imagined he was relaying the sprinkler story for the second time.

I yawned and fired up the Lexus. I was going to find a good cup of coffee, then circle back and drop off the Lexus.

As I pulled away from the curb, a distant crack shattered the morning stillness. The first thing I saw were birds scattering from multiple trees on Stanley's street. My right foot jammed the brakes. I gripped the steering wheel tight with both hands. My whole body went rigid.

The crack was clearly a rifle shot. I glanced toward Stanley's house, holding my breath, expecting to see Stanley Tuchek mowed down on his front door step.

Instead, I watched Johnny Labonte blast off his feet and slam into the side of Stanley's front door.

CHAPTER TEN

WATCHING LABONTE SLITHER down the doorframe got me moving. My right foot stomped onto the gas pedal. I didn't bother making the right turn. The Lexus bounced over the curb and burned across the grass. My eyes locked onto the house as I pointed the hood at Stanley's front door. I witnessed the woman sack Stanley in the midsection and lift him off his feet. The two fell backward and slid across the hardwood, out of view and harm's way. Pepper dropped knee-first to the ground and covered his face with both hands. Labonte's body leaned against the bottom right side of the door in the sitting position. The shot had taken out a portion of his right side, just below his chest. Some intestines had spilled out.

I skidded to a stop in front of the house. There were six concrete steps leading to the front door landing. I inched the Lexus up five steps, jammed it into park, and pulled the emergency brake. The SUV blocked most of the front door and protected Labonte and Pepper.

Yelling at Pepper to snap out of it, I grabbed Labonte under his arms and dragged him inside. Pepper followed suit and slammed the door shut.

"Grab a towel, George, or something to cover up the wound."

"Who are you?"

I turned around and saw the woman had a gun pointed at me. Stanley said something, but it was indecipherable.

I looked at the woman. "Agent Chase, from Long Beach."

She dropped the gun. "Sorry."

"Would have done the same thing. You two move to the back of the house."

Pepper came back with a bathroom towel. I motioned for it.

"No, I'll do it," he said. "You call 911." He flipped me his cell.

While I dialed and waited, I checked for a pulse. I looked at Pepper. "He's got a pulse, but it's faint. Sorry, George."

"He'll make it."

The operator answered and I requested an ambulance, then I turned to Pepper. "You have decent pressure on the wound?"

He nodded.

"How else can I help?"

"I've got it from here," he said. "Go protect the kid. Secure the back rooms. There's two bedrooms and a laundry room back there."

I nodded and hustled to the back of the house. Stanley was sitting alone on a bed in one of the back bedrooms. The woman had drawn the blinds, so the room was a little dark. The walls were a forest green color and there was only a single bed in the room. I could hear the woman rustling about in another room, already securing the back of the house.

"You alright, Stanley?"

He blinked fast. "This can't be happening. This can't be real. Is Agent Labonte dead?"

Before I could respond, the female agent bounded into the room.

"Everything's secure," she said. "And the backyard is clear. We're safe for now."

"The shooter was pretty far away," I said. "I could tell from the sound of the crack. There's a twenty-story apartment complex about 300 yards from here. The shooter must've set up on the roof."

"So he's long gone already," she said. "Probably not a threat."

I nodded. "On the freeway by now. I take it you're from the LA office?"

"Agent Karla Dickerson. Where were you, by the way? How'd you get here so fast??"

I told the truth. "I was in Stanley's Lexus, parked on the corner. Didn't trust Labonte to stay awake all night. I was on protection before the shooting—"

She nodded. "I read your report last night." She turned to Stanley. "You all right?"

"Agent Labonte will be okay, won't he? He's not dead, is he? This can't be happening. This isn't real." Stanley stood, then paced back and forth. He was breathing hard, to the point of hyperventilation.

The ambulance could be heard in the background. All I could think to say was: "The paramedics will be here soon. He's got a chance."

Karla took a seat on the bed and patted the spot next to her. "Come, Stanley, have a seat. We need to calm your breathing." She put an arm around his shoulder and gave him a comforting squeeze.

I tried to process what had just happened. By the look on her face, Karla was doing the same thing.

Why had Labonte been shot? Why him? It didn't make sense with my theory. Shooting Johnny Labonte didn't hurt me, didn't make me look incompetent, it wouldn't be payback for anything. I may have had it all wrong. Perhaps this was about Stanley after all, and what he'd been doing online.

Stanley stopped pacing. "Was that bullet meant for me, Agent Chase?"

"I'm not sure," I said. "The shooter missed badly if it was meant for you."

He pushed up his glasses. "Everything is suddenly spiraling out of control."

"Suddenly?" I said. "What do you mean by that?"

Karla put her hand on Stanley's knee. "It's not your fault. None of this is your fault."

"I want you back on protection, Agent Chase. Promise me that. I don't want anyone else but you protecting me."

That wasn't going to happen, but I tried to stay positive. "We'll see, Stanley."

The kid walked to the corner of the room and started texting.

"Who are you texting?" I asked.

He didn't look up.

"Stanley."

He looked up, but didn't stop texting. "Letting my dad know I'm okay."

I nodded. When he finished texting, I said, "We didn't finish our conversation at the hospital. You up for talking more about your situation?"

"We need to know everything," Karla said. "Talking about it will keep your mind off what just happened."

Stanley sniffed. "What more do you want to know? I feel like I've told you both almost everything."

Karla motioned for Stanley to sit beside her. He did.

"How much money are we talking about exactly?" I asked. "What have you made off the website and sponsorship?"

"To date, 1.8 million."

Karla and I exchanged glances. She pulled out a pad and made a note.

I asked, "How do you know so much about this TV show?"

"I don't have a job, Agent Chase. I spend all week thinking about the show and running different scenarios and theories through my mind. Gives me an advantage over most people. Other than the writers, who else can devote that much time to the show? I know where the writers are going with the show, figured it out months ago. They're pretty predictable actually."

"You're pissing off the network," I said. "That has to be it."

"That's not what I gathered," Karla said. "That's the second thing I checked after meeting with the governor and being assigned Stanley's case yesterday afternoon. I figured the network had the best motive for stopping Stanley, considering the amount of attention he was generating."

I sat on the other side of Stanley. "What was the first?"

"I checked in with Stanley at the hospital, just before he was transferred home. Asked these same questions. After we talked, I went straight to the WBC and met with two execs."

"Why isn't the WBC upset about all this?"

"They're not losing any money because of Stanley. In fact, they're making money."

"How so?"

"All the attention Stanley's site receives draws more attention to the show itself. This generates more viewers, and a higher Nielsen rating. In turn, the network keeps increasing their price for commercial spots. They're happy with what Stanley's doing."

"But what about his theories? Is he not giving some of the show's secrets away?"

Stanley waved his hand. "Guys, I'm right here."

"His theories are not always right," Karla said.

"Only one mistake," Stanley added.

"Plus," Karla continued, "he's not giving away any big secrets."

"Does he even know the big secrets?" I said. "How could he? He's not writing the script."

"Enough." Stanley stood, looked at Karla first, and then me. "I'm right here, you two."

We both looked at Stanley and gave him our attention.

"I'm not going to give everything away," he said, "like who the ultimate villain is. If I did, people would stop visiting my site, which would stop all the hits, which would stop the advertising. I have to play it strategically. So I give away a bit of info each week."

I eyed Karla. "You sure the execs were being truthful? Maybe they were hiding something."

"I know when people are lying to me."

I believed her.

"Sounds like there's some commotion out there," Karla said. "I guess one of us should go and take a look."

I hadn't noticed the sounds coming from down the hall. I wasn't about to leave the kid's side. Karla sensed that and slipped out. Stanley started pacing again. After seeing Labonte's intestines spill out, I imagined he was in shock.

"You okay? That must've been traumatic for you to see."

He didn't stop pacing or look up. "It's all so suddenly real now. I don't know what to make of it."

"You've said that twice. What do you mean by suddenly so real? Wasn't it real after you were shot?"

He hesitated to answer, pushing up his glasses instead.

"What do you mean, Stanley?"

He sighed. "I don't remember much about being shot. I guess that's it. But seeing someone shot with their insides hanging out has really affected me, Agent Chase."

I nodded.

"Does Agent Labonte have family? A wife and kids?"

"No, he's single, not sure if he has a girlfriend or not. I don't know him that well."

"He has to live. He can't die."

"It's bad, Stanley. He may not make it; you have to prepare yourself for that."

"I can't believe this." Stanley whipped out his cell and started texting again.

I was about to question who he was texting, but decided against it. Instead, I focused my thoughts on Labonte. Why had the sniper taken out his right side? Why not blow off his head or shoot dead center in the chest? Did the sniper miss again on purpose, like he did with Stanley?

Ten minutes later, I had no answers, and I had no time to think anyway. Karla came back to the room and told me that Stanley was requested up front. The three of us walked down a narrow hallway toward the living room. When I stepped into the living room, all activity ground to a halt. The living room went deathly quiet.

Frank was in the middle of the room, with Phil Hornsby to his left. Frank looked at me and wiped his brow. Behind Frank, in the corner, stood Anfernee Gates. When Gates saw me, he actually waved, which nobody saw but me.

A deep voice to my left said, "What the hell are you doing here?"

I looked over. The front door was wide open and the governor was standing on the landing. He steamed through the front door. All I could see was his mountainous chest barreling right at me.

I held my ground and braced for the impact.

CHAPTER ELEVEN

THE GOVERNOR STOPPED his charge exactly two feet from me. Nobody said a word. It felt like the air had been sucked from the room and everyone was holding their breath to conserve oxygen.

"I said, what the hell is he doing here?" The governor pointed at me, but looked around the room.

Phil Hornsby stepped forward. "I'd like to know as well."

Frank wiped his forehead with a handkerchief. I didn't know if he was stalling while thinking of what to say, or if he'd simply locked up.

I let out a slow breath and was about to speak, but Karla stepped in.

"I told Agent Chase to meet me here before I started work. That way he could drop off the Lexus and I could give him a ride home."

I looked at her. She was something.

The governor jammed his thumb over his shoulder. "What's with the parking job?"

All eyes diverted to me.

I cleared my throat. "When I came around the corner, the shot went off. I bee-lined it here and used the Lexus to block the front door from additional fire."

The governor glared at me for a few seconds. "What about the shooter? I take it you didn't catch him again." He looked around the room. "Anyone go after the shooter?"

Everyone continued conserving oxygen.

The governor faced me. "Looks like we have ample protection here, Agent Chase. You're dismissed."

I nodded.

"For good," he added.

What was that supposed to mean? Did he have the power to fire me?

"Good day, Agent Chase." The governor waved toward the door.

I started walking that way. As I did, I caught movement in my right eye. I looked over and saw Gates staring at me with an ear to ear smile. He mouthed the word bye, then waved and smiled again.

I lost it. "Something funny, Agent Gates? Is that why you're smiling?"

Gates dropped his arm, and the smile. I wasn't sure if anyone else in the room had caught his mocking gesture.

"Nothing funny about a federal agent being shot and near death," I said. "Is there?"

He didn't say anything.

"Show some respect," I said.

Frank swept in behind me. He grabbed my right arm and ushered me outside. He kept quiet because a lone news van had parked across the street. A camera was already pointed our direction. A policeman was in the process of taping off the crime scene. The cop held the tape up for us as we ducked under. We kept walking until we passed the corner where I had parked the Lexus.

Once we were out of sight, Frank turned to me. "You're lucky she saved your ass."

"What do you mean?"

"You think I buy Dickerson's story? That you just came here coincidentally the second Labonte was shot? You were watching Stanley's house, weren't you? You deliberately disobeyed my orders to leave this alone, didn't you?"

I didn't deny or confirm. "Come on, Frank, you're already down one agent with Labonte. You need me. I can help on this."

He stuck his finger in my chest. "You're done; you've forced my hand. I'm putting you on unpaid leave."

"Frank, I'm sorry for forcing your hand. I get that you're just doing your job. I've been pushing it because I have a lot at stake here. If you put me on unpaid leave, things only get worse for me, especially if Gina or the custody judge finds out. "

Frank took his finger off my chest, but he didn't say anything.

"Please, Frank," I said, swallowing. "Everything's crumbling." I stopped before getting emotional.

Frank turned away and sighed. He smoothed out his hair and put his hands on his hips. Finally, he turned back. "I'll fill out the paperwork, but won't send it to HR, not unless Hornsby or the governor request it. You'd better disappear and not push this anymore. One word from either man and you're done. Got it?"

I nodded.

"Good, now give me your piece."

"Come on, Frank, really?"

"Absolutely." He wiggled his fingers. "I know you have a backup piece."

I reached back and handed over the Sig Sauer.

Frank pointed the butt of the gun at me. "Disappear."

While Frank marched back to Stanley's, I stood on the sidewalk and searched for something to punch or kick. I settled for the curb and took a step toward it, but Karla honked and distracted me. She pulled her blue Ford 500 over to the curb.

"Get in," she said.

"Not a good career move for you, being seen with me and all."

"Get in."

I hopped in. "Thanks for bailing me out back there."

"After the couple of days you've had, I'm happy to. Buckle up."

"I'm fine with going through the windshield."

"I don't want to have to clean that up." She sat and waited.

I buckled up.

"Coffee sound good?" she asked.

"Absolutely. If Hornsby catches us—"

"I don't care. I get the sense you're not going to drop this case anyway. Am I right?"

I shrugged. I knew the risks if I kept investigating, even if it was off the books. I mulled that over for a few seconds. In the end, I knew I had to keep pursuing this. I couldn't sit back, watch things happen, and hope for the best. Not when life with my son was at stake, not to mention my reputation. I couldn't let chance control my destiny.

She pulled away from the curb. "You know a good place for coffee, Agent Chase?"

"I do. And just Chase is fine."

"You can call me Karla."

She didn't look like a Karla, not even close. Karla was a bad name for a woman, especially a cute one. But then who was I to judge, with a name like Garrison?

We drove to Giuseppe's Italian Coffee shop. The place was just around the block from my house. If a person wanted coffee, espresso, macchiato, or an Americano, this was the place. If somebody wanted a shot of caramel in their coffee or a silly fruit flavor addition, this wasn't the place. Giuseppe wasn't above reaching across the counter and strangling a person for such a suggestion.

A deep, earthy aroma hit us when we walked in. Giuseppe carried on when he saw me; a lot of gushing in Italian and multiple hand gestures. Apparently he'd heard about the cops carting me away in cuffs yesterday morning. I ordered two large coffees and handed him two bucks. He told me if I didn't put my money away, he'd stuff the bills into my mouth.

Fair enough.

We sat at a small table in the front corner of the shop. We both took a moment and enjoyed the coffee. As Karla sipped, I noticed her wedding ring for the first time. The ring was small and unassuming, like Karla herself. It didn't surprise me that she was married. In fact, being the quality woman she was, it would have surprised me if she weren't married.

Karla put her cup down first. "So I wanted a first-hand account about Stanley's shooter, about what happened at your place, about your visit to the LB police station. I heard some rumors about that, and it wasn't in your reports."

"Not big on reports."

She smiled. "Figured that."

I took a swallow of coffee, then launched into the details about the break-in, run-in with Gates at headquarters, Stanley's shooting, and my recent conversation with Frank. At first I was in no mood to chat about the case, but the more I talked, the less I thought about Simon and next week's hearing. By the end of my talk, I was in full investigative mode.

"You think this whole thing may be about your past?" Karla asked.

"You heard about that?"

She laughed. It was quiet, but infectious. "Who hasn't?"

"People without internet."

"Who are they?"

"Anyway," I said, "at first I thought this whole thing was about my past, but after Labonte being shot, this whole thing is about Stanley, and not me."

"You sure?"

"Has to be. Labonte and I have no connection. Taking him out doesn't hurt me, doesn't embarrass me, doesn't make me look incompetent, doesn't feed into a payback theory. It has no impact on me."

"Right," Karla said.

"If this was about me and my past, if this person was out for me, they'd have no reason to take out Labonte. So this has to be about Stanley."

I suddenly felt a ray of hope. The fact that somebody from my past wasn't out for payback was great news for me and my custody hearing, though terrible news for Stanley. But if I could prove that somebody was targeting Stanley, and ultimately stop that person, then I could prove to Gina and the custody judge that my past wasn't a problem.

"So why Labonte?" Karla asked. "That's the question. And why not Pepperstein? Or for that matter, why not me? I was right there. Why not take all three of us out?"

"Wrong question."

"What do you mean?"

"This is about Stanley, so why didn't the shooter take him out? That's the question."

"Right." Karla clicked her fingernails on the table. "Pepperstein swung open the door. Stanley was clear in the doorframe. An easy target."

"Exactly. And that was the second chance the shooter had to take out Stanley."

"So whoever is behind this wants Stanley alive, clearly."

I nodded. "And that's the important question. Why do they want the kid alive?"

While I lingered over that question, I walked to the counter. Giuseppe refilled our cups. When he went into the back room, I threw a five-dollar bill over the counter.

I approached the table and said, "Where's your partner, by the way? How come you're working this alone?"

"He's tying up loose ends on a case we just closed. We're supposed to be working this together. Don't tell the governor. I can't imagine what he'll do if he finds out only one agent is working the investigation and not the full-time four he requested. Anyway, that's why I need your help."

"When was the last time the LA field office had four agents working around the clock on one case?"

Karla nodded. We both enjoyed a sip of coffee.

"What if," I said, "this whole thing is a media stunt?"

"What do you mean?"

"We're talking millions of dollars here, in terms of marketing, commercials, and sponsors. And you said the WBC was fine with what Stanley was doing. That his website drew more attention to the show, which in turn drew more viewers, which in turn made them more money. So clearly the network wants Stanley around. But what if they were responsible for Stanley's death threats? Not threats they were actually going to carry through. Maybe they wanted to draw more attention to the whole situation. So they could ultimately make more money."

Karla scrunched up her nose.

"A long shot, I know. But money makes people do things they'd normally never engage in. And we're talking about a lot of money."

"But potentially murder?" she said. "That's what we're talking about. Not just hiring someone to break into your house and to shoot Stanley, which are bad enough. But now we're talking about possibly killing a federal agent."

"You're right, and why Labonte? What would they gain from that? Aside from more attention to the case. Shooting a federal agent means every law enforcement agent in LA County is out for blood. Which means a deeper investigation that needs answers and culprits and fast results. And they wouldn't want that, not that type of attention and scrutiny. No way, no, forget it. My theory's garbage."

Karla leaned forward. "It might not be. Besides, we don't have another plausible theory. And we are talking about lots of money."

"But potentially murder?"

We switched roles, like we'd been working together for years.

"Maybe it's hundreds of millions of dollars," she said. "And it only takes one person at the top of the network to pull the strings. It's not like this is a huge conspiracy among the top execs. Maybe one of them has a shady background and knows the right people."

"Maybe."

"Maybe Labonte stumbled onto something in his investigation and he needed to be taken out."

"Now that I can't buy. Not Johnny Labonte. No way. You met him. He wasn't exactly the finest Long Beach had to offer. He had trouble understanding all of the fantasy football rules."

"It's a theory," she said.

We reflected for a moment, then Karla continued. "Tell me, if you weren't suspended, where would you start if you were in my shoes?"

"Run background checks on the WBC execs. See if anyone has a shady past. Then find out exactly how much money was involved on the WBC end. After that, talk with Pepperstein. Grill him for all the details. Make sure he and Labonte didn't know something that didn't go into their report."

"How do I get you to help on the case without getting you in trouble?"

"I'm already in trouble, more than you know, outside of work as well. So you should stay far away from me. If I could, I'd stay away from myself."

"I'll get to work on Pepperstein and the network execs. But I know you're not going to drop this. What angle are you going to work?"

"The less you know what I'm up to, the better."

"Talk to me, Chase."

I finished my coffee. "I have to be super careful about working on Stanley's case, so I'll let you handle that for now. I want to find out about Anfernee Gates and who he works for. He has a beef with me and I have to find out why. I have a theory about his involvement, and I have to confirm whether it's true or not. But I'm doing it way under the radar. I won't be working in any official capacity. No way can Frank know I'm looking into anything."

Karla nodded. "How long have you been awake?"

"Too long."

"Where are you staying? I'll drop you off."

"Just around the corner. I can walk."

"You look terrible. I'll drive."

"Thanks."

Just as I stood, Karla motioned behind me. I turned and saw an LCD flat screen hanging on the wall. My entire face filled the screen. It was an older picture of me so I had fewer wrinkles, and some hair. The volume was turned down. I had no idea what they were saying about me. A yellow banner at the bottom of the screen said *Special Agent Garrison Chase*. The screen suddenly flicked over to video footage of Frank escorting me out of Stanley's house. I gripped the edge of the table with my left hand and tried to crush the cheap Formica top.

Karla put her hand on mine. Her touch was warm and reassuring. "Are you okay?"

I faked a smile. "You happen to have a hat?"

We left Giuseppe's and walked to her Ford.

Karla unlocked the passenger door. "Tell me, without a badge or gun or access to your computer at work, how are you going find out about Gates? How can you possibly get any details?"

"I have some connections."

She smiled. "I bet you do."

Karla walked around to the driver's door. I stretched, turned my head, and cracked my neck. As I looked down the street, I noticed a car on the opposite side of the street. It was a Crown Vic.

"You're kidding me."

"What?"

I pointed down the street. "Gates. He's still tailing me, in that Crown Vic. Let me drive." I hustled around to the driver's side. "Scoot over, if you don't mind."

"No way," Karla said.

"Come on, I'll be careful."

"I can tail people just fine."

I wiggled my fingers. "I have control issues."

She reluctantly handed me the keys and crawled over the gear shift.

"What the hell is he doing still watching me," I said. "Especially now that I'm off the case?"

"He's probably smart enough to know you're not going to drop this. What are you going to do?"

"Go after him."

"Is that wise?"

I shook my head. "I'm sure it isn't."

CHAPTER TWELVE

KARLA LOOKED AT me and asked, "What are you going to do if you catch up with him and he actually pulls over?"

"Ask some questions."

"What kind of questions?"

"Pertinent ones."

Karla pointed at the Crown Vic. "If you catch up with him."

The Vic shot out onto the street and squealed away. I punched it through the intersection. Karla gripped the passenger door handle as the Ford drafted tight behind the Vic.

"Don't you dare hit him," she said.

I let off the gas, but didn't brake, missing the Vic's bumper by a hand width.

"This is nuts," Karla said. "Seriously, you're chasing a federal agent. Why is that again?"

"Why's he running? That's the question."

"Because you're crazy."

Ignoring the comment, I stared at Gates's squinty eyes in his rearview mirror. I tried to match the intensity of his stare as I pumped the accelerator. "Come on, Ford."

"How do you even know that's Gates? It doesn't look like him."

Gates had a hat on, which was a weak attempt at a disguise. I knew it was Gates because of his eyes, and because his hair puffed out from the sides and back of the hat. Plus, he was in the same Crown Vic. "It's him, I'm positive."

I had the gas pedal pinned, but the Vic started pulling away, first ten feet, then twenty, then thirty. I tried to coax the Ford on with my hips, but it was useless.

"You're never going to catch him," Karla said. "Not in this car. Especially if he gets on the freeway up here."

She was right. In about five seconds, Gates would veer onto the 405 freeway. I grasped the steering wheel and squeezed.

Karla put her hand on my shoulder. "Let's find a better way to figure out what he's up to. No use trying to chase him down on the freeway."

"You're right." I blew past the 405 on-ramp. As I did, I looked right and watched Gates race onto the freeway. "Maybe he'll head back to LB headquarters. He could be working out of that station for some reason. You mind if we head there to see if he shows up?"

"Fine, just slow down."

"Sorry." I braked and slowed to the speed limit. "That guy gets me going."

"I can see that. You don't have to grip the wheel so hard."

I released the tension on the wheel. "If you'd rather drop me off and get to work on the investigation, that's fine. But I have to find Gates and confront him."

"I'll wait with you. Besides, I wouldn't want to miss the confrontation if it happens."

I drove through some back streets and made it to headquarters in about five minutes. I drove around the block twice before finding a parking spot just down the street from the front of the building.

After shutting off the engine, Karla asked, "So what's your theory about Gates? Why he's so interested in you?"

"The governor hired him to watch me; that's the only thing I can think of. To make sure I was doing a good job at protecting Stanley."

"You're not on protection now, so that doesn't make sense."

"That's why I'm fired up."

Karla nodded. We started scanning the area.

After about a minute, she said, "Like I said earlier, maybe he just wants to make sure you're not pursuing this further. Maybe he knows your past, and that you have a hard time letting things go." She smiled.

I cleared my throat. "And what exactly do you know about my past?"

"I know as much as the next person about your recent past. But I mean your past past. Prior to the YouTube thing."

So she had seen the YouTube clip. I was surprised she was willing to get into a car with me. "What do you know about my prior past?"

"Honestly, not much. Your personnel file is pretty sparse, which prompts a lot of questions and intrigue. Maybe that's what Gates is trying to figure out."

"You have access to my personnel file, or had access?"

"I did some digging after reading your report. I had to explore every option. Wouldn't you if you were taking over this case?"

I nodded, appreciating her honesty. "What's so intriguing about me?"

"You never progressed beyond the rank of sergeant, yet you spent all those years with the Marines. And you're obviously capable of being an officer, so that doesn't add up. That was the first thing that interested me."

She scanned the area. "Second, by your own admission, you were involved with some sort of special ops unit. And it was with the Army, that's what your file said, which means you were recruited out of the Marines, which means you were clearly a hotshot in the Marines, enough for the Army to take notice and pull some strings to get you out of there. And if the Army and Marines were involved, that means the special ops unit wasn't limited to one branch of the Armed Forces, it was multifaceted. That suggests to me it was a crack unit authorized by the DOD, probably the Pentagon."

She looked at me and smiled. "How am I doing?"

"Not bad."

"If that's true," she continued, "your unit was likely black ops and off the books. Which ultimately tells me you have some pretty good skills. The intrigue comes from you leaving all that behind and taking an entry-level position with the feds and becoming a desk jockey. That doesn't add up."

"A desk jockey?" I laughed. "Good one."

"Am I right?"

She was good. I smiled. "I could ask you the same question. I can tell you're too smart for this job, that's clear already, yet you're sitting here beside me. We're probably the same classification, right?"

"But I'm a woman, I had to start here. I had no other choice. And I don't have the background that you do."

Fair enough.

We resumed scouring the area. Though we didn't talk surveillance strategy, our eyes scanned opposite areas. She'd look right for a while, while I looked left, then we'd flip flop.

Karla broke the silence. "Tell me more about this black ops unit, if you can. I know it's classified."

"It is, but you're a federal agent, and I'm no longer with the organization. So as long as you don't tell anybody, I don't mind. What do you want to know?"

"You were involved in some heavy situations, I imagine. Was it reconnaissance type work or more of spying and killing?"

"All of the above."

"Why were you recruited? What was your specialty?"

I debated lying and saying something like 'intel gathering'. In the end, I went with the truth. "Shooting. That was my specialty." I looked over to see if she had a reaction. She didn't.

"Was that easy for you?"

I thought about giving a curt answer, but Karla was as genuine as they come. Whatever I told her, I knew she wouldn't go blabbing it to others. And besides, we had time to talk.

"Struggled with it, for sure. Even had a crisis of conscience early on in my career."

"A crisis of conscience? Interesting. What happened?"

I settled into the seat and debated going down that road.

"You don't have to tell me anything; sorry for prying. I shouldn't have."

Telling the story always helped me feel unburdened. Plus, there was something about Karla that made me open up.

"No, it's okay. I'm alright with it." I ran my hand over my head, then started the story. "My crisis of conscience came near the beginning of my career. I was in Mogadishu, the capital city of Somalia. I was part of a small mission to find and kill a Somali general. He was one of the top d-bags in the country's warlord hierarchy. We found the guy on the 16th of January and I was green-lighted to take him out. So I set up in a building directly across the street from where the general was holed up."

"Set up? What do you mean?"

Even though it was a long time ago, I could envision that day like it was yesterday. I took a deep breath. "My shooting set up. I held a Weatherby Mark V rifle while sitting in a rickety wooden chair about ten feet back from a blown-out window. My rifle was perched on top of an even more rickety table. I'd leveled the table out with a couple of sugar packs I kept in my food pouch. I scanned the windows, waiting for the general to make an appearance. I also kept an eye out for 'Skinnies' on the ground. That was what we called the Somali soldiers since they were so emaciated. Anyway, I didn't want to shoot the soldiers and give my position away, so I relayed their whereabouts to the boys on the ground."

Karla nodded and kept watching the street.

I kept an eye out, too.

"About ten to one in the afternoon," I continued, "I spotted a group of enemy militia filing into a room on the top floor of the dilapidated hotel. About ten 'Skinnies' entered the room and sat on the dusty floor. All of them had blank looks. They were literally kids; couldn't even see a whisker of facial hair on any of them. The general waltzed into the room after the kids had settled. You couldn't call him 'Skinny', since he was clearly well fed. He paced about the room and fired up the troops. I sat and waited for a good opportunity to take him out, waited for the prick to pause long enough in front one of the windows – but he never did. The guy had an unbelievable amount of energy. Never stood still."

Karla looked at me. "What did you do?"

"I tracked him for a couple of hours and waited for a clean shot. About every half hour a new group of ragtag militia would file into the room for a pep talk. I didn't know what the general was saying, but I knew he was doing a fine job because the kids left the room excited. They bashed through the doors and hustled down the stairs. The whole thing fired me up even more."

"How so?"

I thought about it for a moment. "The big picture of it all, I guess. The situation was beyond messy. Over 300,000 Somalians had starved to death in this general's country, all because he and the other feuding warlords wouldn't feed and protect their own people. Yet this big prick was getting his fair share of carbs, that's for sure. And here he was across the street firing up the troops, telling these kid soldiers that the Yanks were the evil ones; that the Americans were the ones who deserved to die; that ultimately these kids should give their lives to this bogus cause. It still makes me mad thinking about it."

I paused and cleared my throat. "Anyway, after watching this guy for hours I had his mannerisms figured out. He had distinct facial tics and arm movements that he repeated with absolute precision. I spent a lot of time studying him. Every time the troops left the room, he'd continue firing himself up. He wouldn't stop pacing and talking and shaking his fists at a torn-up American flag hanging in the corner of the room. He actually—"

I stopped because I could see the general's face as clear as can be. The man's face gave me the chills.

A moment later Karla touched my knee. "Go on."

I took a breath. "He actually got more riled up when he was alone. He truly believed in his cause. I mean, deep down in his soul. It was crazy. He totally bought what he was selling to these kids. That got me thinking a lot."

"About what?"

"About right from wrong and how we can ultimately distinguish between the two. Because here I was, directly across the street, dead determined that I was in the right. Deep down I believed that what I was doing was the moral thing. I knew it without question, without hesitation. Yet the man on the other end of my scope thought the exact same thing about his position. So who was right? How do we ultimately judge between two equally determined passions or points of view? That was my crisis of conscience."

"What did you end up figuring out?"

"That there had to be an outside source to determine right from wrong."

"Outside source like what?"

"Like a third party. I got that idea from my mentor in *The Activity*. He'd been preaching his theories to me for six months."

Karla raised her eyebrows. "*The Activity* was your specialized unit?"

"Right, the black ops unit I joined after being recruited out of the Marines. The one authorized by the Pentagon."

She smiled. "Go on."

"The guy who taught me everything about spy work, including shooting and killing, was my commanding officer, a man by the name of Hans Schlimmergaard. He was this crazy German Christian guy. His call name was Bonhoeffer."

"That the same as a code name?"

"Yeah. Hans loved this twentieth-century German theologian named Dietrich Bonhoeffer. Bonhoeffer was this pious Christian who hatched a plan to kill Hitler right near the end of World War II. He believed in killing Hitler for the greater good. The irony was that Bonhoeffer's plan never came to fruition and the theologian was hanged just days before the Germans surrendered. Regardless, Hans was fanatic about the greater good theory. He truly believed in it, which I imagine helped him face the fact that he killed people, a lot of people in his case. And he was good at it. I never thought too much about the greater good theory until that afternoon."

Karla shifted toward me. She was excited about the story and not watching for Gates. "So what ended up happening?"

I paused.

She punched my shoulder. "Don't leave me hanging."

I smiled. "At 3:30 in the afternoon I was still following the general from window to window. He was on his sixth speech to his sixth group of 'Skinnies'. I was in the chair cursing Hans under my breath, figuring all his talk had finally caught up with me. I spent some time in that room thinking about the Bonhoeffer story. In the end, I knew I believed in Bonhoeffer's theory, the greater good theory. I had to. If I didn't, I knew I was killing indiscriminately and wasn't any better than the man on the receiving end of my bullet – the scumbag across the street in my scope."

Karla's eyes lit up. She nodded. "You kill him?"

I cleared my throat. "When the general reached the crescendo of his last speech, I watched the group of young kids jump up and burst out of the hotel room, but I didn't focus on them; I focused on the general. Because at that moment he did something unusual, something he hadn't done the other five times, something totally out of character: He lit a cigarette, walked to one of the windows, and stood right in front of it. There he was, perfectly framed in this open window. Maybe he did it to catch a breeze and cool down, maybe to blow smoke out, or maybe to watch his troops rush out into the street. Who knows? I didn't, and I didn't dwell on it long. I aligned the crosshairs on his face. I can remember the details precisely. I took a slow breath and calmed my heart. Then I cradled the trigger with my finger and took up the slack. Took up two full pounds of pressure – all I needed was three. Then the general took a slow and steady drag on the cigarette, and—"

I paused, remembering the situation in vivid color.

"And what?"

"I whispered to myself, 'For the greater good'. Then I pulled back with another pound of pressure."

"And?"

"And blew his head clear off his shoulders."

The car went eerily silent.

After about ten seconds, Karla said, "Good for you."

A minute of silence went by. I felt like finishing my story and bringing it full circle. "After the incident with the general, I started reading Bonhoeffer's work, as well as some other old theologians and philosophers."

"Impressive for a killer," she said, smiling.

"Don't get too impressed. I didn't understand a lot of what I read. But I did learn that the 'greater good' theory wasn't actually Bonhoeffer's invention. The theory dated back to a Persian prophet by the name of Zoroaster. St Augustine, however, was the one who truly made the theory famous. The Summum Bonum, as he called it, which was Latin for the supreme good or the greatest good. He put things simply, said there must be something outside of ourselves, something by which we measure all things, by which we determined what was good from what was bad. In other words, right from wrong. He believed that was God, that God was the highest good and the thing by which we measure everything else. That made sense, which was why I used Augustine as my code name."

"You're a theist then?"

"I guess. I think I have to be."

"What do you mean by that?"

"I mean, something else besides society and humans must exist. If it doesn't, then everything is relative. Then my missions weren't any better, weren't any more virtuous or right, than the missions of the men I was trying to kill. If everything's relative, I had no good reason to take another human life, other than following my chain of command. Which was hardly justification for killing."

Karla nodded. "Never thought of it like that."

"My commanding officer, Hans, totally got in my head. But in a good way. He helped me clear my conscience about what I was doing. I didn't have a problem killing a person like General Douchebag, for instance, since it served the greater good of the nation. Because I believed he and his fellow conspirators were violating the higher moral code. A moral code established by a higher being, a third party."

"Got it," Karla said. "I understand. Were all of your missions for the greater good? Was every mission black and white like Mogadishu?"

She was sharp. I thought about her question. "It's a fair question, and the answer is no. The longer I was with *The Activity*, the more I became engaged in questionable missions. Near the end, I became pretty disillusioned with the job, if I'm being honest. When my son was born, I saw my out and took it. I didn't mind being a desk jockey if it meant I'd see my son grow up. Much higher value in that than in taking questionable kill orders."

"See, being a desk jockey has some redeeming qualities."

I smiled. "I guess it does."

We resumed scanning the area. I could tell Karla was deep in thought, digesting what I just said, so I stayed quiet.

A few minutes later, she broke the silence. "You know, it doesn't look like Gates is coming, at least not any time soon. You should get some rest. You look awful."

"Thanks."

I fired up the Ford and drove to the *Faded Blue Motel*. It took less than ten minutes.

When I opened the door to room 12, Karla peeked in. "Did you pay extra for the seventies theme?"

"Vintage," I corrected, "not seventies. I had to put down an extra deposit."

"Really?"

"No."

Karla smiled. "Get some rest." Before she closed the door, she said, "Can I ask you something?"

"Shoot."

"Why are you risking it all?"

I furrowed my brow. "What do you mean?"

"I mean, you're risking your career for Stanley Tuchek. And you've been pulled off the case. So it's not your responsibility. I know the kid was shot and Labonte may be on his death bed, and you want vindication for that, but it seems way too risky for you to pursue this when you could lose your job for good this time. If Hornsby or the governor finds out, you may be living here full-time. What's the greater good in that?"

"You don't have all the facts." I reached into my wallet and pulled out a worn picture of Simon and me. He was a year and a half old in the picture. I was wading in chest-deep ocean water with Simon on my shoulders. We had huge smiles. I handed her the picture. "He's three now."

"Super cute. He has your eyes. And for his sake, let's hope not your hair line. What's his name?"

"Simon. I saw him yesterday. The first time in a year. I lost visitation rights after the YouTube thing aired. Next week I have an important custody hearing. Before yesterday, I figured I'd at least get weekend visits back, but after everything that's happened, I feel screwed. My ex-wife will do whatever she can to stop me from being with him. She's even filed a restraining order by now."

"Cold," Karla said. "Really cold. I mean, you're his father. I don't get that at all."

"The only chance I have is figuring out Stanley's case, wrapping it all up before the hearing. That way I can convince the judge that the break-in had to do with Stanley's death threats and not my past. I need to prove that there are no imminent threats on my life, and that I can provide a safe environment for Simon. I'll probably have to commit to being a desk jockey for life, but if it means getting Simon back, I'll do it."

Karla nodded. "We'll solve this."

"I have to stay low profile. You're going to actually solve the case. I'll help in the background. No one can find out we're working together."

"It's our secret. And trust me, I'll do the best I can, I promise." She closed the door behind her.

I drew the heavy curtains closed and plunged the room in darkness. Since Karla was going to work the WBC investigation, I figured I'd catch an hour or two of sleep and wait for one of my contacts to call.

Collapsing on the bed, I put my beeper on the nightstand, then took out the picture of Simon and studied it. Stared at it for as long as I could, until my eyes were so heavy I had to close them. I fell asleep with the picture of Simon on my chest and my hands crossed on top of it. Slept that way for a while. I didn't wake until a knock on the door rattled the motel room. That knock was a first in a series of knocks.

A series of knocks that would keep me up for the second night in a row, and change everything I knew about Stanley Tuchek's case.

CHAPTER THIRTEEN

ANOTHER LOUD KNOCK shook the flimsy motel door. I tucked Simon's picture into my wallet, got out of bed, and peeled the curtains back a fraction, just to be safe. Standing in front of the door was a chubby-faced cop with a warm smile. I opened the door.

"Agent Gates told me you were staying here," Officer Kowalski said. "Thought you might be missing some things. I hope you won't be needing them, though with your past couple of days, who knows?"

He thrust out a case. To the untrained eye, the case looked like it contained a long musical instrument like a trombone; but it wasn't a trombone case. The case held my Weatherby Mark V .308 caliber rifle. The one I used in Mogadishu.

"Thanks, Kowalski. Come on in. I'm surprised I'm getting this back."

Kowalski unclipped the catch on his holster, withdrew a gun, and stepped into the motel room. "This is yours as well. The rifle and gun were registered in your name, and a few others were registered in your father's name. You can come by the station and pick up those ones. We can't give you back the illegal assault weapons. Their serial numbers were scratched off."

I nodded. That was my father for you.

Kowalski whistled and handed over the Smith & Wesson Model 500. "Sure is a beauty."

"Most powerful handgun in production."

"Heard it has three times the muzzle velocity of a .44 Magnum."

"It's a beast."

Kowalski dug into his pocket and handed me five rounds. "It was loaded, and I didn't want to accidentally blow my foot off."

I took the bullets. "You're a fine officer, Kowalski. I mean it."

His face got redder, if that was possible. "Ah, no worries. It's the least I can do to help. That Agent Gates is really out to get you."

I scratched my head. "Any idea why?"

"Wish I knew, but I'm in the dark on most things."

"Did Gates happen to come by your station today?"

Kowalski shook his head.

"Did you find out who he works for?"

"Actually," Kowalski said, leaning in, "rumor has it he works for the CIA."

"The Company?" I scratched at my stubbly chin. "No, he can't work for The Company."

Kowalski leaned back. "I know, CIA agents don't operate on domestic soil. That's why I said rumor has it he works for them. I didn't hear that info from my CO. It's just the rumor that's floating around headquarters."

I eyeballed Kowalski. "Just a rumor then."

"Maybe, maybe not." Kowalski shrugged.

I changed subjects. No way was Gates CIA. The Company operates almost exclusively on foreign soil. "This is a crazy question, Kowalski, I know: You wouldn't have a way to contact him, would you?"

He shook his head. "Sorry, Chase."

We made small talk for another minute, then I patted Kowalski on the shoulder and watched him leave. After closing the door, I slid the Weatherby case under the bed and took the 500 to the kitchen table. Just when I'd finished reloading, a hard knock rattled the entire room. Since I held a loaded gun, I didn't bother getting up to see who was at the door. "Who's there?" I said.

"Karla."

I put the revolver on the table. "Come in."

Karla walked in. Her eyes looked glassy, and I noticed the spring was gone from her step. She took a seat at the chrome table.

"Nice gun," she said. "Where'd you get that?"

"Tooth fairy."

She rolled her eyes.

"What's up?" I asked. "I didn't expect to see you back here so soon."

"So I tried to meet with Stanley—"

"What do you mean, tried?"

"His father put him in protective custody, in WITSEC, can you believe that?"

I ran my hand over my head. WITSEC stood for the Witness Security Program, a solid operation run by the US Marshals. "But you're the lead investigator on this," I said. "How can you not meet with Stanley?"

"Apparently it's temporary, until Stanley is settled. Once they're done processing and relocating him, I'll be able to speak with him on the phone. Hornsby doesn't even know where the kid is right now."

"On the phone? Not in person?"

"Yeah, no FBI agents are to be physically near Stanley, ever."

"Courtesy of his father, I suppose."

"The governor's pissed."

I nodded. "And that's probably an understatement."

"Then again," Karla said, "parents do crazy stuff for their kids, almost anything to protect them."

I eyed her. "They sure do." I walked over to my tiny kitchen. "Want some water? It's all I have."

She shook her head. I filled a cup for myself. Just as I finished, another knock nearly broke down the door.

"Expecting anyone?" Karla asked.

I shook my head and went to the window, thinking maybe Kowalski forgot something. I peeled back the drapes.

It wasn't Kowalski, not even close.

Eva O'Connor stood in front of the motel door. She wore a tight velour track suit. The suit was jet black and had a small zip top that accentuated her upper body. The pants hugged all the right places, too. I stared, not because she looked great, but because I'd figured I wouldn't see her so soon after the restaurant incident. How did she know I was staying here?

Another hard knock.

"Uh," Karla said, "Are you going to get that before the wall collapses?"

"Gimme a second."

I slipped out and smiled at Eva. "This is a surprise."

She gave a wary look, but didn't say anything.

"A pleasant one," I added. "I wanted to apologize about the restaurant. I had a ton of bad coffee earlier in the day—"

"Far enough." Eva held up her hand. "Spare me the details."

"How'd you know I was staying here?"

"Aren't you going to invite me in?"

"Place is a mess." I faked a smile.

"Already? You just checked in, didn't you?"

"Seriously, how'd you know I was staying here?"

"Garrison." She sighed. "I work for the government." She said it straight-faced, so I didn't know if it was a joke or not.

"Right," I said. "Come on in. Another federal agent is here. We're working on a case."

Eva stepped into the motel room. When she saw Karla, her eyes narrowed. "Oh, sorry to interrupt."

"You're not interrupting anything," Karla was quick to say.

Eva backed out of the room. "I'll come back later, Garrison, when you aren't *working*."

"No, it's not like that," I said. "We truly are working."

"Here in a motel room?" Eva tilted her head. "It's fine, Garrison, it's not like we had an exclusive thing going. It's not like we've even been intimate yet."

She said it loud enough to ensure Karla heard.

"Eva," I said. "Nothing is going on here."

She spun and walked toward her car. I followed her.

She turned around about halfway to her car. "Just wanted to hear about the shooting at Stanley's place this morning, that's all. Saw you on TV so I wanted to make sure you were okay."

The words seemed nice, but her tone wasn't convincing.

"Eva, wait. Let me explain."

Before I could smooth things over with her, she hopped into her Toyota Prius and stuck her head out the window.

"Have a wonderful night," she said.

The Prius silently zipped away.

I watched her go, then walked back to the room.

"Ouch," Karla said. "Sorry about that."

"No worries, seriously. That's twice in two days she's stormed out on me."

"Going that well, huh?"

"Yup." I took a seat in one of the chrome kitchen chairs.

There were a few moments of awkwardness. Karla was quick to change subjects. She asked, "So what did you learn about Gates?"

I cleared my throat. "A crazy rumor that can't be true. I won't even bother you with that. My connection hasn't come through yet. What did you find out?"

"That the WBC employs a bunch of upstanding citizens."

"Really? Nothing?"

"Not even a hint of criminal activity. A few parking tickets, that's all. I tried upper, mid and lower management, nobody had a record. So I met with Pepperstein. He was still shaken up, but I grilled him anyway. Like you said, those two don't have the brainpower to figure out much. They didn't have any leads."

"How's Labonte? Did you hear?"

"Touch-and-go for now. He's in the critical care unit. By the way, when I met with Pepperstein this afternoon he kept referring to you as 'Mag'. What's that about?"

I wasn't prepared for that question, so I didn't respond right away.

"Sorry," she said. "I'm prying again. It's a problem for me."

"No, it's fine, you're not prying. It's an honest question. It's just that you already have a tainted picture of me from the whole YouTube thing. So I don't want you refusing to work with me."

"That bad, huh? Now I really want to hear it."

"I'll tell the story on one condition."

"That is?"

"No matter what, you keep working with me."

She nodded. "Talk to me."

"The 'Mag' nickname comes from a story about two years old now—"

Just then Karla's cellphone chirped. She dug it out of her pocket, held out a finger, and apologized.

Figuring it was her husband, I went to the kitchen, turned on the tap, and poured another glass of water. Even with the water running, I could still hear Karla's voice.

"Just calm down," she was saying.

To drown out the conversation, I turned the faucet on full, but Karla's voice grew louder, so loud that I finally looked over and realized she was yelling at me. I turned off the faucet.

"It's Stanley," Karla said, holding out the phone, "and he's freaking out."

CHAPTER FOURTEEN

I GRABBED THE phone. All I heard was heavy breathing.

"What's happening, Stanley?" I said.

"Nobody's here, Agent Chase. Everybody's gone. I can't. I don't—"

"Take a breath, Stanley."

"I'm walking around and can't find anybody. There are supposed to be people here. Where is everyone? I have no clue what's going on."

"Breathe, Stanley."

He took a huge breath, like he was drawing oxygen from his feet. It was so loud in my ear that I actually had to pull the phone away for a second. After that, I put the phone back. I could hear Stanley moving about the house.

"Stop walking around, Stanley. Take a seat and fill me in."

A moment later I heard him pull out a chair and sit.

"Now tell me what happened," I said.

"An hour ago two US Marshals were in the safe house with me, along with my nurse. But now I can't find anyone. What the hell's going on, Agent Chase."

"It's okay. Just keep calm and focus. Tell me everything that happened in the last hour."

He took a quick breath, then launched into his story. "I was in the bedroom working on my computer. The marshals had been checking up on me every half hour. No one had come back for a full hour, so I was getting thirsty and went to the kitchen for a Diet Coke, but I didn't see or hear anyone, and I couldn't find anyone in the house. All I could think to do was call Karla. She gave me her cell number yesterday."

He paused to breathe.

"Are you sure you're alone?"

"I'm all alone?" I heard him get up. "Am I really? Is this for real, Agent Chase?"

I scratched my head. What kind of question was that?

"Listen, Stanley, sit back down. You need to be calm."

I waited for him to sit. No chance he was going to calm down anytime soon, however. I knew the situation was bad. Marshals would never leave a safe house unless there was an imminent threat outside.

"Are you sitting, Stanley?"

A brief pause. "I am now."

"Good," I said. "Now did you look outside? Maybe the marshals are doing a perimeter sweep."

"No, I didn't check outside." He breathed heavy into the phone. "Of course they're doing a perimeter sweep. That must be what they're doing. I'll check—"

"Stanley," I interrupted. "Don't go outside. I repeat, do not go outside."

"Why? What do I do then? And why are you raising your voice?"

His breathing picked up.

"Go to the front of the house," I said. "Stand by the front door, but not directly behind it. Do it now."

"Got it." I heard Stanley scurry to the front. "Okay, I'm there."

"Is the living room to the right or left?"

"Right."

"Is there a window in the room, maybe overlooking the front yard?"

"Yeah, a big bay window, and the curtains are drawn."

"Good, don't go over to the window, though. Stand to the right of the door and the left of the window, with your back against the wall."

A brief pause. "Okay, I'm in position."

"Get down low, on your hands and knees, then peek out the bottom edge of the curtains."

"One second, Agent Chase."

He must've put the phone against his pants. I heard a muffled sound and some scratching. When the sounds stopped, I asked, "Can you see anything? Or is it too dark?"

"I can see; the streetlights turned on not long ago."

"Anyone there? Any movement? Anything out of the ordinary?"

Silence for a few seconds. "No. Nothing out of the ordinary, as far as I can tell."

"Any cars parked across the street?"

"No."

"Anything weird or unusual or out of place? Anything at all?"

"Everything looks normal, Agent Chase. Of course, this is the first time I've been in this house, so I really don't know what normal is."

"Sure, I understand. Just looking for something obvious, Stanley."

What I really wanted to know was whether there were any people lurking around outside or any bodies scattered on the front yard. I didn't want to ask Stanley those questions directly. He'd freak out if I did, and I needed him as calm as he could be. Since he didn't mention anything unusual like a dead body on the yard, I figured the front of the house was secure for the time being.

"Stanley, I need you to check around the front of the house, on the inside."

"For what?"

I paused and debated going down this road.

"I said, for what, Agent Chase?"

In the end, I had to bring up the obvious. "For any signs of struggle, of a fight, or a break-in."

"A break-in? A fight?" He took a big breath. "You're freaking me out. What the hell's going on?"

"Focus, Stanley, check around."

He immediately responded. "I can't see any signs of struggle."

"Stanley, you didn't move. I would have heard you move. Now I need you to move. Go back to the front door and see if the lock has been tampered with. Check the doorframe around the lock, too."

I heard him get up slowly, probably the slowest the kid had ever moved.

"Nothing, Agent Chase. The lock's fine and the door's intact."

"Get a good look around, take your time. It's important."

Stanley didn't say anything for fifteen seconds. He didn't pull the phone away either, so I waited and listened to his strained breathing.

"Nothing," he said. "I don't see anything. Wait a minute."

He paused.

"Wait a minute what?" I said.

"There's something here, above the doorframe. A little piece of electrical wire, and something's stuck into it. It's a loop. It looks like an electrical circuit."

My heart raced. It couldn't be. "Stuck into what, Stanley? What does it look like?"

He didn't answer right away. I almost didn't want him to answer. I was afraid of his answer.

"Like putty, Agent Chase. Grey in color and it's flattened in a circle, about the size of a quarter. It's—"

"Get out," I snapped.

"What?"

"Get out NOW," I shouted. "Get the hell out of the house."

"You said not to go outside."

"GET OUT," I yelled. I couldn't remember the last time I yelled like that.

Stanley fumbled with the lock. I could hear the safety chain jiggling and the dead bolt releasing. A second later I heard the doorknob turn, then the door suck open. Footsteps raced away. The patter of Stanley's feet and his labored breathing overwhelmed any other sound.

Suddenly a huge explosion rang in my ear; so loud I instinctively pulled the phone away, then I quickly put it back.

And heard nothing but static on the other end.

CHAPTER FIFTEEN

I KEPT LISTENING to the static, hoping Stanley's voice would magically return.

Karla put her hand on my shoulder. "What happened?"

I looked at her and blinked. "A big explosion. I'm assuming the safe house blew up."

"Blew up? What about Stanley? Is he okay?"

I swallowed. "I'm not sure."

Karla pried the phone from my ear and listened, then snapped it shut. "Did he get out in time?"

"I think. I mean, I hope. I know he got out of the safe house, but I'm not sure he's okay. It depends on how big the blast was."

I ran my left hand over my head. Maybe the shooter/arsonist meant to spare Stanley again. I thought deeper, eventually shaking my head. No, that can't be. The shooter/arsonist couldn't have known I would tip Stanley off about the Semtex. I blew out a breath. The kid was meant to die this time.

"What do we do now?" Karla asked. "We don't even know where Stanley is."

I pointed at the cell. "This is going to show my ignorance, but can't we just call him back? Doesn't that thing show the incoming call number?"

"Usually, but whatever number Stanley called from was blocked. All it said was private. I'm calling Hornsby."

"Wait." I held up my hand.

She kept dialing.

"Karla, this is an inside job. Think about it. It has to be."

She shook her head. "For Stanley's sake, we have to get someone over there now."

"Fire trucks and cops are on their way. Semtex was used in the explosion, so it was huge. The whole neighborhood heard it. A dozen people probably called 911 by now."

Karla eyed me. "We need to grab the kid and protect him if he's alive. We need to send a team, or at least someone."

"The shooter/arsonist is probably on the inside, Karla. If that's true, and if Stanley's still alive, the inside man could finish him off. Right?"

She looked at the phone, then back at me. A second later she closed the cell. "This is crazy, you understand?"

"I do."

"I mean, you're saying this inside man works for the federal government and is trying to kill the governor's son. Why? Why would a fed be after Stanley?"

I shook my head. "No clue."

"How are you so sure this is an inside job?"

"I'm not 100%, but it makes sense. I mean, we're talking about WITSEC, the US Marshals. They've never had a witness harmed under their protection, at least not ones who played by the rules and followed procedures. They're damn good. Barely anyone, including yourself, knew where Stanley was being housed. Only someone on the inside would know that information."

Karla paced a few steps. "So you're saying the inside man is a compromised marshal or someone dirty on our end?"

"Likely our end," I said. "And if it's on our end, it has to be at Hornsby's level or higher."

She stopped pacing. "No way."

"Has to be, Karla." I held out my hands. "Think about it. You didn't even know where Stanley was being taken, and you're the lead investigator."

She narrowed her eyes. "Who do we trust then? Who do we call?"

The only person I could think to trust was Frank, but if I called Frank...

Karla's cell suddenly vibrated in her left hand. She glanced down. "It says private."

I waved for the cell. She tossed it at me.

"Stanley?" I said.

Some gasping on the other end, then the kid said, "Agent Chase?"

"You okay?"

"You saved my life." I heard him swallow. "Got me out just in time."

"What about the explosion, Stanley?"

"Air from the blast rushed out the front door and knocked me over. The cell flew out of my hand and blew the battery out."

"Where are you now?"

"A couple blocks away. I went back to the house."

I scoffed into the phone. "You did what?"

"Had to, Agent Chase. Had to get my backpack and see if my laptop was still intact."

"That's crazy, Stanley. Listen to me, you can't trust anyone. You have to—"

"It's intact, it's fine. The explosion spared the bedrooms."

"What?"

He cleared his throat. "My laptop, Agent Chase. Everything is okay."

"Stanley, just tell me where you are. Karla and I will come get you."

"You just told me not to trust anyone."

"Anyone but us."

A pause. "I only trust you, Agent Chase."

"Good," I said. "So you can trust my judgment. Now tell me where you are. Are you still in LA County?"

"Is the cell you're using encrypted? Is it a snapcell?"

Not having a clue about these things, I pulled the cell away and asked Karla, "Is this a snapcell?"

"A what?" she said.

"We don't know, Stanley."

"If you don't know," he said, "then it isn't. Is the phone STE encrypted?"

I repeated that to Karla and she shook her head.

"Nope."

"Is it at least STU-III encrypted?"

I rolled my eyes and asked Karla. She shook her head again.

"No, Stanley, apparently the cell isn't encrypted at all. Do you really think Karla's cell is tapped?"

He sighed. "You tap landlines, Agent Chase, not cellphones. Cells are digital wireless signals. You don't tap the cell because it isn't wired to anything. This conversation is out there right now, over the airwaves. You just need to know how to grab it."

"Enough, Stanley."

"I'm not telling you my location, not over an unencrypted cell. You just told me not to trust anyone, which means you don't trust anyone. Which means you think someone in the government is corrupt, and that person could easily be monitoring Karla's cell. Trust me, I know these things. It's why I use a snapcell. It has one of the highest levels of encryption these days."

"How about you call me on the motel phone? Is that being tapped? I just checked in today."

"You never know. How about we meet up somewhere?"

"Where? And how are you going to get there?"

"I'll text you a location. Delete the text as soon as you see it. I'll take a cab there."

"How long will it take you?"

"I'll be there within the hour. It will probably take you about twenty minutes to get there."

"Send the text." I hung up and tossed the cell to Karla. "We're on the move as soon as we get a text from Stanley. Write down the address and then delete the text." I walked over to the bed and slid the Weatherby case out.

"What's that?" Karla asked.

"A little insurance, in case things get hairy. Can I drive?"

Karla sighed, then flipped me the keys. I jammed out of the room. On my way out, I almost knocked over a man standing in front of the motel door preparing to knock. One glance at the man and I immediately wished I'd bowled him over.

Dr. Frances Julian gathered himself and extended his hand. "Garrison."

You're kidding me. I ran both hands over my head. This guy, right now? How did people know where I was staying? Just when I thought the situation couldn't get worse, Gina popped up behind the little man.

"It was his idea, Garrison." She pointed accusingly at Jules. "He thought we should all meet up and talk about stuff. He insisted we come."

I addressed Gina. "How on earth did you know I was staying here?"

She pointed toward the motel office. "The check-in guy is good friends with Stuart Feldman. He called Stuart and—"

I held up my hand. "I get it."

Doc Jules stepped toward me. "It would be good to process our emotions, Garrison. I think it would be highly beneficial to us all to clear the air, so to speak. What do you say?"

"What do I say? I say you better step back, right now, Doc. I don't trust myself."

Since I didn't want to publicly threaten him, I turned just enough for him to glimpse the Model 500 in the back of my pants. The sight of the Smith & Wesson alone was threatening.

"My, Garrison, this is—"

He swallowed and didn't finish the sentence. It was the first time I'd seen my former therapist at a loss for words, but he cleared his throat and quickly recovered. "This is good, very good, raw emotion, true to the heart. We're already making progress. How about we sit and open up some more? I'll mediate."

Mediate? I stepped back and turned away. How can the source of the problem be the mediator? I took a moment to breathe. Sensing I was about to blow, Karla swept in and grabbed me by the waist. She prodded me toward the Ford.

"We have somewhere to be," Karla said.

"Understandable," Jules said. "You need more time, Garrison. I can empathize. I can see how the situation between Gina and me may be construed, how it could possibly portray my actions in a less than flattering light. There's a perfectly good explanation. It's not what it seems."

I turned back. "So you, my ex-therapist, aren't dating my ex-wife?"

"We're just friends," he said.

Gina slugged him on his right shoulder.

"Let me be more precise: Friends who are in the process of exploring one another."

Gina sighed. Karla rolled her eyes.

I pointed at Jules and bit my lip. Karla pried the rifle case from my hand, then pushed my arm down. For good measure, I withdrew the gun and gave it to her as well. I walked over to Jules. Because I was afraid of an accidental strangling, I put my hands behind my back.

"This is the last time I ever want to see you. Understand, Doc?"

Jules shuffled back a step, not saying a word.

I stepped forward and put my finger on his chest. "Hang out with Gina for as much and as long as you like; what do I care? But I'll be watching you, and if I see that you've been around my son, laid eyes on him, for that matter, I'll report you to whatever professional association you're registered with. I'll contact the ethics board or whatever board I have to. I'll make sure everyone's in the loop about you dating my ex-wife just months after our mandatory treatment period has ended. If they don't reprimand you or take away your license, I'll go to the press."

As I leaned in, Jules stepped back.

I grabbed the back of his head and forced him close so the ladies didn't hear. "Truthfully, I won't go to the press. I'll take matters into my own hands, Motel 7 style. You remember that story, don't you?"

Doc Jules was the only one who knew the real story. During one of our last therapy sessions, I made the mistake of opening up and telling him all about it.

He swallowed and nodded.

I relaxed my grip on his head, then walked backwards to the Ford. I turned and faced Karla and handed her the keys. "You'd better drive. I may run them both over."

CHAPTER SIXTEEN

THE TEXT CAME through just as Karla and I got into the Ford. I memorized the address, then deleted the text. Karla used her phone to pull up the location, then handed me the phone to navigate. We didn't talk for the first few minutes of our drive. Every so often I pointed in the direction Karla needed to turn. Since the window was rolled down, the wind cooled my face a little. It did nothing for my internal rage, however. I gripped my left knee so hard it hurt.

Karla glanced over. "That was awkward. Sorry you had to go through that."

I started to say something, but Karla politely waved me off. "I got the gist of the story, no need to say anything else. You're a better person than me, that's for sure. I would've kicked him in the groin."

"I should've decked him, at least drilled him in the gut with my knee. Right?"

"You did the smart thing, with next week's hearing and all."

I shook my head. "I'm screwed at the hearing, no chance. I should've clobbered him."

"Don't say that." She looked me in the eye. "We're going to figure this out and buy you some redemption."

I looked away. "Wouldn't that be nice."

A few minutes later, I pointed and said, "Ahead is the location, it's a 7-Eleven, drive past it and make a left at the next cross street. We'll watch from a distance."

Karla followed my direction and parked the Ford on a cross street about 100 meters from the store. She turned off the car and pulled out her pistol, a Colt Delta Elite. She chambered a round, then holstered it. I was impressed with her choice of semi-automatic.

I scanned the area for a moment, then turned to Karla. "I'm talking hypothetically here, but let's say you break up with a guy on close to mutual terms. It was fairly amicable and there wasn't too much drama involved. Do you think your ex would ever do something like Gina did? Go and date someone like that, someone you spent a year telling your innermost thoughts to? It's cruel, vindictive, and plain unethical. Right?"

Karla cleared her throat. "It's bad, really bad actually. On both of their behalfs. Look at your therapist, how could he possibly think that it's okay to date your ex? I don't get it."

"They're a real pair. I guess they're meant for each other. And, believe me, I don't care that they're dating, seriously. It's my son and his exposure to all this that's killing me. I have to get him back."

We scanned the area in silence for a minute.

"So what are we doing here, Chase?"

"What do you mean?"

"I mean physically here."

"Physically?"

Karla laughed. "Physically in this spot, I mean, parked down the street from the 7-Eleven."

"Oh, right." My face flushed. "Well, I don't want to wait out front of the store. I think we need to hang back and see if the kid's being tailed."

She nodded. "What's our next move once we actually get Stanley?"

"What do you think?"

"The way I see it, it's complicated. If someone's dirty in the Bureau, then I don't want to waltz into the LA field office with Stanley at my side. I don't want to take him there and jeopardize his safety. What about you?"

"Same. If I come in with Stanley, Frank will be on the phone to

Hornsby in a second, no matter what I tell Frank. It would only be a matter of time before the kid's dead."

She looked at me. "We go it alone, then? Don't tell anyone we have the kid?"

I nodded. "It's our only choice, to see this through to the end. Until I'm dead, or Stanley's dead, or you're dead, or we're all dead."

"Or until we figure this out."

"Seriously, Karla, you don't have to do this. You have a husband and a bright career ahead. I'd understand if you bailed out."

She turned as red as Kowalski. "Not a chance in hell you're getting me off this, Chase."

"Alright, then." I climbed out of the Ford. "I'm going to wait in the alley between the two buildings directly across from the 7-Eleven. Once I'm positive Stanley wasn't tailed, I'll bring him back here."

"Where do we go from there?"

"I have an idea. I need to work out the details in my head."

After Karla nodded, I closed the door and made my way to the alley. By the time I was in position, it was thirty-eight minutes since Stanley had called. Eleven minutes later, after I'd worked out the details of my plan, Stanley's taxi rolled into the 7-Eleven parking lot. The kid hopped out. His head bobbed around, searching for me. While he headed into the store, I stayed put and watched passing cars.

Stanley took up a position by the front window of the store. After five minutes I felt confident he hadn't been tailed, so I headed across the street. Stanley scooted out of the store when he saw me. His left shoulder and arm were in a sling, and he had on a backpack.

He held out his right hand. "Am I glad to see you, Agent Chase."

I shook his hand. "I'm glad you're okay. Let's get out of here."

I led him back to the Ford. He skipped along beside me. His excitement was downright annoying.

When we got to the car, Stanley blurted, "Shotgun." He grabbed the passenger door handle. I politely pushed him out of the way and climbed into the front seat.

Stanley slipped into the back and took a seat in the middle. He leaned forward and exchanged words with Karla.

Sensing his excitement and energy flowing up front, I snapped a look over my shoulder. "Alright, kid, what's going on?"

"What do you mean?" He pushed up his glasses.

"This giddy-like-a-schoolgirl thing."

"I'm just excited, Agent Chase."

"You're excited?" I turned all the way around in the seat. "What do you have to be excited about? Excited that a house blew up? That maybe some US Marshals are dead? Maybe an innocent nurse, too?"

Stanley blinked and sat back, clearly deflated. "I don't think the nurse or marshals were in the house when it went up."

Karla turned to face Stanley. "This is serious, Stanley, you need to sit back and think hard about this situation. People may be dead, and more people could die, including yourself, if we don't figure this out soon. We need to know everything."

"Believe me," he said, whining. "I've told you both everything. I wish I had more to tell."

Karla and I stared at Stanley. Stanley blinked and stared back. After a moment, he whipped out his phone and started texting.

"Who are you texting now?" I asked.

He didn't respond.

I reached over and tried to grab his phone, but Stanley was quick. He pulled his phone away and said, "My dad, Agent Chase. He needs to know I'm okay."

Karla changed the subject. "We can go back to my place until we figure out what our next move is."

"No," I said. "I don't want to bring anybody else into this."

Stanley piped up. "What about my place? We can go there."

"We're going to the wharf," I said. "I have a plan; I think it's our best option. But it's risky, real risky."

I directed Karla to the Long Beach wharf. It was just south of downtown and slightly east of the city's harbor. Karla drove the Ford into a large parking structure across from the wharf. Not many cars were there since it was nine at night. We wound our way to the top floor and parked in a darkened area. The parking structure overlooked the waterfront.

Karla shut off the Ford. "So what's the plan?"

I cleared my throat. "What if we use Stanley as bait, to draw out the inside man? What do you think?"

Karla looked straight out the window for a moment, then back to me. "I think it's risky, like you said. Why don't we slow down a little and come up with something less drastic?"

"We could, but I think moving fast serves us best."

"What do you mean?"

"Stanley was supposed to die in the safe house explosion, but he didn't. The inside man screwed up and will want to fix the mistake. And he'll want to do the job quickly, especially if he finds out that Stanley is in a dark, nearly deserted place like the wharf."

"Maybe," Karla said. "What about Stanley? You think he's up for being bait?"

A snort came from the back seat.

I glanced back at the kid. "You alright with the plan?"

"Sure." He pushed up his glasses. "As long as I get a gun."

"What are the details?" Karla asked. "How do we make sure the kid is safe?"

"Seriously," Stanley said. "Do I get a gun?"

I turned to Karla. "You're going to call Hornsby and tell him you have Stanley."

She raised an eyebrow, but didn't say a word.

I continued. "Tell him you're down here at the wharf, but don't tell him where exactly. If he presses for a location, get panicky, tell him you think there's somebody corrupt in the Bureau intent on killing Stanley. Really sell it. Tell him you don't want to talk over the phone about the exact location. If he keeps pressing for a location, ratchet up the tension. Tell him you're scared and fear for your life. If you have to, cut the call short and leave him hanging."

Karla nodded. "I think I follow. Talk to me more about the logic."

I shifted in the seat until I faced her. "Since we're close to the Long Beach Resident Agency, Hornsby will call Frank. He has to, since we're in Frank's jurisdiction. Neither will come charging down here, though, not right away at least. They'll conference call and get a quick plan together.

They'll send a small team, maybe three agents, which will take a little time to assemble. Not a lot of time, but enough—"

"For the inside man to beat them down here," Karla said.

"Exactly. The calls between Hornsby, Frank, and the other agents will be intercepted, which should flush out the insider. If it doesn't, and a small team shows up, we bail, taking Stanley with us."

Stanley leaned forward and poked his pinhead between us. "If I'm being used as bait I need a gun."

I leaned to the left and forced Stanley to sit back. "We know the insider is acting alone, at least so far he has been. With his skills, I'm positive he'll beat the team down here. We're going to have to be ready."

Karla nodded. "Like you said, he's pissed that he screwed up, so he's coming to fix his mistakes."

"Then I definitely need a gun," Stanley announced.

I turned to the kid. "You'll get one."

"Seriously," he said.

Karla eyed me. "Yeah, seriously?"

"I think he should have one," I said. "Just in case things go bad. Plus, it gives Stanley the element of surprise. He can hide it in his sling."

"Sweet," Stanley said.

"I doubt you'll need it, Stanley. It's just for a life-threatening situation, that's all. Cool it with the excitement."

Karla kept looking at me, but didn't say anything. I imagined she was questioning Stanley's ability to handle a gun. I know I was.

"I'll give him a quick lesson, Karla. He'll be fine."

"A lesson?" Stanley said. "You just point and pull the trigger, right?"

I turned and glared at Stanley. Karla sensed me losing it and changed subjects.

"So run me through the details," she said. "Make me a believer."

I climbed out of the Ford and walked to the chest-high concrete ledge in front of the Ford. Karla and Stanley joined me. The parking structure stood at the far western end of the waterfront area. I stretched my arm over the concrete ledge and pointed east. "This whole area is pretty much shaped like a figure eight, running on an east/west plane. You can sort of see the figure eight from this elevation. If we had an aerial view, or a map, you could really see it. It looks like an eight on its side—"

"An infinity sign," Stanley said. "I see it."

"Where the figure eight pinches in the middle." I pointed where I was referring to. "That's the channel where boats enter and exit the harbors. It's the only way in or out. When boats come in, they either go left or right, into one of the two harbors. Right in front of us is the western harbor. The bigger boats, and the tourist ones, dock there. The eastern harbor is where the private boats dock. There's a small public mooring area there. That's where visitors tie up. Most of the activity at night happens there. There's a string of restaurants and bars that curve around the eastern part of the figure eight. I want you two to wait over there." I pointed east. "I want you at the end of the string of restaurants, the very end, sitting at those outdoor tables overlooking the channel. I'll be up there." I traced my finger across the channel. "At the lighthouse."

The western harbor curved as well. Instead of restaurants lining the curve there were a number of moored boats and one tourist attraction, the Long Beach Aquarium. A path continued past the boats and aquarium and wound its way up and around a large grassy area. At the pinnacle of the grassy area, overlooking the boat channel, was a lighthouse.

"Good position," Karla said.

It was. I had a clear, elevated view of the entire wharf with almost no obstructions. The best part was that my back would face the water.

I glanced at Stanley. "I'll be fifty yards away, just across the narrow channel. I'll have you covered through my scope. I'll be able to count how many times you push up your glasses."

"Will my gun have a scope?" Stanley asked.

I ignored the kid and grabbed Karla. We walked behind the Ford. I motioned at Stanley to stay put. "The only soft spot in the plan is behind you. It's a weakness. My view of the parking lot behind the restaurants is partly blocked. But I'll have a decent view of the lot entrance, so if I do see a car come in, I'll be ready. I might not be able to see him sneaking up, but—"

"I'll be prepared," she said.

I believed her.

Stanley asked, "What if the inside man spots you, Agent Chase?"

"He won't spot me," I said. "I'll make myself invisible. This is what I used to do for a living. I'll take him out if he gets anywhere near you guys. I won't miss. You're perfectly safe, Stanley."

Karla nodded.

"So where's my gun?" Stanley asked.

I pulled out my .50 caliber revolver. Stanley reached for it and I batted his hand away. I gave Karla the .50 and motioned for her to give up the Colt. She hesitated, then handed it to Stanley.

"I'll go make the call," she said.

While she walked to the other end of the parking structure, I gave Stanley the rundown on safely operating the Colt. After my demonstration, the kid swung the gun around wildly and tried out different stances. I snatched it away from him, made sure the safety was on, and tucked it into his sling.

"Now leave it alone," I said.

I went to the Ford, opened the trunk, and took out the Weatherby rifle. When I turned around, Karla was back. "You sell it?"

"I think so. I hung up in a panic; made sure not to give any details."

"Good," I said. "So if the inside man doesn't show, and the team does, we need to work out an abort signal. I'll be able to see the team coming from a mile away."

"Why don't you just call us?" Stanley said.

"No open communication. We can't take that chance. For all we know, the inside man is intercepting Karla's cell."

"Do you have a Sony or Ericsson phone?" Stanley asked Karla.

"No, who uses a Sony these days? And why would you need a Sony phone?"

"Because I have an extra snapcell. The snapcell isn't an actual cellphone. It's a device that attaches to the bottom of a regular cell in the spot where you plug in and charge the phone. Snapcell, though, only works on Sony or Ericsson phones. But not to worry..." Stanley started rummaging through his backpack in the trunk, the one he retrieved from the burning safe house. "I have an extra phone and snapcell somewhere;

here it is." He handed it to me. "Press one and the pound sign. It will dial my number." He held up his phone. "Then you can call me and give the abort signal. I'll put it on vibrate mode."

"Stanley, why on earth would you need one encrypted cell phone, let alone two?"

"Because of the death threats, Agent Chase. My father uses snapcell. He got me one and the other is for backup, so we could communicate safely."

"You sure these are safe?"

"So far they are. No one's been able to decipher the encryption, not even the NSA. The military uses this technology now. STE encryption and STU-III are pretty much fossilized systems compared to this."

I shut the trunk and led Stanley and Karla to the parking structure stairwell. We walked down in single file, in silence. At the bottom, I turned and looked at them. "Any questions?"

Neither said a word. Karla nodded. Stanley pulled out the Colt and smiled.

"Put it away," Karla said.

Stanley obliged.

They headed left while I veered to the right. I kept my pace casual, in case anyone was watching me. I didn't want to draw any attention. When I reached the base of the lighthouse, I stopped and contemplated a camouflage idea. Since the inside man had access to Semtex, I figured he might have access to FLIR (Forward looking infrared) technology. FLIR makes it possible to see through foliage, day or night. It senses minute differences in temperature and assigns them various shades of color. It's deadly to snipers, especially since the latest handheld imagers only weigh about a pound.

I scanned the area for a minute, ensuring no one was around. Feeling confident that I was alone, I stripped off my clothes and waded ankle deep in the ocean water. I covered myself in muck from the ocean floor. I wasn't sure if the mud would temper my body heat and help make me less visible to FLIR, but it was worth a shot.

I put my cords back on, but not my shirt. When I reached the top of the lighthouse, I took up a position on the south side of the platform, lying on the metal grate with most of my right side facing the water. I put the rifle in place and used the scope to scan the eastern area, where Karla and Stanley were.

Those two were already in position. Nobody else was in the area. Just down from their location was a noisy bar, thumping out dance music. Karla had her back toward me. Her head swiveled slightly as she scanned the area. Stanley faced me. He touched his face more than usual and occasionally patted his sling, making sure the Colt was still there.

I swept left with the scope, as far west as I could go. I didn't see anything unusual, so I worked back east on a higher plane, concentrating on Shoreline Drive, the road directly north of the waterfront.

When I reached the eastern parking lot entrance by the bar, I watched the activity for a few minutes. A number of cars left the lot and a few cabs entered. Figuring a cab would be excellent cover for the inside man, I zoomed in and studied each one. Nobody hopped out, though, just a bunch of tipsy passengers stumbled in.

I turned the scope back to Shoreline Drive because I noticed a lone car traveling east to west. The car slowed and exited onto Aquarium Way, then headed straight toward the parking structure. I zoomed in with the variable scope. Unfortunately, it was too far away to make out the driver's face. I could see the car, though. It was black with tinted windows and a dead ringer for a motor pool car.

My body tensed when the vehicle wound its way up the parking structure and headed toward Karla's Ford. From the elevated angle I had, the only part of the car I could see was the roof. It parked about five spaces away from the Ford. A second later I heard a car door slam.

I peeled my eye from the scope, wiped some sweat off my forehead, curled my finger around the trigger, then put my eye back to the scope.

The first thing I saw was the upper body of a man walking toward the concrete ledge. Since the parking structure lights were mounted on the outside of the building, and the light from those cast straight down, no light entered the structure itself. I couldn't make out a face. But when the man reached the ledge, he bent forward and leaned over, bathing his face in the fluorescent lights.

I blinked. It couldn't be.

CHAPTER SEVENTEEN

AGENT ANFERNEE GATES squinted as he tried to see past the bright lights.

While I kept my eye locked onto Gates, my mind kicked into high gear. Frank didn't know Gates. Obviously, he wouldn't have called Gates, nor would Hornsby. They wouldn't want another agency to swoop in and snatch Stanley. Frank and Hornsby wanted to grab Stanley first to save face.

I swallowed and pushed out a deep breath. That meant Gates hadn't received a call about Stanley and Karla being at the waterfront. Which meant Gates had listened in on Frank or Hornsby's call. Which meant Gates was the inside man. But why would Gates be trying to kill Stanley? I smoothed the stubble on my head, thinking of Gates breaking into my house, and shooting Stanley. Did my memory of the shooter match his body shape? I couldn't be sure.

There were too many thoughts in my mind, so I refocused on Gates's body. Any second I expected him to pull out a gun, but he didn't. He just stood there, staring over at Karla and Stanley and occasionally patting down his puffy hair.

I watched him for seven minutes. After seven minutes, I decided to do something stupid. I abandoned my post and went after Gates, leaving my rifle behind.

Staying in the shadows, I made my way to the southern end of the parking structure. It took four minutes. At that point Gates was twenty-five yards north of my position, and four levels above. The concrete ledge on each parking level jutted out a few feet, so I was hidden from sight.

I sidestepped along the base of the structure until I reached the stairwell at the far northern end. Gates was well out of earshot, but I crept as quietly as I could up the first flight of stairs.

While ascending the second flight, my back pocket started vibrating. It took a second to realize that it was Stanley's cell. I didn't dare answer it. Stanley would have to wait.

I reached the base of the third flight and felt Stanley call again. I waited for the vibrating to stop, then took another step.

Just as I did, a distant yell caught my attention. I heard footsteps in the distance, then heard another yell. When I recognized the voice, I held my breath. It was Stanley, and he was screaming at the top of his lungs.

I backed down the steps. At the bottom of the stairwell I realized Stanley was screaming my name.

"AGENT CHASE. AGENT CHASE."

I ran toward him, cursing under my breath. The kid had no idea of the danger he was in. For all I knew, Gates was right now pulling out a gun and taking aim.

"GET DOWN, STANLEY."

I motioned toward my left, where there were benches, bushes, and spots for cover. Stanley couldn't see me from that distance, however. The kid raced down the wharf with the Colt stretched out in front. I ran into him at full speed. Scooped him up and slammed him to the ground. We rolled under a concrete bench. I held him tight while he squirmed.

"Agent Chase, we have to get the hell out of here. Back to the car, somewhere safe."

"Not the car. He's by the car."

"What are you talking about? No, he's not. I just got away from him. He has Karla."

"What?"

Stanley nodded fast. I must have been in shock for a few seconds because next thing I know Stanley started shaking me with his good hand.

"Agent Chase, I said he has Karla."

I blinked. "Who?"

"The inside man—you know, the shooter, the arsonist. I thought you had us covered?"

I snapped out of it. "How'd you get away?"

"Because of this." He held up the Colt. "It definitely surprised him."

"We have to get Karla," I said.

"I'm with you. Should I smear mud all over me, too?"

I ignored the question and relieved Stanley of his weapon, then peeked out from under the bench. Gates was gone, which made sense. I was an idiot. The whole thing was a two-man operation all along. Not a one-man operation. Gates was the inside man, but he didn't actually do the dirty work himself. He had an accomplice for that. Gates probably came to make sure his accomplice finished the job.

I kicked the bench, pissed at myself.

Stanley shook me again. "Agent Chase. Karla?"

"Right." I rolled out and glanced at the parking structure again. Gates was gone, and I could hear a car racing away, so I figured it was safe. I led Stanley back down the wharf in the direction he'd come from. While scanning the harbor, some motion in the water caught my attention. I stopped and squinted at the narrow boat channel. Two figures were in the water, swimming in single file. The person behind had one arm out of the water and appeared to have a gun pointed at the back of the first person's head.

The accomplice and Karla. It had to be. The channel between the harbors was only fifty yards wide, so it was a relatively quick swim. I figured the accomplice was headed to the lighthouse to get an elevated view of the area. He'd find the Weatherby on the platform and take us all out. Since they were already close to shore, I had no way of beating them to the lighthouse. I prodded Stanley back in the opposite direction.

"To the back of the aquarium," I said.

When we reached the southwest corner of the aquarium, I motioned for Stanley to stop. There were plenty of trees and foliage for decent cover.

"What are we doing?" Stanley said, pointing toward the lighthouse. "We have to help Karla."

I pointed to the ground. "You're staying put."

"No way, I'm coming with you. Let's go."

I grabbed him by the shoulders. My grip was strong and powerful enough to send a message, but not so strong that I could get in trouble for it.

"For your safety, Stanley, you have to stay here. No discussion." He came toward me and I poked him in the caved part of his chest. Not hard, but not soft either. "I mean it."

He hesitated, narrowing his eyes at me.

"Stanley." I put my finger against his chest and threatened another poke.

He sighed. "Alright."

"Good, now tell me what went down, quickly."

He took a breath. "Karla said she was going to check around the corner. Do a quick perimeter sweep, that's what she said. About thirty seconds later I heard footsteps behind me. I turned, thinking it was Karla, and it was, but a man was behind her, prodding her forward with a gun." Stanley paused and wiped his nose.

"Then what happened?"

"I'm not sure if you noticed, Agent Chase, but I'm pretty quick."

I nodded to keep the story moving.

"Figuring I was a dead man, I went for the Colt. I whipped it out and pointed it at the man. I could see the surprised look on his face, but it only lasted a few seconds."

"Why?"

Stanley's shoulders dropped. "I had the safety on, and he knew it. But the man hesitated, too, so I flipped off the safety and told him to put the gun down. He was also quick. He grabbed Karla and pressed the barrel against her temple. Started making threats."

The kid looked down and away.

I snapped my fingers. "Stanley. What happened?"

"I'm sorry, Agent Chase, but I was more concerned for my own life, so I backed away, then turned and ran for it. Where were you, by the way?"

"I'm sorry, I had you covered for a while. There was another government agent involved. He showed up in the parking garage. I thought he was the shooter so I went after him. Since he wasn't armed, I didn't think there was an immediate threat to you two."

"So there's two of them?"

"There's the inside man and his accomplice, the one who actually does the dirty work. Now stay here and don't move. I'll be back for you soon."

Before he could whine, I took off and headed toward the water's edge. Unfortunately, too much light flooded the grassy area around the lighthouse, so hugging the shoreline was a death sentence. However, the light didn't penetrate past the shoreline. The water was dark, silky, and hopefully forgiving to an approaching shape.

I entered the water, keeping just my head above the surface. To minimize my silhouette, I pressed the Colt flush against the right side of my head, then slowly waded east toward the lighthouse. When I was about seventy-five yards away, I saw movement on the lighthouse platform. I also heard a few sharp whispers float across the water, which was a good sign. It meant the accomplice hadn't slit Karla's throat yet.

I moved another twenty-five yards east. By that point my night vision was coming in and I could see two figures on the lighthouse platform. Both lay flat on the metal grate. Both of their bodies were pointed my direction. Afraid of being spotted, I sank as low as I could go in the water. My nostrils flared wide as I breathed as slow as possible. As I breathed, I contemplated a different plan.

The sound of a subtle click stopped my thinking. Right away I recognized the sound. It came from my rifle. The Weatherby's safety had released.

I tensed and held my breath. Any second I expected a round to tear through my face.

When that didn't happen, I decided to screw the Colt and go under. I blew out all the air in my lungs to get rid of my natural buoyancy, then I started slipping under, first my chin, then my mouth, then my nostrils. Real slow, so I didn't make a sound or draw attention.

Just before my ears slipped under, a voice stopped me.

"Don't move," it said.

I obeyed. Not because the voice asked, but because I recognized the voice. At least I think I recognized it. I hoped I'd misheard.

"Don't move, Augustine. I need time to think. Don't make this worse."

I'd heard correctly. I suddenly couldn't breathe. You're kidding me.

"Aug, please," the man said. "I'll shoot if I have to."

I pushed out the breath I'd been holding. "Gabriel?"

Deafening silence followed. The man didn't respond. All I could hear were tiny waves lapping at the shoreline. Thoughts started coming like a drumroll. I wanted to shake my head clear, though I didn't dare move in case he was serious about shooting.

"I'm sorry, Augustine." The man's voice strained to the point of cracking. "So sorry for all of this."

"Gabriel? Is that you? It can't be you."

No response, only a sigh.

Gabriel was the codename of my former sniper partner. Worse, it was the codename of my best friend, Mick Cranston.

CHAPTER EIGHTEEN

I HELD MY breath, waiting for confirmation, but it didn't come. The man didn't speak. Though I knew it was Mick, I was still holding out a crazy hope that it wasn't my best friend pointing a rifle at me. It's insane how logic can fly out the window when you desperately want something not to be true.

"Mick," I said, breaking the silence. "Is that you? Tell me this is some sort of crazy joke. What the hell's going on?"

Still no response.

"Mick," I yelled.

Finally, he sighed. "It's me, Chase. I have orders to kill Stanley, and you."

"What are you talking about? You're not going to kill the governor's son or take me out. No way."

I rose out of the water and walked forward.

A pop came from the rifle. A millisecond later a sizzling heat whipped past the right side of my face. The round plunked into the ocean and sizzled. The heat of the bullet burned my ear. I grabbed at it to make sure it was still there. I looked up at my best friend and held out my hands.

"This is insanity, Mick. You just shot at me."

"They took my girls, Chase. What am I supposed to do?"

"What? Whose they? Who took your girls?"

"The same people who issued my orders."

"But you work for the government."

"Exactly," he said. "That's how corrupt this is."

"I don't even know what 'this' is." I took a step forward. Before I could take another, a bullet tore through the water by my left foot.

"Damn it, Mick, stop it. Stop shooting at me."

"You stop," he yelled. "Just give me time to think."

"Tell me what 'this' is. Forget thinking and start talking."

Mick took a moment to think, then he said, "You and Stanley are national security threats. I was given a kill order for Stanley and you, and also an order to burn down your house. Apparently you housed highly-classified secret documents that needed to be destroyed."

I scoffed. "You're kidding me, right?"

"I wish I was. That was my directive. That's all I know."

"You know I'm being set up."

He sighed. "Of course I know that. That's why you both are alive and your house didn't burn down. Trust me, I've been stalling for two days. But they took Kimmie and Ruth and threatened to kill them."

Everything suddenly made sense. Mick gave himself away when he broke in because he wanted me out of the house. The detonator didn't malfunction. Mick couldn't bring himself to push the button. I didn't think further about the details because Mick's girls entered my mind. Being a father, I could imagine all too well what he was going through.

I cleared my throat. "They're not going to kill innocent young girls, Mick, no way."

"Maybe," he shot back. "Maybe not. You don't know these people, Chase. They have the power and resources to make anyone disappear. They could make my girls disappear forever, without a trace."

"It's not going to happen. You and I can figure this out and take them down."

"You have no idea who we're dealing with."

"I have a little idea, and they're not that smart."

A brief pause. "What are you talking about?"

"I'm talking about your partner."

"Partner? I don't have a partner. I'm a lone operative, 100% on my own on this one."

"What about Gates?"

"Who's Gates?"

I sighed. "Agent Anfernee Gates."

"No clue. Never heard that name before."

What was Gates doing here then? I ran my hands across my stubbly head. How did he arrive before the Bureau?

I shook off the questions. "Trust me, Mick, we can figure this out."

"I can't. I'm sorry, Augustine. Not with my family on the line. You have to understand. Now where's the kid? I'll trade Karla for Stanley."

"Stop it, Mick. Stop using codenames, call me Chase. You're not going to follow through with this. I'm your best friend."

I was positive he wouldn't shoot me, so I started walking.

The Weatherby coughed again. A whistle hissed by my left ear. I stopped walking, suddenly unsure of my best friend's mental state. Maybe he'd cracked. Maybe he actually thought the only way out was to kill Stanley, and maybe me. With family on the line, who knows? I thought about it more, then shook my head.

"You're not going to shoot me, Mick. You know that's not the greatest good here. You're a father like me. You couldn't live with shooting me and leaving Simon without a father."

"Don't use your philosophy BS with me. You don't know what the greatest good is."

I shot back. "You think the greater good is killing Stanley and following through with a directive you know is corrupt?"

"I won't miss again, Aug, I promise. Just get me Stanley, tell me where he is. You and Karla can walk away. I'll disobey your kill order, but I need the kid. I need some leverage. It's his life or my girls."

"I'm coming to you," I said.

"DON'T," Karla suddenly yelled. "Please, Chase, don't move. He's unstable."

"Listen to her," Mick said.

I didn't listen to either of them. I took a step.

The Weatherby spat. I felt the bullet's path over my head. Positive that it had burned my scalp, I touched my head and looked for blood. Nothing.

But I had Mick. He broke his promise. He said he wouldn't miss again.

So I took another step. Six cracks thundered through the air, shattering the night silence. Four bullets plunked into the ground. The other two sizzled into the water behind me. The mag was empty. It held eleven rounds, but I'd only loaded nine in the clip.

I walked to the base of the lighthouse. Karla flew down the ladder, then she pulled back, whipped out the Smith & Wesson, and pointed it up at Mick. I motioned for her to put the revolver away. She hesitated. I motioned again and she lowered it.

A minute later, Mick eased down the lighthouse ladder with the Weatherby in hand. When he turned to face me, I didn't say anything. I didn't know what to say. I felt half anger, half sympathy for him.

To say he looked haggard was an understatement. Deep wrinkles encircled a pair of darkened eyes. His wavy black hair was messy, almost bedhead looking, which wasn't intentional on his part. Mick was meticulous about his hair. Usually he kept it slicked back like the famous basketball coach Pat Riley, except Mick placed a hard part on the left side.

Mick also looked much leaner than I remembered, which was why I hadn't recognized him the morning I'd chased him.

He spoke first. "I'm so sorry, buddy. I didn't know what to do. I was desperate. I didn't want to make any of these decisions."

My sympathy faded and my anger took over. "But you did make decisions. You shot Stanley and Labonte."

"Hear me out," Mick said. "Before you make any judgement."

"Start talking," I said.

"I had to buy time," he said in a pleading tone. "I had to stall. I know I did terrible things. I understand. For the sake of my girls, I felt I had no choice. You have to understand that." Mick looked at me, then Karla, then back to me. "Obviously I wasn't going to kill the kid, so I shot him in the shoulder, told my superior he moved at the last second. I aimed at you first so you'd dive away from the kid. I didn't want you jumping in front of the bullet if you thought it was coming for Stanley."

"What about Labonte? Why him?"

"Again, buying time. I told my superior Labonte jumped in front of Stanley."

"He may die," Karla stated.

Mick buried his face in his hands. "I had to give them something so they didn't go after my girls again. Labonte seemed like the only choice since he didn't have kids or a significant other." Mick looked at me. "I did everything wrong when I broke into your house. Wanted to make sure you got out. Of course, I couldn't kill you, and I couldn't bring myself to burn down your place. I knew you weren't harboring state secrets."

I nodded. "You let the doorknob click in place."

"I even stepped on that squeaky floorboard."

"Twice," I added.

"I sort of hoped you would've charged out of the bathroom, taken me out, and ended it right there. Put me out of my misery. But I had my girls to think about."

"Does this have to do with our time in *The Activity*?"

"Maybe, I don't know, but I'm not with *The Activity* anymore."

"If this is about your black ops missions," Karla said, stepping in between us, "how does a kill order for the governor's son make sense?"

"She's right," Mick said. "It doesn't make sense."

I nodded. "Tell me about the safe house. What was that all about? Had you changed your mind and decided to kill the kid?"

He shook his head. "No way. Another stall tactic to buy time."

"What about the marshals?" I asked.

"I threw a small pebble at the kitchen window. That lured the marshals into the backyard. I subdued them and dragged their bodies behind the shed."

"Subdued?" I said, raising my eyebrows.

"They'll be a little groggy with a splitting headache, just for a day or two."

I nodded.

Mick continued. "After that, I went into the house and planted the Semtex on the front door. I hid across the street, waited for a while, and wondered what to do next. When the kid came rushing out of the front door, I pushed the detonator when I knew he'd be clear of the blast. I tailed him to the 7-Eleven, then here to the waterfront."

I ran my hand over my head. Mick was good. I hadn't spotted anybody tailing us.

"So who do you work for now?" I asked.

Mick was about to respond, but a blaring siren stopped him.

CHAPTER NINETEEN

MICK HEAVED THE Weatherby onto his shoulder and used the scope to scan in the siren's direction. Nine rounds fired from a .308 caliber rifle could be heard miles away. Not a surprise the cavalry arrived so quickly. I wasn't sure if the sirens belonged to the feds or the local cops.

"Who is it?" I asked.

"Unmarked," Mick said. "Has to be the feds. Have a look." He held out the Weatherby.

I took the rifle and put my eye to the scope. Three unmarked vehicles rushed down Aquarium Way. They must've been on their way already, and then heard the shots. Otherwise, they wouldn't come blazing in like this. I pulled my eye from the scope and looked at Mick.

"Do we trust the Bureau?"

"No way. We trust no one." Mick glanced at Karla.

Karla looked like she was about to sock him, so I cut in. "Trust me, she's fine. Let's move."

We headed west. I led the charge while Karla trailed directly behind. Mick stayed ten yards behind her, running slowly and scanning the area. When Stanley spotted us, he hopped up and down and waved at me with his good arm. A moment later he saw Mick and started running the opposite direction.

"Stanley," I said. "It's fine, he's with us."

The kid kept going, so I doubled my speed and tried to catch him, but I couldn't.

I shouted after him, "Stop, Stanley."

He didn't.

I yelled louder, "Stanley Tuchek."

The kid finally stopped and spun my direction. He shouted while walking backward. "What's going on? I heard shots, Agent Chase. And what's with him?" He pointed. "He took Karla. He's the accomplice."

I reached him a little out of breath. "It's okay, he's a friend of mine."

Stanley scrunched his face. "A friend of yours? What do you mean?"

"A good friend. His name's Mick Cranston. He and I used to work together."

"Work together?" Stanley shook his head. "What's going on, Agent Chase?"

"A massive conspiracy," I said. "It's a long story, Stanley. I'll fill you in when we have more time."

He shot me a skeptical look.

"He's with us now," I said. "Don't worry. There's no time to explain." Stanley still looked skeptical. I put my hands on his shoulders and stared at him. "Trust me, he's fine."

Before Stanley could argue, I took off and headed toward the southwest corner of the Long Beach Aquarium. I stopped running when I reached a locked gate that led to the outdoor section of the aquarium.

I turned to Mick. "Should we hide out or take our chances and keep moving?"

"I hate to hide out, but I think it's our best chance. The area will be swarming with cops any second. It'll be hard for four of us to move undetected."

"I agree."

Mick pulled out a small screwdriver-looking device from one of his pants pockets. While he went to work on the lock, Stanley stood behind him, shifting his weight from foot to foot, looking excited over the turn of events. I debated poking him in the chest again and telling him to calm down. Mick had the lock open in thirty seconds and we were on the move before I could make a decision about calming Stanley down.

Mick led us to the far corner of the aquarium's outdoor center. We passed a shallow petting pool on our right. It contained fish, sand sharks, and manta rays. Somewhere in the background must have been a seal pit, because we heard a lot of barking. On our left was another pool. I believe it was the otter tank, but couldn't see any otters to confirm. Behind the petting pool stood an elevated shark pool. Huge glass windows filled one side of the pool. I saw an ominous shape swimming around, and looked away.

Mick stopped at the back corner of the aquarium, right beside two wooden shacks. The shacks hid the huge pumps and filters for the pools. They cycled on and off and were loud as hell. They were the perfect place for cover. We settled behind the biggest shack and sat in a bed of pine needles.

Stanley pushed up his glasses and shouted at us, so he could be heard over the noise. "This is exciting, isn't—"

Mick and I reached for Stanley at the same time. Mick smothered his mouth while I poked him in the chest and held my fingers there. Karla shushed Stanley.

Everyone stared straight ahead except me. I eyeballed Karla, noticing her chattering teeth. Since she didn't have any fat reserves on her and her clothes were wet from the swim, she had a bluish tinge to her skin. Unfortunately, I didn't have a shirt to give her. Mick sat in a trance. His brow was furrowed, thinking about his family, I assumed. Stanley fidgeted with his glasses and wiped his nose on his sleeve. He glanced over at me and held his left thumb up.

I wanted to break it off. I didn't understand the kid and his excitement. Maybe he was younger and more naïve than I thought. Maybe he really had no idea how bad a situation he was in.

Since I couldn't figure out his mood, I turned my thoughts to the conspiracy. It was hard to comprehend that one federal agent had been chosen to protect Stanley while another agent was commissioned to kill him, not to mention commissioned to kill the protector. Didn't make any sense, not at all. Maybe it was a timing thing. Had something happened since I'd been chosen as protector that changed everything? Were the death threats on Facebook and now Mick's involvement two totally separate things?

I put my hands behind my neck, hung my head, and started massaging my scalp. I didn't know the answers. All I knew was that whatever was going on, none of it justified the government sending one of its operatives after Stanley and me. That was for sure.

After a few minutes of massaging, I stared at my best friend, wanting to question him telepathically. The more I thought about it, though, the more I feared Mick had given me all the answers he knew. On most of my classified missions I didn't know squat beyond my directive. I hoped that wasn't the case with Mick.

Since I couldn't question my buddy, I directed my attention to getting out of the aquarium undetected and where to go from there. That kept my mind occupied for some time. After nearly an hour in the pine needles, Stanley popped to his feet and ran over to me.

"How much longer?" he whispered.

Mick motioned at me, signaling that he was going to scan the area and get an update.

Stanley bent and touched my shoulder. "I asked how much longer, Agent Chase?"

I pulled Stanley to the ground and whispered into his ear. "You need to do some soul-searching, Stanley. Tell me what's really going on."

He blinked at me. "I have, Agent Chase. I've told you a number of times."

"That man is a government operative." I motioned in the direction in which Mick had left. "Commissioned by the federal government to kill you for national security reasons."

Stanley pushed up his glasses. "He was going to kill me? For real? Are you serious? I'm having a hard time believing that."

I sighed. "Yes, Stanley, for real."

"Then how come, Agent Chase, I'm still alive then?" Stanley smirked.

I threw my hands up.

Karla walked over and sat on the other side of Stanley. She placed her right arm around his shoulder. "You need to focus, Stanley. You do realize the severity of the situation, right?"

"I do," he whined. "Trust me. What happened at the lighthouse anyway?"

"We must be missing something," Karla said, looking at me.

I nodded in agreement.

She looked at the kid. "Give me your story one more time."

"Again?" Stanley held up his hands. "What about the lighthouse? What happened there?"

"Later," I said. "Tell us again how the death threats started. You may remember something new if you recount the story, or we may pick up on something new."

After some more whining, Stanley told his story again. It took ten minutes and was exactly the same as his other rendition. Mick was back just after Stanley finished.

"It's clear outside of the aquarium," he said. "I found this." He handed over my shirt.

Karla looked at me. "Anything new from the story?"

I shook my head and handed her my dry shirt.

"Me neither," she said. "You keep the shirt; I'm fine."

"The feds just left," Mick said. "No one's hanging around by the aquarium or parking garage. Most of the activity is at the eastern part of the wharf. A few local cops are there. I think they're taking statements about the shots."

"What's the plan?" Karla asked. "Back to the Ford?"

"No way," I said. "Feds will be looking for you, maybe watching the car. It's not safe."

"A taxi?" Karla said.

I shook my head. "A driver will remember us."

"What then?" Karla asked.

"I have a plan," I said. "Follow me."

"I'll take the rear," Mick said.

"Can I hold one of the guns?" Stanley asked.

"Not a chance," Mick said, stealing my words.

We weaved single file around the backside of the aquarium. Once we'd passed behind the bank of ticket windows, I led the group around the west side of the parking garage. We headed north along Aquarium Way and used the elevated crosswalk to go over Shoreline Drive.

Pine Street was on the other side of Shoreline. It was a touristy area with hip bistros and bars. Plenty of people were around, so we didn't stick out and draw attention to ourselves.

I led the team into the first parking garage I saw. We took the stairs to the top level and I immediately started scanning for an unlocked vehicle. Naturally, I didn't want to steal a car, but it seemed the only option at this point.

I found a nondescript, white Japanese car with the driver's door unlocked. It was popular enough and would blend in nicely on the road. I popped the trunk latch and we loaded our weapons and Stanley's backpack into the trunk, then we all piled in. Stanley and Karla sat in the back. I took the driver's seat, and Mick took the passenger side. Within a minute I had it hotwired and was winding down and out of the garage.

When I hit street level, I turned to Mick and was about to ask him a question.

Stanley beat me to it, however.

CHAPTER TWENTY

"SO YOU WERE really trying to kill me?" Stanley said, leaning between the front seats. "With real bullets and all?"

Mick looked at the kid like he was crazy, then over at me.

I shrugged.

"Yeah, Stanley," Mick said, turning back. "I was sent to kill you. Really kill you. Like dead, dead."

Stanley eased back in his seat, suddenly turning as red as Officer Kowalski. I guessed reality was finally starting to hit. Karla rolled her window all the way down. A good breeze flowed into the car. Stanley snapped out of it a few moments later and pulled out his phone.

"What are you doing?" I said.

He didn't answer.

"Who are you texting?" Mick asked.

"Uh." Stanley pushed up his glasses. "My father."

"Put the phone away," I said.

He didn't.

Karla reached over and tried to swipe Stanley's cell. The kid shimmied to the corner, out of her reach. His fingers kept typing.

"What are you telling your father?" I asked.

Stanley looked up, but kept texting. "Just that I'm safe."

"Put it away," Mick said.

"Right now," I added. "Let's not involve your dad until we know what's going on."

Stanley typed another word or two, pressed send, then tucked the cell away.

I sighed and turned my attention to Mick. I had a number of questions for him. Like, who he worked for, who his superiors were. But Gates was eating at my mind the most.

"So you don't know Anfernee Gates? Never worked for or with him?"

He shook his head. "No idea who he is. Why do you keep mentioning him?"

"Because he was at the waterfront. He arrived around the same time you did. I assumed you two were working together, that he was a dirty agent and you were his accomplice."

"Where was this Gates guy?" Mick asked.

"He was watching everything from the parking structure," I said.

"He may have followed us there," Karla said.

I hadn't thought about that. I hadn't spotted Mick tailing us, so maybe Gates was also good at being invisible.

"What's Gates's story?" Mick asked.

"He's been on my tail the past two days, following my every move. It appears he's investigating me for some reason. I'm not even sure which agency he works for, though there's a wild rumor swirling that he works for the CIA. Can you believe that?"

"The Company?" Mick said, running his hand over his head. "You're kidding?"

I looked at him. "That's the rumor from one of the cops at Long Beach headquarters. But that's crazy. Right?"

"Yes and no," Mick said.

"What do you mean?"

"I sort of work for The Company, at least partly."

"You do?"

He nodded. "I was recruited out of *The Activity* for a position with the SCS."

The three-letter agency didn't ring a bell. "What's the SCS?" I asked.

Karla leaned forward. "The Special Collection Service, right?"

Mick nodded.

"Interesting," I said. "Never heard of the organization."

"Most people haven't. It's a joint intelligence-gathering organization, between the NSA and CIA."

"Wait," Stanley said, leaning forward until he was shoulder to shoulder with Karla. "You're telling me you're employed by the SCS and you, Agent Chase, have never heard of the organization?"

Mick turned in his seat. "Are you not paying attention back there?"

I glanced at Stanley in the rearview mirror. "What's wrong with you, anyway?"

"I need to get out, clear my head, Agent Chase. Plus, I need to go to the bathroom. Can we stop?"

"We're not stopping," I said.

Stanley sat back and fidgeted. His red face had now turned ashen. I guessed the enormity of his situation had fully hit him. Finally. Karla attempted to comfort him by patting his knee.

I looked at Mick. "So Gates obviously doesn't work for the SCS, or you'd know him."

"Actually, he could. I barely know anyone in the organization. And I've never met the executive branch. Most of us, operatives like me, are specialists in our respective fields and work alone. Sometimes we work in teams. We mainly stick to our individual directives. It's a black book operation, so it's all about deniability."

I nodded. "Your directives, and even involvement in the organization, don't really exist?"

"Absolutely," Mick said. "We're completely expendable."

"You're the sniper specialist?" I asked.

"Technically I'm the ammunition and weapons expert. I also train other agents in camouflage technique, how to move undetected, that sort of thing. Been with the SCS for a year and a half."

"I need to go to the bathroom," Stanley announced.

I ignored him. "Tell me about the specific directives concerning Stanley and me."

Mick looked out the window for a moment, then back to me. "It all had to do with national security. Which is crazy, I know. My orders, which come via encrypted email, never elaborated on rationale. The SCS is 100 times worse than *The Activity*, Chase. Top down, don't question a thing. Anyway, Stanley and you were apparently into some activities that seriously threatened our national security."

Stanley snorted. We ignored him.

Mick continued. "His death was supposed to be via a single sniper shot. And it had to be after your death and house burning down. I was told to burn down your house because you had highly-sensitive government intel stored there, which needed to be destroyed immediately."

"Have you ever had a directive like that?" Karla asked.

Mick shook his head. "Absolutely not. Nothing like it, ever. Never any domestic targets, that's for sure."

"I can't comprehend the national security threat," I said. "It doesn't make any sense."

"Neither could I," Mick said. "So I questioned the directive. At least I was on my way to."

I looked at my best friend. "What do you mean?"

"When I received the directive, like you, I was totally baffled. So that night I hopped on a red-eye flight to Baltimore. Our headquarters are in Beltsville, Maryland. I'd never questioned an order before and I wasn't about to do it over the phone or via text. When I got off the plane that morning, my cell lit up. It had been off for the entire flight. My wife had left ten frantic voicemails. Plus, I had two texts. One was a picture text." He scrolled through his phone, then handed me his cell.

I glanced at the picture and furrowed my brow. Mick's wife and his two girls were curled up sleeping on a bed, safe and sound.

I put my eyes back onto the road. "I don't follow."

"That's not a room in our house," he said.

"Okay. I'm still not following, though."

Mick took a deep breath. "Someone broke into our house that night, drugged my wife and children, and relocated them to an abandoned house about fifty miles away. They took that picture and sent it to me while I was in the air. Then they brought the girls back to their own bedroom. Julie woke up alone in the abandoned house, however. At first she was disoriented, then she turned frantic. They left her keys and car, no phone. She raced home just as the girls woke up. Julie has no recollection of the break-in or of the transportation to the abandoned house. The girls don't even know anything happened."

I didn't say anything right away. Instead, I took a deep breath. I couldn't imagine what he was going through.

After a minute, I asked, "How's Julie coping?"

"She's not. And I'm not coping well either. The other text said this." He read the text: "Complete your orders or you'll never see them again. We did it once, we'll do it again. This is your warning."

Suddenly I felt the heat in the car. I rolled my window all the way down. Nobody said a word for about a minute.

Stanley broke the silence. He'd been fidgeting a lot during our conversation. "I've really got to go, guys. I'm sorry, but we must stop."

I glanced at Karla in the rearview mirror. She nodded her approval, so I took the next exit off the 605 freeway and pulled into a Chevron station.

"Make it quick, Stanley," I said. "We're in a stolen car here. Plus, every fed in town is probably on the lookout for you."

He hopped out and poked his head back in. "I need to get into the trunk. My backpack is in there with some cash. I need a Diet Coke."

I pulled the trunk lever, nearly breaking it in the process. Stanley rummaged around in the trunk, then scampered toward the restroom with his backpack.

I turned to Mick. "Tell me more about the SCS."

"What do you want to know?"

"Their history. I need to get an understanding of what we're dealing with."

Mick settled back into the seat. "It started post-Cold War, when the NSA became all the rage in the intelligence arena, which was a result of how effective they were in grabbing intelligence data out of midair. The NSA's abilities made other intelligence agencies, like the CIA, which had too many human operatives, look almost unnecessary. Some people actually thought the CIA was doomed at the time, but a few high-ranking members of the NSA didn't agree. They recognized their own limitations. They knew that there were many places in the world where roving satellites and stationary antennas couldn't reach. They knew the value of having highly-trained human operatives on the ground."

He paused and thought, then said, "To make a long story short, the organizations joined in '78 and created the SCS. The idea was to combine the human ability of the CIA with the computer ability of the NSA."

"These trained operatives," I said, "would infiltrate foreign countries and set up spy gear?"

Mick nodded. "Exactly. The spies would smuggle in parabolic antennas and set them up in areas where roving satellites couldn't reach. The whole purpose was to increase the eavesdropping ability of the NSA."

"Where do you fit in to all this?" I asked.

"Eavesdropping like this went on for quite a while. By the late 1990s, however, things started changing."

"How so?" Karla asked.

Mick shifted in his seat so he could see both of us. "The SCS calls it the shift from information 'in motion' to information 'at rest'. Though countries had gotten better at encrypting information sent over airwaves, many had simply stopped sending it that way. Basically they knew better, because it was too risky. Instead, these countries started storing important intelligence information on computer databases, disks, hard drives, that sort of thing."

Karla nodded. "I get it. Information at rest."

"Right," Mick said. "Now, having highly-trained spies on the ground was even more important because intelligence information had to be accessed remotely through cyberspace, the NSA specialty, or it had to be accessed physically, the CIA specialty. And that's the philosophy of the SCS. That's why they're the go-to intelligence organization these days."

"So your job is to protect the spies?" I said.

"Precisely. On sensitive missions I would travel with an agent and basically be their eyes and ears on the ground. Protect them from a distance if anything went wrong on a mission. If they were being tailed or chased by authorities, that sort of thing."

"You would neutralize the threat," I said.

"Any threat," Mick said, looking out his side window. "I even had authority to take down the agent if they were caught."

Karla put her hand on Mick's shoulder. "Did the agent know this?"

Mick turned and nodded. "I think everyone agreed it would be better that way. Nobody wanted to be tortured for information, then be killed."

Silence filled the car for a few moments. I suddenly thought about Stanley. "By the way, the kid's taking too long, isn't he?"

"I should use the ladies room," Karla said. "I'll go see what the hold-up is." She left the car and bounced her way to the Chevron station.

I turned to Mick. "You said something about an executive branch, and that you've never met them."

"Yeah, the executive branch runs the SCS. There are three members from the NSA, three from the CIA, and a leader named the Chairman. The chairman's role is a three-year stint that rotates between the two agencies. I don't know any members of the executive branch or their names."

"That's odd, not knowing anyone's name or position."

Mick subtly shook his head. "The more I realized the sensitivity of the missions I was assigned, the more it made sense. Since deniability is the unofficial code of the SCS, the less I knew of the executive branch, the better."

I looked out the windshield and thought for a moment, then turned back to Mick. "So Gates could be part of the executive branch, maybe even the chairman?"

Mick said, "I guess so."

"This is starting to make some sense. Let's assume Gates is the chairman and sent you the kill orders. He's the dirty agent behind this conspiracy. He showed up at the wharf to make sure you finished the job."

Mick nodded. "It's a definite possibility, very likely even."

"Now we have to figure out why he sent you after Stanley and me. Why would a federal agent want us dead? I think we…" I stopped mid-sentence because Karla jammed out of the Chevron station and raced toward the car. By the time she reached our vehicle, Mick and I were standing on either side of the hood.

She gasped a little. "Stanley's gone."

"What do you mean 'gone'?" I said.

"I mean, gone, gone," she replied. "He crawled out the bathroom window on the other side of the station. It was left wide open."

"What? Why?" Mick said.

Karla motioned us toward the bathroom. "You have to see this."

We followed her into the men's bathroom. I stopped when I saw the message hastily scrawled across the mirror with a soapy finger.

It read: 'DONT KNOW WHAT'S REAL ANYMORE. SORRY'.

CHAPTER TWENTY-ONE

"WHAT'S NOT REAL?" I said. "I don't get this kid. Not at all. What reality is he unsure of?"

Mick looked out the bathroom window. "We need to find the kid and ask him. He's only had a five-minute head start. He must've gone north out the window, otherwise we would have seen him. I'll go on foot."

I followed Mick out of the bathroom. "Karla and I will take the car. We'll drive straight north for five, then grid our way back. Let's meet back here in twenty minutes or so."

Mick nodded and took off. Karla beat me back to the car. I jumped in and peeled out of the parking lot, only to stop a second later.

"What's wrong?" Karla asked.

"I have a bad feeling about something."

I hopped out, popped the trunk, and rummaged around. After a thorough search, I slammed the trunk and crawled back into the driver's seat.

"He took a gun," Karla said. "Didn't he?"

I nodded. "Your Colt."

"That punk," Karla said. "So that's why he took his back pack. What is he up to?"

I jammed on the accelerator and headed north on the street directly in front of the gas station. "I don't know. All I know is the kid was acting strange when we got into this car. I'm not imagining that, right?"

"You're right. He was even more fidgety than usual."

"And it wasn't that hot in here, was it?"

"No, he was clearly stressed. He wanted out of this car, using the bathroom as an excuse."

"Don't know what's real anymore." I drummed my fingers on the wheel. "Strange thing to write, isn't it?"

"Sort of."

"What do you mean, sort of?"

"Well, he kept asking Mick if he was 'really' trying to kill him."

"True, the kid was having a hard time with reality."

"Why would he think none of this was real, though? That's what I don't get."

I nodded. "What I don't get is if the kid had finally started to grasp the reality of his situation, why would he leave us? We're trying to protect him. Does he think the Colt is going to protect him better than us?"

Karla eyed me. "There's more to his story than he's letting on."

"Absolutely. We have to find him."

"We will."

"Another odd thing; he left his laptop in the trunk."

Karla scratched her head. "That is weird."

I nodded. "I have no idea what Stanley Tuchek is up to."

I drove north for another two minutes, then turned and headed east for a couple of minutes. After that, I headed south until the next cross street. I turned right onto that street and worked my way west for a few minutes, then headed south and turned east. I followed that same pattern and worked back toward the gas station. Karla and I didn't talk. We kept glued to our respective side windows. It took twenty-three minutes to arrive back at the Chevron.

When I pulled in and parked, I turned to Karla. "He's gone."

"Little jerk," she said.

"Maybe Mick tracked him down."

"No such luck." Karla pointed past me, toward the station.

Mick trotted out of the bathroom and headed our way. A moment later, he slipped into the back seat.

"No sign of him?" I asked.

Mick shook his head. "What's this kid up to? We've got to find him. We've got to end this. For my family's sake, for everyone's."

"We will." I pulled out the backup snapcell Stanley had given me. I dialed his number. Turning to Karla, I said, "It's worth a shot."

No answer, however. I didn't bother leaving a voicemail. Instead, I dropped the gearshift into drive and squealed out of the lot.

"Where are you going?" Karla asked.

"The kid's not stupid enough to go back home, is he?"

"There'll be a team at his house," Karla said. "I don't think he's that dumb. Should we call it in? Do we trust Hornsby or Frank?"

"I trust Frank," I said. "But I'm not ready to call him yet. I have a better idea."

Karla looked at me. "Which is?"

I thought for a second, just to make sure it was a good idea, then said, "We go to his father. We can trust him. We know he's not involved in a plan to murder his own son. Plus, he may have an idea where Stanley's scampered off to."

Mick leaned forward. "There'll probably be a team there."

"Good point," Karla said.

"Where would the governor be?" Mick asked. "I know he's in LA because of Stanley, but his home is in Sacramento, isn't it?"

"He has a big place in the valley," Karla said. "Hop north on the 605, I know where it is. I met the governor there yesterday. He wanted to meet before I ran the investigation."

It took twenty minutes to get there. Along the way, we theorized about what Stanley was up to. We came up with nothing promising. No decent theories at all. We all agreed we simply had to find Stanley and grill the kid.

When we arrived at the governor's house, I drove past the front gates and parked down the street. His place was beyond big; gargantuan, in fact. The property was hillside and surrounded by old sycamore trees. A six-foot iron fence encircled the whole perimeter. The actual house was nowhere to be seen from the road.

"If we don't trust the feds," Karla said, "we can't drive up to the front gate and announce our presence. Everyone will be tipped off before the gate opens."

"If a team is here," I said. "They could have left by now. It's late."

"Someone is likely to be around," Mick said. "Why don't you guys sit tight and I'll go see what vehicles are here."

Karla nodded.

Mick was the obvious choice for reconnaissance. We didn't need to remind him to be careful. Staying undetected was what he did for a living.

After Mick closed the door, Karla and I sat in silence for a few minutes.

Finally, she turned and said, "I've been thinking."

"Uh-oh."

"You never did tell me about the 'Mag' nickname. You were about to, but we got interrupted."

"You're right," I said. "The kid interrupted us with his call, didn't he?"

"Let's hear the story then." Karla shifted and put her back against the passenger door.

I unbuckled my seatbelt and turned to my right. "You already know the YouTube story, so I might as well." I smiled. "I'm sure your opinion of me is awfully low, and this story will keep it there."

She smiled back. "I admire your vigilantism."

"Perhaps you'll admire me more then. This story makes it look like I went easy on that soldier."

She waved her hand. "Go on then."

"The nickname comes from a case I worked a couple of years ago." I paused because it felt weird telling the story. The only person I'd told the full story to was Doc Jules.

"Which case?"

I cleared my throat. "I was lead investigator on the Giovanni Russo case." I didn't say anything else, wanting to see how long it would take Karla to connect the dots.

Exactly twelve seconds. That was when her eyes went wide.

"So you were that guy?" she said. "You were responsible?"

I nodded.

She did something I didn't expect; she smiled.

Her eyes lit up. "Tell me how it went down. It's been a couple of years and my memory is a little foggy."

Barely anyone knew exactly what had gone down. There was a lot of speculation over the incident, and still was, so I laid the truth out for her.

"As I'm sure you know, Giovanni Russo owned the nationwide Motel 7 chain, which he made a decent living from. But the real money he made came from the deal he had with the government."

Karla nodded. "He took in criminals and gave them a place to live, I remember that."

I held up my finger. "But not just any criminals. Violent sexual offenders were his specialty, offenders who had recently been released from prison or paroled. The freaks that no cities or neighborhoods or communities would take. But Russo saw a good business opportunity. His West Coast motels were suffering a lot since the 2008 economic meltdown. On average only 35% of the rooms were booked on any given day. So Russo knew he had plenty of space to house these criminals. Since the problem of where to house the criminals was nationwide, every state struggled for placement. Russo knew that California would be a big draw for these perverts. Which makes sense. Wouldn't you rather live in California than the middle of Nebraska?"

"Absolutely," Karla said.

"So Russo brokered a deal with the prison system and parole board. He'd take these criminals into his motels—"

"For a big price tag, I imagine."

"Sure," I said. "A huge kickback from the feds. Initially, everything appeared above board. Lengthy contracts were drawn up and huge stipulations were in place."

Karla furrowed her brow. "Like what?"

"The housing was to be transitional. Three months at most. Only a limited number of criminals in any motel, in any location, at any given time. Nowhere near an elementary school, that sort of thing."

"Got it. So what happened?"

I paused for a moment, then said, "Pico Rivera happened."

Karla looked out the side window. "Right, a child was abducted and raped from that school in Pico Rivera. I remember that." She looked back.

I nodded. "And the culprit was a registered sex offender. Except the guy was registered in Iowa. He was supposed to be living in some sleepy little city in the middle of that state. But he turned up in California doing his dirty business. That fact triggered the feds' involvement. Which is where I came in. I was with the Violent Crimes division of the local field office at that time. I was tasked with the investigation."

"This was before the YouTube affair, I guess." Karla tapped my knee.

I laughed. She had a knack for getting away with things. I imagined she could call me Gary and I wouldn't mind.

"It was," I said. "Anyway, it was a long, drawn-out investigation. I spent every waking hour figuring out the racket. Wouldn't let any detail go."

"What was the gist?"

"Russo's motels had become flooded with violent sex offenders. He housed approximately 1,000 offenders, but he was only supposed to have a hundred, maximum. Of course, the official books said he only housed a hundred, so those books were clearly being cooked. It was basically a giant shell game. If you went online to look at where these offenders were living, everything looked spread out across the country. But in reality, nine hundred sex offenders were living where they weren't supposed to be. And Russo was contracted to receive two grand a month per offender."

Karla held out her left hand. "Wait a second. Two grand a month per offender, and he had unofficially a thousand. That's two million a month."

My eyes went big. "I know."

She squinted at me. "How'd they get away with this? Must've been a huge government conspiracy. Right?"

"That's where things get tricky."

"Tricky? How so?"

"Clint Clemens, the head of the third branch of government, the federal judiciary, had his signature and handiwork all over this thing. He and Russo were supposedly in cahoots."

"Just the two of them?"

I shrugged. "Clemens probably had a few other officers to help with the paperwork. But when the officers were questioned, they naturally pointed up the chain and said they were just following orders. Nobody really knows who Clemens involved, it's still speculation to this day. Clemens's office had a second set of books and files for these nine hundred offenders. In these files, paperwork for a California transfer was completed and signed, except no dates were on the form. So if anyone questioned why a registered offender wasn't in the proper locale—"

"Clemens would falsify the date, then produce the paperwork."

"Exactly. Clemens would simply say the paperwork was just filed and the offender's whereabouts hadn't been updated in the system yet."

Karla leaned forward. "You mention the books. What about the money?"

"The accounting appeared legit, but ultimately the funds were funneled through a variety of shell organizations and sent to a few offshore and Swiss accounts which were traced back to Russo's name."

Karla cocked her head at me. "Sounds like a major conspiracy still."

"It is, and the feds knew it, but still it's a little tricky. The director and deputy director of the FBI wanted Clemens big time. They knew they couldn't absolve the government of any wrongdoing; they were well beyond that stage. I'm sure ideally they wanted to pin everything on Russo, but since they couldn't do that, they wanted to pin everything on Clemens. In particular, they wanted to stress that he acted alone in this, that there was no widespread conspiracy. Here was where it got really bad—"

"Let me guess," Karla said, shaking her head. "They turned Russo against Clemens."

I banged my fist onto the steering wheel. "Yup, they were willing to cut Russo a lightened sentence if he turned state's evidence against

Clemens. The bastards even approached me and told me to offer Russo the deal."

Karla's eyes went wide. "Did you?"

"I had to. I was lead investigator and this came directly from the top. And Russo, the slimy prick, had the balls to negotiate with me."

"What do you mean?"

"He wanted to dictate the terms to us. Said he would turn over all the evidence on Clemens provided he got no jail time and the feds didn't touch his money."

Karla sat back. "This guy is something else."

"I'm not sure who's worse, Russo or the feds. Because the feds basically agreed to all his terms."

She blew out a breath. "You're kidding."

I banged the wheel again. "I'm not. They agreed to no jail time and said he could keep his offshore money. The feds didn't want to admit it was there anyway. They made Russo sell the motel chain, which he made a fortune off of, then they made him leave the country. He's not allowed back into the U.S., ever. That's the only original term they stuck to."

"Unbelievable," Karla said. "But it still sounds like a pretty cut and dried conspiracy. You said Clemens was supposedly in cahoots with Russo. What do you mean by supposedly?"

"In all this, we, including me, thought Clemens was beyond corrupt, that he was skimming money or getting a kickback from Russo. Somehow the guy must've been profiting from all this corruption. Otherwise, why do it? The problem was we couldn't find a trace of any money coming back to him. In fact, the guy was squeaky clean and living pretty much below his means. Most of his salary went toward college tuition payments for three of his kids. The guy drove a four-year-old Subaru Outback and his wife drove a five-year-old Honda Odyssey. And they hadn't been on a vacation in over six years. It didn't add up. Also, when Clemens was arrested, he totally shut down. Never sought legal counsel, never made a formal or informal statement about his involvement. Never claimed innocence. It was strange. He represented himself at his arraignment, too."

"Naturally you followed up," Karla said.

I nodded. "Of course, but initially Clemens wouldn't even let me visit him in prison. So I visited his family. Right away I knew something was wrong."

Karla narrowed her eyes. "How so?"

"They seemed nervous that I was even there. And I was asking pretty innocuous questions, nothing to get nervous about. After ten minutes, I figured it out; they weren't nervous, they were scared, terrified really. That's when it dawned on me that Russo had probably threatened Clemens or his family, or both. He was blackmailing Clemens. As soon as I asked if Russo had threatened them, the eldest son demanded that I leave. Actually, he pointed at the door and told me to get the hell out. I didn't want to upset them more, so I left. Went right back to the prison, but Clemens refused to see me again. So I bribed a guard to pass a note to Clemens."

Karla smiled. "I love how nonchalantly you say 'I bribed a guard'. What did the note say?"

I paused, remembering the exact words. " 'I know Russo threatened your family. Let's talk'."

"And that worked?" Karla asked.

I nodded. "Sure did. Clemens met with me within five minutes of getting that note. And he came right out of his shell. Begged me to drop everything and leave him alone. Like his son, he told me to get the hell out and stay away. I wouldn't, of course, but Clemens wouldn't talk either, about anything specific or acknowledge any threats that had been made. We reached a stalemate. By that point, though, I knew for sure Russo had him by the balls because Clemens was terrified, just like his family. I could see it in his eyes. I could tell he would probably never talk. In the end, we struck a deal. If he talked and told me the true story, I promised not to pursue Russo nor go public with anything; to basically drop everything and periodically check in on his family."

"Obviously you felt there was no other choice."

"Yup. It was either walk away empty-handed or at least know the truth, but do nothing about it. And I can't not know the truth."

Karla nodded. "I get it. So what had happened between Clemens and Russo?"

"Clemens was following the book with Russo for about the first six months of the deal, then Russo put the gears to him. Or to his daughter, I should say."

I stopped, not sure whether it was appropriate to tell this part to a female.

"I can handle it, Chase," Karla said. "I'm a big girl."

"Okay, fine," I said. "Russo got a couple of his thugs to go after Clemens's eldest girl. She was twenty-two and finishing up college. These guys tailed her home late one night when she was leaving the library. They hauled her into a car and took her to an undisclosed location. Stripped her naked, tied her, beat her up, took it right to the verge of raping her, then they stopped. The punks recorded the whole incident, with the daughter screaming for daddy and all, then they sent the video to Clemens's cellphone, with the message that if Clemens didn't agree to Russo's terms, or if he went to the authorities, next time the thugs would finish the rape, kill the daughter, and dump the body in Long Beach harbor."

Karla pushed out a breath. "The man is evil."

"It gets worse."

"How could it possibly?"

I took a breath, then launched into it. "Naturally Clemens freaked out about the situation. Didn't know exactly what to do. He knew Russo had the mafia in his back pocket and could call on them anytime. Anyway, when Russo approached him with the deal to house these extra criminals, Clemens didn't respond in the affirmative right away. He was too concerned about the welfare of his daughter and how to handle the situation. Like should he go to the authorities, knowing his family would likely spend the rest of their lives in WITSEC, looking over their shoulders." I paused. "I guess Clemens spent too much time thinking because, two days later, the thugs grabbed his wife on her way home from the grocery store. In the middle of the day, mind you. They did the exact same thing to her, then sent the video to Clemens with the message that he had an hour to decide or his wife would be raped and killed. Of course, he agreed to the terms."

Karla shook her head. "This is horrible. And Clemens never told anyone?"

I nodded. "Most men will do anything to protect their family, and Clemens was no different. He knew how powerful and evil Russo was. Clemens didn't feel like his family would be totally safe in WITSEC. Russo had the means to get to anyone, and he knew that first-hand. So Clemens agreed to the scam, but wanted no part in the money. Things ran to Russo's plan for a while. But then, eventually, Clemens cracked."

"He cracked? What happened?"

"Pico Rivera happened. That's when Clemens couldn't live with himself or the situation any longer. Knowing he had played a major part in a child rape and abduction sent him over the edge. He told me he was willing to die to uncover the Russo scam. Except he knew that Russo would punish his family, not him, so he had to think of a way to discreetly reveal what had been going on."

"Makes sense."

"Right. So when Pico went down, Clemens, instead of giving the authorities the forged transfer paperwork, he gave them the original paperwork. He knew that would trigger an investigation as to why the rapist was living in California and not Iowa. Clemens knew that it was more than likely the whole Russo scam would be revealed by this detail. Which is exactly what eventually happened."

Karla eyed me. "Wasn't he afraid of Russo retaliating?"

"He was, but Clemens told me that Russo really had no idea how Clemens was managing the paperwork and books. Russo didn't know that Clemens could have simply provided the false transfer paperwork and everything would have been fine."

"That's risky."

"Yup," I said. "And Clemens knew that, but it was a risk he was willing to take because he couldn't live with the deal any longer. While everything was going down, Clemens consulted with a lawyer to get an idea of how much jail time he would be facing. He found out it would be somewhere in the ball park of ten years, but with good behavior he could potentially be out in five. He figured five years of hard time would be better than living in fear for the rest of his life. So Clemens convinced

Russo that he had nothing to do with helping the feds and, to prove it, he would take the fall and do the time, provided his family was safe. Russo agreed and said that if Clemens talked and broke his promise, his whole family was dead. Clemens knew that, with Russo's ties, Russo could make that happen no matter if Russo was in jail or in a different country."

Karla tapped my knee. "That's why Russo had the balls to negotiate with you and the feds. Right? He knew Clemens was never going to give him up."

"Exactly. So that's why I said this situation was tricky. It's not such a cut and dried government conspiracy. Russo was really pulling the strings and responsible for almost everything. I guess Clemens should have gone straight to the authorities. But if he did, I wouldn't have been surprised if some or all of his family died. It's a tough ethical dilemma."

"It is. And I guess you didn't follow through with your promise to Clemens." Karla smiled. "You didn't drop everything, did you?"

I raised my eyebrows. "I guess I didn't. I'm not proud of how I handled things."

"So tell me how the next part of the story went down."

"I wish I could take it back. It's not flattering."

"I can take it."

I sat back and looked out the windshield. "Once I knew the truth, I couldn't let it go. I knew we couldn't take Russo down on legal matters because Clemens wouldn't cooperate, out of fear. But I just couldn't let Russo get away without some sort of punishment. It goes against every-thing inside me. I couldn't live knowing Russo basically got off and Clemens was the fall guy doing hard prison time. So, yes, I broke my promise to Clemens, but I imagine he's okay with it."

"How'd you get Russo alone?"

"I knew he had this late-night ice cream obsession. Once a week, like clockwork, Russo would head down to the local creamery. The creamery was on a busy main street, so Russo's driver had to drop him off about a block away, in a parking lot behind the main street. Since Russo always went right before closing, which was around one in the morning, I knew the parking lot was pretty much deserted. When they pulled into the lot that night, I ran over to the car with a balaclava and gloves on and knocked out the driver. Then I climbed in the back and knocked out Russo.

"I drove to his Motel 7 billboard, the one right off the 605 freeway in Pico Rivera. I threw Russo over my shoulder and climbed the rungs to the top of the billboard. There's a narrow platform up there. Once we were up top, I smacked him around until he woke up. Then I politely grabbed him by the ankles and dangled him over the ledge."

Karla grabbed my knee. "You're kidding?"

"Nope," I said, smiling. "I dangled him there for quite a while. Sometimes I used just one arm, you know, to conserve energy and give my other arm a rest. I swear Russo screamed louder than a middle-aged woman at a Rod Stewart concert. We were so high up nobody could hear. I also stressed to Russo that I was acting alone. I wanted to make sure there were no ramifications for Clemens's family. Anyway, once Russo lost his voice, I told him I'd let him live if he agreed to a few things."

"What things?"

"An anonymous donation to the Pico Rivera school, enough to build a whole new state of the art facility, and a million-dollar anonymous donation to the Clemens family. Of course, he agreed to everything. But who wouldn't, right? Hanging upside down over the freeway like that. So I pulled him up onto the platform and enforced everything again with my fists. I'd brought a flashlight to shine in his face when I was talking to him, in the hope that he wouldn't recognize my eyes. Not sure if that worked or not."

"It's my understanding that he had to have facial reconstruction. Is that true?"

"I don't know – there's some speculation over that part of the story. The reconstruction could be so people don't recognize him, can't be sure. Anyway, I thought I was done after the facial beating, but something inside me wouldn't let me finish. I didn't think he'd come through on the anonymous donation deal, so I couldn't let him off so easily. It boiled me inside that he suffered no repercussions; no prison time and no huge public outcry about how evil he was. The guy wasn't even out of money."

Karla nodded excitedly. "So what did you do?"

I paused and looked away. "To make a long story short, I stripped him naked and hog-tied his ankles to his hands with his own necktie. Then I shoved the flashlight between his upper legs where his thighs meet his butt cheeks and left it there. With the bulb end shining right on his billboard."

I looked at Karla. She had no reaction. All she said was: "I'm assuming the flashlight was a Maglite."

I nodded. "Indeed it was, the big one with four size D batteries. Hence the nickname, 'Mag'. For the record, Pepperstein and Labonte have no proof that I was involved. Obviously, I'd be in a lot of trouble if anyone could prove it was me. Anyway, I left Russo on the billboard catwalk to contemplate his life choices. Honestly, I didn't know Russo would be so visible when the sun came up. I didn't know the freeway would back up like it did."

"Four hours," Karla said, smiling. "If I remember correctly, that's how long the 605 was basically at a standstill. I can remember the news footage of the helicopter taking Russo out of there. Unbelievable. People were out of their cars, standing on the freeway, watching the whole thing, many of them recording it on their phones."

I nodded along. "I was surprised it went so public."

"And now Russo's the *butt* of many jokes."

"Good one," I said. "You're quite the *crack up*."

She smiled. "Ouch, you hit rock *bottom* with that one."

"*Ass*-cuse me?"

Karla laughed. "I can't believe that was you."

"Another shining moment for me."

She leaned forward. "So did Russo ever follow through on your deal?"

I held up a finger. "Actually, he did follow through on one thing: the school donation. Pico Rivera received two million, but the Clemens donation never came through."

"That's something, I guess. So where's Russo now?"

"Europe. Italy, I think. He's probably back in his hometown. All I know is he hasn't stepped foot on American soil since the incident."

"So does Frank know you were responsible?"

"There were a lot of rumors, of course. Labonte and Pepperstein assumed it was me and kept those rumors alive. Frank pretty much knew it was me, and he was livid about it until we struck a deal."

"Which was?"

"He'd bury the case if my name ever came up, as long as I agreed to a demotion. At least that's how I saw it. Frank called it a voluntary lateral movement. He wanted me in the office, stuck behind a desk so he could keep an eye on me. That's why I was transferred from Violent Crimes to Cyber Crimes."

"Cyber Crimes, eh? Doesn't sound like you."

"Yeah, that didn't work out too well for me. I can't be cooped up like that, which is probably why I exploded on that Marine."

"Right, *To Catch a Pervert.*" She smiled.

I shrugged.

"So nobody knows for sure you're responsible?"

"Well, now you do, and my former therapist. You have to promise not to tell anyone, even your husband."

Karla blushed and opened her mouth to say something, then she stopped. Before I had a chance to prod her, Mick cracked open the car door and slipped into the back seat.

"Everybody get down," he said, breathing hard. "NOW."

CHAPTER TWENTY-TWO

KARLA AND I ducked at the same time. I scrunched as far down in the seat as I could go. Karla buried herself in the foot well.

"Hope we're not about to be shot," I said.

"Nothing like that," Mick said. "Hornsby just left. His car should be at the gate by now. I ran back to warn you since I didn't want him turning right out of the driveway and catching you guys with his high beams."

I pushed out a breath. "Got it."

We waited in silence for thirty seconds.

"All clear," Mick said.

I sat up and looked back at Mick. "Anyone else there?"

He shook his head. "We're good to go."

"Should I roll up to the gate and hope for the best?" I looked from Mick to Karla. "Any objections to that plan?"

Nobody said a word, so I drove up to the front gate, rolled down my window, and pushed a button on the intercom.

"Agents Chase and Dickerson here to see Governor Tuchek."

No response for twenty seconds. I was about to try again when the speaker crackled on.

"The governor wants to know if his son is with you."

"Negative," I said. "That's what we're here to talk about. It's important. Please relay that to the governor."

Another few moments of silence, then the gate suddenly buzzed, and the metal wheels screeched on their track. The bars grated open. A moment later our car barreled through and wound its way up the driveway. It was a steeper incline than I'd imagined. I figured the house was perched on the apex of the hill, overlooking the city.

Once we'd wound through the sycamores, the mansion materialized in the distance. It was Spanish style, maybe 10,000 square feet, possibly more. The roof was clay-colored adobe tile and the curved driveway in front was made of ancient-looking cobblestones. I didn't see more details than that because my eyes were drawn to the front door. Ernesto Tuchek nearly filled the entire frame of the double front doors. His hands were square on his hips and his lips were pursed.

I parked and looked at Karla. "This should be fun. He loves me."

"Maybe I should do the talking," Karla said.

"I second that," Mick added.

I turned to my best friend. "Well, it definitely shouldn't be you talking, since you tried to kill his son and all."

"Point taken," Mick said.

We exited the vehicle at the same time. Karla sprang to the front door and shook the governor's hand. Tuchek didn't offer his hand to Mick or me.

Instead, he looked right at me and said, "What the hell happened this time, Agent Chase? Where is Stanley? And by the way, you guys know everyone is looking for you, right?"

"We do," Karla said.

The governor stroked his beard. "Maybe I should get Hornsby back here."

I wanted to remind the governor that he was the one who insisted I be pulled off protection, which meant that Stanley wasn't technically my responsibility, but I stepped toward him instead, and took a more political approach. "Give us five minutes to explain, sir, before you call anyone. Please."

"It's important, Governor," Karla said. "We don't know who to trust right now, except for you. Give us a chance to tell you what's been going on."

The governor eyed us for a moment, then stepped back and let us through the front door. He ushered a couple of staff members away and pointed us toward a sitting area to the right of the front door. Karla and I sat on the lone dark brown leather couch, while the governor and Mick took two red wingback chairs.

"Alright," the governor said, squeezing into the chair, "start explaining."

"As you know," Karla began, "Special Agent Chase was chosen by Stanley to protect him." The governor cleared his throat and was about to say something, but Karla held up her hand. "We understand your opinion on this, sir, but hear me out. Special Agent Chase was protecting your son from Special Agent Mick Cranston." She motioned at Mick.

The governor shot looks between Cranston and me, but didn't say anything. Finally, his brow scrunched and he said, "What do you mean? That sounds crazy, you understand that?"

"We do," Karla said.

The governor continued. "You're saying the government sent *my* son death threats, then actually decided to follow up on them? This is preposterous. Why? Why would they do that?"

"We're not exactly sure yet," Karla said. "The Facebook death threats and Stanley being targeted by the government could be two separate things. What we do know is that Special Agent Cranston was given orders by the Special Collection Service to kill your son and Agent Chase, for national security reasons."

"I can't believe it," the governor said. "Makes no sense, not at all. Stanley certainly hasn't been into anything of this nature. I don't even know what the Special Collection Service is."

"It's a joint intelligence organization between the NSA and CIA," I said.

The governor eyed me. "You're saying my son, the son of a United States governor, is being targeted by the federal government? I just can't comprehend that. Why? What do they think Stanley's done?"

"It's true, sir," Mick said. "I was commissioned to take out Stanley. Direct orders from the chairman of the SCS, unequivocal. I couldn't believe it myself, and that's why he's still alive. Obviously I didn't follow through with my orders, sir. I was also directed to kill Agent Chase and burn down his home. He and I worked together in the past, and he's one of my best friends."

The governor shifted forward in his chair and massaged his temples. "Do you know for sure Stanley's alive right now? Because if what you're saying is true, which I still can't believe, maybe they sent someone else, another agent, and that person has killed my son."

"No, sir." Mick shook his head. "Tonight I was sent to kill Stanley at the waterfront. But the four of us slipped away undetected because we were unsure which parties we could trust. Then your son gave us the slip after we pulled over for a restroom break. He's more than likely still alive."

The governor stabbed his finger at Mick. "More than likely? More like, he'd better be." The governor took a deep breath and settled back into the red chair. "You said this is all for national security reasons. What does that even mean, especially as it relates to Stanley? How is my son a threat to national security? And who gave you the order anyway?"

Mick cleared his throat. "My job, sir, was to kill your son to protect the security of our nation. My orders didn't come with an explanation or rationale of what Stanley had been doing to justify that order. That's what we're trying to figure out now."

The governor pushed himself out of the chair and stood. He looked at Mick. "So you're basically a government hit man then, doing their bidding?"

"Essentially," Mick said. "This is the first time I've been directed to eliminate a domestic target."

The governor began pacing the room. "Stanley has done nothing wrong, certainly nothing to warrant his death." He stopped pacing and looked at us. "You guys agree with that, right?"

"Governor," I said, "we know this whole situation is completely illegal—"

"A major conspiracy," Mick added.

"Right," I said, "a conspiracy. The fact that I was targeted too definitely proves that. I've done nothing to compromise national security. I know that much."

The governor jabbed his finger toward me. "So you think Stanley did then?"

"I highly doubt it, sir, and that's why we're here. We want to know more about your son so we can figure out this conspiracy. We need to find Stanley and speak with him."

"Well, I don't know where he is. In fact, he hasn't checked in with me for a while."

I thought back to our recent car ride, when Stanley was texting. When Mick questioned him, he'd told us he was texting his father.

"Did he not text you about two hours ago, sir, and tell you he was safe?"

"No, he definitely did not. He never texts me. He calls."

I exchanged glances with Mick and Karla.

"What is it?" the governor snapped.

Nobody said a word.

"I'm taking it my son's been lying, then, is that it?"

"He told us he'd texted you to tell you he was safe," Karla said.

The governor pulled his phone out. "Maybe I missed it. Maybe he couldn't talk at that time."

There were a few moments of awkward silence as the governor rifled through the messages on his phone.

I broke the awkwardness. "Never mind the text, sir. Do you know where Stanley would go? He was having a hard time grasping the reality of his situation, with Agent Cranston commissioned to kill him and all, which is understandable. I'm guessing he panicked over it all so he gave us the slip at a gas station. We're not exactly sure why he left us. That's why we really have to find him soon. Is there any place you think he might be?"

The governor paced a few steps, then looked up. "Other than his house or the Long Beach State coffee shop, I can't think of any." He looked at Mick. "You never did tell me who specifically gave you your orders."

179

"I'm not exactly sure," Mick said. "My orders came via encrypted email from the chairman of the SCS."

"And the name of the chairman?"

"Actually, sir, field agents like myself don't know the names of the executive branch of the SCS. Because of the secrecy of our missions."

"Plausible deniability," the governor said.

"Basically," Mick replied.

"What can you tell me about this chairman?"

"The chairman is the head of the executive branch of the SCS, which is a rotating position; CIA for three years, then the NSA. Currently, the chairman is from the NSA. That's about all I know."

The governor walked back to the chair and wedged himself in.

I wondered if I should tell the governor my theory that Agent Gates was the chairman. After a quick thought, I decided to keep that to myself until I had more proof.

The governor looked at the three of us and said, "Why would Stanley's former employer want him killed? Stanley told me he left there on good terms. I don't get it."

I leaned forward on the couch because I thought I'd misheard. "What did you say, sir?"

The governor looked at the three of us. "By the looks on your guys' faces, you obviously didn't know some key facts."

"No, we didn't, sir," Mick said. "We sure didn't."

"My boy made history," the governor said, beaming. "Stanley was the youngest employee ever at the NSA."

CHAPTER TWENTY-THREE

I TUNED OUT my surroundings and collapsed into the couch. My mind replayed the conversation I'd had with Stanley at the coffee shop. I remembered questioning Stanley about what he did after deferring acceptance to MIT. He said it was classified. I'd laughed at his quick wit and didn't pursue the line of questioning. Obviously, I should have pursued it further.

Smoothing my hands over my head, I looked at the governor. "Stanley works at the NSA, sir, really?"

"Worked," the governor corrected. "And briefly, I might add. I'm not sure if he left of his own accord or not. He wouldn't, or perhaps I should say couldn't, let me in on the details. Never did tell me much about his time there."

Karla had collapsed backward at about the same time I did. She leaned forward and asked, "Sir, can you go back to the beginning and tell us how your son got involved with the NSA? We had no clue. We're all a little in shock here."

"Sure." The governor paused and thought for a moment. "It all started after Stanley graduated high school, which was at the age of fifteen, by the way. I'm not sure if you know this, but the NSA recruits high school grads, mainly the top mathematical students across the country. They invite these students to an intensive summer intelligence training program in Maryland." He looked at us. "Did you guys know that?"

"No, we didn't, sir," I said.

"Even though Stanley was young," the governor continued, "he was still the top mathematics student in the nation. So the NSA extended him an invitation. From what I understand they'd been following Stanley's academic path since he was about twelve. Crazy, I know. Anyway, after the summer training session, the NSA extends full-time offers to the top students in the summer class. Those students go on the payroll for the agency and subsequently enroll in the NSA's National Cryptologic School. Other students choose to go the more traditional college route first, which the NSA doesn't mind since they'll foot the college bill if the student agrees to work for the agency after graduation. Not surprising, Stanley was the top student in his summer program. But he was too young to go on their payroll. So he started taking courses in their Cryptologic School, without pay, though the courses and his expenses were covered. Stanley breezed through every course the school offered. When he turned sixteen, he officially became the youngest employee ever at the agency. I'm not too sure what happened from that point on, only that one day, over a year ago, he suddenly quit."

"Or was terminated, maybe?" Karla said.

The governor stroked his chin. "Perhaps. Stanley never told me why he left or what was going on at the agency. He said he was forbidden to talk about his particular situation, and the agency in general. Considering that it was the NSA, I didn't think it was strange. Besides, the whole time Stanley was there he didn't seem happy. So I wasn't bothered by him quitting or being fired, whatever the case was."

"Do you know why he wasn't happy?" Mick asked.

The governor looked away for a second. "No, but Stanley alluded to the fact that he'd probably go back. He said something about the timing not being right. That's all he mentioned."

"What about MIT?" I asked.

"MIT?" the governor said. "What about MIT?"

"Stanley told me he deferred acceptance. Did he go to MIT after the NSA?"

"No idea what you're talking about. He and I talked about MIT, but Stanley never deferred acceptance. As far as I know he never applied."

I felt Karla's eyes boring into the side of my head. The kid had lied about a lot.

"Listen," the governor said. "Stanley took the whole NSA thing seriously. I believe all NSA employees and ex-employees are forbidden to talk about the agency, so it doesn't surprise me that Stanley would make up a little white lie to detract from what he really did."

I wanted to ask the governor if Stanley was a habitual liar, but knew if I did I might meet one of his fists, so I refrained.

Mick didn't. He looked right at the governor and said, "Did Stanley make it a habit of telling white lies, sir, or of stretching the truth?"

Tuchek pounced. He struggled out of his chair and took two long steps in Mick's direction. While towering over his chair, he said, "Watch it, Agent Cranston. My son has had death threats made against him, has been shot by you, and now is who knows where. A couple of lies to you three is the least of my concerns, and should be the least of yours too." He pointed a stumpy, sausage-like finger about a foot from Mick's face.

Mick held up both hands. "I apologize, sir, you're right. I've been under a lot of pressure as well."

For a second I thought Mick might tell the governor about his daughters being taken, but he decided against it and stayed tight-lipped. Mick's silence seemed to calm the governor down.

Karla helped by changing the subject. "So what did Stanley do after his time with the NSA?"

The governor dropped his hand and turned to face Karla. "Loafed around the house, mainly. He spent far too much time on that damn computer of his. I pressured him for about a year to get a job. But then he started making money on his website because of that TV show. What was I to tell him at that point? He was making far more money doing that than at any job I could help him secure. Anyway, the death threats started, then I requested protection – and here we are."

Just then a cellphone in the governor's pocket started ringing.

"Maybe that's Stanley," he said. The governor pulled out a snapcell, looked at the screen, and shook his head. "Not Stanley, a different phone." He reached into another pocket, pulled out an iPhone, and looked at us. "Hornsby."

While the governor walked out of the sitting area and took the call, Karla leaned over and said, "This kid is something else."

"How many times has he lied?" I asked.

We sat in silence, trying to process what we'd just found out. After a minute or so, Mick walked over to the couch. "Stanley must be into something really bad. We have to find the kid."

"We'll find him," I said. "It's our number one priority. I'll waterboard the kid if he feigns ignorance again."

"I'll hold him down," Karla said.

The governor breezed back into the room. His eyes were glued on me as he walked past and struggled into his chair.

"Now I've started lying," he said. "Damn you three, you've put me in a bad position by being here."

Since he was looking right at me, I said, "Lied about what, sir?"

"To Hornsby. He and a team of agents are at your office right now. They're confiscating your hard drive, Agent Chase. Apparently they received some tip about incriminating evidence being stored on your computer. What've you been up to?"

"What kind of incriminating evidence?" I said.

"Hornsby wouldn't say. It was a courtesy call, that's all. He asked me to let him know if I see you or if you try to contact me. He said they have a BOLO and an APB out on you. Your whole office and the Long Beach PD are searching for you at this moment."

"I'm being set up." I looked from Karla to the governor, then to Mick. "Trust me. The most incriminating evidence I have on my computer is my lack of response to emails. I promise."

"Did Hornsby specifically ask if you'd seen Agent Chase, sir?" Karla asked.

"No."

"Did you tell him anything about us being here, or what we've just discussed?"

"No, I told him I'd let him know if I hear from or see Agent Chase. That's all."

"I'm not sure if this helps," Mick said, "but you really didn't lie, sir. Just withheld information. It's a nuance, I know, but not a direct lie."

The governor glared at Mick, then turned back to me. "The only reason I didn't tell Hornsby about you three is that I'm paranoid now as well. I'm not sure who to trust in the Bureau, or the Agency either. Plus, I know that you're risking everything to be here and that you want what I want: to find Stanley. So let's make that our mission."

"Agreed," I said. "Did Hornsby say anything else at all about the supposed evidence on my hard drive?"

"Not a word."

Karla stood. "Has anything else come to mind, about where Stanley could be?"

He thought for a few seconds, then shook his head. "If my son is going to make contact, it will come via this phone." The governor held up the snapcell phone. "I'll call you right away if he does. Now this may sound rude, but you three have to get out of here now. I don't want anyone knowing you were here."

"Two more quick things," I said. "If Stanley calls you, be sure to call me on his backup snapcell." I held up the phone Stanley had given me. "I'm sure you have the number."

The governor nodded.

Now that I felt the governor was 100% on our side, I thought it best to bring in my Gates theory. "Also, sir, we need you to pull some strings and find out as much as you can about a federal agent by the name of Anfernee Gates. It's a distinct possibility that he could be the chairman of the SCS. Rumor has it he also works for the CIA."

The governor looked at me. "The CIA? How could they be involved? They don't operate on American soil. They—"

I held up my hand. "I understand, governor. I'm hoping you can pull some strings and find out anything you can on the man."

The governor eyed me, then nodded. "What's the story with Gates, anyway?"

"He's involved in all this, perhaps the mastermind behind it. He was at your son's place after Agent Labonte was shot."

"I don't remember him."

"He's a darker-skinned gentleman," Karla said. "Puffy hair and tight grey pants."

"His face looks like he ran into the back end of a porcupine," I added.

The governor smirked. "Right, he was at the hospital, too. He was the one who told me you dove in the opposite direction when Stanley was shot, Agent Chase. I figured he was with the Bureau. Why exactly do you think he's involved?"

I answered the question as succinctly as I could. "He showed up at the waterfront when we were trying to lure Mick out. Gates could be the chairman and showed up at the wharf to ensure Mick completed his orders."

The governor scowled at me. "What do you mean, lure Mick out? What exactly happened at the waterfront?"

Damn. I'd shot my mouth off without thinking. At least I hadn't told the governor that we used his son as bait.

"It's a long story," Mick said. "Probably not the best time, governor, since we need to get out of here immediately."

He dropped the scowl. "You're right." The governor walked to the front door and opened it. We followed in single file. As we walked out the door, he said, "No more contact from you guys, understand? I'll do the contacting."

"Understood," Karla said.

"I'll call on Stanley's backup cell if I hear from him, or if I learn anything about Agent Gates."

Before anyone could respond or say goodbye, the governor of California shut the door in our faces. We brushed it off, loaded into the stolen car, and barreled down the driveway. While negotiating the curves, I tried Stanley on his cell again. By the fifteenth ring, I gave up and jammed the cell into the console.

Karla leaned forward and put her arms on the bucket seats. "So what do you guys think?"

Mick turned to his left. "I think the kid has been lying to us from the start. I think he's into some super-serious illegal activity. He'd have to be, right? To be targeted by the SCS like this. I just can't imagine what."

"What about the whole TV show thing?" Karla asked. "Do you think this is all about the show?"

"How so?" Mick said.

"Obviously Stanley had some incredible computer skills," Karla said. "Skills taught to him by the NSA. Maybe he was hacking into the network's server and finding scripts for the *Stranded* show. That's how he was able to predict the show's outcomes and gain all those followers, which in turned generated financial support by his website sponsors. And the NSA found out Stanley was doing this."

"Sure," Mick said. "That's illegal, a serious felony even, but not exactly a national security threat that would necessitate his death."

"You're right," Karla said. "What do you think, Chase?"

"I agree. The TV show thing, if true, doesn't constitute a national security threat. Maybe Stanley is into some other spying stuff that *does* constitute a threat. Like Karla said earlier, maybe the Facebook death threats and the kill order from the SCS are two totally separate things. Or maybe the Facebook death threats were a ruse to draw attention away from the real attempts on Stanley's life that were being planned. What I don't get is how I'm targeted in all this. I have no incriminating evidence stored at my house, or on my computer. It makes no sense that I was part of Mick's orders. Even if Stanley isn't who we think he is and he's selling secrets to the Russians or something, there's no reason to burn down my house. Stanley and I haven't been colluding on some evil plot. I was simply chosen as his protector. Yet I'm being framed with some sort of illegal evidence…"

I scratched my head and thought about Simon's hearing next week. I was screwed. Even if my name was miraculously cleared by then, the damage may not be reparable. Maybe I'd lose visitation rights forever. Could a judge do that? Suddenly I found my right fist gripping the car's center console. Karla put her hand on my shoulder, which stopped the tension in my body.

Looking back at her, I said, "If we find the kid, you should do the talking. I seriously may waterboard him."

CRAIG N. HOOPER

"So what's the plan?" she said. "Talk to me about that."

"We need to dump this car," Mick said. "As soon as we can."

I nodded. "Bars have been closed for a while now. The owner has probably called the cops already. And we stole this right by the water-front, so it won't take the cops long to put two and two together and issue an APB on the vehicle."

"We need to get off the road and find a base of operations," Mick said.

Karla looked at Mick. "A base of operations?"

"Yeah, some sort of headquarters," he said.

I knew where Mick was going with this. "A seedy place, naturally."

"Of course," Mick said. "Sketchy at best."

"A place where Visa and MasterCard are shunned," I said.

"And they've never even heard of American Express," Mick added. "Cash only."

"Alright, fellas, enough with the boys' club. What are you talking about?"

I looked at Karla in the rearview mirror. "We can't keep driving around, we're too exposed. We need to find a shady motel."

"Somewhere where prostitution and drug deals happen on a regular basis," Mick said.

"Got it," Karla said. "Some place where the check-in clerk is tight-lipped and hates cops, right?"

"I know the perfect place," I said.

After the video of me 'disciplining' the Marine went viral, the press showed up at my front door and camped out for two weeks. I'd holed up in a seedy motel in the heart of Compton. Nobody had bothered me there.

I drove to Compton in complete silence. Karla and Mick were deep in thought, as was I. About fifteen minutes into the drive, as we traveled south on the 710, we saw the amber alert. The sign stretched from one side of the freeway to the other. The vehicle color, description, and plate number were spot on. Nobody said a word about it. I casually exited off the freeway and took surface streets to the motel. It was creatively named: 'MOTEL'.

"Pull around back," Mick said. "Try to find a parking spot in the darkest area."

I found a good spot and shut off the car.

"You two check in, then meet me back here. I'll take care of the vehicle situation and the weapons." Mick rifled through his pockets and pulled out a small screwdriver. Karla looked confused, but I knew what he was doing.

"Come on," I said to Karla, "I'll fill you in later."

Sure enough, the check-in guy barely looked up. I peeled sixty bucks out of my wallet. The clerk grunted something and handed me a key. When we returned to the car, Mick was sitting on the back seat with the rifle case on his lap. Karla and I took the front seats.

Mick handed the .50 caliber over the seat.

I tucked it into the back of my pants.

"Alright," he said. "I gotta leave you two for a few hours. Need to check in on Julie and the girls. I'm sure they're fine, but I'm a little nervous if I'm being honest."

"You stash them far away?" I asked.

"Not too far. They're in Big Bear at a remote rental cabin my dad and I used to fish from. They have no cell coverage or internet there, so I have to check up on them in person."

"Of course," Karla said. "Chase and I should have this figured out by the time you get back." She smiled.

Mick did, too. "Okay, so I need to steal a different vehicle for the time being. While you were gone, I swapped some license plates around. This car now has clean plates, so it won't draw any attention, but don't take it anywhere. Just wait for me to get back. I'll dump my stolen car as soon as rental agencies open in the morning. Then we'll use that vehicle if we need to get around."

"You can't pay for a rental in cash," Karla said. "And they'll track your credit card."

"Not to worry, I have a couple of aliases that are untraceable. Trust me."

I looked at Mick in the rearview mirror. "Get outta here. Hug your girls for me. I'm sure they're doing fine. We're in room eight."

As soon as we stepped into the room, Karla scrunched up her nose. "Whoa," she said. "Definitely sketchy, not sure we needed the smell."

I plugged my nose. "Smells like a hundred dirty diapers are hidden somewhere." Just to be sure they weren't, I checked under the bed and in the closet. When I walked into the bathroom, the smell nearly knocked me over. "Here's the source." I closed my eyes and flushed the toilet.

Karla was right behind me and backed out quickly. "Close that door."

I wedged the door shut while Karla opened the windows. Just as I was about to sit on one of the double beds, the snapcell in my back pocket rang. I looked at the number, then over to Karla.

"It's Stanley," I said.

CHAPTER TWENTY-FOUR

I STABBED THE talk button. "Where the hell are you, Stanley? We need to talk right now."

A brief pause.

"Stanley," I snapped.

The kid sighed. "I know, Agent Chase, I'm sorry I ditched you guys. I'm so sorry. I'm so confused."

"You're confused?"

"We can't talk on the phone." He spoke in a hushed tone.

"You said these phones are safe, super-encrypted or STU-encrypted or something like that."

"I don't know what's safe anymore, Agent Chase."

"What's going on? What did your message on the mirror mean? Why don't you know what's real?"

"Not over the phone. Let's meet and talk. I'll send you a text with location."

"Last time you were tailed, Stanley. You need to be more cautious. Drive around in circles before getting to the location. Make sure nobody is following you."

"Will do, Agent Chase."

"Listen, right now I don't have a way to get there and—"

"You'll find a way. You're resourceful."

"Listen, Stanley—"

"I'm freaking out, Agent Chase. And this conversation is freaking me out even more."

"Calm down."

"I'm heading to our spot now. I'm sending the text. Delete it."

"Wait, Stanley."

"I'm out the door. I'll meet you around back of that place."

"Stop."

"See you there." Stanley hung up.

I snapped the cell shut and glared at Karla. "I can't believe this kid. He just took a play from our playbook."

She furrowed her brow. "What do you mean?"

"Remember at the waterfront when I told you to call Hornsby, and if he pressed you for a location or information, to get panicky, to tell him you're freaking out and then hang up?"

Karla nodded.

"That's what Stanley just did."

"He didn't say anything else?"

"Nope, he wouldn't. He wants to talk in person."

"I guess we have to go."

I shrugged. "I guess."

The text came through. I memorized the location, then deleted the text. After a mini debate about how to get there, we decided on the stolen Japanese car. The plates were clean and the car was common enough to blend in. Karla drove and I lay low in the back seat, since every law enforcement agent in the county was on the lookout for me.

The location was a mom and pop convenience store on the west side of Long Beach. Karla parked in the rear parking lot. I moved into the front passenger seat. Stanley wasn't there yet. The only things around were two large dumpsters, a bunch of broken-down cardboard boxes, and about ten red milk crates stacked against the convenience store rear wall.

Karla looked at me. "Still want me to do all the talking?"

I shook my head. "I think I've calmed down enough. The kid's safe, unless he starts lying again."

"He'd better not, or I'll be the one strangling him." Karla brought her hands up and mimicked a choking.

I nodded in agreement.

A minute later, a maroon Chevy Tahoe pulled into the lot. Stanley was in the driver's seat. He proceeded to back the vehicle into the spot to the right of ours. Since he was parked on my side, I rolled down the window. He didn't look at us. Instead, the kid's head snapped side to side while his eyes bounced around, clearly looking for something. I waved at him until he made eye contact, then I motioned for him to roll down the window and he did.

"Shut it down and hop into the back." I motioned to our back seat.

"No way." Stanley shook his head. "It's safer for us to be in separate vehicles, Agent Chase. I tried my best, but someone may have followed me. And if they did, we can peel out of here in different directions. I don't want to endanger you guys any more. You have a son and Agent Dickerson has a husband."

Karla leaned over. "Listen, Stanley, you have to cut the crap and tell us everything. We just met with your dad and he told us all about your NSA recruitment. Why did you never mention that?"

Stanley looked at Karla, then back to me. "I have to ask you one question before I say anything. You have to answer me truthfully. It's important."

I didn't respond right away. It was hard to let him dictate the terms of our conversation.

"Please, Agent Chase."

I looked at the kid and held up a finger. "One question, and it had better be quick."

Stanley unbuckled his belt and leaned my direction. "Did you apply for a position with the SCS? Tell me you did. Please tell me that."

I squinted at him. "That's your question?"

"I have to know. It's important."

"No, Stanley, I didn't. Before today, I didn't even know the SCS existed."

Stanley squinted back at me. "You're not just saying that, right? To keep it secretive or to throw me off?"

I sighed.

Karla intervened. "He said he didn't, Stanley, so leave it at that. Tell us what you're talking about."

Stanley sat back in the seat. It was the most deflated I'd seen the kid. He stared straight ahead and didn't say anything.

"Stanley," Karla prodded. "What's going on? We need answers."

He turned slowly and looked at me. "They told me this was all a field test, Agent Chase." He paused.

"A field test? What field test? Who's they?"

"I was told that this was *your* field test, that the last couple of days were all about testing you. I swear that's what I thought."

I shook my head. "You're not making sense."

Stanley adjusted his hair, looked around, then back at me. "Let me back up." He took a breath through his nose. "I was told you'd applied for an operative position within the SCS. I was told all candidates who applied for this job were put through an extremely stressful situation, a situation that wasn't real but appeared very real to the candidate. In other words, a real-life field test, Agent Chase. The whole point of these last couple of days was to test you, to see how you reacted to threats against me, to know if you could handle the line of work you'd applied for."

"Talk about crazy," I said. "This is crazy talk. Tell me the truth, Stanley. Now."

His eyes went big. "I am, Agent Chase, I promise. At first, I was excited to be a part of it all. But things got hectic right away, with me being shot, then Agent Labonte being shot. Every time I questioned what was happening my contact told me it was part of the field test; that it absolutely had to be as close to real as possible."

He looked away and banged on the steering wheel. "I'm an idiot. I know that now. Everything was so elaborate and over the top that I was having a hard time believing it. But I was told this was how it worked, that you'd applied for one of the most intense jobs on earth and the government would go to any length to test a candidate for readiness.

When I asked why on earth I was shot, for example, they told me it was to see how you reacted to the sniper. They told me the shot was deliberately aimed at my clavicle to minimize damage and ensure complete recovery. My contact told me that Agent Labonte's shooting was staged. The gunshot was a blank. Apparently Agent Labonte had fake blood and guts taped to his stomach under his shirt. When the blank went off, he pierced the bag and faked being shot."

I looked at Karla. She shrugged like she had no idea what was going on.

Stanley continued. "Any time I had a question or doubt, I was given an answer and reason for everything. And I was being tested in all this, too. That's important to know. I knew they were watching me to see how I reacted. They wanted to know if I could take a bullet, too."

Karla leaned in my direction. "What do you mean, you were being tested?"

Stanley ignored the question. "When Agent Cranston joined our gang and said he was sent to kill me, I started freaking out. It suddenly felt like a thousand degrees in that car. Remember how crazy I was acting then?" Stanley looked at me, then at Karla. "And remember how I asked Agent Cranston if he was really sent to kill me? I texted my contact, not my father as I'd told you guys, and asked about Agent Cranston and what was really going on. The reply was straightforward, that he's lying, that it's part of his cover."

I looked straight out the window, trying to process his story.

Stanley carried on. "That's when I bailed out of the car – because I didn't know what was real anymore. I went to the bathroom to calm down, but I couldn't. Agent Cranston seemed to be telling the truth, which freaked me out even more. Because that meant I'd been fooled, and for some reason was really being targeted by the SCS. Say something, Agent Chase. Please."

I couldn't.

"Trust me," Stanley said, pleading. "I wanted to tell you guys everything, but then I thought, what if Agent Cranston was an incredible actor, or just an incredible liar? If I told you guys everything, I would be blowing his cover and the entire operation. The only thing I could think to do was scrawl that message on the mirror and bail. I didn't know what was real anymore. That's why I had to ask you that question right away, Agent Chase. I absolutely had to know if you'd applied for an SCS position."

I finally looked at the kid. "Trust me, Stanley, I didn't apply for any job like that. And now I'm the one having a hard time with reality, at least your version of it. You do know the government doesn't test candidates like this, right? You understand that I hope?"

Stanley blinked at me and nodded. "I do now. I feel so foolish. So stinking foolish."

"Stanley," Karla said, "you need to go back to the beginning. Explain how you became a part of this, and what you meant by being tested."

I looked at Karla and nodded in agreement.

Stanley looked around again, his eyes darting left and right.

"Nobody's around," I said, sighing. "A car hasn't even driven by since you got here."

"Okay, good." Stanley wiped at his nose. "So I was recruited by the NSA out of high school. How much did my dad tell you anyway?"

Karla responded. "He said that you'd been recruited out of high school, then attended the summer training program. You did really well in training, but were too young to go on the payroll. So before they hired you, you took a bunch of courses in their Cryptologic School. After that you quit."

"Or were fired," I added.

"I wasn't fired," Stanley said. "What my dad didn't tell you, because he didn't know, is that the top student in the summer training program is promised a job in any division within the NSA. Which was a huge bonus, and we all competed heavily for that perk. I graduated top of the class and, sure enough, was promised I could start my career in any division. So I took my time and did some research before making the decision. I had a whole year of taking courses at their school before I could request where to start."

Stanley quickly looked around.

Before I could say anything, he said, "To make a long story short, the Agency was impressed with my computer and math skills from the very beginning, so I was concerned that I'd never see any field action or do any real spy work. And that's all I wanted to do. If I didn't choose wisely, I figured I'd be placed behind a computer for the rest of my life."

He banged on the steering wheel again. "And I definitely didn't want that to happen." He ran his fingers through his hair to calm down. "Anyway, in my research about the organization I learned of the NSA's role within the Special Collection Service, so I requested to be transferred there. But they denied my transfer, citing all kinds of lame excuses. Excuses like I was too young, that technically the SCS wasn't a division within the NSA, that I didn't have the physical skills." He paused.

"What did you do, kid?" I asked.

"I pushed back a few times, but was repeatedly denied the transfer. I won't lie, Agent Chase, I was pretty upset by it all. But then I had a thought. Why don't I prove to them that I have the necessary skills to be an SCS agent? So I broke into a secure portal and—"

"Wait," I interrupted. "How did you do that? This is the NSA after all."

"True, but they trained me really well. As I got to know more of their systems and protocols, I saw some holes, some ways to access their systems. I actually let them know a few things I'd discovered. That freaked them out and caused a number of internal changes within the NSA. I didn't tell them every potential problem I saw, which came in handy. It enabled me to access this secure portal and download some highly-classified information about the SCS, mainly just the names and roles of the agents involved. That's when I discovered who the chairman of the organization was."

"Wait, what?" I put my hand out to stop Stanley. "You know the chairman?"

"Sure," he said.

"It's Anfernee Gates, right?"

"No, it's not Gates. It's the woman you're seeing, Agent Chase: Eva O'Connor."

I lost all sense of time again, the third time in two days.

CHAPTER TWENTY-FIVE

I STARED STRAIGHT ahead without blinking. Eva O'Connor was the chairman of the SCS? The thought seemed completely outlandish, so crazy I couldn't process it.

While Karla shook my shoulder, Stanley rambled on in the background. I didn't hear a word he said. Thoughts consumed me, spiraling in different directions. Eva O'Connor commissioned my best friend to kill me and to kill the son of the California governor? Why? It made no sense, none at all.

I finally snapped out of my daze and looked at Stanley. "Whoa, kid, stop talking. I haven't been listening. Back up. And how did you know I was dating Eva O'Connor?"

Stanley paused for a second, then said, "Eva's my contact; the person I've been texting. She told me she was dating you. In fact, she told me they went to great lengths to screen candidates. And that she had no problem pretending to date a candidate because it gave her a true sense of the applicant. She said the best way to really know a candidate is to interview the person when he or she didn't know they were being interviewed. She also said she never led a candidate on or got physical."

"You bought that, Stanley?"

"She got physical, really? She said she didn't."

I sighed. "No, I mean, you bought that she was dating me to secretly interview me?"

He nodded. "Well, in the context of shooting people, the dating-as-interviewing technique was actually easier to believe. I just want to say to you two, now that I know what I know, I realize how naïve I was. And I'm sorry, I shouldn't have believed anything. I feel like a complete idiot."

"It's okay, Stanley," Karla said.

I looked at Karla, to see if she was being real.

"Finish your story," she said. "Go back to the beginning so we can work this out in our minds. You said you'd accessed a secure portal and gotten names of SCS members."

"Right. So after finding out Eva was the head of the SCS, I made an appointment with her and let her know I knew she was the chairman."

"How'd she respond?" Karla asked.

"She denied it at first, but then I showed her the document I'd downloaded. I thought she'd be impressed. Instead, it infuriated her and she told me to leave the office. I did, because she was really upset and needed to calm down. I figured after some time she'd come to truly appreciate what I'd done. Sure enough, about a week later, she contacted me and told me she'd changed her mind."

"Seems odd," I said. "Why'd she do that?"

Stanley looked away for a moment, then back at me. "She probably realized the skills it took to hack into an ultra-secure database. She didn't come right out and say that, but that's my guess. Anyway, she told me that I would have to wait until my eighteenth birthday to join the SCS. Primarily because the SCS requires military action, and I needed to be at least eighteen for that. Eva also said I'd have to leave the NSA first, then be officially hired by the SCS on my birthday. Basically, she didn't want to have to explain a transfer from the NSA to the SCS. She wanted to keep everything as low-key as possible. So that's why I left the Agency."

"When did you turn eighteen?" Karla asked.

"A few months ago. I put in my request on that exact day. But two months went by and I hadn't heard from Eva, or anyone else in the NSA or CIA or SCS. So I demanded to meet with her. When I finally got an appointment, I asked her what was going on with my request, and she refused my transfer again. This time she said it had to do with budgetary concerns and because the NSA was under a ton of scrutiny for some alleged privacy violations. I won't lie; I was upset, even more so this time." He paused.

"What did you do, Stanley?" I said, prodding him again.

"I had put my life on hold for a shot at the SCS, Agent Chase. And just like that I'd been denied again." Stanley held out his hand, then opened his mouth, but didn't say anything.

"Speak, Stanley," I said.

He sighed. "I'm not exactly proud of this, Agent Chase, but I felt it had to be done, to prove once and for all that I was more than capable of being an SCS agent. I broke into Eva's personal work computer."

Karla and I didn't react, so he continued. "All I wanted to do was grab a document off there and show her how good I was. While I was rooting around, though, I came across some alarming evidence." He stopped and looked around.

"We're fine, Stanley," I said. "No one is around. What kind of evidence are we talking about?"

"Evidence of foreign arms dealing," he whispered. "To three anti-American groups: ISIS, Hamas, and the Russian-backed separatists in Ukraine. There was a detailed email chain between three people. The emails provided these anti-American groups with intel about arms exchanges, about where and when our government was providing weapons to our allies. Of course, the email addresses were untraceable and used nobody's real name. But the evidence suggested Eva was behind it all. I didn't know what to do at that point, Agent Chase, so I sat on the information for a while. Then I started receiving death threats on my Facebook site."

"So that's what the death threats were about," Karla said.

"Yes," Stanley said, "and this is where things get even more interesting."

I ran my hands over my head. "How so?"

His eyes went big. "I was able to trace those threats back to the NSA. Not back to Eva's computer itself, but I figured she knew I'd hacked into her computer. And she knew that I knew she was responsible for sending me the death threats."

"So what did you do?"

"I met with her again. Told her I knew she'd sent me the death threats and that I had evidence of her providing intel to anti-American groups."

"Oh, kid," I said. "You blackmailed her?"

Stanley got out of his car and scurried over to my passenger side window. "Absolutely not, Agent Chase, no way. I just sort of presented the arms evidence to her."

"What does that mean?" Karla asked.

"It's okay, guys," Stanley said. "It turns out it wasn't that big of a deal. At least that was what I thought at the time. Eva laughed when I showed her the evidence. She explained that it was actually forged evidence, totally fabricated, a recent project she was working on."

Stanley leaned closer toward me. "Apparently the SCS has fake evidence they can plant to incriminate certain individuals, or blackmail them, but only if they absolutely have to. And the government rarely uses it. She said the primary use of the evidence is for training situations. She told me the head of the SCS is responsible for developing the fake evidence and for its safety and whereabouts. She told me all spy organizations need evidence like this as leverage."

I glanced at Karla, to see what she thought. She looked skeptical.

"Guys," Stanley pleaded. "This is what I was told. I've watched enough movies to know that this kind of stuff probably happens. That's why I believed it at the time. Anyway, Eva finally admitted that she was impressed by my skills. She said the death threats were completely harmless and were actually a test for me."

"A test?" I said.

"Yeah, Eva wanted to see if I could trace the threats back to the NSA, which I did, of course. She also said she was impressed that I'd confronted her with the knowledge. Then she said she had a plan to test me further, just to ensure that I was capable of being a real agent. She told me that you, Agent Chase, had applied for one of their top, covert operative positions. She wanted to use me in your vetting. That's what she called it."

"She wanted to use *you* in my vetting?"

"I promise you, Agent Chase, this is true, at least what I believed to be true at the time. Eva was planning on putting you through what she called Operation Crucible."

"Crucible?" Karla said. "Come on, Stanley. Really?"

"Yes, that's what she called it. It was intended to test Agent Chase's strength, determination, and resolve. That's exactly what Eva said."

"I understand the pretext, Stanley. What was your exact role in all this?"

"Please don't be mad, Agent Chase. I really believed at the time that this was all a field test and not real."

I motioned for him to go on.

"She wanted me to plant the arms evidence I'd found on her computer onto your computer, Agent Chase, to see if I could incriminate you, to see if I could pull off that kind of computer manipulation. That was my test. Since the Facebook threats got the attention of my father and he requested protection, Eva instructed me to request you as my protector. Then she told me that you'd be late for the first day of protection. I was to head to your agency, wait in your office, and plant the evidence."

I put my hands behind my head and leaned back. "Unbelievable, Stanley."

He continued. "Once my part in planting the evidence was over, I was supposed to watch and learn from you."

I didn't look at him. "I was supposed to be dead at that point, kid. And Mick was supposed to kill you at the coffee shop, right after you framed me. She just made up Operation Crucible, Stanley. I hope you see that. She totally used you."

"I'm an idiot. I'm so sorry, please believe me. At the time I had no idea I was being lied to. And, of course, you won't be incriminated for anything because I'll vouch for you, Agent Chase. I promise."

"Thanks, Stanley, that's kind of you."

Karla grabbed my shoulder. "This sounds so crazy, so preposterous, it may be true."

I took a moment to digest all the information. I could feel Stanley's bug eyes digging into the side of my head. While awaiting my response, the kid didn't fidget or look away. It was the stillest I'd seen him.

I looked at Karla because I wanted to see if she agreed with my theory. "If what Stanley's saying is true—"

"It is, Agent Chase," Stanley blurted.

"That means I'm in big trouble, and so is Stanley. Because we know the field test theory is complete garbage. Obviously I didn't apply for some covert operative position. And clearly the American government doesn't 'field test' potential agents by sending someone to date them, then try to kill them. So what's truly going on is that Eva O'Connor or the SCS or NSA or whoever is framing me as a traitor." I looked at Stanley. "And they want you dead, kid. That was Mick's directive, which he deliberately disobeyed." I looked back at Karla. "Am I missing something?"

"Sounds about right," she said. "The question is: why? What have you guys done? Or what has one of you done?"

I nodded. "Why is Eva going to these incredible lengths? I can't fathom a response right now."

"I'm sorry, guys," Stanley said. "It must be me. Hacking into a highly-secure NSA mainframe database wasn't the smartest idea. That's probably the cause, and now I'm on some hit list, a liability that Agent Cranston was supposed to deal with. I'm sorry I've endangered you two. You have a husband, Agent Dickerson." Stanley pointed at me. "And you're a father. I never meant for any of this to happen. You have to believe me, please."

I looked at Karla. For some reason her face was all red.

"We believe you," she said. "And I'm not married, Stanley. Let's just get that into the open so you can stop worrying about it." She took off her ring. "It's cubic zirconia. I wear it in the office so guys won't hit on me." She looked at me, shrugged, and mouthed the word *sorry*.

That made sense. It explained why she kept getting embarrassed when Stanley or I mentioned her husband.

"Stanley," Karla said. "What you just said explains why you were targeted, but not why Chase is mixed up in this. It doesn't explain at all why Chase is being framed."

I had a sudden thought. "The arms evidence is real," I said. "That's the explanation. It's not faked at all. Eva's probably a traitor and arms dealer, and she used Stanley to pin the evidence on me, obviously making up the whole story about the field test as cover. She wanted Stanley and me dead so we couldn't refute any of this."

Karla nodded. "She's been using you all along, rather than actually dating you."

"Why would she use Mick, though? I asked. "She must've known we were former partners and good friends."

"This is crazy," Stanley said. He scurried back to his Tahoe and fired up the vehicle.

"Turn it off," I said. "Stay put."

"I have to confront Eva," he said. "Find out what's going on."

I held out my finger. "I'll do that, Stanley, not you."

"No," he snapped. "I need to make this right, Agent Chase. I feel so stupid, unintentionally framing you as a traitor like that. No, I have to make it right. That's what I have to do. I can't endanger you guys anymore." He stuck the gear shift into drive. "You still have my laptop, Agent Chase?"

I'd totally forgotten about it. "It's in the trunk."

"Don't leave it there, please. Keep it somewhere safe. The original arms evidence is on there."

"You're not going anywhere," Karla said. "Chase and I will handle this. Shut off the car."

Stanley didn't comply, so Karla fired up the stolen car.

"Turn it off," I shouted to Stanley.

He fidgeted around on the front seat, looking for something. His vehicle was higher than ours, so I couldn't see his hands or what he was trying to reach for.

"I'm sorry, guys, really sorry," he said.

"You've apologized enough," Karla replied. "Stop it, just shut off the car."

"No, I mean sorry about this." He whipped out the Colt Delta Elite pistol, aimed it out the passenger window, and fired a shot into our front passenger tire. The tire exploded and the car listed to the right.

Then Stanley Tuchek jammed on the gas and squealed out of the parking lot.

CHAPTER TWENTY-SIX

I SMASHED THE dashboard with both hands. "I can't believe this kid."

Karla shut off the car. "Neither can I. We need to bail right now. That gunshot and tire pop were pretty loud. Somebody will come to investigate."

I cranked open the car door, then got out and back kicked the door shut.

Karla pointed across the street. "There's a small city park just over there. A couple of the park benches are in the dark. We should take a seat and lay low for a bit."

I led the way. "I doubt he'll pick up, but I'm going to call anyway."

I tried Stanley on his cell as I walked toward the park. It rang all the way to the park bench that we eventually sat on. His voicemail never picked up.

Snapping the phone shut, I turned to Karla. "I'm having a little trouble with Stanley's story."

"You think he made it up?"

"You think he's telling the truth?"

She paused. "Actually, I think he is. He seemed genuine in his apologies, and he is a kid after all. I know he's a mathematical genius, but that doesn't mean he has street smarts. You can be academically smart but lack common sense. Eva probably knew that about Stanley, that he'd be gullible enough to buy her field test story."

I nodded. "I agree, but Eva setting me up like this is hard to swallow." I held out my hand. "Before you say anything, I know she wasn't affectionate with me, but I can't believe she was trying to kill me, and also Stanley. That's a whole other thing that requires incredible acting and an evil motive. Plus, why would she use Mick for the deed? I know he's an SCS agent, and as the chairman she could deliver that kind of order. But she knew we were best friends and that it would be hard, if not impossible, for him to harm me in any way. She had to have known that."

"And what about Gates?" Karla said. "How is he involved in all this? Now that we know he isn't the chairman." She suddenly put her hand on my knee and shifted closer. She motioned with her eyes to my right. I slowly moved my eyes that way. A man was walking his dog on the sidewalk encircling the park, about fifty feet away. She put her arm around my shoulder, snuggled even closer, and whispered, "So we look like a couple and don't draw attention to ourselves."

I gave a quick smile. It was the closest, both in a physical and an emotional sense, that I'd been with a woman since my divorce. It felt good. Her touch momentarily took my mind off things. I whispered back: "And here I thought you were doing it because you're suddenly not married."

Karla blushed. "Listen, about that. I'm—"

I held up my hand. "I'm teasing. No need to explain, not at all. I know how the guys are in the office. If I was a woman, I would've done the same thing."

The dog walker passed by. Karla pulled her arm back. "Thanks for understanding."

My heart beat fast, which was an odd feeling for me, so I changed the subject. "Any thoughts on Gates?"

Karla looked away and thought for a moment. "He probably does work for the CIA or SCS. Maybe he caught wind of something and was investigating. Whether it was Eva or you, who knows? But if it was an internal thing, the CIA would look into it. They don't generally operate on American soil, but I'm sure they launch internal investigations on domestic soil."

"Right. Gates was probably investigating me. Maybe Eva tipped him off about me, told him I was a traitor, and they were gathering evidence against me, something like that. That's why he had such a bone to pick with me."

Karla looked back. "Maybe."

"I'm going to call Eva. Why not? It's midnight, but she's a night owl. I'll confront her with the allegations and see what her response is. Maybe I'll get to her before Stanley does. If so, she'll be caught totally off guard. She won't have any time to make up a cover story or lie."

Karla jostled her head side to side. "It could work."

I thought about it further and said, "Let's go back to the car and make the call from there. I'll put the call on speaker so you can hear her reaction and explanation."

Karla looked around. "I think we're clear. Nobody's investigating the noise."

I grabbed her hand and hauled her off the bench. As we walked toward the convenience store, we held hands for two steps, then we suddenly let go at the same time. It was awkward and natural at the same time. Neither of us said a word about it.

A minute later, I hopped into the driver's seat and Karla into the passenger one. Flipping open the phone, I turned to Karla and said, "It's worth a shot."

She gave me the fingers crossed sign as the phone rang. I pushed the speaker button and waited. On the sixth ring, Eva picked up.

"O'Connor."

"Eva, it's Chase."

"Chase? What number are you calling from? It said unlisted."

"Does it matter?"

"Do you have me on speaker? It sounds like it. Why would you have me on speaker? Is someone else there?"

I thought quickly. "No, I just got into my car." I cranked the ignition to keep up the ruse. The car purred to life. "I don't have Bluetooth or ear buds. The last thing I need is to get pulled over for talking on a cellphone."

She sighed. "Listen, I ducked out of an important meeting for this. An emergency meeting, in fact. That's why I'm at work so late. I have to get back, unless this is incredibly important."

"It's important, trust me."

I paused, suddenly realizing I should've thought more about how to transition into accusing her.

"Garrison, please, speak or I'm going to hang up and get back to my meeting."

I suddenly blurted, "Stanley told us everything."

A split-second pause, then she said, "Everything about what?"

I took a quick breath. "About your supposed 'field test'. About you being the chairman of the Special Collection Service. About the Facebook death threats. About framing me, and how you sent my best friend to kill me and burn down my house, then kill the kid. About—"

"Stop, Garrison. I have to go somewhere private if we're going to have this conversation right now. I'm putting the phone down."

I wondered if she was stalling for time, which would be a pretty wise tactic. She was on the move, however, and not standing still and thinking. The cell must have been by her thigh because I could hear the constant swishing of her skirt as she moved somewhere fast. She didn't walk far. After a few moments of skirt swishing, I heard a door shut.

"A 'field test'?" she said. "That's what Stanley came up with to explain everything? I can't tell if that was ingenious of him or a pathetic attempt at a story."

I didn't say anything.

"Your silence suggests that you're buying his story. Maybe it was ingenious of him after all."

"So Stanley's lying?" I said. "Is that it? You didn't convince him that I'd applied for an SCS position and you wanted him to help in my vetting?"

"Garrison, let me ask you, before Stanley told you whatever crazy story he made up, how many times had he lied to you?"

I didn't respond.

"How many?"

She waited, but I didn't say anything because I knew where she was going.

"By your lack of response, I'm assuming a lot. Now how many times have I lied to you?"

"Your point?"

"My point is, at least give me the benefit of the doubt, more so than Stanley Tuchek. I'm already on better ground than him. You should hear me out before making any sort of judgment. Trust me, you have no idea what Stanley Tuchek is capable of. You'd be surprised."

I looked at Karla. She motioned for me to carry on. "Point taken about the lies," I said. "Tell me everything then."

"Actually, I'm interested in how Stanley spun all this. You said he claimed this was a field test. How so? What else did he say?"

As a man who made his former living as a spy, I wasn't about to fall for her trick. Or at least what I thought was a trick. Eva probably wanted me to tell Stanley's story, which would give her time to think and respond appropriately to whatever I said.

Karla sensed it as well. She shook her head and mouthed the words 'don't do it'.

"Actually," I said, "I need to hear your version of what's going on."

Eva didn't respond right away. She didn't sigh or breathe heavily either, nothing but silence from her end. She was probably debating whether to continue the battle of wills over who should go first.

"Fine," she said with a huff. "Stanley was recruited by the NSA, at a pretty young age if I remember correctly."

"He was," I said.

"He did well in his summer training program, top of the class in fact, so he was promised he could start his career in the division of his choosing. To our surprise, he chose the SCS. We'd never had any student ask that before, and we certainly had no intention of following through with the request. So we denied him right away, to get that idea out of his mind, but he was pretty insistent about it. The little brat then accessed a highly secure and confidential database on our servers. He probably didn't tell you about that, right?"

"No," I said, "he did actually. Said he accessed a database and got some information about the SCS, mainly just the names of the agents involved. That's how he found out you were the chairman."

Eva laughed, a rarity for her.

"That wasn't all, Garrison, not by a long shot. He had all the names and positions of agents, management, an organizational chart, information about past missions and their outcomes. All kinds of classified information he shouldn't have had. It jarred us, to be frank. Sent us spinning, in fact."

I glanced at Karla. Her mouth was open and she was shaking her head.

"You have to understand," Eva continued, "we weren't dealing with a run-of-the-mill employee, or a civilian for that matter. This was the governor's son, so we had to tread lightly. Any other person and we would've dealt with it pretty severely."

"Arrested them?"

"Probably not. We wouldn't have wanted to draw attention to an internal breach of security like that."

"What would you have done?"

"It doesn't matter. What we did do is buy some time with Stanley."

"You promised him a position with the SCS, right, but not until his eighteenth birthday?"

"Exactly."

"But you had no intention of letting him work for the SCS."

"True."

"So why lie and string him along like that?"

She paused for a second, then cleared her throat. "We wanted to track his every move, see what he did, what he was capable of outside of the Agency. If he continued hacking secure computers and breaking the law, we could deal with it more effectively as an external threat. And, as you said, maybe arrest him if need be. Then we wouldn't have to deal with him wanting to join the SCS. We could make it go away quietly, without involving the authorities or the governor."

"Okay, makes sense. So the kid turned eighteen and then what happened?"

"I knew he'd contact me on his birthday. But after a year of monitoring him we didn't have much evidence against him. Stanley had been a pretty good boy until his eighteenth birthday."

I furrowed my brow at Karla. "What changed?"

"Just after his birthday I discovered he was hacking a TV network's server. He was downloading information from that Gilligan's Island parody. He had access to all the writers' and producers' emails as well as the scripts for the show. Bet he didn't say anything about that to you. Am I right?"

I didn't respond, just stared at Karla. She gritted her teeth and made a fist, as mad as me at Stanley. He'd conveniently left out that piece of information.

"I take it from your silence, Garrison, that he didn't mention the domestic spying. Anyway, a couple of months went by and we had a solid case against him. Not only was he hacking into the network's database, but he was also profiting heavily from it. Millions were involved. When he met with me and demanded to join the SCS, I confronted him with the evidence and told him we'd drop any domestic spying charges if he stopped the SCS demands and went away quietly. We promised him that his father and the authorities would never know a thing, but he had to stop his demands and walk away from the NSA for good."

"Did he take the deal?"

She sighed. "I thought so. When I confronted him with the domestic spying evidence, I thought he was embarrassed. He went completely red and couldn't speak. As I look back on it, considering what he ended up doing, I now know he was furious with me, not embarrassed by it at all. I totally misread his emotions. That was my mistake."

"What did he end up doing?"

"Another thing he obviously didn't tell you. He broke in to my personal work computer and planted evidence on it, in an attempt to frame me."

I ran my hand over my sweaty head. "Let me guess, the evidence he planted had to do with arms dealing."

"How'd you know?"

"He told me about that."

"He admitted to that?"

"No, not at all. According to him he found the evidence on your hard drive. Didn't say anything about planting it, obviously."

Eva scoffed. "Right, I'm an arms dealer. I have ties to Hamas, ISIS, and Russian-backed separatists. Please. How does this fit in with Stanley's field test story? I don't get it. What exactly did he tell you?"

"The kid said that after he'd found the arms evidence on your computer, he confronted you with it. He also confronted you about the Facebook death threats. Did you really threaten his life?"

A brief pause. "That I wasn't too proud of. Yes, I did threaten his life. Technically it was cyber bullying and, of course, I wasn't going to follow through with it. When I found out that the kid had broken into my computer and planted evidence on it, I got livid. In an emotional fit, I sent those threats. It was a mistake, a total unprofessional move on my behalf, but I needed him to back off and I wasn't thinking straight at the time. But back to Stanley's story. In his twisted version, how did I respond to the arms evidence?"

"You responded by saying it was fabricated evidence that the SCS kept in case they needed to frame someone. Stanley said you told him you were in the middle of vetting me for a top SCS position under the code name 'Operation Crucible', and you wanted the kid's help with my vetting. You asked him to plant the faked evidence on my computer, to see if he has the skills to manipulate evidence like that. That was his test and, if he passed, you promised him a position with the SCS."

"I take it back," Eva said. "That was pretty ingenious of him. But still a complete lie."

"What happened then? Did Stanley blackmail you with the planted evidence? How did he get that arms evidence anyway?"

"I don't know how he got it, seriously, but he indeed blackmailed me with it. He said he wouldn't tell anyone about it—can you believe that?—as long as I made him an SCS agent. To make a long story short, Stanley Tuchek was ushered out of the building and told never to step foot in the Agency again. He was told if he pursued anything further, he'd be arrested on the spot."

"Were you worried about the evidence he'd planted?"

"Not really. I have an entire agency at my disposal, and was pretty sure one of those computer experts could prove that Stanley hacked into my computer and planted the evidence. I wasn't entirely sure, to be honest, so that's why I had him ushered out and not arrested. I honestly thought I'd never hear from him again."

"But you did."

"But not directly."

"What do you mean?"

"Stanley was furious with me, and out for revenge. That's the only theory I can think of for why he wouldn't let this go. Now that you've told me his story about the field test, everything makes sense."

"So Stanley's behind all this. Stanley Tuchek?"

"I told you you'd be surprised."

"You really think he's behind this?"

"He is. Garrison, Stanley had access to my personal computer, so he could send an email in my name. Plus, he had previously accessed the secure SCS database. And part of the highly secretive and confidential information he downloaded was our directives and kill codes. So he had the ability, and the proper information, to send the kill directive against himself and to set these events in motion. Stanley's revenge was to say I was as a traitor, and that I'd used one of my own agents to try and kill him because he'd found out that I was dealing arms. He even had evidence that I sent those death threats to back up his story."

I looked at Karla. She was looking my way, but staring right through me. I could tell her mind was spinning.

"Okay," I said. "So Stanley is furious with you for repeatedly denying his request to join the SCS. For the sake of argument, as you said, let's say his motive is revenge, to make you pay or whatever. If this is all true, and Stanley is behind everything, why did he pick me for protection and then issue my kill order?"

There was silence on Eva's end for about fifteen seconds, then she said, "Three reasons, I think. First, to keep his story realistic, he would want protection. To add more credibility to his story, he'd also want the protector to be targeted as well. Second, and this is undeniable, Cranston was under my command and Stanley had the list of all agents under my command. That's a fact, part of the information he stole off my computer. Third, and this is my theory, but the most important part, Stanley probably researched my agents. He likely discovered that you and Cranston had worked together and were friends. I bet he chose you because he knew Cranston wouldn't believe you were part of a national security threat, so Stanley knew Cranston wouldn't kill you or actually burn down your house."

"But Mick's directive included killing Stanley. You're basically saying that Stanley sent Mick a kill order that included killing himself."

"I think so. I know it's hard to believe, but after all, Stanley was right, right? Cranston couldn't kill either one of you. Stanley knew Cranston wouldn't act irrationally. Stanley's much smarter than you're giving him credit for, Garrison. Maybe he took a risk, but it was a calculated risk in his mind. And it worked out for him. Remember, Stanley's story frames me as the traitor who needed to cover up everything and tie up the loose ends. And Stanley was the loose end who needed to be disposed of. So, of course, he had to be part of the kill order."

Karla mouthed something to me, but I didn't understand. I think it had something to do with Mick.

"Garrison, if you don't believe me, you need to talk with Stanley. You know he's lied to you many times already. Ask him about the SCS evidence he downloaded and exactly what information he had access to. Ask him about spying on the TV network and how he made his millions through domestic spying."

"Trust me, I will. You think Stanley set this in motion for revenge? That's your take?"

"Partly. But I believe he was also scared of doing jail time for spying on the network, and I had evidence that proved his guilt. So he wanted to frame me for revenge, but also as insurance against being incarcerated. That's his major motive."

I thought about it. "What about this? Maybe in his twisted mind this is all about proving to you that he has the ability to be an agent. From the beginning he's been trying to convince you that he has the requisite abilities to be an SCS agent. Twice before he's tried to demonstrate his abilities to you."

"Sure, but it's gone way too far now for me to believe that's his main motive."

"Maybe the kid can't stop what he got rolling."

I heard a faint tap on Eva's end of the phone.

"Hold on," she said. "Someone's at the window to this office." She muffled the cellphone.

A few seconds later, she was back. "I've gotta go, Garrison."

"No way, Eva, we have more to talk about."

"I know, but I have to go. I've already been gone too long. They just sent someone to locate me. Everyone's waiting on me. Let's meet later."

"Absolutely."

"Listen, Stanley's called me twice in the last hour so I'll make sure he comes to the meeting. I may have to lie to get him there. We'll clear up everything at the meeting, then arrest Stanley. I think we need to meet somewhere private."

"Private? Why private?"

"We're dealing with the governor's son, Garrison, who is himself a public figure and recognized by many people. And, from what I under-stand, you're a wanted man right now and can't be in public. We need to be secretive. I know a place in Long Beach. It's an old federal dead drop place that hasn't been used for years."

She had a point. "You're not going to ask me to come alone, I hope."

"Bring whoever you want. In fact, be sure to bring Agents Cranston and Dickerson. I insist."

I glanced at Karla. "You bet I will."

"Good. The dead drop is at Pier 42, right by the Long Beach docks. There's an old abandoned warehouse near the end of the pier. It's big and private and you can't miss it. How about 3:00 a.m.?"

"We'll be there."

Eva hung up without saying goodbye.

I dropped the phone and looked at Karla. "I don't know what to believe anymore."

She nodded. "I'm going to kill that kid."

CHAPTER TWENTY-SEVEN

I SHOOK MY head at Karla. "Not before I do. If Eva's telling the truth, we'll have to fight over who gets to the kid first. I'm thinking about strangling him; it's more personal. You?"

"Holding him under water until he drowns. But back to reality, this is a lot to take in, right?"

"It is," I said. "By the way, you were trying to ask me something a moment ago."

"I wanted you to ask about Mick's family being threatened."

I thought for a second, then sighed. "Of course, I should've questioned her about that. I should've asked about Gates, too."

Karla nodded. "Eva's explanation of everything, or close to everything, makes sense. And she didn't hesitate to explain anything or stumble over any facts."

"It does appear the kid's guilty. She made a convincing case."

"But Mick's family being threatened doesn't make sense. It makes me question her entire story."

I nodded. "I agree. If Stanley chose Mick because he believed Mick wouldn't follow through with the orders, how does the coercion of Mick's family make sense? That doesn't follow, not at all."

Karla looked at me. "Exactly."

"My other problem is whether Stanley Tuchek could pull this off. Is he really capable of all this? I understand he has amazing computer skills and could break into an NSA mainframe and Eva's computer and download stuff from the TV network. I don't have a problem believing that. My problem is with him drugging and threatening Mick's family, which led to Labonte being shot. Not to mention sending his own kill order. Really? I suppose he has the money to hire people to do anything, but is the kid that vindictive that he would go to these lengths? I realize I've only known him a day or two, but this is a maniacal plot I'm having a hard time believing he's responsible for. Plus, where would Stanley get arms evidence to frame Eva with? What did you think?"

Karla leaned back. "The main problem I have with Stanley is the lying. He's lied a lot to us. I don't trust his version of events either."

"You think Stanley just lied to us about everything?"

She thought for a moment. "Possibly. Think about it. The kid lied to you about MIT; he's been lying to us all along about the network and the death threats; he never told us a thing about his involvement with the NSA; he even lied about texting his dad in the car, a few times. The list goes on."

"You're right. I really have no idea who Stanley is."

"So what's going on? Whose story do you believe? Stanley or Eva?"

"Honestly, I don't know. I do know I have to speak with Stanley again. Ask him about spying on the network and blackmailing Eva. How about—"

Headlights suddenly flashed in the rearview mirror. The beams lit up the inside of our car. Karla glanced quickly at me. Her eyes popped. We both slinked down in our seats, hoping the lights would disperse.

They didn't.

We kept still. The muffler of the idling car behind us burbled away.

"It's probably a cop car," Karla whispered. "Could be running our plates, which don't match this vehicle."

"Could be," I whispered. "Could be anybody." As discreetly as I could, I put my hand behind my back, slipped out the Smith & Wesson, and placed it on my lap.

"That's not going to help if it's a cop."

I eyed her. "But it will if it's not."

We waited in silence. After a minute, I said, "You're right, it must be a cop."

Karla nodded. "Probably having a hard time reconciling the plate and vehicle description." She reached across, took the .50 caliber from my lap, and eased it under her seat. Just as she finished, the car's high beams flashed quickly, then red and blue lights flipped on and started circulating. The car filled with a dizzying array of colored lights.

"We're finished," I said.

"Let me do the talking," Karla said. "Maybe I can talk my way out of this."

The cop car's speaker crackled on. "Driver, put your hands on the steering wheel. Passenger, put your hands on the dashboard. We're approaching the vehicle. No sudden movements."

I wasn't positive, but it sounded like Officer Palmer. I slowly sat up and put my hands on the wheel. "I think I know these guys."

Karla put her hands on the dash. "Is that a good thing or bad thing?"

"I'm not sure."

Now that I was sitting up I could see everything in the rearview mirror. I was right. Officer Kowalski struggled out of the passenger seat. Palmer was already out of the vehicle. Both cops had their weapons out, but not drawn. The guns were pointed straight down at their sides, not threatening, but ready for quick action. Palmer approached my side of the car, while Kowalski took Karla's. They moved cautiously. I waited for instructions.

Palmer stopped four feet from the driver's door. He raised his pistol. "Slowly, with your left hand, driver, open the door and get out."

Kowalski gave similar instructions to Karla.

I turned, just slightly, so Palmer could see my face.

He reacted, lowering his gun a bit and taking a step forward. "Agent Chase? What are you doing in this car? Shots have been reported in the area and—"

"Officer Palmer, we're not armed," I said. "Take a peek inside if you don't believe me. I'll get out slowly and explain everything. Not sure that there's a need for your drawn weapon."

"I'll determine that," he said.

Palmer shuffled closer. He checked out the back seat, then peeked in the front. He ordered Kowalski to do the same. When Kowalski was finished, he stepped back and holstered his weapon, then he actually opened the door for Karla.

"I take it you're Special Agent Dickerson?" Kowalski said.

"I am. Appreciate the courtesy, Officer." Karla stepped out and Kowalski brought her around to my side of the vehicle.

Palmer wasn't as courteous. He lowered his gun, but didn't holster it. He commanded me to get out slowly. I did. Karla was to my right and Kowalski stayed by the front hood.

"What the hell is going on?" Palmer asked. "There's an APB on you, Chase, and I think this car has been reported stolen. The plates don't match, so I assume you switched them. Plus, two gunshots were heard. We got a tip they came from this general location. What are you up to?"

"I can explain," Karla said.

"I asked Agent Chase," Palmer said, without looking at Karla.

"It was one shot, actually," I said. "The other bang was our tire popping, on the passenger side. Check it out."

Palmer motioned at Kowalski. Kowalski waddled around and checked. "Looks to be the case," he said.

I told a modified, quick version of the events. "Someone's been trying to kill me and the governor's son. To make a long story short, we think it may be an inside job, so the two of us have gone off the radar because we don't know who to trust."

"A crooked cop?" Palmer said. "Is that what you're saying?"

"No, likely someone in government intelligence is dirty, not the cops. We didn't want to communicate with our superiors until we've figured out who's behind the conspiracy. We knew our own vehicles could be tracked easily so we stole this one and switched the plates."

"What's the APB about?" Palmer said.

"I'm not sure," I said. "I imagine because the dirty intelligence officer is trying to find us and stop us."

"What about the shots?" Kowalski said.

"It was Stanley—"

"Stanley Tuchek has a gun?" Palmer said, interrupting. "And he shot out your tire? The governor's son?"

I didn't want to tell the cops our theory that perhaps Stanley was behind everything, so I said, "Let me explain, Stanley gave us the slip because he didn't want to endanger our lives any more than he already had. We obviously didn't agree with him on that point, so we've been trying to track him down and we finally did. We met him here to discuss what to do next. After we talked a while, Stanley, in all his juvenile wisdom, shot out our tire so we couldn't follow him. He gave us the slip again because he thinks he can figure this out on his own. He doesn't want our help because he thinks we'll be in danger. Which is crazy, I know."

"Where'd he get a gun?" Palmer asked.

I didn't want to admit it was Karla's gun, so I shrugged.

Palmer eyed Kowalski to see if he had any thoughts. Kowalski didn't.

"I don't know," Palmer said, sighing. "I'm not sure what to believe."

"Makes sense to me," Kowalski offered.

Karla jumped in. "Why don't you call the governor himself? Besides us, he's the one person who knows about the inside job. We just visited him. He can vouch for our story."

"I'll call him right now," I said, fishing out the cell from my pocket.

Palmer didn't respond. He did ease his stance, though, and holster his weapon. I hoped he didn't take me up on the offer.

After a moment of eyeing us, Officer Palmer walked over to Kowalski. They whispered back and forth for a minute. Finally, Palmer turned toward us. "You two want us to let you go. Is that what you're going to propose next?"

I stepped forward. "It'd be a courtesy I wouldn't forget."

Palmer rubbed his head. "So we pretend this whole interaction never even happened, I guess?"

"You never even saw us," Karla said.

"It's fine by me," Kowalski said.

"That's a surprise," Palmer shot back. He looked at us. "So our stories are straight. We never saw you. We investigated the shots and found this abandoned car. And you never saw us either. Got it?"

We both nodded.

"You guys have to get out of here now, on foot," Palmer said, pointing at us. "If this comes back to bite me—"

"It won't," Karla interjected.

Palmer nodded and walked toward the cruiser. Kowalski waddled behind him. Before reaching the cruiser, the radio on Kowalski's hip squawked. "All duty officers, we have an update on the APB for Garrison Chase. Consider the suspect armed and dangerous."

Palmer turned in our direction.

The radio continued. "A warrant has been issued for his arrest. Apprehend the suspect on sight."

Kowalski turned to face me.

I held out my hands.

Kowalski unclipped the radio from his belt and pushed the side button. "This is Officer Kowalski. What's the warrant for Agent Chase concerning?"

"We're pulling a body from his '86 Chevy Caprice as we speak. It's in the trunk, two bullets to the head. It's Agent Anfernee Gates. Witnesses spotted a tall, bald man by the trunk earlier."

Kowalski cleared his throat. "So the warrant is for murder?"

"Affirmative."

Palmer came toward me with his hand on his weapon. Kowalski just looked at me with disappointment in his eyes. I stood with my mouth open, unable to respond.

"It's a mistake," Karla blurted. "The same person on the inside is trying to frame Chase. We're trying to figure out who, guys."

"Please," I said. "I had absolutely nothing to do with this. I have to figure out who's after me."

"You can explain that to someone else," Palmer said.

"I'm his alibi," Karla said. "I've been with Chase all night. We were at the governor's house before this. Call him, please."

Palmer scoffed. "You could obviously be in cahoots with Chase, couldn't you, Agent Dickerson?"

"You're making a big mistake," Karla said.

"Maybe so," Palmer responded. "But we can't walk away now. I'm not turning my back on a warrant for murder. If you guys are innocent, then everything will work out. That's how I see it, and that's how it's going to play out."

I could tell that Palmer had his mind made up and wouldn't crack, so I turned to Kowalski. "Give me the benefit of the doubt. You know I couldn't kill a federal agent like Gates, right?"

Kowalski shrugged. "Honestly, I don't know what to believe, Agent Chase."

"Kowalski," Palmer snapped. "We're taking them both in. No more talking. Take Agent Dickerson."

Palmer pulled out his cuffs. "Let's not make this difficult, Chase."

I held my hands out in defeat. While Palmer loosened the cuffs, I glanced at Karla.

"Officer Kowalski," she said. "Let me grab my badge from under the car seat. I can't leave it in this vehicle obviously."

Kowalski hesitated, but then shrugged and said, "Sure."

I tried to make eye contact with Karla to stop her. I knew what she was going to do and I didn't want her in more trouble than she already was, but Karla didn't look my way. She went straight for the seat.

Kowalski didn't stand a chance. After grabbing the gun from under the seat, Karla stood and suddenly spun around Kowalski's body. She kept the gun hidden from sight during the spin. The move reminded me of a running back spinning around a tackler. Before Kowalski knew what was happening, Karla was behind him with the gun pressed into the middle of his back.

"I'm sorry, Officer Kowalski," she said. "You guys gave us no choice."

Palmer looked at Karla. In doing so, he failed to finish cuffing my right wrist, so I raised my left hand and whapped him in the face with the dangling cuff. As soon as his hands went up to grab his face, I relieved the officer of his weapon and pointed it at his chest.

"Karla's right," I said. "You've left us with no choice. I'm sorry, Officers."

Palmer rubbed his eye and blinked a few times. His face was redder than Kowalski's.

"I'm sorry, Palmer," I said. "I really am."

Palmer glared at me. "You're already wanted for murder. Now you want to do this? Are you sure?"

"Add it to the list," I said. "I have to clear my name on worse charges than assaulting an officer. I wish it hadn't come down to this. I'm being set up. I hope you guys believe me."

I grabbed the key from Palmer, undid the cuff on my left hand, then cuffed Palmer's hands behind his back. Karla relieved Kowalski of the radio and his service piece, then cuffed him as well.

"I can't believe you guys are doing this," Kowalski said. "Agent Chase, I brought you your guns back."

"You're a good officer, Kowalski. I promise, when everything comes to light and I clear my name, you'll understand why we had to do this."

I looked at Karla. "What's next in your plan?"

She motioned toward the cruiser.

"All of us?" I said.

"I was thinking just you and me."

I looked at Kowalski. Feeling bad for him, I said, "We can't leave them here. It'll be embarrassing for them. We have to extend a little professional courtesy. We'll take them with us. I've got an idea."

Karla eyed me. "So we steal a cop car—"

"Borrow," I corrected.

"So we borrow a cop car and put the cops we've handcuffed in the back seat? And a man wanted for murder drives them around. Tell me that's not your idea."

"My idea is to help the officers save face. Let's go. We'll chat about it when we're on the move."

I prodded Palmer toward the cruiser. Karla sighed, but did the same with Kowalski.

As I pushed Palmer's head down and positioned him in the back seat, he said, "This is your idea of professional courtesy?"

"Do you want me to leave you here?" I said. "Is that a better option?"

Neither Palmer nor Kowalski responded to the question.

I hurried to the stolen car and retrieved Stanley's laptop from the trunk. I climbed back into the driver's seat and fired up the cruiser.

Turning to Karla, I said, "We'd better figure out this conspiracy. If not, we're screwed."

She nodded. "Otherwise, no doubt we're going to jail for this."

CHAPTER TWENTY-EIGHT

I BACKED OUT of the parking lot in the cop cruiser. Kowalski stared at me in disbelief through the rearview mirror. Palmer looked like he wanted to get personal and drown me, or strangle me, not sure which way he was leaning.

I grabbed the mirror and pushed it straight down so I couldn't see anything behind me, then I headed to Compton.

"This is bad," Karla said.

I laughed. "It was your idea to stick a gun in Kowalski's back. What did you think would happen?"

"No, I mean your situation is bad. The arms evidence on your computer frames you as a traitor. Now you're being framed for the murder of a federal agent."

I glanced at her. "Bad is a severe understatement."

"So who killed Gates? What do you think?"

"Not sure. Who are our suspects?"

Karla leaned back into her seat. "Obviously not Mick or us. That leaves Eva or Stanley."

"Maybe Stanley is more sinister than we think. Maybe he actually did hire someone to threaten Mick's family. Maybe the kid is super vindictive and wanted to pin that on Eva, too."

Karla nodded. "Maybe, but I doubt it. Even more so now that Gates is dead. Why would Stanley want to frame you for that?"

"I have no clue. Even though he's dead, we have to find out about Gates. Exactly how and why he was involved in this. He's key."

"Maybe the governor will come through for us."

"You think he'll call me if he finds out something?" I looked at her. "Now that I'm wanted for Gates's murder?"

"Maybe, maybe not. He does know about the conspiracy and that you're being framed. Maybe he'll see these new allegations as another attempt at framing you."

I shrugged. "Maybe."

The snapcell in my front pocket buzzed. I dug it out and looked at the screen. "Got a text." Since I was driving, I gave it to Karla.

She read it. "Pier 42 tonight. 03:00 a.m. Be sure to bring my laptop. Everything will be cleared up then. Stanley."

"That's it?"

She nodded.

"Text back and say we need to meet before then. It's urgent."

Karla tapped out the message and pressed send.

While I drove to Compton, we waited in silence for a return text. Every few seconds Karla glanced at the phone, but ten minutes passed and there was no response. At the outskirts of Compton, I pulled off the road and into the parking lot of an abandoned Foster's Freeze restaurant. We were about three blocks from our motel.

Karla tapped out another message and pressed send.

Another five minutes passed without a response. While staring at the phone, willing it to ring or buzz, I had a thought. "Text messages, Karla. We should have asked to see Stanley's phone, to see if he was lying. Why didn't we think to ask him?"

She furrowed her brow. "What are you talking about?"

"Stanley said he had been texting Eva, asking her questions about Mick and what was real. Remember? Cells keep records of texts, don't they?"

"Absolutely." Her eyes lit up. "You're right, we should've thought about that. We could've looked at Stanley's cell to see if he actually sent those texts to Eva, and what Eva said in return."

"If Stanley's telling the truth, he'll have a log of all those texts. We have to meet him right away."

"I don't think he's going to respond."

"Neither do I, but we have to find him. We have to at least try."

"First," Karla thumbed over her shoulder, "we have to do something with Kowalski and Palmer. What was your idea?"

"Let's talk outside."

We got out and met at the front of the cruiser.

"Let's split up," I said, "and meet back at the motel. It's about three blocks east of here. You head west, then double back, keeping out of sight. I'll head south for a couple of blocks, then work back toward the motel. That way our backseat friends will have no idea which direction we actually headed."

"Are we just going to leave them in the cruiser cuffed?"

"I think we should put the handcuff key in one of the foot wells. They'll have to work together to pick it up. I'm sure they can figure out how to release each other's cuffs."

"It'll buy us time to get out of sight. I like it. Good plan."

I nodded. "It'll buy us at least ten minutes or more. Plus, I'll leave the car keys so they have wheels and aren't stranded in the middle of Compton. And I'll leave their pieces, too, in the front."

"Maybe they won't pursue charges because it will be embarrassing for them to admit we got one up on them."

"That was the idea."

We stood and looked at each other for a moment, then Karla nodded.

I broke the silence. "Let's go, you first. I'll meet you back at the motel."

Karla handed me Kowalski's gun. "I'll stop at a convenience store and grab some snacks. I'm starving." She headed west without saying another word.

I walked back to the cruiser. I grabbed Stanley's laptop and left the service pieces in the glove box, then I opened Kowalski's door and dropped the handcuff key at his feet. I apologized and took off before he or Palmer could plead their case.

I arrived at the motel nine minutes later. Opening the door to room eight, I expected to see an empty room.

It wasn't empty, however.

A huge, bald man sat on the corner of one of the beds with a slight grin. His right elbow rested comfortably on his knee while his right hand gripped a silenced pistol, which appeared to be a Glock. The gun pointed at my chest.

"And where is your partner in crime?" he asked.

He spoke with a heavy Italian accent, but it wasn't Brooklyn-Italian. It sounded like he was straight off a plane from Italy. He reminded me of a wise guy, maybe a Mafia hit man.

"You mean the lady?"

"Yes, the lady."

As I debated how to respond, I gave him the once over. He was deeply tanned with a head as shiny and bald as mine. What jumped out at me were his eyebrows. They were a deep black color and looked to be an inch and a half thick. He reminded me of a bald Antonio Banderas, but with Martin Scorsese's eyebrows.

"I ditched her," I said. "I didn't want her involved in this any deeper than she already was."

"Such a gentleman." He motioned at the laptop in my hand. "I see you have what I've been looking for."

Just then I noticed that the man had ransacked the room. Some of the dresser drawers were open. The sheets and comforter from the bed were balled up on the floor. One of the lamps was lying on its side, minus its shade. The mattress was slightly skewed.

"This is all you want?" I held up the computer. "Seems to be pretty popular. Who sent you anyway?"

He didn't respond. Instead, he patted the bed. "Drop it here, Agent Chase, nice and slow."

"Who are you working for? Eva O'Connor?"

No response.

"Ah, it's Stanley Tuchek then? To maintain an air of innocence, he entrusted me with the laptop. But he knew he'd get it right back. I get it."

Again, no response.

"How did you know we were here?"

He sighed. "I've asked nicely. Don't make me start shooting. I'll start with your knees and work my way up."

"Maybe you work for Anfernee Gates, the man you recently killed and stuffed into my trunk?"

"Last chance." He patted the bed again.

I shrugged and held out my hands. "Why won't you tell me? You're obviously not going to let me leave here alive, so why not?"

"Actually, it's your lucky day. Any other time and you'd be a dead man by now. But you have somewhere to be tonight, am I right?"

I smiled. "You are, and you just gave away your hand."

His eyebrows rose a little. "How so?"

"You admitted your orders don't include killing me. Obviously I'm needed at the pier tonight, so nothing deadly is going to happen. Am I right?"

He didn't respond.

"Why don't you put down the gun? We'll settle this like real men. Last man standing gets the laptop. How about it?"

He scoffed. "Really?"

I didn't want to fight him, but I also didn't trust that he was telling the truth. For all I knew he could be here to kill me, and I didn't want to die, not until I'd cleared my name anyway – and seen Simon at least one more time. Plus, I didn't want to just hand over the laptop. It was important.

"You've got both inches and pounds on me," I said. "Don't tell me you're chicken. Are you afraid? Is that it?"

The thug pulled the trigger and the pistol let out a muffled pop. I flinched as a bullet flew over my right shoulder and lodged into the door.

"I'm not here to play games, Agent Chase. Hand it over."

"You won't fight me? A big guy like you? You'd rather hide behind a gun. You drug and threaten innocent women and children, like Mick

Cranston's family. That was you, wasn't it? Is that your M.O.? Is that how you operate?"

I waited for a response. His eyebrows were angled in, so I could tell I was getting under his skin. The brows were so prominent that they gave away any emotion he had. He'd make a horrible poker player.

"Come on," I said, egging him on. "I'm gonna tear your face off. Which would be an improvement actually."

He rose slowly, methodically. I got a good look at him. He was thick everywhere, not just in his eyebrows. He probably had two inches on me, at least. Probably bested me by twenty or thirty pounds, too. I'd have my work cut out.

"You still want to do this?" he asked, pronouncing 'this' like 'deece'. "Give me a good look, Agent Chase. I don't think that's wise. You're a big guy, but I'm bigger, substantially so."

"I'll hit you so hard in the mouth, hopefully I'll knock that stupid accent out of you."

That did it. He dropped the pistol onto the bed, lowered his head, and charged at me like a Pamplona bull. As he ran, his gorilla arms scraped either side of the narrow hallway. Since I stood just in front of the door, I had nowhere to go. All I could do was brace myself for the impact.

A moment later his right arm snagged me at the waist and lifted me into the air, nearly two feet off the ground. Just before slamming into the hotel door, I tossed the laptop onto the bed to protect it. My back smashed against the hard door. I felt every vertebra in my back groan; but I hit the door flush so the impact was spread out along my spine. The hit brought me alive and heightened my senses.

Wasting no time, I grasped both hands together and clubbed him on his back as hard as I could swing. I tried two more seal clubs but, honestly, it didn't faze him. Probably didn't even hurt him. I felt like I was wailing on a frozen cow carcass.

The thug was in the perfect position to flip me over, so he did. I tumbled forward, tucked my head, and rolled across the floor. Since I'd landed by the bathroom door, I scrambled in there on my knees. The bathroom door swung inward, so I grabbed the edge of the door with both hands. When the thug rushed in after me, I swung the door closed like I was swinging for the fences.

He stepped back and tried to get out of the way, but at some point he realized he couldn't avoid the impact, so he lowered his head and took the blow on the forehead. The door was cheap wood and it splintered around his head. It was like a scene out of Stephen King's *The Shining*. Seriously, I could see part of the thug's face through the door. The man was spewing and red-faced and downright pissed.

Since I was already on the floor, I scrambled back and braced myself against the side of the bathtub. Placing both hands on the ground, I cocked my legs toward my chest, then exploded them at the door. The door slammed shut and the thug's face peeled away. He reeled back and smashed through the hallway closet, shattering the full-length mirror.

The cramped bathroom was my death sentence. I had to come out swinging, but not with my fists. My fists wouldn't do anything to this bald ape, so I pried off the toilet top, the rectangular part made of heavy porcelain. I held it in my left hand. With my right, I grabbed the door handle and swung it open. Then I used both hands on the heavy, porcelain top and threw it at the thug with everything I had.

It slammed into his chest at what seemed like a hundred miles an hour. I swore I heard at least two ribs crack. The thug grunted and gasped, but the blow didn't stop him. He stormed toward the bathroom in a rage. I managed to sidestep his charge just as he exploded through the doorframe. The thug almost ripped the door off its hinges as he crashed into the bathroom.

I glanced to my right and reacted, grabbing the small glass coffee pot off the tiny vanity. Fortunately, the thug's back was turned to me, so I ran at him and lifted the pot over my head. I used the pot like a tomahawk and smashed it over the back of his skull. It shattered into a hundred pieces. Three large shards dug into the top of his head.

The thug didn't drop. Unbelievable. Instead, he turned to face me. That was when I noticed his knees starting to give, so I used that opportunity to try and exit the bathroom, but he lunged toward me and grabbed my right ankle before I could get out. In response, I bicycle kicked him in the face with my left foot. I actually felt the cartilage in his nose mush into the sole of my shoe.

The blow didn't faze him, and he didn't let go of my foot. In fact, he was able to get a hold of my other foot after the face kick. He pulled me toward him like I was on a zip line. As I slid on my belly, I pivoted my upper body so I was on my side. When my feet jammed against his body, I used the momentum and sprung forward and planted my right fist into his busted nose. He yelped and finally let go of my ankles. I proceeded to kick him in the chest with both feet. The kick wasn't very hard. But it wasn't soft either. It had just enough power to send him backwards, to land between the toilet and tub. His head bounced off the bathroom wall. Lucky for me, one of the glass shards jammed deeper into his skull. While he winced and pulled out the shard, I scrambled out of the bathroom.

On my way out, the thug clawed in my direction and caught my shirt tail. I pumped my knees and dragged him out of the bathroom, ripping off the bottom half of my shirt. Suddenly I was free, however, so I jumped toward the bed and swiped up the gun as I slipped off the corner of the mattress. My chest broke the fall.

As I turned and pointed the gun, I figured it was over. I'd won. I had him.

I was wrong.

All I saw were four hairy knuckles coming at my face, and I had no time to react. My head snapped back. It felt like my face split in two. It was by far the hardest punch I'd ever taken, and I've taken a lot of punches over the years. If I'd been on my feet, I would've at least dropped to my knees, maybe even fallen over, but I was already on the ground when he hit me, so I simply flopped backward and landed on something soft. It took a moment to realize I'd landed on top of the comforter and bed sheets.

Somehow I managed to keep my grip on the gun after the punch, but before I could draw, the thug stamped on my right hand. The crushing weight of his boot forced me to drop the gun. He kicked the gun away, then my forehead met the sole of his boot. It wasn't a pleasant meeting.

"You're gonna like this," he said.

He jerked the comforter from underneath me. Tossing it over my head, he rolled me up like a cigar. It happened quickly, and since I was dazed from the punch, I didn't react in time. Suddenly I found myself rolled up tight in the blankets with my arms straight at my sides. The thug jumped on and straddled me.

He assaulted me with his fists. There was no pattern to his thunderous punches. Two in the face, then one in my gut, three to my side, another to the face, then back to the gut. It felt like ten men were punching me. Fortunately, as the blows came, the comforter loosened, so I was able to wiggle around and get into the turtle position and protect myself a little. The thug was in such a fury he didn't stop to adjust the comforter. When I felt like there was enough slack in the comforter, I waited for a gut punch, then made my move.

After taking a blow to the stomach, I used both hands and latched onto his retreating fist. With a quick turn, I snapped his wrist. It sounded like popsicle sticks breaking. The man howled. At that point, I grabbed the comforter and pulled it off my face. Immediately the thug clamped onto my throat with his good hand, his left.

I reached up and tried to grab his throat in retaliation, but the thug arched his head back, which left me clawing at his stiff left arm. The man had all his weight and strength bearing straight down on my throat, so I couldn't budge his arm. I clawed, pinched, and punched, but nothing worked.

I was in trouble. I had no oxygen coming in and not much time before I passed out, or maybe died. Desperate, I reached out and tried to grab his busted right hand, but the man was too smart. He put his hand behind his back and focused all his attention on choking me with one arm. All I could do was wedge my hands under his armpit and try with all my strength to counteract his leverage.

It worked, just a little. I was able to take a breath, which gave me some life.

We remained in deadlock for minutes. Or maybe it was seconds, I don't know. Honestly, after seconds, or minutes, whichever it was, everything started to fade. I tried to fight against it, but it didn't help. It felt like everything was about to end. My life. My legacy, whatever that was.

All I'd truly wanted was to be the exact opposite of my dad, to be there for my boy, to help him grow up right in this world. But that didn't seem to be on the cards for me and Simon.

Just before I blacked out, I had a thought; a thought about my son growing up without a dad. It wasn't the end of the world for a boy to grow up without a dad, but what about a boy growing up with a dead traitor for a father? One convicted of murdering a federal agent. How would that affect a boy and his psyche?

That thought sparked new life in me. Suddenly, I was able to keep the counter pressure going again. I closed my eyes and hung on with everything I had.

Suddenly a cracking sound filled the room. Following that, tiny glass shards rained down on my face, sprinkling over me like heavy raindrops. The weight on my lower body gave way and the death grip on my throat relaxed.

As I gasped for air, my eyes fluttered open and I saw the thug toppling to his left.

There, right behind where the thug had been, stood Karla Dickerson. She gripped the base of a lamp. Its bulb was shattered and the end of the lamp was bent back at a near ninety-degree angle.

She smiled. "I smashed that one out of the park."

CHAPTER TWENTY-NINE

KARLA TRIED TO help me up, but I waved her off.

"I'm fine." Halfway to my feet, I stumbled and fell to my knees.

"Yeah, real fine." She helped me up.

Once on my feet, I said, "I had him right where I wanted him."

She laughed. "Looked like it."

"Thanks, Karla, you saved me, big time. You have a hell of a swing, too."

"No time for small talk. I heard you guys smashing around in here before I walked into the building. We have to get out of here. Even in a dive this bad, I bet somebody's on their way to check out what all the noise was."

I motioned at the thug. "Let's check his pockets first."

While Karla felt for a pulse, I rifled through his pockets.

"You didn't hit him that hard," I said. "Did you?"

"He's fine," Karla said. "At least I hope he is. I did aim for one of those shards in his skull. That's probably why he dropped instantly."

A moment passed. "Got a pulse," she said.

All I found were car keys in his pants pockets.

Karla found a cell in one of his shirt pockets. She swiped at the screen, then shook her head. "It requires a password, obviously."

"Take it anyway."

She pulled a rectangular badge out of his jacket pocket and looked at it. "No way, no freaking way."

I looked at her. "What?"

"It's an NSA badge." Karla handed it to me; her hand shaking slightly. "He works for the Agency."

"Can't be." I looked at the picture on the badge. It was indeed the bald, bushy-eyebrowed thug.

"Gustavo Enriquez," I said. "The name doesn't surprise me, but working for the NSA does."

"Now we really have to get out of here, Chase, and fast."

"Should we take him with us? Maybe when he wakes up we can waterboard him for answers."

"How are we going to get him out of here unnoticed? We'd both have to carry him. And where would we take him?"

I thought about rolling him up in the comforter and throwing him over my shoulder.

"Leave him right here and don't look back," Karla said.

I didn't want to deal with Gustavo when he woke up. Plus, he probably wouldn't talk anyway. "I think you're right. Let's go. We can take his vehicle for the time being."

Karla ran to the door. I grabbed her before she made it out. "Let's be casual and not draw any attention."

"You're right," she said.

I grabbed Stanley's laptop, then we walked to the parking lot, not slow, but not fast either. Fortunately, the keys had a fob attached. I pushed the lock button and saw some lights flash from a grey Chevy Suburban in the rear part of the motel lot. The SUV was a couple of years old and had regular plates, not government plates. The windows were tinted, which was a bonus.

After piling in, Karla asked, "Are you okay? Your nose looks bad and both eyes are turning black already."

"I am. Did you catch a glimpse of his face? His wasn't pretty either."

"Was he waiting in the room or did he ambush you? Tell me what happened."

I fired up the Suburban and pulled out of the lot. As I drove, I relayed the story to Karla.

When I finished, she said, "Good thing we didn't pay with a credit card. You two did some serious damage to that room. How did he know we were there?"

I glanced at her. "I've been thinking about that. We didn't call or text anyone about finding a base of operations. Stanley wasn't with us when we decided to go to the motel, and Eva had no clue of our whereabouts. So he must've tailed us from the governor's place. I didn't notice anyone tailing us, but that's the only explanation I can think of. He either picked up our tail at the governor's house or he was tailing us before that and I just didn't see him."

"Who was he? Did he say anything?"

I shook my head. "Not about himself or his employer. I tried. All he wanted was Stanley's laptop."

"Interesting," Karla said. "What about Mick? We need to warn him not to show up at the motel."

"Text him." I handed her the snapcell. "Tell him to meet me at the abandoned warehouse on Pier 42 in Long Beach."

"Just you? Not us?"

"I have a plan for you."

She eyed me. "Which is?"

"It's pretty late for any agents to be at your field office, right?"

She nodded. "You think I should go back to my FO?"

"We need to find out as much as we can about Gates, and also this Enriquez character. Eva O'Connor, too. Since we can't trust anyone else for intel, I think you should go to your FO and see what you can dig up. You haven't been named in the APB or arrest warrant. It's just me they want. I don't think you're in any trouble, or at least not too much trouble. Plus, you have some time right now to come up with a story about where you've been the last twelve hours, in case you run into someone at the office."

"And what are you going to do?"

"I need to check out the pier and come up with a plan. Something tells me our meeting won't go smoothly. Who knows what's going to happen."

"This is a conspiracy I couldn't have dreamed up. For all we know, it's a huge setup. I'll see what I can find out at the office. Maybe I can crack the password for this phone. I'll meet up with you and Mick as soon as I come up with some useful intel."

I nodded. "We're on, then. Text Mick and let him know what's up."

She did, then I let her have some time to think about a story.

It took eighteen minutes to get to the LA field office. Mick texted back during the drive, saying he was on his way back and would meet me at the pier. When we arrived at her FO, Karla said she had a good story to tell about her recent whereabouts in case anyone asked. She grabbed my hand, squeezed it, and told me to be careful. She left before I had a chance to reply.

On my drive down the 710 toward Long Beach, I thought about the Enriquez character and who was giving him orders. Was it Eva, or Stanley, or someone else?

I couldn't come up with an answer or a decent theory, so when I arrived at the docks I shut my mind off and studied the surroundings. The Long Beach harbor was massive. There were an inordinate number of docks, tankers, cranes, and shipping containers. Even a few cruise ships were moored there. The farther I drove, the less busy it became. When I reached Pier 40, I pulled over and parked because I wanted to walk the rest of the way to Pier 42. Not only so I could do reconnaissance of the area, but also so I wouldn't draw attention to myself. I had no clue what was waiting for me at the abandoned warehouse.

As I approached the warehouse, I studied the run-down structure. It was definitely abandoned. The once-red paint was faded and peeling. Beneath the paint were planks of worn, weathered wood. Not a soul or car were in the immediate area. The place was deserted, and had been for some time. It was a good place for a discreet meeting.

The wooden warehouse was large, probably fifty feet wide by a hundred long. It was perched right at the end of the pier. No other structures were on the 200-foot length of dock. Half of the moorings on the pier were ripped out, which meant a boat couldn't tie up, at least not a big one. Nobody had set foot on the pier in three years or more. That was my guess, anyway.

From my current viewpoint, there were only two visible windows on the structure. The windows were twenty, maybe twenty-five feet up on the west side of the warehouse, near the top of the building. Both windows were crusted up by the salty air and impossible to see through. There was one set of sliding, heavy steel doors on the west side of the building.

I walked past those doors, wrapped around the north end, and saw that there were no doors or windows there. There was, however, a steel door in the middle of the east side of the building. A rusted padlock dangled below the handle. There was only about a three-foot walkway behind the building. The west side was clearly the front of the building and would have received the shipments.

After a full perimeter sweep of the building, I tried the sliding doors. They were big enough for a large truck to pass through. To my surprise, the doors weren't locked. I grated them open, slipped in, and quickly shut them behind me. A sliver of moonlight forced its way through the crusted windows, helping to light up the warehouse.

The first thing I noticed was a giant shipping container in the middle of the warehouse. Along every wall were towering metal shelves, like the kind used in Costco. On the shelves were tons of empty pallets and various sizes of shipping containers. Everything had an inch-thick layer of dust on top and the place smelled like a musty, old dog.

I walked to the eastern side of the building and examined the locked metal door. Essentially there was only one way in or out of the warehouse. That made for an easier plan.

To the left of the metal door were two construction lights. They were about six feet tall and had their own base of support. I plugged one in and was shocked to find the building still had power. The light cascaded across the floor, casting a large shadow around the shipping container. I plugged in the other light, then maneuvered both so they pointed directly at the sliding doors. Anyone entering the warehouse would be blinded. My hope was to control the meeting from the very beginning.

Since I really didn't know what was going on, or what to expect, I needed to call the shots.

Next, I climbed the shelving in the northeast corner of the building. The tops of the shelves were about thirty feet in the air. Before anyone arrived, I planned to be tucked away high in the corner, the farthest point from the light, alone and in the shadows. I also planned on having a rifle and scope in hand. One way or another, I was going to force Stanley and Eva to come clean.

I sat on top of the shelf in the northeastern corner for a few minutes, surveying the scene until I felt confident in my plan. While I was sitting, my beeper buzzed. I'd forgotten it was in my pocket. I fished it out and saw Gina's number scrolling across the screen. Why was she calling so late? It must have something to do with Simon. Maybe she had changed her position concerning the restraining order. A long shot, I knew, but it was good to be hopeful. I made a mental note to call her back as soon as the meeting was over.

While climbing down the shelves, I heard footsteps outside the building and assumed they were Mick's. Just to be safe, I hid behind the large shipping container in the middle of the room and drew my weapon. The footsteps circled the building slowly, then stopped in front of the sliding doors. The doors opened a fraction and the blazing lights split through, lighting up Mick's face. He quickly closed the doors.

I stepped out and lowered my gun. "It's just me, Mick." I walked over and pointed the lights away.

The doors screeched open and closed. Mick slipped in. "That's pretty good. Definitely going to put anyone entering the building on edge."

"How are Julie and the girls?"

"The girls are fine. They think they're camping. Julie's a little on edge."

"Understandable. But everyone's safe?"

He shrugged. "They are for now. We just need to figure this out fast."

"We do. And it's gotten way more complicated since you left, way more. I don't even know where to begin."

Mick walked over. "I can tell by your face."

I started to update Mick on the latest, but he stopped me.

"Let's talk on the way to my Bronco. I brought some supplies."

Mick had parked a pier farther away than I did. Along the way, I recounted what had happened with Eva and Stanley, then the cops, then Gustavo Enriquez. I kept things broad and to the point, not dwelling on every detail. Mick didn't ask one question. He listened intently to the whole story.

When I finished, he stopped walking. He calmly turned toward me and said, "Let me get this straight; you've been dating my boss, the actual chairman of the Special Collection Service? Who I ultimately take orders from?"

I nodded.

"And she may be responsible for all this; my boss, that is. And if she's not involved, then the kid is. The son of the California Governor."

He paused. I let him digest the information.

Mick rubbed his temples. "I don't know what to say. This is a lot to take in."

I nodded. "It is."

"You were really dating the chairman, chairwoman, whatever? And Stanley originally thought she was trying to vet you for an SCS position?"

"I know it sounds crazy."

"Doesn't *sound* crazy, it *is* crazy."

"I know."

"The chairman thinks Stanley is behind everything? That he broke into her computer and planted incriminating arms evidence on her computer, then sent the kill orders to me?"

"That's her story."

Mick scratched his head. "Why? Why would either of them do this?"

"That's what I don't know and have to figure out."

"So we really don't know who's responsible for the kill orders and setting you up? What does your gut tell you?"

I paused and thought a moment, then said, "The problem with Stanley's version of events is that he's a liar. I can't trust what he says. But Eva's version asserts that the kid is some sort of mastermind, a criminal genius."

Mick nodded. "Which I have a hard time believing, too."

"Maybe Anfernee Gates and the Italian thug are behind all of this, though that's the least plausible theory in my mind. Karla's working on that angle."

Mick looked at his watch. "I guess we're going to find out soon."

"We're going to find out something. So we need to be prepared for anything."

"We will be."

Mick walked another fifty feet and stopped at his vehicle. He opened the Bronco's trunk. There were two rifle cases, a few handguns, some night binoculars, and some communication equipment.

Mick grabbed an earpiece and handed it to me. "You and I should probably split up. Obviously you need to be in the warehouse."

Grabbing the rifle case, I said, "I'll set up in the northeast corner with the Weatherby."

"I think I should be outside the warehouse, scanning the area. That way I can relay information to you about who's showing up. And let you know if anything odd is happening."

I nodded. "Sounds good."

Mick pointed at a loading crane on Pier 40. "I'll set up on the crane. It'll give a wide, elevated view of this whole area." He took the other rifle case. "I'll have you covered."

"Like the old days," I said.

Before we could discuss any further plans, the snapcell rang. I dug it from my pocket. I didn't recognize the number, so I figured it was the governor.

"Governor Tuchek, is that you?"

I heard heavy breathing, then: "It's Karla, Chase. I'm in trouble; big trouble."

CHAPTER THIRTY

"WHAT'S WRONG?" I said.

"He's here." Karla took a quick breath. "The NSA agent from the motel, all battered and bruised, with a crooked nose and some dried blood on the back of his head."

"Where are you? Still at your FO?"

"In my office. He just showed up, along with Frank and Hornsby."

"Have they seen you?"

"Not yet, but they've been pointing in the direction of my office, so I'm pretty sure they're here for me."

I thought about the implications. Hornsby and Frank being called in so late to Karla's FO was terrible news for us. "You gotta get out, Karla."

"That's part of the trouble. I can't."

"What do you mean?"

"My office is in the corner of the building. And they're all in the conference room, which is basically a fishbowl of windows. I have to walk by that room to hit the exit. There's no other way in or out of the building."

"Shoot."

"Worse," she said. "They're leaving the conference room right now and are headed my way."

"Can you hide?"

"Not really. They'll find me quickly, then it'll look really bad."

I ran my hand over my head. "Right."

"Do I come clean, Chase? What do you think? I don't want to say anything in front of the NSA guy."

"You don't. Is Frank with them?"

"He is."

"Try to get him alone and explain everything, but only to him. He's the only one I trust. Did you find out anything, by the way?"

She sighed. "Couldn't hack the phone. Sorry, Chase. Gustavo Enriquez is a complete mystery. It doesn't appear he works for the NSA, not according to any federal intelligence database. I couldn't find any hits for his name on the NSA interlink. That's all I know. I gotta go, they're here."

Karla put down the phone, but didn't hang it up.

"Agent Dickerson," Hornsby's voice said, "the NSA has some questions for you, and apparently you have some questions for them as well. Agent Enriquez says you've been on their interlink for the past half hour from this very location. You need to go with him now."

"But, sir—"

"That's an order."

"I can't go now," Karla said.

"As I said, it's an order, Agent Dickerson."

There was brief silence, then the phone hung up. I stared at the cell.

Mick nudged my shoulder. "Who was that?"

"Karla. The NSA thug from the motel room, the man who probably drugged your family, just showed up at her office looking for her."

"She going to be alright?"

I shook my head. "I don't know, I really don't. Like you said, we need to figure this out fast. That's the only thing I know."

"We will. Let's stay in touch." Mick pointed to his earpiece.

We did a quick sound check, then went our respective ways. Since I couldn't wait any longer, I called the governor on my walk back to the warehouse. He didn't pick up.

After placing the lights back in position, I climbed the shelving. The snapcell buzzed just as I reached the top. I stabbed the talk button.

"Governor?"

"I'm taking a big chance calling you, Agent Chase."

"I understand. I'm glad you called. And I appreciate the risk you're taking. Did you find out about Gates?"

"You do know the feds think you killed him, right?"

"You have to know that's not true."

The governor didn't respond.

"Someone's framing me, Governor. I promise I had nothing to do with killing a federal agent."

He cleared his throat. "What about my son? Have you heard from him?"

I wasn't about to tell the governor about Stanley's involvement, not until I figured out his exact role, so I said, "We're meeting soon, sir. He and I are about to have a heart-to-heart and figure everything out."

"Don't you dare hurt my son."

"Of course I won't, sir. We're just talking. What about Gates? Did you learn anything?"

"It took some probing, but I found out a little. He definitely worked for The Company. Apparently he was on special assignment. My understanding is that the CIA had been given information that somebody in the SCS was dirty. That somebody had been selling arms secrets. Gates was assigned the investigation. So it's not like it was a spy operation on American soil. It was an internal investigation."

"I suppose you don't know who Gates was specifically investigating?"

"That's what I meant by a little, Agent Chase. That's all I know about the situation. It took all my connections and political clout to get that far. I hope it's somewhat helpful."

I paused and took a breath. Pieces were starting to fit. I could rule out Gates now. It appeared he was trying to figure out everything, just like I was. "It definitely helps. Thanks, Governor."

"For the record, Agent Chase, if it wasn't you who killed Gates, then who did?"

"That's what I'm planning to find out."

"You think Stanley might know? Is that why you're meeting him? You don't think he's involved, do you?" He scoffed into the phone. "That's preposterous."

"I'm not sure what to think right now, sir. That's the honest truth. But I'm going to find out."

"And I should be the first to know. Promise me that."

"I promise."

Sensing the governor was about to hang up, I continued. "One more thing, sir. I need one more favor."

There was a pause and quick sigh. "What is it?"

"I had a contact gathering intel on two people, but that contact has just been detained, so I need some help."

"Intel on whom?"

"Two NSA agents: one by the name of Eva O'Connor, and the other called Gustavo Enriquez. Any information I can find out about those two would be extremely helpful."

I heard him writing down the names.

"I'll see what I can do," he said. "But on one condition."

"Anything, sir."

"You bring Stanley immediately to me after your meeting. Got it?"

"Agreed."

He hung up without saying goodbye.

After the call, I unloaded the Weatherby and adjusted the scope, dialed in the turrets, checked my field of vision, chambered a round, then double-checked my work.

My beeper buzzed after I'd finished. I was surprised to see it wasn't Gina's number. It was a familiar one, though, and it took a moment to realize who it was.

It was my ex-therapist Doc Jules.

Are you kidding me? Really? Why would my snake of a former therapist want to talk now? Why would he think I'd ever want to talk with him anyway? Then I realized – something must be going down with Gina or Simon. My pulse quickened, but my ear piece suddenly crackled, forcing my attention away.

"You in position, Aug?" Mick said.

"We're using codenames now?"

"We're on a mission, pal. Like old times, as you said."

"Ten-four, Gabe. That's affirmative on position."

"Good, because the kid is on his way. He's barreling right toward us in a maroon Chevy Tahoe. I can see him through the scope. His bug eyes are bigger than normal. You want to handle him alone? If you want, I can intercept him before he makes it to the warehouse."

"I'll handle him. You stay in position."

"Ten-four, here he comes."

I heard the Tahoe's engine humming as it approached. A moment later, the brakes locked and Stanley skidded the Tahoe to a stop close to the front of the warehouse. I heard a car door open, then slam shut.

"He's got a gun," Mick said into my ear. "And it's drawn, Aug. What do you want me to do?"

"Hang tight."

"I can take out a knee, just let me know."

I didn't think Stanley was a threat but, just in case, I brought my eye to the scope and pointed the rifle at the doors. "I've got it covered, Gabe."

The doors opened, just a fraction. I saw Stanley lift both hands to protect his eyes from the bright lights. I could've popped the kid in the chest, maybe even re-racked and planted another round into him, that's how long he stood frozen by the lights.

Finally, Stanley reacted and stepped out of view, but he didn't close the doors.

"It's okay, Stanley," I yelled. "It's just me in here. Come on in."

"What's with the lights?"

"Don't worry about it. Get in here, but not with that gun drawn."

"You're sure it's just you?"

"Get in here, kid."

Stanley walked in and scurried to the left of the bright lights. He stuffed the gun into his shoulder sling. "Where are you, Agent Chase? Did you bring the laptop?"

While watching him through the scope, I sighed. "Yes, I have it."

"Good. Eva just called. She needs it. It's our deal. We agreed on a trade; if she gets the laptop she'll come clean. That's what this is all about. Apparently she's going to make everything crystal clear at this meeting, as long as she gets the laptop. Those were her exact words."

"Do you really believe that?"

"I do," he said.

I had to look the kid in his eyes to see if he was really buying his own story. I dropped the rifle, grabbed my handgun, and shimmied down the shelves.

When I reached the ground, I said, "You'd better not reach for that gun, Stanley. I need to look you in the eye."

"What?" Stanley held out his good hand. "Why would I ever shoot you?"

I hustled toward the kid. "Listen, before you dig yourself into even deeper lies, you need to know that I had a long conversation with Eva, right after you shot out my tire."

He wiped his nose. "I'm sorry about that. I felt like I had no other choice. You really got hold of Eva?"

"You bet I did. And she had quite a different version of events than you did."

"When did you speak with her?"

"What does it matter? You lied about a lot."

Stanley narrowed his eyes. "What did she tell you? I'm confused."

"I see it now, Stanley. I didn't before."

"Didn't see what?"

"That you're an actor, and a decent one. You have this whole naïve persona down pretty pat."

"What? I'm not acting. What did Eva tell you?" He blinked twice and looked genuinely confused.

I put my hand on his shoulder and gripped it tightly. "You didn't find the arms evidence on her computer, that's what she said. She said you planted it. Didn't you?"

"That's crazy. No, I didn't. Where would I get evidence like that?"

"And you blackmailed Eva for an SCS position, right? Used that arms evidence for coercion."

He stepped back and jerked his shoulder free. "Absolutely not, Agent Chase, I promise I didn't."

I pointed at him. "You were hell-bent on revenge, weren't you? Totally pissed at her for repeatedly denying your transfer."

He swallowed. "I was upset, yes, but not hell-bent on revenge. No way."

"Will you admit that you were spying on the TV network? Using your talents for domestic spying and making millions from it? You never mentioned a thing about that to me."

He opened his mouth, but didn't say anything.

"Well?"

"Okay, I failed to mention—"

"NO! You lied, Stanley, say it." I stepped forward until my finger was almost touching his chest. "Say it now, say you lied."

He pushed up his glasses. "Okay, I lied about that, Agent Chase, I did. I broke some laws and spied on the network—"

"And profited a lot. Don't forget that." I dropped my arm.

"I did, you're right. And Eva confronted me about it, told me to drop the transfer request and get the hell out of the NSA for good. She even had me ushered out of the building."

"I know, she told me that. That move really fueled your fire, didn't it?"

"It did, but not for revenge. It fueled my fire to prove to her that I was the best asset she could have. That's why I broke into her computer."

I raised my brows. "And blackmailed her with what you found."

"No, if that's what Eva said, she's lying. That's not what happened, not at all. I told you what happened with the information. I presented it to her and she was initially mad, but then she came around. Eva told me I had the skills to be an agent and she wanted to involve me in Operation Crucible."

I took a deep breath. "That's not her recollection, Stanley, not at all. When you first broke into the NSA database, you said you found the names of the SCS members and the chairman."

"That's true, I did."

"So you didn't find mission information, organizational charts, kill codes, and then used that information to send Mick kill orders?"

"Kill codes? What? No way. I didn't get information like that. Why would you say that? Besides, if I got access to kill codes, they'd changed the codes, right?"

I hadn't thought about that. Stanley was right. Unless, of course, Eva hadn't changed the kill codes because then she would've had to admit that Stanley had broken into her computer.

"Cellphone." I wiggled my fingers. "Let me see your snapcell. You can't keep lying to me. Your text records should confirm some things. In fact, it will clear everything up. It will prove whether you've been lying to me or not."

"Why? What for?"

I sighed. "Let me see it. Let me see your texts to her. Show me now. You said you've been in constant contact with her."

Stanley's mouth dropped. He stood motionless.

"Come on, let's see it." I beckoned with my hand.

He blinked and looked away. "Now I get it." He looked back. "Now I understand why she insisted I get rid of my cell. She's ingenious, Agent Chase. She really is."

"What are you talking about?"

"Eva said she'd explain everything tonight at this meeting. She said you and Karla would be safe. I just needed to bring the laptop because the original arms evidence was on there. She wanted to destroy the evidence herself, once and for all. She also told me to destroy my snap-cell, so there were no communication ties between her and me. I didn't think much of it until right now."

I gripped his good shoulder again. "You don't have your cell? You're kidding me?"

"I don't, Agent Chase. I destroyed it, like she asked. The last text I sent was to you about this meeting. I did everything she asked because I wanted to ensure Karla and you were safe."

I squeezed his shoulder a little tighter. "I needed to see those texts to Eva, Stanley. You understand that? You understand it would've helped me believe you?"

His head drooped. "I do now, Agent Chase. I'm sorry. Please, I'm so sorry."

I stared at him, balled my fists, then released them. I did that three times.

"Walk with me, kid."

I prodded him toward the middle of the warehouse. As we walked, I thought about what Eva said on the phone. She told me she was going to lie to Stanley to get him to the meeting. She also said she'd clear everything up, then we'd arrest the kid.

I still didn't know who to believe.

We stopped in front of the shipping container. The door was halfway open.

"You understand, Stanley, that I have two conflicting stories about what's going on, your version and Eva's version. And both of you are pointing the finger at each other."

"I get it. But you have to believe that Eva has been manipulating me from the very beginning. It doesn't make sense, Agent Chase. It's not like I sent a kill order to Mick. How could I? Think about it. Mick was supposed to kill me! So obviously I'm not involved."

"I actually agree with you, Stanley, many things aren't adding up. I really don't know what to believe."

I pushed him into the shipping container. Not hard, but not soft either. He stumbled back and looked stunned.

"I need to figure this out," I said. "I'll let you out after I've spoken with Eva." Then I slammed the door and latched the metal bar shut.

Stanley yelled something and banged against the door. I ignored him and walked toward the shelves. My beeper buzzed along the way. I looked at it and saw my mom's number scrolling across the screen.

My mom? What?

Something must be seriously wrong for her to call me this late. Mom didn't stay up past 9:30. Ever. I used the snapcell and called her number.

Mom picked up on the first ring. "Hon, is that you?"

"It is, Mom," I said, breathing hard. "What's going on? Are you okay?"

"I'm fine, dear. I'm calling about Simon."

"Simon? What? Why?"

A brief pause.

"Mom, what's going on? Talk to me."

She took a breath, then said, "He's missing, Gary."

CHAPTER THIRTY-ONE

"MISSING?" I STOPPED breathing. "What do you mean, missing? What's going on, Mom?"

She immediately replied, "So he's not with you? I was hoping he was with you."

"No, he's not with me. What do you mean he's missing?"

Mom paused for a split second too long.

"Mom!" I snapped. "I'm freaking out here."

"Sorry, dear. Gina called ten minutes ago and woke me up, said she was looking for you. She told me Simon was gone. She went in to check on him before bed and Simon wasn't in his room. She tried to get hold of you on your beeper, but when you didn't call her back she assumed that you'd taken him. She's furious, hon."

"Of course I didn't take him." I said it much too forcefully, however. I took a deep breath. "He's missing, really? Did she check everywhere in the house? He used to love playing hide and seek, I remember that. He loved that game."

"I assume she did, dear. She said you guys had an incident at a restaurant and that you left upset. She figures you took him out of spite. She wanted me to get hold of you to let you know that she's called the cops.

She's accused you of abducting him. You haven't done that, right? Obviously you haven't. This is awful."

"Abduct him?" I pulled the phone away for a second, then put it back to my ear. "Are you serious, Mom? She thinks I abducted Simon?"

A pause, then: "She does. You should call her back right away and straighten everything out."

There had to be a logical explanation for Simon's disappearance, not a sinister one. I thought about it. The thug who'd abducted Mick's wife and girls couldn't have taken Simon. No way.

"How long does Gina think he's been missing?" I asked.

"She doesn't know for sure, maybe a couple of hours at most."

The thug had been busy the past couple of hours. After he woke in the hotel room he must've gone straight to the LA field office. There hadn't been time for him to drive to Gina's and abduct my son. I visualized the route he would've taken and the time he needed to do it. It wasn't possible. His recent whereabouts were accounted for. It couldn't have been him.

Sweat beaded on my forehead. I wiped it away. Maybe Simon had found a really good hiding spot. Maybe Gina had freaked out and wasn't thinking straight and didn't thoroughly check the house. Or maybe there was another explanation, maybe a crazier one, like sleepwalking. Are young boys prone to sleepwalking? What age does that start?

"Hon," my mother said. "You need to call her straight away."

The phone beeped, alerting me to an incoming call. I pulled it back and looked at the screen. The number was unlisted, and I assumed it was the governor.

I put the phone back. "Listen, Mom, you can't begin to believe what I'm going through right now. I'm tied up at the moment—"

"Tied up? At this time? What could you possibly be doing? And what's more important than this?"

I hesitated for a moment.

"Talk to me, hon."

"You're right, Mom, absolutely nothing is more important than Simon. It's just that I'm on assignment and can't leave right this second. Believe me, if I could, I would, without question."

"You're working now, at this hour?"

"I am. As soon as I'm done I'll head straight to Gina's and figure this out. For the time being, can you call her and let her know I had nothing to do with Simon? Tell her I'll be over as soon as I can. Maybe Simon is hiding or sleepwalked to the neighbors or something like that. There must be a simple explanation. Were there any signs of a break-in?"

"She didn't say."

The phone beeped again.

"Mom, please do this for me. I need you."

She sighed. "Sure, dear. Call me when you know what's going on. Heaven knows I won't be going back to sleep."

I thanked her and tried to swap the calls, but the other caller had hung up. I immediately thought about abandoning the meeting and heading straight to Gina's. After a moment of deliberating, I figured that was the wrong move. If Simon had been abducted, I knew that it must be either Eva or Stanley behind it, and so my best chance of getting Simon back was sticking right where I was. Plus, I absolutely had to figure out what was going on. I had to clear my name and prove I wasn't a traitor, fugitive, and murderer. If I didn't, I'd never see my son again.

I stayed put and refocused the Weatherby's scope on the warehouse door.

The snapcell buzzed again. I picked it up.

"Governor?"

"It is."

"That was fast," I said.

"I haven't looked into Gustavo Enriquez yet. I started with Eva O'Connor. Did you know she was a West Point graduate?"

"I didn't." West Point was America's top military academy. It was a bit of a surprise that Eva was a graduate, but I wasn't sure of the relevance.

"She was actually the first female graduate of the program."

"Really?" I said.

"She was. When I found that out, I knew that a colonel friend of mine who still works at West Point would know all about her. And he always works late. So I contacted him and he did me a huge favor."

The governor paused. I didn't know if it was for dramatic effect, so I prodded him on. "Which was?"

"He sent me her personnel file. All documents of former West Point graduates have been scanned and logged into a centralized database, so it was easy for him to send me the file. It's large and contains not only her academic records, but tons of personal and financial information as well, at least about her earlier years. Nothing, of course, about her time after graduation."

"Anything of interest?"

"That's the thing, I just glanced through it quickly. I haven't really dug into it. It's late, Agent Chase, so I thought I'd send it directly to you and you can go through it in detail."

"Makes sense, but I don't have access to the internet or a computer right now, and I'm a little tied up."

He sighed.

"Anything jump out at you at all?" I asked.

"A couple of odd things, that's all. Nothing alarming, though."

"Give me an example."

He paused. I heard him clicking on his mouse. Then he said, "Eva grew up in a bad part of Baltimore, basically the projects. Her mom worked a couple of waitressing jobs to support her."

"Okay. What's odd about that, though?"

"From her upbringing to where she ended up seems a little strange to me."

I thought for a moment. "Sounds like a classic American success story to me. A poor girl, but highly intelligent, overcomes her upbringing and gets accepted into a top school."

"What's odd is that West Point is difficult to get into. Typically, applicants need a letter of support from a member of Congress."

"I didn't know that. That is a little odd. You're right. Maybe she was a community activist and frequently wrote to politicians as a high school student, something like that."

"Maybe."

"Maybe one of her relatives was a politician?" I said.

"Again, maybe, Agent Chase."

"What else? You said there were a couple of odd things."

The mouse clicked again. "Eva O'Connor went to a private boarding school in upper Maryland during her high school years. I know the school pretty well. It's an incredibly expensive place, a place her mother definitely couldn't afford. She listed it on her West Point application."

"Maybe they had scholarships or financial aid for her to attend boarding school."

"Even so, it's really a place only the super wealthy can afford. Not even a mom working ten waitressing jobs could afford to send a kid there, even if the kid received multiple scholarships."

I smoothed out my bald head. "What about her father? I'm assuming they were divorced. Maybe he paid for boarding school. Maybe the mother used alimony to pay for Eva's education."

"Let me check." I heard the governor click away. "Let's see. Okay, here it is: she left her father's information blank on the West Point application."

"Really?"

"Yes, really."

"Maybe she had a wealthy grandparent or uncle or some other family member that helped her pay for it."

"Maybe, but there's no other family information listed."

"You said there was a lot of personal information listed in the file. Is there a copy of her birth certificate?"

"Let me check. There's a folder listed 'personal documents'."

I waited, listening to the governor's breathing and the clicking of computer keys.

"Here it is," he said. "A copy of her birth certificate. Her mother's name is Beth O'Connor and her father is listed as Johnny Russo."

The governor said a few more things, but I didn't hear him. I couldn't. As soon as I heard the 'Russo' name I went rigid. The name commanded my attention every time I heard it.

My mind spiraled for a second or two. Within moments, however, everything suddenly became clear. It all made sense. I collapsed onto the shelf, then rolled onto my belly, still holding the phone to my ear.

Johnny was a nickname for John. And John was the American equivalent of Giovanni in Italian.

Giovanni Russo, aka Johnny Russo, was Eva's father.

Eva O'Connor was actually Eva Russo.

I dropped the phone.

CHAPTER THIRTY-TWO

"AGENT CHASE, ARE you listening to me?"

The entire plot unraveled in my mind. I'd been completely set up, duped and manipulated by Eva Russo for months now. I banged the back of my head on the shelving.

"Agent Chase?"

How long had she been planning this? I put my hands over my face. Stanley had lied about a few things, but he had been telling the truth about Eva. It wasn't Stanley bent on revenge; it was Eva, for what I did to her father. I dropped my hands and banged both palms against the shelving unit. The cell popped in the air from the force.

"AGENT CHASE," the governor shouted.

His harsh tone snapped me from my thoughts. I picked up the phone.

"Sir, sorry about that. I know what's going on. I know who's setting me up."

"What? Just like that? All of a sudden you figured it all out?"

"It's a long story, sir."

Muffled shouts came from the shipping container. I'd trapped Stanley in there and needed to get him out.

"That's all you're going to say?" the governor said. "I deserve more explanation than that."

The governor did, so I ignored Stanley's cries for the time being. "Johnny Russo is Giovanni Russo, sir. That name may ring a bell."

I waited to see if the name registered with him.

A moment later, he said, "You mean the Italian man who used to own the Motel 7 chain? The man found on the freeway billboard with the, uh—"

"Yes, that man," I said, interrupting. "He and I have some history together."

"History? What do you mean by that?"

"I was the one who..."

The governor cleared his throat. "Oh, I see. Really, you were responsible for the—"

"Eva Russo is setting me up, sir, for my part in her father's deportation."

"And humiliation," he added.

"Fair enough. She's the inside person, Governor. She's the one who's been trying to kill your son. And she's trying to frame me for everything. That's as much as I can explain for now. I have to attend to Simon."

"Understood. Go to it, Agent Chase, protect my son. Have him call me as soon as he can."

"Will do."

I hung up and started climbing down the shelves. Mick's voice filled my ear on the descent.

"Aug, inbound car traveling at a good clip. You ready? In position?"

"Is it Eva?"

"Haven't made an ID yet. Remember, I don't know what she looks like. Describe her."

As I quickly described her, I heard the car's engine racing toward the pier. It would be here in seconds. I didn't have time to fill Mick in on everything. "Eva's behind it all, Gabe. Stanley's telling the truth."

"What do you mean? How do you know that?"

"The governor just fed me some intel about Eva. It confirms she's been lying all along. I don't have time to explain. Give me a confirmed ID as soon as you can."

"Roger."

While climbing back up the shelves, I heard the car screech to a stop near the front of the warehouse, then a car door open.

A moment later, Mick said, "Affirmative, it must be her. Slim, high cheekbones, dark hair. It's strange, though, she's wearing a large coat. Looks like a trench coat or something like that. Looks like she's hiding something."

"Hiding what?"

"I can't tell from this angle; she has her back to me."

"You think she has a bomb or something?"

"Not sure. It's something big. Wait, she's opening the trunk."

She'd parked so close to the front of the warehouse that I could hear her opening it.

"She's taking off the coat," Mick said. "She definitely has something strapped to her front."

"Strapped? What does she have? A bomb?"

"I don't know. Her back is still toward me. Hold on, she's turning now."

Mick went silent.

I thought our communication link had dropped. "You there, Gabe? What's going on?"

Still no response, so I checked the earpiece. It looked fine. I said, "Gabe, you there?"

A moment later, Mick said, "I'm here, Aug." His voice was different, though, almost trembling. Maybe it was my imagination.

"Talk to me," I said. "Tell me what's going on."

"Do not, I repeat, do not do anything rash when she comes in. Finger off the trigger, Chase. In fact, lower your weapon right now."

"What the hell is going on?"

"Just wait for me, buddy. I'm coming. I'm abandoning my post. You need my help."

"Stop being cryptic. What's going on? What aren't you telling me?"

"I'll be right there."

"No, STOP. Tell me what she's hiding. You need to prepare me."

"She has something."

"Has what? Spit it out. This is crazy, Mick, just tell me."

He cleared his throat. "She has someone strapped to her chest."

"Someone? What do you mean? How can she have a person strapped to her? How's that even possible?"

He paused, then said, "It's a small child. A, uh, boy."

My son instantly popped to mind. "Simon? Tell me you're kidding. She can't have my son. It can't be him." I sucked in a breath and held it.

Mick didn't respond right away, so I knew it was Simon. It made sense since Simon went missing a few hours ago, but I still couldn't believe it, or didn't want to.

"It can't be," I said, exhaling and shaking my head. "It can't be."

"I'm pretty sure it's him, Chase. Just want to prepare you. He has a blindfold on. I haven't seen him in a year or so, but..."

My heart thumped. I swear you could hear it beating at least ten feet away "A blindfold? What?"

The trunk slammed shut.

"Just try and remain calm," Mick said. "Don't do anything rash. I'm coming. I'll figure something out."

I tore the earpiece out. Of course I wasn't going to do anything rash. I did have a hard time calming down, however. My breathing bordered on hyperventilation. I couldn't remember if I'd ever hyperventilated before. With all my previous training, I was usually a picture of calm on missions. Now I had to put the rifle down because my hands shook and my chest heaved uncontrollably.

While deepening my breaths, I heard solitary footsteps approach the sliding doors. Part of me knew it was Simon strapped to Eva's chest. Another part of my mind kept telling me it was some other boy. It had to be.

Then I had the most selfish thought of my entire life.

Let it be someone else's boy. Please, please, let it be someone else's boy.

The doors screeched open a fraction, then stopped. So did time. I waited until Eva made another move, but nothing happened for a long time.

It was silent outside the warehouse. Inside, all I could hear was my pounding heart. It was so loud it seemed to echo throughout the big, empty space. I put my hand over my chest in an attempt to muffle the beating.

I refocused my attention on the sliding doors, which were lit up by the construction lights. One beam shone through the crack in the doors and flooded a small section of the pier. There were no shadows out there, and no movement.

Suddenly the doors flung open and Eva Russo slipped in. She pulled the door shut while sliding to her left, keeping her back to the wall. Her movements were a bit of a blur because I was focused on the boy. It took a split second to confirm that she had Simon on her chest.

My heart paused, then sank. Maybe even disconnected from my arteries. It literally felt like that. As if my heart needed to be told to beat again. Willed to beat again.

Simon had a black blindfold on, and I could tell right away that he was unconscious. His chest moved slightly, so I knew he was alive, but she must've drugged him with something pretty strong. The sight of my son made me gasp. I couldn't help it.

Eva heard the gasp. She swung her head toward my corner. "There you are, Gary. I figured you'd be up in one of the corners."

The disdain in her voice was palpable. Eva gripped a gun in her right hand. I didn't identify its make as I usually did, and I didn't respond to her comment either. I was too focused on Simon.

My son was strapped to Eva with what looked like a modified baby carrier. Crude slits were made up the sides of the carrier, allowing his legs to fit through the once-small holes. A swath of duct tape wound over his abdomen and around the back of Eva. Another band of tape wrapped across Simon's upper shoulders and the lower part of his neck. The same piece of tape wrapped around Eva's back, securing his upper body to her chest. She had her left hand placed under Simon's throat, effectively holding his head in place so it didn't bobble forward.

It took everything in me not to shimmy down the shelves, launch at Eva, and tear Simon free, then plant two bullets into her forehead. But I didn't know what Eva had planned for Simon.

I did know she was using him as a human shield. The top of Simon's head was parallel with the top of Eva's nose, just under her eyes so she could still see. There were only a few inches of Eva's head protruding above Simon's. Way too small a target. The shot was far too risky. Eva knew exactly what she was doing.

"In shock, Gary? Can't speak, can you? I understand this must come as a hell of a surprise. You must be going crazy right now."

I took one last look at Simon, then shifted the rifle and focused on Eva's eyes. "What kind of sick person uses an innocent child to protect themselves? As a human shield. You're a coward, beyond a coward. Who are you?"

"I'll tell you who I—"

"A person with a twisted and demented father," I interrupted, not wanting to give her the satisfaction of revealing her true identity. "You're a Russo through and through. Obviously it runs in the blood."

I saw her eyes jump a little. The flinching eyes confirmed I'd caught her off guard.

"You're smarter than you look. Obviously you *just* figured that out. You had no idea about your boy, I bet."

Eva used her gun hand to pick up Simon's right arm and fake a wave. "Wave to Daddy, Simon."

I dropped the rifle and looked away, then took a deep breath and addressed Eva.

"Like father, like daughter. If you harm a hair on Simon's head, you're a dead woman, except I'll torture you first."

She scoffed. "Pretending to date you has been torture enough. By the way, the only reason I dated you was to find out more about you so my father and I could orchestrate the perfect revenge. It didn't take me long to learn the only thing you cared about in this world is Simon. For the record, I have no intention of killing your son. Unless, of course, you make a stupid move and force me to. Then I'll have to kill him, but his blood will be on your hands, and on your conscience. Not mine. I'm not a child killer; let's make that clear. For now, he's my insurance policy against you taking a shot."

I pulled my eye from the scope and unbuttoned the top two buttons of my shirt. It felt like the warehouse was 100 degrees. A sheet of sweat moved down my face. I used the back of my palm to wipe it away.

Keeping a level head was crucial. I absolutely had to keep my emotions in check. Most important, I had to keep Eva talking until Mick came through with something.

"What's your plan anyway, Evangeline? You really think you're going to walk away from all this?"

"It's Eva," she snapped. "And I am going to walk away from all this, trust me. And you're going to die. You'll be known as one of the worst, if not *the* worst, American traitor in history. Now tell me where Cranston is."

Just then a metallic boom rang out. Another followed, then another. It took me a second to realize that it was Stanley banging on the inside of the shipping container.

"I take it that's Stanley?" Eva said.

I didn't respond.

Eva grabbed my son's foot and bent it to an unnatural angle. Not enough to break anything, just enough to get my attention.

I winced and held my breath.

She seethed, "I asked if that was Stanley."

"It is," I said, still holding my breath. "Now let go of his ankle."

She did.

I exhaled.

"Now tell me where Cranston is," she said.

I cleared my throat. "How would I know?"

"Spare me, Gary, I know he's around somewhere. Use your radio or whatever communication equipment you have and get him in here."

I didn't respond or call Mick. Stanley started banging louder and faster.

Eva grabbed my son's foot again and bent it.

"Stop," I shouted. "You're not a child killer, agreed, but you're a child abuser, just like your pedophile father."

Eva suddenly swung her gun my direction and fired a shot. It ricocheted off the shelf's metal frame. I scrambled to the back of the shelving unit so she couldn't get the correct angle to hit me. Unfortunately, though, the shot drew Mick out. I heard the sliding doors jam open.

Glancing over the shelf, I saw two muzzle flashes, then two booms followed. The bullets were aimed in the opposite, lower corner from where I was set up. Mick fired the shots as a distraction.

Stanley immediately stopped banging.

I watched my best friend dive into the warehouse. When he hit the ground, he rolled forward and came to his feet. He stayed in a squatting position with his arms extended, holding a pistol. He quickly found Eva and pointed the weapon at her.

To Eva's credit, she didn't flinch. From the moment the doors opened until Mick found her, her only movement was a slow turn toward Mick. With her left hand she kept Simon's head up to block Mick from blowing her head off. She calmly used her right arm to raise her weapon and take aim at my best friend.

"First things first," she said. "We need to go over the rules of engagement."

Mick jabbed his hand gun at Eva. "You kidnapped my girls and threatened their lives. How could you? I can't believe you run the SCS. What the hell is this about anyway?"

"Like I said, rules of engagement first. Now drop that weapon, Agent Cranston."

"I'll never take orders from you again," he said.

Eva motioned at his gun. "Lower your weapon now."

"Why would I?" Mick said. "I heard you when I was outside. You said you don't want to kill Simon, you have no plans to. I'm sorry, Chase, I don't think it's best to give up my piece. I won't take a shot because I don't have one, but I'm not giving up my gun."

"It's okay," I shouted, and I meant it. Eva had given too much away about her intentions. She had no leverage to make either of us drop our weapons. Though I still didn't know what she was thinking or planning.

"I thought you might play that card," Eva said. She pulled a cellphone out of her pocket and addressed Mick. "One call to my associate and you may change your mind. You think I don't know about the little cabin in the woods, in Big Bear? The one where you've stashed your wife and girls?"

My view of Mick was from the side, so I couldn't see his face, but I could see his usually steady gun arm start to shake, just slightly. I was positive he was freaking out, or raging, or a combination of the two.

He stabbed his piece at her again. "How do I know you haven't already sent someone?"

"You don't. But I have no intention of harming your family, just like I have no intention of hurting Simon. Your girls served my purpose, which was to set you after Stanley and Chase. I don't need the girls anymore, unless you don't comply. Now drop that weapon and kick it over here."

Mick shook his head. "You drop the phone first."

I picked up the rifle and put the scope on Eva. She took a second to think about Mick's proposal.

"That's fair," she said. She dropped the cell to her right side and kicked it, but not very far. She could get back to it if she had to.

I focused on Mick. His whole body quivered. Everything in him wanted a shot at Eva. Eventually, though, he dropped the weapon and kicked it toward her.

"How could you?" he said. "You're the chairman of an inter-agency spy operation dedicated to protecting the American people. Yet you've kidnapped young girls and threatened my wife and sent me to kill the governor's son, and my best friend. Did you really think I would do it?"

Eva pointed her gun in Mick's direction. "None of this was originally supposed to include you or Stanley. My father and I had it all figured out, the perfect revenge for what Chase did to him. Only Chase was to suffer and die, nobody else. My father's associate, a hitman who also specialized in abduction, arrived from Italy a week ago. He was going to abduct Simon, then lure Chase to this warehouse with the promise of getting his son back. But only if Chase came alone. We were going to send a video of Simon in that shipping container where Stanley is right now. When Chase arrived, and determined nobody was waiting to ambush him, he would've rushed in and opened that shipping container. Except Simon wouldn't have been inside. On the tablet would've been a ten second video message from my father telling Chase he never should've messed with him. Then, from a safe distance, my father's associate would've blown Chase up, along with this warehouse. Chase would've died never knowing if he son was safe or not. Of course, we had no intention of harming an innocent child, so we would've returned Simon safely to his mother."

"What happened then?" Mick asked. "What the hell changed?"

She waved the gun at Mick, then up at me. "Here are the rules of engagement, gentlemen: You make a move toward me, Agent Cranston, and you're dead. I won't hesitate to shoot you. And, Gary, if you take a shot at my legs or feet or some other body part, I'll kill your son in a heartbeat. Then I'll lock you two in here and raze this warehouse to the ground."

She tucked the gun into her pocket, pulled out a small device and held it up. "Semtex is in all four corners of this building. One push on this detonator and the warehouse will be consumed in thirty seconds. Look above you, Gary, if you don't believe me."

I didn't want to look up, but I did anyway. It took a few seconds to spot the Semtex. The material was stuck in the corner of the warehouse, between two adjoining pieces of wood. Since the wood was faded and grey, the Semtex was hard to see.

I grabbed the edge of the shelf and tried to crush the wood and metal frame together. I'd walked right into her trap, like a complete rookie, like a total idiot.

"Why are you doing all this?" Mick snapped. "Who are you?"

I focused the scope on Eva. She put the detonator away and pulled her gun back out. She didn't answer right away, so I did.

"She's Eva Russo, Mick. The daughter of Giovanni Russo."

Mick slightly turned my direction. "How could the daughter of that monster be employed in our government? How could we let that happen?"

"The feds didn't know she was his daughter," I said. "She kept her mother's last name."

Eva whipped the pistol toward me and fired. The gun roared and the bullet splintered through the wooden planks behind me.

"Shut your mouth, Gary. You don't get to tell my story. This is my moment. Neither of you have any idea of who my father truly is."

I shifted back on the shelving unit. Eva was dying to reveal her story.

The fact that she sacrificed a bullet to stop me from talking was proof. We had to keep her talking until she made a mistake.

Mick prodded her on. "Then tell me your story, Eva. Tell me about your father. I want to know."

Mick and I had fallen into the classic good cop/bad cop routine, which was the only strategy we had. Good cop/bad cop kept a suspect on an emotional roller coaster, and suspects tended to make mistakes when they were being emotionally jerked around.

"You two are like everyone else," she said. "Judging someone from what you've seen in the media. You have no idea."

I scoffed. "Remember I investigated your father, Eva, and met him face to face. I know firsthand what a scumbag he—"

"Shut it," she said. "The feds approached him for help. They approached him." She stabbed her gun in my direction. "They needed a place to house those criminals who served their time, and my father was willing to work with them. But they screwed him over, which was the second time the feds had done that."

"Screwed him over?" I laughed. "Unbelievable. Your father manipulated them, lied to them, threatened Clint Clemens and his family, endangered innocent children, and was ultimately responsible for a child being molested. It's the other way around, Eva, that's for sure."

Mick deflected. "The second time the feds had screwed him over? What do you mean, second?"

She turned to Mick and took a breath. "My father and his wife immigrated here when he was in his early twenties. And when he arrived in America, all he knew was the Italian way of life, the Mafia way—"

"And he made quite a name for himself," I interrupted.

"Maybe too big of a name," Eva said. "Because the feds made him the prime target in one of their investigative stings. They followed him, photographed him, bugged his house, harassed and threatened him, all in an attempt to extort information from him. The worst part was how they filled his wife's mind with poison against him, which eventually destroyed their marriage, though they never did divorce. Fortunately, my father found love again."

I put the rifle down and thought for a second. Pieces started to fall into place.

"With your mother, right?" I said. "Your mom was Ms. O'Connor, the illicit mistress, and you're the illicit daughter. It all makes sense."

"You're quite the genius, Gary," she said.

I prodded her some more. "Tell me, Evangeline, was it a one-night thing with your mother, or ongoing. Did Russo even care about her?"

She trained her gun on me, but didn't fire. "You know, Gary, when I was plotting my revenge and entertained the idea of involving your son like this, I almost didn't do it. I had second thoughts about involving an innocent child. But now I don't; I made the right decision."

"What about your mother?" Mick said, deflecting again. "Tell me about her."

Eva shifted toward Mick, but didn't lower the gun. "They were madly in love at one point. My father was trying to get out of the Mafia and become a legitimate businessman. He wanted to lead a normal life. The feds, however, insisted he stay in and become their informant. But my father was not, and never would be, a snitch. Never in a million years. In an attempt to extort him into service, the feds approached my mother and poisoned her against my father, just like they did with his wife. They showed her all this supposed evidence of people he murdered and maimed, which they completely fabricated, by the way."

"Fabricated?" I gave a short laugh. "Come on, Evangeline. They wouldn't need to fabricate anything."

She ignored me. "My father tried to undo it, but the damage was done. My mother broke off their relationship and fled to Baltimore. Wanted nothing to do with my father. What she didn't know at the time, and wouldn't find out for another two months, is that she was pregnant with me. My father didn't find out about me until I was five years old. Once he found out, he relocated to the area so he could be near me."

"To brainwash you, too" I said. "From an early age. To poison you against your own country."

She shook her head at me. "Such a simplistic view, Gary. The type of view that comes from a delusional American who thinks the federal government is innocent and pure and could never engage in corruption."

"I could say the same about you, Evangeline, about your simplistic and childish view of your father. Your crazy idea that he is basically a good man and has done nothing wrong, a poor victim of our horrible government and his unfortunate experiences."

Eva scoffed. "The point is that he was trying to become a legitimate, stand-up businessman, but the feds kept dragging him down. They wouldn't let him move on from his past. His past wasn't his fault; he was born in Italy, into the Mafia. It was the only way of life he knew until he moved to America. And then America destroyed everything he loved, twice over. He was trying to do what was right."

"So he used you as his weapon of revenge," I said. "Is that it? Put you through the best schools and molded you in his image. Got you a government job so you could spy on and betray your own country."

"I have my own mind. I make my own decisions. My father made sure I had an incredible education. He sent me to the best boarding school and college money could buy. Having the best education means I can think for myself. As I moved through the ranks in the intelligence community, I witnessed all kinds of government corruption. My father didn't 'brainwash' anything into me. I saw the corruption first-hand."

"You're unbelievable. So you abused your position in the intelligence community and got into arms dealing, into dirty business with your dirty father. Everything Stanley found on your hard drive was true evidence of your involvement, wasn't it? You sold secrets about arms deals to America's enemies for payback, for what the government did to your father."

She stabbed the gun at me. "This isn't just about my father—"

"What evidence on the hard drive?" Mick said. "What are you talking about?"

I hadn't given Mick all the details about Operation Crucible. "Stanley had—"

Eva fired a shot into the shipping container out of anger. I held my breath, hoping the kid didn't get hit. A second later I heard Stanley scrambling around inside.

"I'll kill the kid, Gary, if you don't shut up. He's the reason this has gotten more complicated. He's certainly expendable. In fact, you're all expendable." She turned back to Mick. "The feds froze all my father's assets and deported him back to Italy with just the clothes on his back. They didn't honor the deal they promised, to let him keep the money he'd funneled offshore. And because of what Gary did to him, the humiliation has continued in his homeland. When he got home he was shunned by the Mafioso, couldn't even show his face in the local village. He had to hide out in his own villa, and pretty much still does to this day."

I was about to antagonize her more, but decided against it. For Stanley's sake.

"My father," she continued, "had a certain lifestyle he was accustomed to, but he had no way to make a living to support himself or even cover the expenses of his villa. So, yes, he and I went into business together. I have access to all the intel, and he has the foreign connections. It was a good match."

Mick shook his head and held up his hands. "You didn't have a problem selling out the country where you were born and raised?"

"You have a naïve understanding of arms trading, Agent Cranston."

"How so?" he said.

Eva thought for a second, then said, "Historically speaking, our government has funneled arms to many countries. And many of those countries have eventually become our enemies. America always arms the lesser of two evils in any foreign squabble, but those same arms our government donates or sells will end up being given or sold to anti-American groups or countries at some point. My father and I had no problem speeding up the process, so to speak."

"And no problem benefiting from the betrayal," I added.

Mick jumped in before Eva responded. "How did you do it; sell the arms, that is?"

She smiled. "It was easy because of my maximum-security-level clearance, and how good I am at digital eavesdropping. I'd find out locations and times for when our government was planning to deliver arms to our allies. I'd give that information to my father and one of his associates, and they'd broker a deal with certain groups. The groups would then intercept the arms. Those groups would pay a pretty penny for the information we were selling."

"Those groups?" I said. "You can't even say their names, can you? Is that how you justify this in your mind? Just convince yourself you're selling information to some innocuous group and not a group like ISIS that beheads innocent civilians. Unbelievable."

Eva trained her gun on the shipping container. "I wouldn't expect either of you to understand, not with your nice, suburban, middle-class upbringings. I don't need to justify anything to you two anyway."

Mick redirected. "How did Stanley get involved in all this? Where did the kid come into play?"

Eva lowered the gun a little. "Stanley had hounded me for a job for almost a year. Naturally, I had to handle the situation delicately because of his father. The kid crossed a line, though, when he hacked my computer and found the arms evidence. I sent him death threats, and thought that was the end of everything. But Stanley wouldn't let it go. What he probably didn't tell you Gary is that he sent the CIA an anonymous email stating that he believed somebody within the SCS, most likely on the NSA side, had been selling arms secrets. In the email, he included a few incriminating lines from emails between me, my father, and my father's associate, with the promise that more emails could be sent. So now I had a huge problem with Stanley, and with the CIA since they sent Gates to investigate. The kid had the original evidence and wasn't scared to use it."

She waved the gun in my general direction. "When the governor requested protection for Stanley because of my death threats, I saw the perfect opportunity to deal with him and Gary. I knew Stanley was book smart, but not very street smart. The kid was naïve and pretty gullible. So I sold him a grand story about how the arms evidence wasn't real. About how I was field testing Gary for an SCS position. And the kid bought it. He was in way over his head."

"Now I understand," Mick said. "You promised Stanley a job if he planted the arms evidence he'd discovered on Chase's computer, essentially framing him for your crimes."

"It was brilliant," Eva said, smiling. "The email evidence that Stanley had implicated three people, so I needed three people to frame. I knew the CIA wouldn't rest until they figured out who was selling arms secrets. Three people needed to go down as traitors, and it certainly wasn't going to be me, my father, and my father's associate."

I shook my head. "So it was me, Stanley, and Mick."

"It was perfect," Eva said. "Stanley had the hacking ability to break into secure government mainframes and steal arms information. The fact that I had evidence of him spying on the TV network made that assertion of Stanley completely plausible. Since Stanley's email to the CIA mentioned that an insider was involved in selling secrets, quite possibly from the NSA side, I had to shift the investigation away from me."

Mick stabbed his gun at Eva. "To me, obviously."

She nodded. "Exactly. When the CIA got wind of somebody selling arms secrets, they immediately confiscated the computers of every SCS member, including mine and yours, Agent Cranston."

Mick clenched his fist. "I wondered what that was about."

Eva looked at Mick and continued. "Fortunately, I'd wiped all incriminating evidence off my computer immediately after Stanley hacked my computer. And I knew the CIA wouldn't find any direct evidence on your computer, but what if they found the evidence on your best friend's computer?" She smiled, waving her gun toward my corner. "So the third person involved in possibly the biggest traitorous act in American history, and the man with all the incriminating evidence on his computer, is Mr. Garrison Chase. Who isn't employed in the NSA or CIA and therefore not smart enough to wipe his computer clean." She grinned. "It's good practice telling this story; I'm going to have to do it again in a few hours."

Everything in me wanted to take her out right then. But I had no shot.

She kept going. "So Stanley is the computer hacker and eavesdropper, the one who will be tied to my emails. The emails from my father and his associate will be linked to Cranston and Gary. Which makes sense since you guys are friends and were both involved with *The Activity*. So you'd be aware of seedy foreign groups to approach and broker deals with."

She paused, probably to let it sink in, or just to gloat.

I didn't say anything. I couldn't. All I could think about was how beyond screwed I was. Eva had been meticulously plotting her revenge. She'd set me up as the fall guy for her traitorous actions, and it appeared she had an airtight case against me. I looked at Simon, strapped to Eva's chest, and felt grief pour through me. What kind of life would Simon lead, with a dead traitor for a father?

Mick blasted on with questions, interrupting my thoughts. "So you bring me into this and implicate me in the story because you need a corrupt inside agent within the SCS. Did you really believe I would kill the governor's son, my best friend, and also burn down his house? Why not use your father's associate to do your dirty deeds? He's your father's paid hitman, right?"

Eva stabbed her gun in the direction of the shipping container. "Get the kid."

Mick stood still.

She jabbed the gun again. "Get him now, he'll help explain. He's the reason why you're involved."

Mick walked over, unlatched the arm, and opened the door. I sort of expected Stanley to burst out of the container, but he didn't. In fact, Mick had to coax him out, which was understandable the more I thought about it. He was probably terrified, now that the reality of his situation had finally settled in – and because a bullet had ripped through the container just minutes ago.

"Let's go, kid," Mick said.

Stanley shuffled to the door and peeked out. Mick politely helped him all the way out of the container.

Stanley looked up at Mick. "I'm sorry, I was naïve."

Mick just shook his head.

Stanley turned in my direction. "Agent Chase, I told you I wasn't lying about Operation Crucible."

I sighed. "I know, kid, you bought her crazy story. I get it now. You sent that email to the CIA, didn't you?"

He nodded. "But—"

"Stanley," Eva interrupted, "we wouldn't be standing here right now if it wasn't for you. You understand that, right? If you hadn't poked your pointy little face into everything, and sent that email to the CIA, you three wouldn't be on the brink of burning to death." She thought for a second. "Well, at least not you and Mick. Gary certainly would be."

The kid stomped his foot. "It was my right to have a position in any intelligence group. My absolute right. And you're blaming me for this?"

Eva laughed. "Don't think you're innocent in all this, Stanley? You broke many laws, spying on the television network, breaching secure NSA databases, violating numerous privacy laws, and blackmailing me—"

"I never blackmailed you," he said.

She scoffed. "What was the email to the CIA all about then? Did you honestly think I wouldn't have found out about that? Within a day of you sending that email, Anfernee Gates was in my office questioning me and confiscating my computer. Sending that email was your way of trying to control the situation, to make sure you had leverage over me, to make sure you got what you wanted. But I wasn't about to let you control anything, Stanley. Your amateurish game brought Agent Cranston into this. Now he has to die today and leave a widow and kids behind."

"What?" Stanley said, almost screeching. "Don't put that on me?"

"It will be on you, and so is Agent Gate's death. He was starting to put the pieces together and needed to be taken care of. If you hadn't sent that email, kid, he'd still be alive. Although his death will be blamed on Gary, it should be on your conscience."

While Stanley whined to Eva, my mind processed all the information I'd just heard. No wonder Gates had such a beef with me. Maybe he thought Eva and I were in cahoots because we were dating. Or maybe because Mick and I were friends and former partners. Nothing mattered about that situation now because Gates was dead. If something miraculous didn't happen soon, the three of us would be dead too. That would leave only Karla alive to untangle everything and clear our names. Nobody else knew a thing. Karla, however, was likely in the hands of Eva's hitman right now.

I clenched my fists tight, blew out a frustrated breath, then refocused the scope on Eva. I searched for any possible shot. She somehow had to be stopped.

Unfortunately, I had no shot. The only way to take her out was to also take out my son. I wiped away another sheet of sweat moving down my forehead.

Mick took a step toward Eva. His body had a slight shake to it, so I knew he was raging. "Why threaten my family and terrify my wife to death? I get it that you needed three people to frame, and one of them needed to be me since I work for the SCS, but why not have your father's hitman kill Stanley and Chase. Why put me, and my family, through all that?"

He took another step. "Tell me."

Eva extended the gun. "Stop right now."

Mick shuffled closer. "Just tell me and I'll stop."

"Stop first or I'll shoot. I'm in control here."

Mick pushed it and took another step.

"Fine," she said. "I told you I'd shoot." She jerked the gun to her left, dropped the barrel six inches, then pulled the trigger.

And shot Stanley Tuchek.

CHAPTER THIRTY-THREE

I HEARD STANLEY drop, but I didn't focus on him.

I looked at my son. The gun had gone off only a foot from his ear, but Simon didn't wake up. I wondered if she'd drugged him so bad that he was dying. Surely a gunshot should have woken him. Right? He had to be okay. He just had to be.

Sweat sheeted down my face, so I put down the rifle, tore off my shirt and wrapped it around my forehead like a bandana. Stanley started howling, which commanded my attention.

I put my eye back to the scope and found the kid. He was crumpled on the ground, holding his left side. It looked like the bullet had torn clear through the left side of his stomach.

Mick was at Stanley's side. He had ripped off his shirt and was applying pressure to the wound. Blood had already soaked the shirt and was pooling underneath Stanley.

The kid struggled to say a few words. It sounded like he was saying, "She's crazy, she's crazy."

I wanted to abandon my post and help, but I knew I had to keep the rifle on Eva. Any mistake she made, I'd have to capitalize on. Otherwise, Stanley would bleed out, and Mick and I would burn to death.

I refocused on Eva. She hadn't moved an inch. Her face was blank and devoid of any emotion.

She carried on explaining things to Mick, as if she hadn't just shot the governor's son. "My father and I debated heavily over that very point, Agent Cranston. Here's the thing: The associate my father sent was more skilled in abduction. He wasn't as finely skilled as a killer as we would've liked. We didn't trust him to cleanly take out all three of you. Killing three people is far too risky. Way more opportunities to screw up and be seen and leave evidence behind. We wanted our associate to have limited involvement so that nothing could point back to my father. Basically, Agent Cranston, we needed you to do the dirty work."

Mick shook his head, then spat in her direction. I'd never seen him spit before.

"Plus," Eva continued, "the story is more plausible if you're personally involved, Agent Cranston. And the details, especially the death threats, make more sense. Think about how the story plays out. The three of you are complicit in selling arms to terrorists. But there's a massive internal fight among you guys, some serious issues, maybe money, maybe somebody grows a conscience, it doesn't matter what it's about. All that matters is that it fractures your group. Stanley and Gary end up on one side of the divide, and you on the other, Agent Cranston. You turn on your partners. You send death threats to Stanley, which prompts the governor to request protection. Remember, those death threats can be traced back to our organization."

She motioned at Stanley's crumpled body. "Naturally, he advocates for Gary to protect him. Then you, Agent Cranston, go after the two of them. You try to kill your best friend, and also burn down his house. The more personal it gets, the more plausible the story becomes. After that, you try to kill Stanley at the coffee shop, then his house."

"You'll never get away with this," I said. It was far from intelligent, but I didn't know what else to say. Eva had clearly thought everything through.

"I will," she responded. "And that's the point. The plan is brilliant."

Stanley lifted his head and pointed his finger at her. "My father will never let this go. He'll never believe I was a traitor."

"Let me ask you, Stanley, how good a job did you do planting the evidence on Gary's computer?"

Stanley thought for a second, then laid his head back.

"Exactly," Eva said. "Nobody will doubt that those emails came from Gary's computer. For what it's worth, kid, you do have the skills to be an SCS agent."

In the distance, faintly, I heard the sound of an outboard motor, which seemed to be getting louder.

Eva didn't pay attention to the sound. "I'll be the only one alive who knows the truth. So I'll be able to shape the story how I want it, and I know the evidence supports my version. I'll even look like a hero, not that I care about that. Everyone will know I was on to Gary's involvement. That's why I was dating him. To gather evidence against him."

The drone of the motor grew louder. The boat was definitely heading toward the pier. Eva still didn't acknowledge the sound. I didn't know if she was unfazed by the sound or if she was too wrapped up in gloating about her deception to notice the approaching boat.

"Did you really think I'd do it?" Mick asked. "Kill Stanley and Chase?"

"I didn't know what you'd do, Agent Cranston. It was fifty-fifty for me. I do know we all do crazy things for our family. Look what I've done for my father. And we all know Gary will do anything for his son. So, yes, I thought there may be a chance you'd follow through with your directives since your family was threatened. At the time I thought that if you did follow through, that would be perfect, so much easier for me and my father. But if you didn't follow through, I wasn't that concerned. And I had no reason to be, because it's worked out in my favor, hasn't it? It clearly looks like you tried to kill Stanley and Gary. And even though you didn't succeed, it still bodes well for my story. At any rate, I had this warehouse rigged for my original revenge plan. After Stanley sent the email to the CIA, the new plan was to lure you, Agent Cranston, and whoever you didn't kill to this warehouse. And make sure nobody left alive."

Eva turned in my direction. "Get a good look at your son, Gary, one last time. I can't imagine anything worse than a father knowing his son will grow up with the burden of his father's sin. Think about the shame and humiliation this will bring to your son. This is our revenge."

I scoffed. "Except it isn't my sin—"

"But your son won't know that," she said. "Nobody will know that."

The Weatherby's barrel bounced up and down. I couldn't keep my eye on the scope anymore. My arms shook in rage. Unadulterated, raw emotion coursed through my body. I'd never been so out of control in a kill situation. I'd never wanted a target to die as badly as I wanted Eva to die.

The boat motor pulled me from my rage. The engine suddenly cut off, then I heard someone jump onto the dock.

Eva still didn't respond to the sounds.

"The thing is, Gary, you can end this all now, can't you? I'm sure you've thought about that already, right? All you have to do is pull the trigger and I'm dead. Then you, Mick, and Stanley live to tell the true story. Except that your son dies in the process. You sacrifice him for the truth. Like Abraham and Isaac in the Old Testament. Ask yourself: can you do it, Gary? Can you put a bullet through your son to stop me? You can end this right now."

"Stay calm," Mick told me.

"You talk about the greatest good," Eva said. "What's the greater good here, Gary? The truth, or your son's life?"

"Shut it," Mick snapped at Eva.

Two sets of footsteps hit the dock. I could hear them over the thump of my heart. The footsteps continued toward the front of the warehouse, then seemed to fade away. I waited for the doors to slide open or a bullet to break through, but nothing happened.

I refocused the scope. Naturally I wouldn't kill my son, never in a million years. I'd sacrifice my legacy for my son's life, without question. Even so, knowing that Simon would grow up with stories about his father being a traitor gutted me. The shame, humiliation, and denial my son would go through was too much to think about.

So I listened for more footsteps instead. Maybe it was Karla and Frank.

"Do it, Gary," Eva said. "End this. The truth is always the greater good."

"You know he won't," Mick yelled.

"I know," Eva said, smiling. "But wouldn't it be great if he did? I'd die for that story. I've thought hard about it. It would be worth it to know you killed your only son, Gary, just to clear your name. You'd have to live with that choice and all the judgment and condemnation from the rest of the world."

I kept my finger on the rifle's trigger and pressed my other forearm against my forehead. The bandana was soaked through and couldn't stop the sweat from entering my eyes. I positioned the crosshairs on the only part of Eva's head I could see, the upper right side of her forehead. The target was only about a cubic inch, though. The shot was far too risky, especially with my breathing out of control, so I took my finger off the trigger and aligned the crosshairs on Simon's face instead. I wanted to see him up-close one more time.

My son's mouth hung open a fraction and his hair was messed up. I imagined that was exactly how he looked curled up in bed.

The sound of a car engine distracted me. It grew louder, clearly aimed toward the warehouse. Eva didn't respond to the sound. A moment later the vehicle's high beams lit up the tiny warehouse windows. The vehicle stopped right in front of the building, and two car doors opened. Seconds later, the warehouse doors screeched open too.

I swung the scope to my left and watched Karla step into the warehouse. For a split second my body relaxed, but it didn't last.

The Italian hitman stepped in behind Karla, a gun pressed into her back.

CHAPTER THIRTY-FOUR

THE HITMAN TUGGED on Karla's shirt and inched her backward. Karla's teeth were gritted and her fists were clenched. The hitman wrapped his hairy forearm around her neck and pulled her close. I pounded my fist on the shelf. I had no shot.

"Perfect," Eva said. "Now everyone who knows anything is here. Only one more loose end to tie up." She looked at Stanley. "Laptop, now."

Lying in his blood, Stanley managed to lift his head and sputter, "Never."

"Spare me," Eva said. "I know you have it on you, or it's somewhere close. I know you kept the original arms evidence on it. It's the last piece I need. Stanley, I'll kill Karla first, then Cranston, then Gary, in that order, until you cough it up."

"I don't have it with me," Stanley said.

Which was true. I had it in the back of the Suburban.

"Fine, if you want to play that game." Eva turned to her right and pointed the gun at Karla. I watched Eva's movements in my scope. She was serious. There was tension on her trigger finger, too much tension.

"Wait," I blurted out.

I knew we were all going to die, either by fire or bullet. It was only a matter of time, so I needed to stall. For what? Maybe a miracle. I didn't know. All I knew was I couldn't watch Karla die.

"I've got it," I said.

Eva released the tension in her trigger finger.

"It's in the Chevy," I said. "A few piers back."

"No, it's not," the hitman said.

What? Why was he arguing with me?

He looked at Eva. "The Chevy's out front."

Right. They must've walked to the Chevy after getting off the boat, then driven it closer. My admission had bought no time. I was about to lose any leverage I had.

"Go check," Eva said. "He may be lying to stall. Drive the Chevy in here; it's going to burn, too."

The hitman backed out of the warehouse, with Karla pressed close. A minute later the SUV fired up and drove through the double sliding doors. He parked it in the middle of the warehouse. Karla was in the front passenger seat; the hit man had handcuffed her wrists to the ceiling handle.

He turned to Eva and rolled down the window. "Laptop's here." He held it up.

"Run it over," she said.

So he did, about ten times. Back and forth until only small bits remained.

When the Chevy shut off, Eva said, "Now grab Cranston and handcuff him in the back seat."

The thug hesitated, motioning toward my corner.

"Gary," Eva said. "Tit for tat. If you shoot my man, I'll shoot yours." She trained her gun on Mick.

I had no interest in the hitman. My attention was on Eva, waiting for some type of mistake, yet so far she was flawless. She kept her gun on Mick while the hitman led him to the Chevy and handcuffed him in the back seat.

I saw Mick's face through the scope. His outward appearance looked calm, but I knew him too well. He was itching to snap the man's neck and go after Eva, but he didn't. Like me, he knew Eva wouldn't hesitate to shoot him. He had no play.

"All set," the hitman said. He walked around and stood by the driver's door.

"One last thing," Eva said to the hitman.

"What's that?"

"Earlier I stashed a gun under your vehicle's seat. I need you to get it."

"Sure thing." He opened the driver's door and searched under the seat with his hand, then looked back at Eva. "Nothing here."

"Right," she said. "I must've left it under the passenger seat."

The hitman leaned all the way into the vehicle. He pinned Karla's legs against the door with one hand and searched under the passenger seat with his other hand. I had an elevated angle and could see everything through the passenger window. I heard some movement and swung the rifle toward Eva. She had shifted a little to her right, her gun pointed toward the Chevy.

"Nothing here either," the hitman said.

Suddenly Eva's gun coughed.

Karla shrieked.

The gun coughed again.

I looked back at the Chevy. Karla had blood splattered all over her shirt, but she was okay. She frantically pushed the hitman's head off her lap, at least what was left of it.

"Karla," I yelled. "You okay?"

She nodded. She picked up her feet and placed them on the car seat. The hitman's lifeless body slumped into the foot well.

Meanwhile, Mick scrambled around in the back seat, trying to pull the ceiling handle free. The whole Chevy rocked back and forth.

I swung the rifle toward Eva. "Incredible. I didn't think it was possible, but you're worse than your father."

"That was the final loose end," she responded. "And you can blame his death on Karla, I suppose."

"What?" Karla shouted.

"You can't even take responsibility for that?" I said. "What we just witnessed you do?"

She jabbed the gun in Karla's direction. "Everything was going fine until she decided to go back to her FO. We needed her here at the warehouse. I'd given him a fake NSA badge and fake name and told him to only use it in an absolute emergency. When he showed his face to agents at Karla's FO, he signed his own death warrant. No loose ends. My story is airtight. I couldn't risk him being identified and linked to me or my father and ruining the story."

She dangled the detonator. "His charred body may be found, but he'll never be identified. Investigators will probably assume he was a foreign asset hired by Cranston or you, that's my guess."

I pulled the soaking wet shirt-bandana off my head. The monster had thought of everything.

Eva tucked her gun away, pulled out a decent-sized padlock, and shuffled to her right. In seconds she'd close the warehouse doors and padlock them shut, then blow the place up.

I still didn't have a shot, so I lied out of desperation. "Frank knows everything. You won't get away with this."

"Nice try." She backed out the doors. "I've monitored all your communications, Gary, from the very beginning."

Before she shut the doors, I shouted, "Karla told Frank everything at her FO."

"Nope," Eva said. "I checked with my man before he got onto the boat. Karla said nothing to Frank or Hornsby." She took one last look at me. "You should never have messed with us."

I ignored her comment. My attention was on my son. I watched him through the closing doors. When the doors closed, I shut my eyes for a split second and burned the picture of my son's peaceful face into my memory. Then I threw the rifle onto the warehouse floor, jumped up and ran along the shelves to the middle of the warehouse. I needed to get far away from the corner, from where the Semtex was plastered.

Reaching the middle of the shelves, I got down on my belly and started to shimmy down. The first explosion rocked the warehouse and stopped my descent, however. My right side slammed against the warehouse wall, then the shelves started crumpling underneath me. I free-fell about twenty feet, landing flat on one of the shelves, about ten feet off the ground. Every ounce of wind was knocked from my body.

I curled up and protected myself as the second, then third, then final blast came. They were staggered by a few seconds. The sounds were thunderous in the warehouse. I was thrown left, then right, then back-ward, losing my handgun in the process. When the explosions stopped, I was buried in a pile of rubble.

As I pushed shelves and debris off me, I smelled fire and heard it crackling. Once free, I looked up into the night sky, since most of the roof had been blown off the warehouse. Smoke from the fire quickly blotted out the starry night sky.

Amidst the chaos, I swear I heard pounding on the back door. I glanced at the door, but it was still sealed shut. Figuring I was delusional, I turned my attention toward the Chevy. Mick was pounding on the back window with his right shoulder, trying to break the window. I wasn't sure he'd have enough leverage to do so. Karla's head slumped forward and her arms dangled from the ceiling. The blast had smashed her head against the glass. I could see the cut on her right temple. My eyes found Stanley. He looked unconscious, too.

Meanwhile, fire raged inward from the four corners, or from where the corners of the warehouse used to be. The explosions had torn four huge holes where the Semtex had been placed. What was left of the roof started collapsing in random pieces. Flames spread quickly to the standing walls. The floor beams had yet to catch, but it was only a matter of time. Smoke was billowing, thick, descending downward and filling the warehouse.

I struggled to the edge of the collapsed shelf, then rolled off and fell the final ten feet to the ground. Landing in a heap, I started crawling toward the Chevy, then I stopped.

A huge thud echoed throughout the warehouse. Another one followed. I looked behind me. The back door suddenly crashed open.

Frank Lemming stepped in, wielding a gun in one hand and a giant pair of bolt cutters in the other.

CHAPTER THIRTY-FIVE

TOO SHOCKED AT the sight of Frank, I couldn't move. I couldn't speak. I remained on all fours in the middle of the warehouse floor.

Frank ran toward me and helped me up. He patted me on the back.

I looked at him. All I could say was: "How?"

"Thirty years I kept this bolt cutter in various cars, thinking I may need it one day." He held up the tool. "Finally came in handy."

Frank propped his shoulder under my arm and held me up.

I motioned at the Chevy.

While Frank helped me limp there, I said, "No, I mean how did you know we were here at the warehouse?"

"Karla slipped me this note, discreetly." He dug out a small yellow sticky note from his pocket and showed me. It read: 'Pier 42 – 03:00 a.m."

Thank you, Karla.

Right then a huge ceiling beam cracked and gave way above us. Frank pushed me out of the way as the beam crashed where we had just been standing.

I got up, thanked Frank, then motioned at the Chevy. "We have to get them out."

Frank ran to the back seat and started cutting Mick free with the bolt cutter.

I struggled to the passenger door about ten seconds later. Along the way, I found my rifle and picked it up. When I reached the Chevy, I opened the passenger door and shook Karla until she stirred awake.

After freeing Mick, Frank cut off Karla's cuffs. Mick grabbed his gun, then ran over and scooped up Stanley. We all headed toward the back door that Frank had broken down. We had to dodge ceiling beams and flames, and stay low to avoid the smoke. Frank helped Karla to the door. I was the last to make it. By the time I reached the door, I had my wind back, but I was choking on smoke. Mick dragged me through the open door, then slammed it shut.

Outside, Frank grabbed me by the shoulders. "Go get your son. Hurry. There's a boat at the end of the dock." He handed me his gun. "Karla and I will get Stanley to the hospital. We'll call for backup."

Before I could respond, Frank picked up Stanley and handed Karla his phone.

"Let's flank her on either side of the warehouse," Mick said. His eyes were wide. He was ready to take her down.

I nodded. "I'll take this side."

Mick still had his earpiece in, so I grabbed mine from my pocket and put it in.

"First one with a clean shot takes her out," Mick said.

"Agreed."

Mick took off.

I ran as fast as I could to the corner of the warehouse. I had to scramble around piles of debris and a number of fiery wooden beams. The dock would catch fire soon. Fortunately, the fire was raging out of control so I didn't have to worry about being loud and giving my position away. Eva would never hear me approaching.

When I reached what was left of the corner structure, I stayed low and crouched onto my belly. I put the scope to my eye and immediately found Eva. She was working on releasing the stern line to a large cigarette boat, which was already fired up. The deep, throaty sputter of the engine could be heard over the fire. Eva had released the bow line, so the boat drifted perpendicular to the dock.

"I have no shot," I said to Mick. "Her back is to me. You in position yet?"

"Almost."

Ten long seconds later Mick said, "Okay, I'm in position, but no shot either."

Eva struggled with the knot because of Simon. I realized it would be hard for her, if not impossible, to unwind all the duct tape and release Simon from her chest. She couldn't bend over very far. She was a little frantic trying to get the final line free. Her frantic movements made for an even riskier shot. I took controlled breaths, calmed myself, and waited for the shot.

It didn't come.

So I waited for her to free Simon. Maybe she had a pocket knife and would cut the duct tape. She wasn't going to take Simon with her, was she? I patted my bald head, wiping sweat away in the process.

Suddenly Eva turned sideways, kneeling down to get a better angle on the stern line. Her front faced Mick, so I knew he had no shot.

Mick confirmed it. "No shot here. You, Aug?"

It was fifty-fifty for me. Unfortunately, I couldn't hold the rifle steady. Too risky for Simon. I pounded on the dock. "I don't think so. She's a pretty small target, kneeling down like that."

"Maybe we let her go then," Mick said.

"No way," I replied.

"Think about it, Chase. We have her. We're all alive. Her story won't hold water against all of us. Stanley will probably make it. The four us will tear apart her story. Stanley will admit he planted the evidence on your computer at the request of Eva. It's over. We win."

"It's not, not by a long shot. We can't let her get on that boat with Simon."

"She said she's no child killer."

"No," I snapped. "We let her on that boat with my son and he dies. Guaranteed."

"I don't think so, buddy."

My mind raced. "I do. We're all alive, and that's the problem, Mick.

Think about it. She'll likely be monitoring the police scanners, so she'll discover we made it out alive. Karla was already calling for backup. As soon as Eva learns we made it out, she'll know it's over for her. And if she finds that out while holding Simon, she'll kill him, then disappear forever. That will be her revenge. There's no question in my mind. She won't let this go without avenging her father. Think of the lengths she's already gone to."

Mick didn't respond. He knew I was right.

Eva finally released the stern line, then she stood, holding the rope in one hand and the gun in her other. Simon's head dipped forward slightly. I still only had a partial side view of her. Still a risky shot.

"I'm going out there, Mick, no gun. She's not freeing Simon."

"Don't you dare. It's a death sentence. She'll shoot you immediately."

"Maybe, maybe not. She'll be shocked at least. I'll try and get her to talk for a second, try and distract her. She may turn and give you an angle."

"It's too risky."

"Maybe, probably. If she does shoot me, you know what'll happen. Her head will tilt back from the recoil. That's your opportunity. Simon's head is already drooped forward. When—"

"It's too dangerous, Aug, stay put."

"When her head goes back, Mick, there'll be a safe distance between her head and Simon's. Take the shot. I trust you."

A brief pause, then he said, "You don't have to do this."

"I have to. It's the greatest good, laying down my life for my son's. If I die, there's no other way I'd rather go."

"Stop that talk. We can come up with a better plan."

Even though Mick couldn't see me, I still shook my head. "We don't have time, buddy. We have to do this now. Bury her when she shoots me. And then clear all our names." I paused and cleared my throat.

"Make sure Simon grows up right," I said. "Take care of him, Mick. I'm trusting you for that. I wouldn't want anyone else to be a surrogate father for him."

A split second of silence from my best friend. "Of course I will. At least take your rifle and get her on the defensive."

"I can't have her put a gun to my son's head. No way. She's likely to kill him now that we've got out. I need her attention on me. If she sees me with the rifle, she'll immediately think about killing Simon."

"At least take Frank's gun. Put it behind your back."

"I will."

I stood and left the rifle behind. While walking toward the boat, I stuffed Frank's handgun into the back of my waistband.

"There's a better way, Aug, there must be."

"No time to figure it out, Gabe." I ripped out the earpiece and dropped it onto the dock.

"Eva Russo," I shouted.

Right before getting into the boat, Eva stopped and turned. I took a tiny bit of joy from her expression. Her lips were slightly apart and her eyes jumped. She stood speechless.

Suddenly she jabbed her gun in my direction. "Stop right there, Gary."

I didn't, because Eva wasn't turning. She stood parallel with the edge of the dock, not moving. Mick had no shot, so I side-stepped to my right, to get her to turn toward me and give Mick a decent angle.

She didn't turn.

Instead, she shot me.

I dropped to my knees. She'd winged my left shoulder. I wasn't sure if she'd meant to wing me, or if she was just a bad shot.

"I told you to stop," she said. "Who else made it out?"

I didn't answer. The gunshot had stirred Simon. I saw my son move for the first time all night. He started wriggling in the carrier. Eva had removed his blindfold.

I watched and waited for his eyes to flutter open. Before I died, I wanted to look into my son's eyes. If my last vision was Simon's face, I'd die in peace.

But I didn't get to see his big, blue eyes.

Eva shot me again.

I flopped onto my back. She'd shot me in the left shoulder again, about two inches below the other bullet. She was a good shot.

"I asked, who else made it out."

I struggled to sit up. "You're going to kill me anyway. Why would I tell you?"

"No, I'm not. That would be too easy. I'll kill your boy and let *you* live. You need to experience pain and suffering like my father, for the rest of your life."

She pulled the gun off me and pointed it at Simon's temple.

"NO," I screamed.

Mick suddenly jumped into view with his palms extended. He'd had his gun stuffed behind his back. He pulled it out and pointed it at Eva and moved side to side, trying to make himself a tough target.

Eva was stunned at Mick's sudden appearance. I could see it on her face. The shock caused her to make a mistake. Her one and only mistake. The one I had been waiting for.

She turned toward Mick.

Instinctively, I reached around with my right arm and whipped out Frank's pistol. Taking aim at the side of her head, I used her slightly larger than normal ears as a target. In my peripheral vision, I could see Mick moving erratically.

Her gun coughed.

From the corner of my eye, I saw Mick drop, but I kept focused on Eva. The energy from the gunshot transferred from her hand to her forearm, then up her arm and through her shoulder. I watched her head kick back, just like I knew it would.

I concentrated on the middle of her ear, tracking it backward a few inches. When her head reached the farthest point from Simon, I pulled the trigger.

The bullet drove through the middle of her ear. Pink mist sprayed from the other side of her head, clouding my vision for a moment.

When the pink mist cleared, my body finally relaxed.

Eva's lifeless body dropped to the dock.

But I didn't get to celebrate, not for long. Because everything changed a moment later. I saw it coming, the unintended consequence.

The momentum from my bullet carried her body backward.

Eva plopped onto her butt, right near the dock's edge. The stern line was already floating in the water. The boat was unmoored and slowly drifting away from the dock. I gasped and held my breath.

With my son strapped tight to her chest, Eva Russo's body toppled backward off the dock and plunged head-first into the Pacific Ocean.

CHAPTER THIRTY-SIX

I SCRAMBLED TO my feet and charged toward the ocean.

While my damaged left arm swung erratically at my side, my right arm pumped as fast as it could. When I reached the dock's edge, I launched into a dive, barely missing the boat. I broke the water's surface with my good arm.

Fortunately, the raging warehouse fire lit up the ocean's surface, so I could see a few feet underwater. I spun left, then right, looking for Eva. Finally spotting her, I swam toward her sinking body. When I reached her, I grabbed a swath of duct tape with my right hand and stopped her body's descent. I knew I couldn't rip Simon free with one hand, so I kicked with everything I had and headed to the surface.

After breaching the water, I spun Eva around and checked on Simon. His eyes were closed and he wasn't breathing. I wasn't sure if he'd fallen unconscious again, so I tried mouth to mouth, but I kept sinking with every breath. Treading water and holding up two bodies with one hand was next to impossible. Simon's mouth dipped underwater every few seconds.

Trying not to panic, I wedged my good shoulder under Eva and scissor kicked to keep everyone above water. The strategy worked for thirty seconds. After that, my legs couldn't keep up the pace and we started sinking again.

Desperate, I tried ripping the duct tape with my mouth. With every bite, however, I took in water and sank a little farther. All I wanted was to rip Simon free and watch Eva sink to the bottom of the Pacific, but I couldn't do that. Each kick got harder, like I was drowning in a pool of cement.

After twenty, maybe thirty seconds, my thighs started aching, burning, like someone was holding a torch to them. Another twenty seconds later I couldn't feel my legs anymore. In fact, I wasn't sure if I was still kicking. I looked down and confirmed that they were moving, but just barely.

Soon my entire body was submerged, even though I continued to kick. I held my right arm straight over my head and wedged my palm in the middle of Eva's back. I knew if she was above water, Simon was safe. My heart and will were committed to saving Simon. Unfortunately, my legs weren't.

Before long, my hand started dropping below the water line. I kicked harder, but my legs made no progress and my lungs screamed for air. I sank farther. My legs felt disconnected from my body, like they weren't even there. I needed oxygen everywhere in my body. The burning torch had moved from my thighs to my chest. I felt like my chest was going to cave inward. If I drew a breath, however, it would be deadly for Simon and me.

As I kicked, the water took on a viscosity like quicksand. It felt like a thousand-pound weight was attached to my ankles, drawing me deep into the ocean's depths. When I looked down at my legs, to will them to keep moving, Eva's weight suddenly fell away.

I panicked. For a split second I thought she'd toppled off my hand. I didn't see her body sinking, however, so I scrambled to the surface. I crawled through the water with my good arm and exploded through the water's surface, gasping uncontrollably. Immediately I looked for Eva and Simon, frantically looking left and right.

They weren't there.

I looked up and found them above me.

Mick held Eva under her arms, struggling to get her body onto the dock. My son's head drooped forward, staring down at me with lifeless eyes.

Simon didn't look like he was breathing, so I jumped out of the water and latched onto the dock with my good hand, but my body was dead weight, and I was exhausted. I couldn't pull myself up with one arm, not a chance.

Fortunately, Mick helped. His face appeared over the dock's edge a moment later. He grasped my forearm and yanked me up. I slithered onto the dock while Mick collapsed backward. I could see that Mick had been shot on the right side of his chest. A steady stream of blood poured from a clean bullet hole. He must have jumped to the left just as Eva pulled the trigger. If he hadn't jumped left, he'd most likely be dead.

Mick motioned at his pocket. He struggled to speak and breathe. I realized his lung had probably collapsed.

"Pocket," he said.

I coughed out the words: "Don't talk, buddy, save your energy." Then I scrambled over and pulled a knife from his pocket. Using my teeth to open it, I turned to Simon and cut him free from the duct tape.

Sirens wailed in the background. Fire cracked and popped behind us, as three of the four warehouse walls had toppled and were now in a raging blaze.

I pried Simon off Eva. "Help is coming, son. Wake up. Stay with me." I straddled my son and started chest compressions. After five, I bent over and delivered a big breath.

Nothing. No response.

I did five more, then another breath.

Nothing.

Mick gurgled and coughed up a pile of blood.

Turning to Mick, I said, "Hang in there, pal, you're going to make it."

I turned my attention back to Simon and did five more compressions, then another breath.

No response.

"Damn it, breathe," I yelled.

After the fourth breath, just as I pulled my lips away, Simon coughed and gurgled up water. I quickly turned him on his side.

As water poured from his mouth, I collapsed to his side and cradled him. When all the water was out, Simon coughed again.

I hauled him on top of me, chest to chest. I cradled his head and waited. Moments later, his eyes twitched and fluttered open.

Then I finally saw my son's blue eyes, but only for a moment as tears burst from my own eyes, clouding my vision.

I smiled and grasped Simon with my good arm, maybe a little too hard. He coughed a few times, then placed his cheek to my chest.

The sirens were super loud now.

I squeezed Simon, vowing to never let him go. To never leave his side. To never let anything like this happen again. When I finally let up on my hug, my son pulled back and looked at me.

He cocked his head to the side. "Is that you, Dad?"

I was too choked up to speak, so I simply nodded.

Then my son embraced me as hard as he could.

CHAPTER THIRTY-SEVEN

KARLA RAPPED ON my front door, then barged in before I could say anything. I guess we had that type of relationship now.

"They buried it," she stated, dropping the papers in her left hand onto my kitchen table. "They buried the entire story. Like it never even happened."

I had just finished plunging a French press and was about to take a sip of good coffee. I hadn't had a decent cup in a couple of days. Hospital coffee wasn't even slightly palatable.

"Of course they would," I said. I took a quick sip of coffee. "We knew they would. It's amazing what federal agencies can do when they actually work together. We are talking about the CIA and NSA after all. No way would they want a story aired about one of their own being a traitor."

"I know, it's just frustrating." She grabbed one of the papers and waved it. "Our esteemed local paper. The warehouse fire made page three."

She picked up another paper. "The *LA Times* has the story on page nine. Page nine! Can you believe that? I think it's about a hundred words long. Here, read it."

I'd been in the hospital the past two days and hadn't seen a newspaper, so I took the paper and read the quick blurb. The article mentioned the old warehouse, that it was abandoned, and that the dock eventually went up in flames. Nothing about the dead body of an Italian henchman, of course. Or about a dead, corrupt NSA agent who had sold arms secrets to terrorists. According to the article, nobody was harmed. Nobody was even there when it burned down.

Karla pulled out a chair and took a seat. "When did they get to you?"

I thought for a moment. "Before the hospital, if you can believe it. They redirected the ambulances from Long Beach to a veteran's hospital in South Orange County. They put Stanley, Mick, and me in the same hospital room after we got patched up. In fact, we had the whole wing to ourselves. They wanted to limit our exposure to the public as much as possible."

"How do you think that happened so quickly? How did the feds know to contain you guys?"

"Gates. It had to be Gates. He was piecing everything together before he was murdered. He must've told someone else, one of his superiors probably. The Agency and The Company were on high alert after his murder."

Karla nodded. "That has to be it. They had agents questioning me within hours. A couple of hours after that, they sent in some federal prosecutors. Hired NSA lawyers, I imagine. They gave me the riot act about national security and made me sign some confidentiality papers. I heard that those lawyers met with every single cop and fireman who showed up at the warehouse that night."

"I've seen those same lawyers more than the Army doctor over the past two days."

She reached across the table and touched my hand, held her own there. "How is your shoulder by the way?"

I shrugged my good side. "Apparently I get to use it again, so that's good."

She squeezed my hand. "What about Simon? Is he okay? You hear anything?"

I squeezed her hand and collapsed back into the chair. "Not directly. After a night in the hospital, he was stable, so they took him directly to his mother. The governor did me a solid, though, and visited Gina yesterday to try and smooth some things over."

Karla winced. "How'd that go?"

"He said as good as can be expected."

"What did he tell her?"

"Not much, because he couldn't. He and I worked up a story before he went over. Just to keep up the pattern of lies, you know."

I smiled to ease the pain, then continued. "He told her I was working on a case of national security interest and that a credible threat was made toward my family. That's why I acted in haste, broke in, and took Simon for his protection, until the threat had abated. From her perspective, it explains the break-in and potential arson at my home. Of course, the story has tons of holes. The governor didn't explain much more than that, citing confidentiality when she questioned him. You know how that goes."

Karla nodded.

"It was the best we could come up with," I said. "The truth, or any version of it, was worse."

"So what about the custody hearing?"

"That was yesterday afternoon. The governor sent his lawyer in my place and requested a three-month extension, in light of my injuries during service."

"How do you feel about that?"

I ran my hand over my head. "Good, I think. It gives some time for things to blow over, and maybe I can repair my relationship with Gina. That would be good before we stand in front of a judge. I'm hopeful for weekend visits back."

Karla smiled. "You deserve it. I'll be there at the hearing, to back up your story or for moral support, whatever you want, whatever you need."

Before I could respond, a loud knock rattled my front door.

"Chase, it's Frank."

Frank? What was he doing here?

I looked at Karla. She shrugged.

"Come in," I said.

My boss steamed into the house. "I'm going to make you buy a cell-phone, Chase." He held up his phone. "This is ridiculous."

"What's going on?" I said.

"Stanley Tuchek is what's going on." Frank glanced at Karla and smiled. "Good morning to you, Agent Dickerson. Or maybe you two is what's going on. Good thing you two work at different offices." He waved his hand between us. "That way this isn't a problem."

Karla blushed right away.

My face went hot too.

Frank turned his attention to me. "Apparently Stanley's being released from the hospital."

"So?" I said, not sure I wanted to spend any more time with Stanley, ever.

Frank waved his phone. "He's called three times. He wants me to get you to come pick him up. He wants to go to his coffee shop."

I held out my hands. "You're kidding, right?"

"I'm not," Frank said.

"No way," I said, crossing my arms.

Frank pushed up his sleeves and leaned on the table. "We're doing it, Chase. We'll all go together. I'll buy the coffee and we'll debrief a bit. That's a direct order, by the way."

"Come on," Karla said. "You and Stanley need to talk it out anyway."

I looked at Karla. "You sound like my ex-therapist." I turned to Frank. "And you're acting like my boss. But last time I remember I was suspended."

"True, but not anymore." Frank pulled out my service piece and handed it to me.

After that, he dug out a new badge and extended it my direction. "You're back in."

I didn't take it. "You're assuming I want back in."

He scoffed. "What else would you do?"

I motioned at my kitchen. "I'm a decent cook. Maybe I'll open a beachfront restaurant and cook for a living. Something low-key like that."

Karla laughed, walked over, and hauled me up by my good shoulder. "Come on, let's go." She made her way out the door.

Frank flipped the badge at me.

I caught it.

While Frank followed Karla out the door, I turned the badge over and over in my hand, wondering what to do. Wondering what was best, not for me, but for my son.

A minute later, Frank honked the horn, which snapped me from my daze. I pocketed the badge and headed out the door.

Still unsure what I was going to do.

AUTHOR'S NOTE

Dear Reader,

Thank you for taking the time to read my book. I hope you enjoyed THE GREATEST GOOD. If you did, I'd be grateful if you'd consider leaving a review on Amazon.com and/or Goodreads.com. Reviews are extremely helpful!

If you'd like to learn more about me, the Garrison Chase thriller series, or sign up for my newsletter, please visit my website at:

craignhooper.com

I'm also giving away a free ebook to all my fans! FALLOUT, the prequel to the Garrison Chase series, is FREE when you sign up for my newsletter. Please visit my website to get your free copy.

If you have any questions or comments, please don't hesitate to reach out at craig@craignhooper.com. I absolutely love hearing from fans!

-Craig

ALSO BY CRAIG N. HOOPER

Fallout (Free*)

A Thin Line

All the Good Men

The Baja Directive

The Garrison Chase Series (Books 1-3)

* To get a free copy of Fallout, please visit Craig's website at

www.craignhooper.com.

Made in United States
North Haven, CT
29 December 2023

46791736R00172